I0760801

SELFIES

Book One
MANIFOLD SERIES

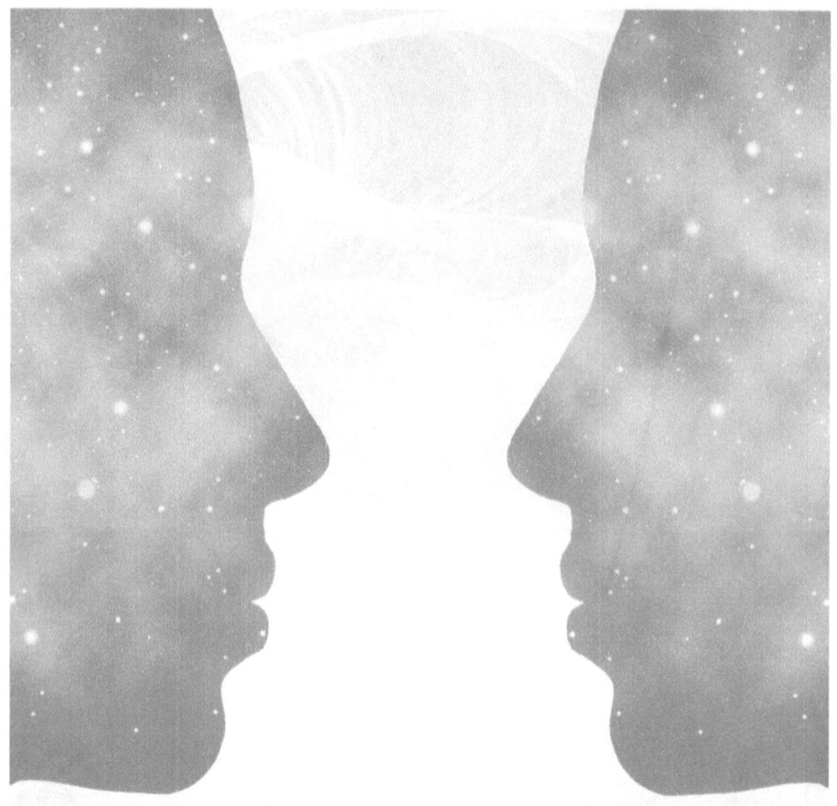

SCOTT A. YOUNG

ISBN: 978-1-964323-02-2
Paperback ISBN: 978-1-964323-01-5
Ebook ISBN: 978-1-964323-00-8

Cover Art by Jason Gurley
Interior Art by Scott A. Young

For Susan.
If it weren't for your support and devotion,
this book would not exist.

PART ONE

Indent

"This is the way I think the world will end—with general giggling by all the witty heads, who think it is a joke."

Søren Kierkegaard (paraphrased by Stephen Baxter in **Manifold: Space***)*

"Selfies are our reflections but with all the imperfections introduced by a camera lens."

Professor Phileas Gray: **The Measurement of Light**

1

Manifold

WALLAS TRAPMORE'S DEATH came suddenly.

A surge of potent power slammed through him with a light so perfect and bright its brilliance melted his eyes, seared his muscles, and turned his bones to dust. Trapp, like every Indent, knew this day would come. Even if the promise of an expunged criminal record and full Terran citizenship were worth the risk, working beside the Manifold was a suicide mission.

Such a death would be a noble one, perhaps the most noble of all. Each Indent's death averted a world war a little longer. Trapp was okay with that. His life hadn't amounted to much. He'd wasted most of it seeking an elusive purpose; had died a million times over.

Still, he had one regret.

No one would live to solve Jessi's murder.

"Trapp!" a familiar female voice said. It must've been a hallucination, the tendrils of his organized thoughts imagining it as they broke into a trillion waves of energy.

Perhaps this was even the afterlife. Trapp had never believed in one but if one presented itself, he'd gladly accept it—assuming it wasn't eternal hellfire. The woman's pleading voice returned, along with other more distant, overlapping words and phrases that meant nothing to Trapp.

"Leave me alone, you ghosts!" he shouted.

"Trapp!" the voice said again. "You're alive?"

"I'm dead," Trapp said, arguing with this she-devil.

Still, his disintegrating brain began to parse that logic. He was still thinking, which might mean something. He opened his eyes. Tiny lights were dappled onto a swirling black canvas. The vision was recognizable only because it was wrong. Those lights shouldn't be spinning like that. They weren't real. None of this was real. Not even the voice of…

"Erika?" he croaked, suddenly connecting the name with the voice.

"You sound like you're—" Erika said.

"Warning!" a robotic voice screamed over her. *"Battery failure imminent. Plug suit into outlet immediately."*

"—oxygen deprived." Erika completed her sentence.

"What happened?" Trapp asked groggily.

"The Manifold jolted you with enough electricity to kill an elephant—a *hundred* elephants. You're one lucky bastard. No one's ever survived the Manifold."

Trapp looked down at his spacesuit. Pinpricks of stars traced a slow ballet between his boots. Erika was right—none of this made sense. He should be dead.

"How do you feel?" she asked.

"Woozy. Last I remember, I was on the robot arm's platform. I must've been thrown off. Thank god I tethered in."

Just then, a kilometer-long cylinder came into view. Bristling with antennae, girders, stanchions, and dozens of illuminated portholes, it was the *Eos*. His home. And it was dropping away from him.

"Uh...about that," Erika said as Trapp peered around frantically. "Your tether snapped."

"Impossible. Tethers are constructed of self-retracting memory aluminum sheathed in carbon fiber."

"Warning! CO2 scrubbers offline. Recharge suit immediately."

"Apparently," Erika said, clearing her throat, "tethers *can* fail. Especially if they're subjected to enough force."

"Like a surge from the Manifold," Trapp said. "At least the suit's computer is still working." And repeating that obnoxious warning about how he was going to suffocate, he thought with a grimace.

Suddenly, a gigantic diaphanous copper mass floated into view.

Large enough to envelop a small village, it was one of many energy collectors licensed under the Manifold™ patent in orbit near Sol. "Solar Collectors on Steroids," the *Terran Times* had characterized them. Their inventor and original patent-holder, Doctor Phileas Gray, they called "Thor, incarnate." About the Manifold, they said, "With its ability to recharge enough high-voltage batteries to power whole towns, The Professor's invention single-handedly ended the Carbon War by rendering fossil fuels obsolete." Never mind the staggering number of Indent deaths, Trapp thought. It took two missions last year to recover his friend Rory's body after a Manifold surge.

"Are you sending a SLED?" Trapp asked Erika.

"SLEDs are for recoveries only. You know that!"

"For dead people, yes. But I'm alive."

"Sorry. The ISC regs on this are clear."

"What am I supposed to do, then? Just wait till I'm dead?"

"What about your hand thruster?" Erika asked.

Trapp shook his head. "Right! Of course."

Trapp swiveled his eyes down. The pistol-shaped device flew out from his body at the end of its tether. Wrangling it into his outstretched glove, he studied its status screen.

"Dead," he said.

"Damn." Erika's voice was tense.

"Warning. CO2 level at 5,000 PPM. Recharge suit immediately."

"I'm gonna end up like Rory, aren't I?"

"We're working the problem. Just give us a few minutes."

Trapp imagined her licking her lips in that way that she didn't know was sexy. He looked out into the abyss. A glint caught his eye. A planet or comet, perhaps. No. It came from below. He glanced down.

"I have an idea," he said. "Stand by."

Trapp turned his attention to the thruster. Hidden in its grip was a detachable cover for the battery compartment. A tiny aluminum screw gave access. As if winking at Trapp, it had just caught a stray photon.

"Maybe this thing isn't completely dead."

He removed the multi-tool from its holster and worked open the driver. The bit was too fat, though, and he wasted precious seconds trying to get it to fit into the screw head.

"Warning! CO2 level at 10,000 PPM. Recharge suit immediately."

The *Eos* came into view again, followed by the Manifold. Trapp had no idea if the gun held enough propellant to get him to the ship, which was shrinking away. He held the thruster as still as possible in one hand while working the tip of the multi-tool's knife into the housing seam. The blade slipped from his grip and almost skewered his glove. Thankfully, it caught at the end of its tether. Gasping, Trapp tried again.

This time, the knife tip plunged into the case, and the cover cartwheeled away.

"Got it!" he exclaimed.

"Got what?"

Ignoring Erika's question, he studied the battery. An intact wire was still attached to the small neon-colored cuboid. The other wire's outer casing was puckered and blackened, revealing the location of the short.

"Warning! CO2 level at 20,000 PPM. Recharge suit immediately."

Rolling the knife back and forth over the puckered wire, Trapp carefully cut into it. The blade slipped from his grip numerous times. Eventually, he exposed two copper ends of the singed wire. He wound these together using his thick-gloved fingers as best as he could. The connection was loose, but it held as he positioned the battery back into the housing.

"Here goes nothing," he said.

"Arrest your spin," Erika said.

"Excuse me?"

"Your spin will make your return vector too unpredictable. You need to arrest it before you attempt to come back."

"Won't I use up too much propellant?"

"I don't believe so, no."

Approximating his spin vector, Trapp aimed the gun in the opposite direction and pulled the trigger. Nothing. He tried again. Same result. Was the propellant gone? Did someone forget to refill it before he went out on this EVA? Was a stupid oversight like that going to kill him? Pushing the thought aside, he squeezed his glove harder and pulled the trigger. The jet came out so fast that it overcorrected his spin.

"Shit," he said.

"What?" Erika asked in a ragged voice.

"Stand by."

Feathering the trigger, he finally brought his spin to a halt relative to the *Eos*.

"Warning! CO2 level at 30,000 PPM. Charge suit immediately. Three minutes to lethality."

The *Eos* looked like it was retreating even faster now. But at least Trapp could eyeball a return trajectory. Although a much smaller target, the robot arm's platform was only 400 meters away. It had a charging station where he could get his CO2 scrubbers back online if the problem was only with his batteries. If the scrubber motors were fried, well… *game over*. On the other hand, there wasn't enough time to fly down to an airlock and wait for it to fill with oxygen.

"Damned either way…" Trapp muttered to himself.

He aimed for the robot arm and opened the thruster to full. Seeing he was off target, he adjusted once, then a second time. The last of the gas sputtered out in stochastic jets of sublimating particles.

"Thruster's empty," he said.

"Calculating your trajectory," Erika said. "Stand by… stand by…*Shit!*"

"What?" Trapp asked.

"You're off course."

"I still have a few meters of the tether. Maybe I can lasso —"

"No," she said in desperation. "You can't."

"Give it to me straight."

"You're going to miss the robot arm by twenty meters."

THE DEAD ROBOT arm approached rapidly. Trapp calculated that his trajectory was even farther off than Erika had predicted. From this distance and velocity, the platform looked frustratingly small and unobtainable. He was about to fly past it.

"Relay a message for me, will you?" Trapp asked. "I haven't spoken to my grandfather in a decade."

"Stand by," she said.

"Tell him I'm sorry for being so hard to raise."

"Trapp. I need to—"

"Please just tell him that. And tell him—"

"Would you shut up! I'm trying to tell *you* something."

"More important than my dying words to the man who raised me?"

"Yes, dummy. The robot arm's back online. It's moving to intercept you. I need you to focus, to guide me."

"Uh. Sure. Okay. Thanks."

"Warning!" Trapp startled at the now familiar voice, half forgetting that he was about to be asphyxiated on top of everything else. *"CO2 level at 70,000 PPM. Charge suit immediately. Two minutes to lethality."*

He looked down at the fast-approaching *Eos*. The arm rocketed upwards from midship.

"Left five meters," he told Erika.

Erika moved the arm right.

"*My* left!" he shouted. "Not yours!"

"You mean starboard?"

"Whatever. Kinda running out of time up here. A little frazzled."

The arm skittered over to his left. It was now only a dozen meters below and coming up fast.

"Two meters positive Z," he said.

"Enough?" she asked after extending it more.

He reached out for it. "I think…It's gonna be close."

His wrist connected with the robot arm below the platform. It flipped him around, and his feet came up, impacting the bottom of the plating. He bounced off toward open space. A black strip floated in front of him. He grabbed it even before realizing it was the other half of his broken tether and still attached to the robot arm. It slipped through his stiff-gloved hand as he slid out to its frayed end. Bearing down with a grunt, he stopped with scant centimeters left. A dark halo of oxygen deprivation filled his periphery.

Holding his breath, he yanked hand over hand, approaching the platform with each pull. He reached the rail, almost allowed it to slip from his awkward grip, then hoisted himself onto the platform. His boots thunked onto its magnetic plating.

"Warning! CO2 level at 100,000 PPM. Charge suit immediately. Fifteen seconds to lethality. Fourteen. Thirteen…"

Finding the pressure suit auxiliary cord on the control panel, he slid open its hatch. A retractable cord flew out, and he plugged it into the bypass port on his belt. If the batteries were toast, this would power his suit directly. He lifted his arm to check the wrist controls. The status light blinked red. The robot arm's control panel must have been fried by the Manifold, too. Trapp was out of options.

Erika had already begun to lower the robot arm.

"It's no use," he panted. "Running out of oxygen. No time left. Give Pop my message. Tell him I'm sorry for…"

"…Six…Five…Four…"

"…everything."

Lights illuminated, startling Trapp and making him cry out. Air blew across his face, accompanied by the pleasant hum of the *CO2* scrubbers coming back online. He only realized he was crying when tiny transparent spheres floated before his faceplate. The platform's control pad winked to life and cycled through a reboot.

"You did it!" Erika shouted, hurting his ears. "Man! That was way too fucking much. Two close calls in one day! I'm bringing you in."

"Negative," Trapp said, clearing his throat. The little tendrils of oxygen starvation disintegrated from his vision. "I still have a job to do."

"We'll send someone else."

He punched in the commands, and the arm moved up.

"Sorry. I *need* to do this. It's my last mission, and if it's logged as a failure…" Trapp gulped. "For Rory. I have the chance to be the first to complete my—"

"Don't say it! You'll curse it. Just get it done." Erika's voice was as emotional as his.

During last year's burial, they'd held hands and sobbed as Rory's lifeless body was jettisoned into space, and the *Eos* set off streamers for the benefit of the online audience.

The robot arm approached the Manifold and its emitters. Each of these was separated by a hundred meters, and, together, they formed a circle over three kilometers in circumference. The resulting magnetic field collected high-energy particles ejected from Sol. Resembling molten copper, the Manifold rippled with billions of strikes like a pond bombarded with stones. These ripples transmitted energy waves back to the *Eos* to charge a million batteries, a process that was a thousand times more efficient than other sustainable methods. Later, the batteries would power homes, businesses, cars, and factories—an entire planet.

Trapp moved up and beyond the emitter array. The robot arm pinpointed the debris; a piece of loose cable was trapped in the Manifold's intense magnetic fields.

Trapp saw something strange out of the corner of his eye.

"Why is there a SLED out here?" he asked, watching the small two-person cargo scow on a course away from the Manifold and toward the *Eos*.

"SOP for Indent-involved Manifold bursts. They were supposed to recover your body."

"Sorry to disappoint them."

Trapp chuckled. He now remembered that the ISC only retrieved Indents for ceremonial space burials broadcast on the Plexus—PR stunts to remind the public where their energy came from. Indents were worth more dead than alive. And this small victory, the ISC using up precious thruster fuel on an Indent, was almost worth it.

"The Manifold is still reading at a ground state," Erika assured him.

"Roger that." Trapp pulled a tool off the platform. It was a non-conductive pole with an articulated grabber at its business end. The piece of cable rotated several meters above the field. "Retrieving debris now."

A few misses and a grab later, he brought the cable onto the platform and secured it in a bin. He typed in the controls, and the robot arm moved away.

Soon, he was lowering down to the ship.

"You're the first, you lucky bastard," Erika said as Trapp felt an uncontrolled grin spread across his face. "Try not to let freedom go to your head."

He nodded to himself. He wasn't going to waste this second chance. From now on, he would do his utmost to get Jessi's case reopened—staying within the law this time, of course. It wouldn't matter if all of Terra believed he should get over it. Twenty-five years was long enough to wait—*way* too long.

Trapp owed at least that much to his mother.

2

Fabricant

BAM-BAM-BAM!

Trapp woke to a strange sound. After listening a while and hearing nothing, he guessed he must have dreamed it. Drifting back to sleep, he lost himself on the wings of a memory. It was his last night on the *Eos*. A warm body with soft curves materialized in his bunk next to him. "Don't talk," Erika said in a throaty voice as she placed a finger on his lips and slowly unzipped his flight suit…

Bam-Bam-Bam!

Trapp opened his eyes again.

A few seconds passed before his groggy head cleared and he remembered where he was. That night with Erika had been four weeks ago. He was now at the Space Corps Miami Base, in his bunk, recovering from space flight. His roommates weren't there. They'd probably gone to breakfast without inviting Trapp. Some friends they were! Suddenly remembering another, more loyal, friend, Trapp's hand patted frantically at the outside of his pocket.

It was still there! A small tag crudely embossed with several digits and letters but without a name. Trapp didn't need one. He knew whose dog tag it was. He'd kept it in his IndentSkins for the last six months as a memorial and a reason to finish his Indentureship.

"Rory," he whispered, running his fingers over the fabric that separated the dog tag from his touch.

Bang-Bang!

So he hadn't imagined the noise. Someone was at his door.

"Coming!" Trapp croaked as he sat up.

His nerves ached, and his head spun from the Zero-G flu, an artifact of months in space. He dropped his feet to the floor and stood. The room twisted. After a few seconds, it righted itself.

"Open up!" a man's voice shouted.

"Cool your thrusters!" Trapp shouted as he staggered across the cell and, reaching the door, yanked it open. "What's the nature of your malfunction!"

Three human forms stood silhouetted against the bright corridor lights. Trapp realized they were MPs, the people Indents called Demons due to their black NanoSkins, helmets, and opaque SmartVisors that hid their faces. His heart rate skyrocketed as he noted that they were also cradling bolt rifles. Then he understood who they'd come for. His roommate's loud bluster about breaking out to score drugs and cheap hookers in Little Havana had finally caught up with him.

"Danny's not here," Trapp said. "Check the mess hall."

He pushed the door shut. A booted foot was thrust in its way, keeping it ajar.

"We're not here for him," Demon One said. "We're looking for Wallas Trapmore."

"This is our guy, boss," Demon Two announced, apparently having identified Trapp on his SmartVisor.

"Indent Trapmore," Demon One said as he lifted his gun a few centimeters. "You're under arrest."

A numb sensation crept up Trapp's spine.

"Uh," he said, barely hearing his words over the buzzing in his head. "This is some kind of mistake. I'm scheduled for a debriefing and to get my discharge papers today."

"I'm afraid Liberty Day's been canceled."

"But I haven't committed any crimes." Trapp sputtered. He was about to vomit all over Demon One's boots. "I was on the base and couldn't have..." Then, his perspective changed. He even managed a smile and a small laugh. "Fuck me, you guys got me good! You don't even sound like yourselves. Is that you, Danny?" He tapped Demon One's SmartVisor. "Where the hell did you get the VoiceSynth? Must've cost a bundle, as well as those freaky Demon suits."

He reached over to grab a fold of Danny's NanoSkins. But Briggs and McNabb, Trapp's other bunkies, suddenly brought their guns up. The smell of oiled metal told him they were real.

"Alright, alright!" Trapp raised his hands in mock surrender. "Let the hazing begin. Just go light. I'm still fucked up from the Zero-G flu."

Lowering their rifles, Briggs and McNabb tugged brusquely at Trapp's hands, thrusting his arms behind his back before slapping MagnaCuffs on his wrists. Where they got those was anyone's guess. Trapp was about to comment on their attention to detail when one of them kicked at the back of his legs, causing him to crumple violently to his knees.

"What the—" he protested. "I said go easy."

"Shut the fuck up," Danny hissed.

Trapp huffed. "Fine. But let the record show you guys are the biggest assholes in the galaxy."

"Stipulated. Now, if you would let me read you your rights." Danny held up his HoloPhone. "You have *no* right to remain silent. Anything you say *will* be used against you in a court of law. As property of the International Space Consortium, you have *no* right to an attorney, although one will be provided. You have the right to a hearing to determine if you will be extradited to the Terran United Republic..."

"Extradited to the TUR? Where do you guys come up with this stuff?"

"...at which time your Indentureship Contract will become null and void. Do you understand the rights that I've just read to you?"

"Okay, okay." Trapp struggled to stand. "This isn't funny anymore."

"Do you understand the ISC rights I've just read to you?"

"I'm not fucking kidding, Danny."

Danny threw a sudden and unexpected uppercut to Trapp's cheek, toppling him backward to the floor. It happened so fast that Trapp's mind barely registered it. A high-pitched ringing blasted his hearing.

Briggs and McNabb pulled him back to his knees.

"Do you understand the ISC rights that I've just read to you?" Danny asked.

"Of course," Trapp muttered, moving his jaw back and forth.

Briggs and McNabb pulled Trapp onto his feet. Several barracks mates, apparently back from breakfast, arrived and watched from the hallway, their faces a mixture of humor and shock. Among them were Danny, McNabb, and

Briggs. Their eyes were big, and it was now dawning on Trapp.

"This is a serious arrest, isn't it?" he asked Demon One, now clearly not Danny.

"As serious as a fart in a spacesuit."

The three hustled Trapp down the hall as the other Indents moved against the wall to make a path.

TRAPP'S ATTORNEY WASN'T human.

After surrendering his IndentSkins for inmate NeonSkins, Trapp was brought by Demon One, whom he'd recently titled 'Fake Danny,' to a claustrophobic, windowless room with no door handle on the inside. A lanky lieutenant dressed in Space Corps blue coveralls sat at a single table in the small room. Their stark white hair was cut to a few millimeters and blended nicely with their bone-colored, smooth skin.

Trapp stifled a groan. A *Fabricant*. It wasn't that Trapp was a human supremacist or anything. He just didn't feel comfortable being this close to a non-feeling human analog.

Fake Danny chuckled disdainfully. "Good luck," he said, nodding toward the Fab. Then he shut the door.

Trapp sat across from the machine. "There's obviously been a mistake here. I couldn't have committed any—"

The Fab raised a finger to quiet him. They were staring at a HoloPhone, apparently lost in something mind-blowing. Perhaps it was news of a FabDrab sale. Trapp began to get impatient.

"No one will tell me what's going on. I'm supposed to be at my debriefing in an hour. If I miss that, I'll have to wait another week before getting my walking papers—another week as an Indent. You're supposed to be *my* attorney. Can't you do some of that lawyer stuff for me?"

The Fab raised their head precisely and leveled their blue-white eyes at Trapp. It was a bit unnerving.

"You can call me Malph. My pronouns are 'he' and 'him.' I'm not, in point of fact, *your* attorney. Technically, I represent the ISC, arguing on the side *against* extradition. But I'm as close to a defense attorney as you'll receive."

Malph stood and glided across the small room. He took meticulous steps, like an ibis poking through a swamp. "If your arrest had come a day later, the ISC would've been off the hook. You'd be going to one of those Terran United Republic prisons instead. No doubt Prague. Or Kyiv." Malph shuddered, perfectly mimicking the proper emotion of horror. "You're quite lucky. The ISC takes care of its own."

"I'm not their own. I'm an Indent."

"You're critical to the ISC. They've invested quite a bit in you."

"I was about to be released, though," Trapp muttered. "Don't you think for a minute that they care a lick what happens to me. And you still haven't told me why I'm here. Why have I been arrested?"

Malph retook his seat. "The TUR has charged you with murder one."

"Um. Say again?"

"Last Tuesday, you allegedly left Miami Base, boarded a Loop to the scene of the crime, murdered your victim, and returned to the base undetected."

"Murder?" The word sucked the saliva from Trapp's mouth. "I left the base? Impossible."

Malph touched his HoloPhone. It projected a HoloPic of a dark-haired man with dark eyes above it. "Is this you?" Malph asked.

"Looks like me, I guess. Where did you get that?"

"It's all over the Plexus. *#MurderSelfie*. Millions of views already and climbing. When you killed The Professor, you didn't have the foresight to keep your head down as you fled MAU's quad."

Trapp barely heard Malph's words as he stared at the HoloPic. It looked like him with his too-big forehead, which he always hated in HoloPics and was why he kept his bangs long. There was that same stupid expression. He looked ridiculous, even in the mug shots. This guy had looked right up at the EYE.

And then some of Malph's words broke through.

"Wait!" Trapp said. "Did you say MAU? As in Mid-Atlantic University? In Raleigh?"

"Yes."

"I killed a professor there?"

"Allegedly. And it wasn't just any professor. It was *The* Professor."

Trapp gazed at the Fab, dumbfounded. "Doctor Gray?"

"Doctor Phileas Ivan Gray, yes."

"He's dead?"

"Yes."

"I couldn't. I didn't...I've never even met the guy. Nor have I been anywhere near MAU. And the tracker in my ankle will confirm that I was on base the whole time." Trapp pointed his nose at his ankle.

"That is, technically, not ISC's problem," Malph said. His second use of the word 'technically' bolstered Trapp's unease. Malph was only a Fab, a non-feeling robot with a sophisticated MESH brain that gave him autonomy.

"It's an alibi," Trapp said weakly. "I'm innocent until proven guilty, right?"

"As an attorney representing the laws of the United States, I'm programmed to follow that doctrine of 'innocent until proven guilty.' Unfortunately, you will be prosecuted under the World Court's doctrine of 'guilty until proven innocent' from the Third Charter of the Budapest Peace Accords."

"Which means exactly what?"

"If the ISC chooses extradition, your Terran United Republic defense lawyer must prove you *weren't* at MAU during the crime. This means they will also need to prove that the EYE, an irrefutable source of evidence for half of a century, somehow got it wrong."

"But how could I have even gotten to the Loop without detection? I would've had to have been gone from the base for the better part of a day. Someone would've noticed that. Not to mention the alarms that would've gone off when I left."

"Where there's a will, there's a way. And the Murder Selfie is damning."

"Don't call it that."

"Whatever you call it, I calculate at least a ninety-seven percent chance that you are the subject in that picture." Malph stared at the floating 3D picture of Trapp's look-alike fleeing the crime scene. The scene of the murder of, arguably, the most-revered man on Terra. *Thor, incarnate.*

"How screwed am I?" Trapp asked.

"I estimate that number to be closing in on 100%. We better get to work on your defense."

3

Admiral

TRAPP STARED AT a sweaty man who'd introduced himself a few minutes ago as Captain Ban Whylee. Presumably, he was arguing *for* Trapp's extradition to the Terran United Republic.

Taking a sip of water, Trapp gazed around the courtroom. He was sitting on a hard chair facing a raised platform where three judges sat and looked bored. One of them was none other than the famous Admiral Margery Stockwell. Or *infamous*. The first captain of a Manifold ship—the *Sentinel*—which exploded on its maiden voyage. Somehow, she saved her entire crew and barely made it to the escape pod herself. Some said she was promoted to admiral so that she would never be able to captain another ship.

It was her case that was the catalyst for the Indent program. No one wanted to risk innocent people's deaths like that again.

"Does the witness need me to repeat the question?" Whylee asked.

Trapp turned back. "Yes, please."

"If you're innocent, how do you explain the 'Murder Selfie'?" Whylee waved toward his HoloPhone, which was projecting the HoloPic.

"I can't explain it. I just know it's not me."

Whylee sneered at Trapp disdainfully. "You stated during Attorney Malph's questioning that you were in the barracks on or around the time of the Professor's murder."

"Yes. I never left the base."

"Do you have any witnesses? Did anyone see you in the barracks on, uh," he looked down at his ScribePad, "last Tuesday, between 20 hundred hours and 23 hundred hours?"

"My bunkies, others who live on my floor, people who saw me in the bathrooms."

"Any Regulars?"

"Regulars don't mix with Indents. As far as they're concerned, we're still a threat, the dregs, throwaway people."

Whylee looked up at the three JAGs. "Your honors, please instruct the witness to keep to the facts."

The three turned to each other and spoke in whispers. Soon, they sat back in their big leather chairs.

"Overruled," Admiral Stockwell said. "Ask your next question."

Whylee's eyes darkened. "Under Section 42 of the Space Corps Unified Code, Indentured personnel cannot be considered reliable witnesses due to their sub-human status. Furthermore—"

"Objection." Malph was on his feet. "The captain is testifying."

"Sustained," Stockwell said. "Mr. Whylee, we know how the TUR views Indents. A damnable policy, I might add. Move on."

Whylee nodded. "Were any HoloVids from the Miami Base found to prove you were there?"

"No," Trapp said. "I was in my room all day suffering from Zero-G flu. And there are no EYE cameras in the personal spaces."

"That seems very convenient, don't you think? We have to take you at your word that you never left."

"It's very *inconvenient*. Since I was too sick to even leave my room, much less travel. Or have you never heard of Zero-G flu? And why was a DNA scan not done on the Loop carriages that ran from Miami to Raleigh that day? They'd prove that I wasn't there."

"I'm not the one who answers questions, Indent Trapmore. But since you asked, under Section 15 of the Third Charter, Paragraph 437, '...the lack of a suspect's DNA cannot be deemed proof of innocence. DNA can only be used to prove guilt.'"

"Objection," Malph said. "The captain is testifying again."

"I was only answering his question," Whylee pouted.

"Does the prosecution have another question for the witness?" Stockwell asked, gazing at Whylee warily.

"Just one more," Whylee said with a devious grin. "Indent Trapmore. Who was Jessica Brown Trapmore?"

"My mother." Trapp looked down at his hands.

"Is she still alive?"

"She died when I was five."

"How did she die?"

"Objection," Malph said. "Relevance?"

"I'll allow it," Stockwell said. "Please answer the question, Mr. Trapmore."

"Murder," Trapp said with a grimace.

"Was it ever solved?" Whylee asked.

"No."

"There was a suspect, though, wasn't there?"

"Yes."

Whylee turned to his ScribePad as if to read who the person was. Of course, he knew. Everyone knew. He looked up.

"Who was the prime suspect in the murder of Jessica Trapmore?"

"Objection, your Honor," Malph said, standing up in a feeble attempt to come to Trapp's rescue. "This line of questioning is immaterial to this extradition proceeding. Mr. Trapmore—"

"Overruled," Stockwell said, lowering her eyes at Trapp. "The witness will answer the question."

Trapp swallowed hard several times, choking on the name. It was why he was here. It was why the World Court believed in his guilt, even without the Murder Selfie.

"You can say it," Whylee said. "We all know. It's been all over the Plexus these last several days—as if anyone needed a refresher course on your sordid history. Who was the suspect?"

Trapp knew how guilty the answer would make him sound. Still, he had to say it. He cleared his throat. Then spoke in a whisper.

"Professor Phileas Gray."

❖ ❖ ❖

TRAPP WOKE THE morning after the hearing to Malph and MagnaCuffs. The Fab walked him out of the cell block as the wisps of a dream floated in Trapp's sleepy mind. There was a young woman. He couldn't place her, although he thought he knew her well. No, that wasn't right. He knew *of* her. He just couldn't remember how. Thinking that a verdict had been reached, Trapp asked Malph where he was leading them. But the Fab spoke little and kept the purpose of the trip to himself. They came through the empty courtroom to a back hallway with three offices, and Malph removed the MagnaCuffs. Then he returned to the courtroom and shut Trapp into the hallway.

"Come in, please," a voice said from beyond a slightly-opened door.

Peering in, Trapp spotted a tomb-sized desk and oak paneled walls decorated with dozens of citations, medals, and 2D HoloPics of Admiral Stockwell standing beside famous people.

He stepped inside.

And there she was, a living icon after whom schools had already been named. Before yesterday, Trapp had never seen her in person. And perched in her JAG cabinet, she'd seemed like a deity.

"Admiral Stockwell," he said, keeping his eyes lowered.

"Please sit," she said, waving her hand at a leather chair adjacent to hers. She was seated at a table, sipping what appeared to be tea. Trapp took his seat as he rubbed his wrists from the memory of MagnaCuffs.

"Tea?" the admiral asked. "Water? I can rustle up just about anything you'd like. Even contraband coffee."

"I'm fine, ma'am," Trapp said, despite his sudden loss of saliva. He struggled not to stare as he sat straight up in the chair.

"What do you think of my assistant?"

"Do you mean Malph?"

"Yes. After I inherited him, I encouraged him to study law. Did you know he's the first Fab to earn his Juris Doctorate?"

"I didn't know that. How long have you had him?"

"Over twenty years."

Trapp sat up straighter. He looked from her face to his hands and back up again. He placed his hands on the armrests and then back in his lap. Then back on the armrests again.

"At ease, Mr. Trapmore. You're making both of us nervous."

"Yes, ma'am. Permission to speak freely?"

"Of course."

"Why am I here, ma'am? Have you reached a verdict?"

"Not yet." She crossed her arms and peered at Trapp intently. "I'm leaning toward one. But, first, I wanted to ask what you think I should do."

"Me? I have no idea."

With a half-smile deepening the lines on her face, she watched him for a while as if she were trying to read his mind. And maybe she could.

"I knew your mother. We were, in fact, very close once. And I've put off this meeting for too long. For that, I'm truly sorry."

"That's okay. I'm fine."

Stockwell glued her eyes on Trapp. "It can't have been easy for you to know that justice has gone unserved all this time."

With an effort, Trapp pulled his gaze away from her intense stare. "I try not to think about it. It's been a long time since I had the right to ask for justice. I became an Indent in the hope that I would earn that right. Full citizenship. Then I'd get a lawyer to help lobby the Pols to reopen her case."

"Getting the International Police to do that would be a Sisyphean task, don't you think?"

"How so?"

"Because of the man who was supposed to have killed her."

She picked up her HoloPhone from the tea table and swiped on the screen. It projected a rotating HoloPic of an older man laid out on an examining table. The picture of Professor Gray was blurry and off-center. But there was no doubt he was dead.

"Did you kill him?" she asked.

"No, ma'am."

"If you did, I'd hardly expect you to admit it."

"Yes, ma'am."

"The powers-that-be are falling all over themselves to put your head on a spit. The trial of the century. I've heard that they plan to broadcast your execution live on the Plexus. Perhaps Albretta will even come out of hiding for the big event."

"Albretta Gray?" Trapp's face flushed. She was the girl in his dream, he now realized. Professor Gray's granddaughter. The man had raised her after her parents had died in that accident. And she immediately became the most famous granddaughter in history. Trapp hadn't thought about her in years.

He came back to the moment. Stockwell was nodding slowly.

Trapp sighed. "I'm innocent."

"I've always thought that the presumption of innocence was one of the things that made America great. Too bad we gave that up in the Budapest Accords."

"We gave up a lot," Trapp nodded.

"Maybe I can help you."

"How?"

"Your Indentureship. There's no need to end it."

"Ma'am?"

"If I rule against extradition, you'd stay here, completely out of reach from the Pols. I can furthermore see to it that you never fulfill your contract."

"You're suggesting I stay an Indent for the rest of my life?"

"Even *I* can't change your status. But... at least you'd *have* a life." She smiled.

"I promised myself I would never go back up there."

"Space?"

He nodded. "I'm the only Indent who survived an encounter with the Manifold. I don't plan to test those odds out again."

"What if I were to assign you to desk duty?"

"We don't even know each other. Why would you risk your career to help me?"

"I won't be doing it for you." She lifted her teacup and took a long sip, tears rimming her eyes. "I'd be doing it for Jessi. I owe her that much."

Stockwell changed the projected HoloPic to Trapp's criminal record and began to read aloud. "Stabbed several times. Beat up while resisting arrest. Brawls in prison. Bar fights. Possession. It seems like you've been trying hard to end your life yourself. Why?"

"To be honest, I don't know, ma'am. I guess I just felt that the dagger hanging over my head would bring about my end soon enough."

Stockwell sat up and set her tea down. "Dagger?"

"Half the world wants me dead because I could bring down their beloved Professor. The other half because I'm too weak to avenge her death." He looked away.

"Honestly, if I were alone with him in a room, I don't know what I'd do. Maybe I'd interrogate him or torture him into telling me the truth of what happened to my mother. Maybe I'd just act as jury and executioner." He looked up again. "But I've never had that chance. I wasn't there. I didn't do it."

She nodded. Then she walked over to her desk and raised her ScribePad.

"The extradition order. Say the word, and I'll reject it. The other two JAGs will follow my lead. You will never be free, never be able to seek the truth about her death—assuming you had planned to do that and weren't going to disappear with the money."

Trapp looked from her back to her pad and back up again.

"What would you do if you were me?" he asked.

"I guess I might try to escape." She laughed. "I'm a take-control person, though. And, as we said, I don't have much of a reputation to protect anymore."

Trapp could hardly believe what he was hearing.

Then she laughed and waved her hand.

"I should remind you," she said. "If you were to escape—which would be nearly impossible—I would be forced to order the Demons to come after you. They're the best at finding fugitives—even ones who've had their faces altered. You have no reason to risk your life to find your mother's murderer. And, if you wish to take your chances with the World Court, you might even get lucky. A jury could find you innocent."

She looked up at him.

"On the other hand. I've always wondered what happened to your mother all those years ago. What was it that caused the falling out between her and Gray? And does his death have anything to do with that? Are the two somehow linked?"

Trapp shook his head. He'd not considered that possibility. It was an intriguing question.

"Maybe," she added, "in finding the answer to who killed Gray, we'll find Jessi's murderer."

She laughed and waved away the notion. She thumbed her ScribePad. Malph appeared.

"How are you going to rule, ma'am?" Trapp asked as the Fab MagnaCuffed him again.

"I really don't know," Stockwell said.

She lowered her head and started to type something on her ScribePad.

A CHOICE?

Never in all of Trapp's life had he been given one. Until now. Space Corps? Indent forever? Stockwell had been friends with Jessi? Or was it more? Trapp had seen it in the admiral's eyes. Stockwell and Jessi may have even been lovers. She thought she was doing Jessi's son a favor by offering him a lifetime of servitude. He'd survive, sure, but as a member of the lowest caste on Terra.

Snick!

Trapp sat up. His eyes weren't night adjusted, and he couldn't make out a damned thing in his cell. Even the LEDs, which usually lit the corridor outside, were doused. A waft of air chilled his face from the air conditioning, the most likely source of the sound.

Trapp lay back down.

This was all Jessi's fault. Not for her untimely murder when Trapp was five, of course. That was some other asshole. Maybe Gray, maybe an unknown assailant. Still, his mother was partially to blame for his current laundry list of troubles. Starting with her choice of husband. Brady Trapmore was never destined to be a parent, much less a single one. He'd all too willingly signed away his parenting rights to Nan and Pop after Jessi's death.

Fizz!

Something moved near Trapp's ankle, tickling the skin slightly. He glanced down in panic, thinking it was a cockroach or a rat. Instead, he spotted the faint outline of a human. Trapp sat up in terror.

"Who's there?" he asked.

"Shh!" a voice said, giving away its owner.

"Malph?"

A hand flew up and covered Trapp's mouth.

"Speak only in whispers," Malph said before removing his cold, robotic hand.

"What are you doing?" Trapp whispered.

"Disabling your tracking device."

A mysterious cone of purple light hovered over Trapp's ankle. His skin sizzled slightly, and he smelled a pungent odor of burning flesh.

"Done," Malph said, now standing. "Let's go."

"The guards," Trapp muttered. "How are we—?"

"Shh!" Malph angled the door ajar and pushed a befuddled Trapp out of his cell. There were no Demons at the guards' station as Malph yanked Trapp out into the main hallway and to the elevator.

"Where is everybody?" Trapp whispered.

"Let's leave the Q&A until later."

The elevator opened, and they stepped aboard. They reached the basement and entered a garage with a dozen parked FleetCars fitted with unlit blue and red beacon lights. Malph led Trapp past them to an opening blocked by a security grill leading to a ramp that ascended into the night. As they neared it, the grill trundled upward, pattering loudly enough to draw attention. But there was no guard in the station outside. After the gate had risen high enough, Malph forced Trapp's head down and pulled him under.

"Fab programming forbids you to disobey orders," Trapp argued as the two moved up the ramp, and Malph stopped to peer around the building's corner.

"I *am* following orders," Malph said.

Then he yanked Trapp into a trot toward the barracks a hundred meters ahead. The moon emerged from behind a bank of clouds, making Trapp's NeonSkins glow in the open exercise field surrounded by EYE cameras. Malph's MESH brain must've suffered from a computer virus to commit this brazen act of criminal misconduct. And yet, Trapp followed in stunned silence as Malph turned toward the main gates.

"There are at least a dozen guards up there," Trapp argued. "They'll shoot first, ask questions later."

"*You* ask a lot of questions," Malph commented.

"Here's one. What the hell are we doing?"

"Escaping."

"No." Trapp yanked free from Malph's grip. "I'm not."

"Minutes ago, the front gate guards were called away to help quell an Indent uprising. It may have just been a false alarm sent by a hacker. It may even be a real threat, depending on who you ask. In either case, all hands were deployed. And when they discover it's nothing but a false alarm, they'll rush back here. I could take you back to your cell if you'd like. Or we could try to get out before they return."

Trapp shook his head in confusion.

"If it helps," Malph said in an even tone, "I'm doing what Admiral Stockwell wishes."

"She's not keeping me here? Or extraditing me?"

"Turns out, she took the third option. And my orders are clear. We need to move our asses."

Malph turned, and Trapp followed willingly.

"Technically," Trapp said, "you don't have an ass. Nor have I ever heard a Fab use that word before."

"Didn't realize you were an expert on Fabs. We have servo-electric glutes designed to mimic the locomotion of homo sapiens."

They approached the gate.

"The EYE logs will show you helped me," Trapp said. "Your ass, such as it is, will be in a lot of hot water."

"When they check the EYE logs, all that the Demons will uncover are several minutes of live feed of an Indent snoring away under his covers. You really should get that checked out."

"What?"

"Snoring could indicate many life-threatening possibilities. I'd see a medic if I were you."

Trapp guffawed while Malph entered the guard house. He stood outside as a breeze bit into his thin NeonSkins. Far-off rumbles hinted at a storm forming over the ocean. A loud clang startled him. Unbelievably, the main gate began to roll open. Malph returned, and the two ran out into the night.

They crossed a narrow highway and crouched behind a stand of pampas grass. The steaming bog behind them led to a meandering stream that glinted in the moonlight. Trapp wondered if there were alligators.

He glanced over at the base. This was the first time he'd seen it from the outside. The ramjet port glowed several kilometers to the south. White beacons flashed at intervals to the top of its tall runway, angled 200 meters into the sky.

"The Loop is four point three kilometers to the east," Malph said, pointing down the road. "It's oh-four-hundred now. You need to get there by oh-five-thirty. You'll catch the northbound Loop to Grand Central Station."

"New York? I'm the most recognizable face on the planet right now. I wouldn't get five kilometers."

"There's a rudimentary disguise in here." Malph pulled a dark rucksack off his back. "I suggest you immediately go abroad once you get to New York. Catch the Munich Loop. Or Amsterdam. A few hours under the Atlantic should get you to somewhere safe."

"The admiral's sure to be arrested for treason for programming you to help me."

"I didn't help you. All of this will be deleted. I won't even remember it. Furthermore, the admiral has already signed the order for the Demons to search for you."

Trapp gritted his teeth against another strong gust of wind. The rumble in the sky was growing louder.

"She signed my death warrant?"

"She had no choice. She learned through a source that the ISC plans to kill you. They'll make it look like a failed escape attempt. A real escape was the only way to avoid that fate. Ironic, huh?"

"Why wouldn't the ISC just extradite me?"

"Frankly, I'm surprised it took them this long to determine the risks of such a decision. If you were extradited, your conviction would most likely result in criminal prosecution for the entire ISC administration—you being their property."

"Damn!"

"Worse, such unilateral action could bring down Space Corps. Manifold production will immediately halt while the TUR works out the particulars of Space Corps's disposition."

"But the Manifold is the only thing keeping the peace," Trapp said.

"Which is why the admiral thinks your escape is the only thing that can cool things down. The manhunt will take everyone's attention. It won't matter if you live or die. The ISC will be off the hook either way."

"Sounds like the admiral *wants* me to die."

"On the contrary, she's instructed me to tell you that she strongly suggests you use this new-found freedom for a bigger mission. Find Professor Gray's murderer. Prove your innocence. And all of this goes away."

"Impossible. I have none of the skills needed to track down a murderer. And what if I just say a big 'fuck you' to her and go permanently underground?"

"Then you will be indirectly responsible for starting the Second Carbon War. Millions will die. But sure, go for it. You be you and all that. Nothing is stopping you. Well, except for the hundreds of Demons looking for you. And the Pols. Every police agency on Terra. As the days go by, the bounty goes up. And then there are the oligarchs."

"Russians? What do they have to do with any of this?"

"When the bounty reaches a certain amount, even with their riches, they'll be compelled to send out armies to find you. You're about to become very popular."

"What if I take my story to the press?"

"It better be a PlexusCast with its own army." Malph smiled wryly. "Almost every option before you will result in your death. Except for proving you didn't commit the murder. And for you, job one is to stay alive." Malph looked down at the rucksack. "Things you'll need in that endeavor can be found inside. Good luck. Don't let the admiral down. Or I may just come and kill you myself."

Malph smiled, patted Trapp condescendingly on the head, and bolted for the fence. When he reached it, he leaped into the air and cleared the concertina wire by a meter. He alighted on the other side with the slightest sound before disappearing into the darkness.

"Whoa!" Trapp exclaimed.

He inspected the contents of the rucksack. Among other things, it contained his IndentSkins. He elected to pull these over his NeonSkins rather than leave his clothes behind for someone to track his movements.

He patted the arm pocket. Rory's tag was still there.

He also found his HoloPhone. It flashed to life as he lifted it.

"Indent," the citizenship status stated.

"Great!" Trapp grunted.

The admiral said she couldn't change his status. Apparently, she wasn't lying. A quick search of his HoloPhone revealed that his felony record was equally unaltered. He was still an ex-con.

Yet, Stockwell seemed to have understood Trapp couldn't get very far without terros. She'd loaded the HoloPhone with enough to go anywhere or do anything he wanted. Could he hide out for the rest of his life? Avoid the Pols, Demons, oligarchs, and every crackpot with a HoloPhone posting a sighting on the Plexus?

A sharp pain hit him in the stomach.

He knew what he had to do.

"Solve Gray's murder," he said.

Follow Admiral Stockwell's implicit orders. Honor her wishes because she was Jessi's lover? Perhaps even solve his mother's murder in the process? Stop a fucking war?

Trapp was no hero.

A strong wind gust accompanied a blast of thunder and lightning.

"Job one," he said. "Stay alive."

Trapp trotted off to the east and the coastline.

4

Fugitive

TRAPP STOOD IN front of the ancient brick building.

Held together by a carapace of brown-scorched graffiti and patches of translucent, non-fossil-fuel-based PlayStyx covering broken-out windows, the old building appeared to be near collapse. Which was precisely how it had looked the last time Trapp had been here. Descending a sunken stairway that reeked of death and sewage, Trapp came to a heavy steel door with a pop-up keypad and a retinal scanner.

"Shit!" he whispered, gritting his teeth.

Tentatively, he moved his eye to the scanner, which he remembered had been programmed to poke a needle into any retina it didn't recognize. The latch buzzed, causing Trapp to recoil. But his retina was still in the database. And, with a shaky hand, he reached for the knob.

The door flew open. Trapp was met with the business end of a contraband shotgun.

He threw his hands up in surrender. "It's me."

"How can I be *certaine*?" the voice said in a familiar French-Swiss accent.

"Because of Stockholm."

"What about Stockholm?"

"We were...we shared a bed in a hostel there, once. It was colder than a witch's tit...you asked me to spoon so we could—"

The person pumped the shotgun, silencing Trapp.

"I asked you something else, didn't I?"

"That I never speak of that night again." Trapp grinned despite the imminent threat of double-aught buckshot blasting a hole in his face.

"*Emmerdeur!*"

"*You're* the pain in the ass," Trapp said. "Cut the shit. Let me pass."

The weapon lowered. A shadowy figure blocked most of the doorway and the dim yellow light of bootleg incandescents. Arnault retreated a pace, allowing Trapp entry. As the door slammed behind them, Trapp grabbed the bear of a friend and planted a kiss on his forehead.

"That night in Stockholm wasn't an invitation for more," Arnault said, irritably pushing him away.

"I know," Trapp said. "I'm just fuckin' happy you're alive."

"I'm not sure I feel the same way about you. Why can't you use the front door like every other asshole?"

"The EYE cameras down below are for shit."

"How do you know the Pols haven't upgraded them while you were away?"

"As if."

The two men now studied each other. Arnault, who was close to Trapp's mass at their last meeting, looked to have gained almost another person. He was sporting a five o'clock shadow, and his receding hairline had given way to a silvery sheen.

Still, the big man wore a grin.

Arnault turned and led Trapp into the cellar of his house.

"You're trying to get us both killed, aren't you?" he asked as they climbed rickety stairs to the first floor.

They entered a galley kitchen and Arnault waved Trapp over to a small well-used table with mismatched chairs.

"Tea?" he asked.

"You got something stronger?" Trapp asked. "I've had a pretty rough few days."

"I'll bet," Arnault said, placing a pot of water on the stove. "But no liquor. I cut that shit out a long time ago. Being in the *putain taule* will do that to a man. Especially after the second time."

"You spent time in prison? I hadn't heard that."

"Last year. Six months. But I'm a reformed *Suisse* now. One hundred percent."

Trapp leveled his vision at his old friend, searching the man's bright blues for deception. Arnault returned the stare. When the teapot started to whistle, he looked away. Pouring two mugs of tea, he handed one to Trapp, filling the small space with a savory aroma of oolong.

"I went too far," Arnault said after joining Trapp at the table, his chair groaning under his weight.

"Fake IDs?" Trapp asked. "Counterfeit terros?"

"*Non*. F'art."

"Excuse you?" Trapp asked, blowing steam off his tea.

"Faux Art," Arnault said in a low voice. "Oils are illegal now, you know. Because of those damned Accords, even though art paint isn't made with petroleum. But say the word 'oil,' and everyone becomes triggered. So, they passed a law. Only PlayStyx paints. Except for restoration artists. And, of course, the old masters are allowed to be bought and sold as is, the new laws tripling their worth, I might add. Which seems like not so much of a coincidence to me."

"Yeah," Trapp said, sipping his tea.

"The nouveau riche can still cover their castle walls with art and are permitted to feel as superior as ever over the *bourgeoisie*. And what can I say? I saw a business opportunity."

"What'd you do?" Trapp grinned knowingly.

"Let's just say that if someone were to discover a painting in their *grand-mère*'s garret—Vermeer, Renoir, Magritte, for instance—they would suddenly need an enterprising so-and-so to get it to auction for them. For a fee, of course."

"That seems like a legitimate business model."

"The problem is, there aren't many paintings out there that haven't already been discovered. And what is a broker to do if he, say, wants to find a way to earn enough terros that he can retire in the South of France?"

"You got caught selling forgeries?"

"I know," Arnault said with a grin and a wave of his hand. "*Stupide!* But my counterfeiter was a *conservateur du musée*. One of only a hundred people worldwide who can purchase oil paint, legally."

"He wasn't really a conservator, was he?"

Arnault peered over his mug with a sheepish grin.

"You forged his license," Trapp said with a nod. "And who painted the paintings?"

"Yours truly. Pretty good shit, if I say so myself."

"I always said you could've been a legitimate artist."

"Where's the fun in that?" Arnault's glare indicated his question was a dead-serious one.

"What happened with your new business venture?" Trapp asked.

"Sophie gave me two black eyes."

"Sophie?"

Arnault smiled and thumbed his HoloPhone, bringing up a smattering of HoloPics of a thick, attractive blonde posing in various positions, many of which were nearly pornographic. He swiped them away. Then, with a serious look, he projected the Murder Selfie above the table.

"Murder, *mon ami*?" he said with a low whistle and a slow shake of his head. "A bit out of your league, isn't it?"

"That pic is not of me."

"That's not what my software analysis says. And if you're right and I'm wrong, the Pols must've deep-faked your face. We'd all be fucked. They could frame anyone for anything at any time…"

"I didn't do the crime."

"Maybe someone drugged you, got you to do it without your knowledge."

"I have a different theory."

"Which is?" Arnault asked.

"Surgical alteration." Arnault's eyes narrowed. "And, if I'm right, there's only one person in the world…"

"Get out!" Arnault shouted, standing up so fast he knocked his chair to the floor with a thud. "That you'd think an *ami* would fuck over another *ami! Frères d'une autre mère!*

"Are we?" Trapp asked, standing up. The two men stood chest to chest. Arnault was big. But Trapp had better fighting skills.

"What?" Arnault asked.

"Are we brothers from another mother?"

"I thought so. Until this moment."

Arnault stared Trapp down as if debating which part of the smaller man's body to rip off first. Then his eyes went moist, and he looked away, his jaw pulsing.

"I had to ask, bro," Trapp said in a low voice. "You'd have suspected me too if the tables were turned."

Arnault glared down at Trapp.

"*Non!*" he said. "I would've trusted you."

"Perhaps. But you've never been charged with murder. Never been on the run from a million people who want you dead."

"*Certainment!* And, for that reason alone, you're not currently lying in pieces on my *sol de la cuisine*."

"Sorry," Trapp said, raising his hands in surrender. "You're right. I was way out of line."

"You know I would never cooperate with the Pols." Arnault's lower lip stuck out in an ursine pout. "Even if it were to save my own ass."

"I know, man. I know. I guess I just had to hear you say it."

They stared at each other for a long time.

"You don't have an evil twin out there, do you?" Arnault asked.

Trapp laughed.

"Even if I did, the match is too perfect. Or imperfect. The face has my same crooked front tooth, freckles, and moles, the same stupid eyebrow cowlick. Besides, according to Doyle, it's never twins."

"Doyle? Is that the guy you used to run with in Spain?"

"No. He was a famous author. Wrote all those Sherlock Holmes novels?"

Arnault's eyes were big with bewilderment.

"Never mind." Trapp waved a hand.

Thankfully, Arnault's HoloPhone chimed and he looked down at it. Then he projected a news article HoloPic. "You better find the guy. And quick."

Trapp read the headline.

"I thought I'd have at least another day before the ISC admitted they'd lost me."

"They're asking for a bounty that's the highest in history," Arnault said, studying Trapp closely.

"Better not be thinking what I think you're thinking."

"Nah!" Arnault grinned widely. "Of course not. And, to answer your next question, you can't stay here. My ass will already be in a sling with the Pols for not turning you in."

"I'm not staying, anyway. I need to go back. I need to prove my innocence."

"*Stupide idée.* And if you're not here to find a place to hole up, I'm not sure how I can help you."

"There's one thing, I think, you can do for me."

Trapp smiled and nodded. He pointed at his face.

"*Non, non, non!*" Arnault said. "I haven't done that in years. And Sophie will kill me if I get caught."

"You're the best in the business. And I'm pretty sure you still have a few tricks up your sleeve."

Arnault looked Trapp up and down critically.

"There's one idea I've been itching to try," he said. "And you're not gonna like it."

Without another word, Arnault headed back down to his cellar.

"EXCUSE ME, SIR," someone said to Trapp.

He had taken the window seat in the back of the Loop carriage to avoid confrontations. He'd kept his head down and studied his HoloPhone, trying to be inconspicuous. Still, someone was trying to get his attention.

Trapp looked up.

A porter stood next to a cart laden with sandwiches, pieces of fruit, SynthCrisps of varying flavors, urns of hot tea and cold, and recycled water.

"Yes?" Trapp asked, trying not to react to the food.

"I'm sorry," the porter said, blanching. "I didn't mean to interrupt."

"It's quite alright. Did you need something?"

"I was going to offer you a snack," the porter said. "But, I mean…not that it's any of my business. Clearly, I was mistaken. Of course, you wouldn't want—"

He trailed off, completely mortified.

"Why wouldn't I want one of your offerings?" Trapp asked, having a little fun with the thin man. His stomach rumbled in protest, trying to give him away. But the carriage trucks bounced on their cushion of magnetic levitation and made an ambient sound that masked his stomach's betrayal.

"You're a—" the guy whispered. "I mean, aren't you?"

"A Fab?"

The guy turned gray, his face collapsing into a small, nauseated ball.

"I'm sorry," he said, gagging on his own words. "It's not appropriate to ask."

"It's fine," Trapp said, letting the guy off the hook. "You're correct. My kind doesn't require food." He pointed to the cable that ran out of his midsection and was plugged into the outlet on the seat in front of him. Another detail that Arnault felt was necessary to complete the disguise. "I'm getting enough fuel from this."

"Forgive the intrusion," the porter muttered as he moved his cart onto the next passenger.

Trapp hid a smile behind his phone.

He was half-tempted to send Arnault a HoloText, confirming that his disguise of ultra-white skin, shaved head, and yellow contacts lens had passed the flight test. Trapp had encountered many people on the way to the Heathrow Loop. Most ignored him. A few gave him a second glance as if they weren't quite sure *what* he was. One guy, whom Trapp had seen a few times as he made his way through the station, had stuck out like a sore thumb himself. He wore dark jeans and a black T-shirt to match his slicked-back jet hair—a goth. And, when Trapp made eye contact with the man, he glanced away quickly, giving himself up as a gawker. Trapp dismissed it for what it was. Trapp was tall for a Fab, which was one part of the disguise he couldn't change. Still, Arnault had been a master. And the encounter with the porter proved Trapp was safe to travel.

He lowered his head and waited as the Loop flew west at a thousand kilometers per hour, hundreds of meters under the sea.

5

Gothic

TRAPP WAS BEING followed.

As he stepped off the train in New York's Grand Central Station, he became aware that everyone was looking around, every eye scanning for a fugitive. Furthermore, the place was teeming with a greater-than-usual number of Loop Security agents, all on high alert. No one seemed to recognize him. Still, Trapp kept his head down on the way to the Southern Concourse. But then, there he was. Standing in a duty-free shop, the goth guy from Heathrow was admiring an expensive bottle of scotch and glanced up. Trapp made eye contact. Goth Guy looked away a little too quickly again. And Trapp knew. The man was tailing him.

Trapp ducked into a nearby shop.

He picked up a bag of something vaguely vegetable-based and hid behind a sign with a big green leaf on it. Goth Guy couldn't be a Pol or a Demon. Otherwise, Trapp would've already been locked in a scary room with lights shining into his face and angry voices threatening him. Goth Guy could be an agent of the oligarchs. Perhaps, as Malph predicted, the bounty had gone up enough to draw the Russians in.

"I didn't know Fabricants smoked weed."

Trapp shot a look toward the speaker. A ginger-haired young man wearing a rainbow T-shirt stared at Trapp's hands. Trapp followed his gaze. Inadvertently, Trapp had picked up a bag labeled "Norwegian Gold," which touted its contents as having a boysenberry opulence with a sandalwood-structured smoke. He froze at his ineptitude. But then he looked up at the kid.

"Maybe you should check your human supremacy at the door," he said. "What business of it is yours if we smoke weed?" He lowered his voice to a conspiratorial whisper. "You know, we do it secretly behind buildings when all the humans aren't looking. We get high and plan our take-over of Terra, mostly because of insensitive pricks like you."

The kid raised his hands in surrender. "S—sorry, dude. Take the pot. No charge. Just don't post this on the Plexus. I can't afford another one star review."

Trapp tossed the bag to the kid. "I don't want your crappy cannabis."

He turned and huffed out of the shop. For a moment, he was so overwhelmed by human supremacy he'd forgotten himself and what he'd been doing.

"Damn!" he whispered.

Shaking off the angst, he moved to the Southern Concourse security line.

And why was he so nervous? His plan was solid. He'd made it this far without being recognized. He knew how to get into the building, how to defeat its security protocols. It was the best place to go. And he was just one Loop ride away from putting this whole thing to bed. He would find the answers, would clear his name. So why was he obsessing about Plan B? That required a trip of thousands of miles in the opposite direction. It would almost certainly fail, too. His contact was more likely to call the Pols than to provide sanctuary and help.

"The line's moving," a woman from behind said. She was carrying a crying baby in a pack on her chest.

Trapp moved forward. "Sorry, ma'am."

"Where are you headed?"

"DC."

"Me too. My wife is with the reformed US military…" Her words suddenly drifted away as Trapp saw something. Goth Guy was ten people ahead. He was boarding Trapp's train! "…she's held the post for ten months," the woman continued.

Trapp nodded before stepping up farther. What was he going to do? He most certainly couldn't get on that train. And, if he ducked his head…*Oh shit!* Goth Guy turned around and looked directly at Trapp. In a mock salute, the man nodded and put a finger to his eyebrow.

"…advocate for the rights of all humanoids…" the woman was saying loudly so she could be heard over the screaming of her squirming child.

"Ma'am," Trapp said, interrupting. "Perhaps, instead of worrying about the rights of human analogs, you should attend to the needs of the tiny human in your care."

"So you're fine with the FTA?"

"I have no feelings about the Fabricant Transition Act either way. We were designed to serve. And, since we often outlive our owners, it's logical that we be given to another upon their death."

"It's just that..." She shooed Trapp forward. "I don't think we should be so cavalier with the rights of our servants."

"I'm not your servant."

"No. I guess not. But you do look familiar. Have we met before?"

"I don't see how," Trapp said, turning away as his heart rate shot up.

"I never forget a face. Do you work with my wife?"

"I don't think so." Trapp could barely hear his own voice through the thudding in his ears.

"I know I've seen you somewhere. Recently. Just give me a minute and I'll get it."

Trapp shook his head and checked on Goth Guy.

Talking frantically on his HoloPhone, he was just two positions back from the scanner. Several guards stood behind the MoleScan and studied the line while glancing back and forth at their phones. Apparently, they were comparing faces to Trapp's picture.

He glanced back at the woman. She smiled and tapped her forehead, telling him she was still trying to place him. Soon, she would shout it to the masses. The Selfie Murderer was in their midst. The Plexus would call her a heroine. And Trapp would be arrested.

Goth Guy reached the MoleScan. He was still on his HoloPhone. The woman guard at the head of the line pointed at his phone and then the conveyor belt. Goth Guy ignored her and continued to speak on his phone. The woman motioned for him to step out of line. Goth Guy shook his head in refusal. The guard grunted and spoke more forcibly. Goth Guy responded with loud refusals. The guard's hand moved to her holstered bolt gun.

Goth Guy raised his hands while smiling in surrender.

That's when Trapp saw it. So did the guard. Goth Guy was wearing a holstered 9-millimeter Glock. The guard pulled her weapon and pointed it at the guy while talking into her shoulder-mounted radio. Guards turned away from their search for Trapp and, with guns drawn, moved to her aid.

This would've been the perfect opportunity for Trapp to flee. But he couldn't take his eyes off the scene. Even the woman with the screaming child went silent. No one moved. Goth Guy spoke in terse, short words while slowly lowering his HoloPhone. The guards shouted at him, indicating that they were about to shoot. Ignoring them, he began bringing his phone back toward his face.

Several guns cocked loudly. Goth Guy's HoloPhone projected an image—a badge of some sort. Trapp couldn't read its inscription but knew it wasn't a Pol or Demon badge. It was one he'd never seen before. Somehow, its presence calmed the guards. They holstered their guns. Goth Guy removed his weapon and laid it on the conveyor belt to run through the X-ray machine.

But then things got weirder.

A young woman, perhaps a teenager, sprinted by Trapp for the front of the line. She reached Goth Guy and they hugged. The guard now did something extraordinary. She smiled and nodded at the little girl. Then she made the girl take a Selfie with her as if she were a celebrity. This put the whole incident into perspective. The girl was a Plexus influencer or a child actor and Goth Guy was her bodyguard. His vigilance toward potential threats had made him extra aware of strangeness. This was why he watched Trapp so intently. A very tall Fab would be enough of an anomaly to require extra monitoring.

Trapp smiled. Still, too much had happened to throw off his confidence.

Plan B was not only the safer option but the best one. If Celebrity Girl and her bodyguard were headed South, Goth Guy would continue to watch Trapp. He might even realize who Trapp was and contact the Pols. This was a scrutiny Trapp didn't need.

"Fuck!" he muttered as he turned out of line.

"Language!" the baby-toting woman said.

"Fuck that," Trapp said.

"Fuck that," the child said in a high-pitched voice, mimicking Trapp.

Trapp fought to keep his laughter at bay. As he headed out of the security area, the tension in his stomach eased, giving him a sign.

Going to MAU had been a bad idea.

Alaska was the right play.

"I'M SORRY," AN old man's voice said, crackling in the rusty speaker posted by the doorway of the small house. "I'm not accepting solicitors at this time."

"I'm not selling anything," Trapp said to the speaker. "I'm here to..."

To what? He knew what. But he didn't know how to say it. To gain entry to this place, which hadn't changed in years. Of course, the paint had faded and was peeling. And the cracks in the sidewalk were wider. Or was that an illusion? Had he expected that this time-traveling moment would result in such changes? Just like the house.

To say it was tiny would be generous. And why had Trapp remembered it having the interior space of a European castle?

"Fabs aren't welcome here," a male voice said, crackling from the antique intercom system, ancient vocal cords, or both.

"I'm not a Fab. It's just a disguise to keep from being arrested."

A long silence followed.

"No!" the voice finally whispered. "You can't be him! He died a long time ago."

"I'm alive. And I'm right here."

Trapp stared at the doorway next to the little speaker and tried to will it to open. The man would be in his mid-eighties by now, although Trapp couldn't remember the exact year he was born. And why did he believe Trapp had died? Was he suffering from dementia?

The front lock buzzed and clicked.

The door creaked open on hinges that screamed for lubricant.

A bent man stood in the darkness as a hint of decay tinged with urine issued from the house. The man's white hair, which had only been graying when Trapp last saw him, had all but disappeared from the top of his age-spotted scalp, leaving only a few pen-strokes of whiteness to cover the leathered skin.

"You look like a ghost," the man croaked.

Trapp laughed. "It's a disguise."

"I'd have been just fine if you'd have left me be."

"I need your help."

He looked up at Trapp. Trapp was almost half a meter taller than the man. Still, he slumped, feeling like a child again. The man cleared his throat, which did little to arrest the croak that came out.

"You better come on in then, grandson."

Pop turned and hobbled back into the darkness.

6

Lab

THE OLD MAN led them into Trapp's childhood home.

Stacks of papers and empty food containers lined one side of the hallway, boxes of clothes on the other. The carpet was worn, especially next to the doorway that led to the attic. Apparently, Pop had been going up and down those stairs a lot. Perhaps to purge Nan's stowaways. Trapp had been forbidden to go up there as a kid. A rule he'd broken a thousand times.

"After your grandmother died," Pop said as he heated two meals in the kitchen microwave, "I had to learn to cook."

"Sorry to hear that," Trapp said, thinking that microwaving was hardly cooking.

"It's okay," the old man said, waving a gnarled, age-spotted hand. "I could barely stand her cooking anyway."

The microwave beeped. Holding a tattered towel, Pop slowly extracted two bubbling dishes and brought them to the table. He made a racket as he rummaged through a drawer and came up with two mismatched forks. The old man dropped into his seat with a groan and then plowed into his meal, eating like it was his first food in days. Which, by the gauntness of his frame, was probably not far from the truth.

Trapp's stomach growled at the sight of the gray meat and beige veggies, completely unidentifiable as food. As a fake Fab, he'd not considered that eating something might give him away. He took his first bite of the mystery meat tentatively. It was some of the best food he'd eaten in a while. He dug in graciously.

"I can barely stand to look at you in this get-up," Pop said, pointing at Trapp's disguise.

"It was a necessary evil. I'm the most popular subject on the Plexus these days."

"I'm guessing you came to Alaska for the cabin, then. I haven't been up there in years. I'm not even sure it's still standing. But you can use it, such as it is."

"Thanks." Trapp's words were garbled as he wolfed down the food. He was now convinced he was eating fake beef and synth potatoes. "But I've been running my whole life—a walking disaster area. I can't run away anymore."

Pop stopped eating and pointed his fork at Trapp. "You lost your mother. It's not your fault that you felt the need to act out. I understood that. Although I didn't always like it."

Trapp gulped down several bites, holding back tears. Satisfied, he pushed the tray away and swigged some water.

"Why are you here?" Pop asked. "If not to hide out?"

"To find clues to Jessi's murder. I heard a recent theory that Gray's homicide might even be related. If I hope to solve his murder and clear my name, I must first solve hers."

"I'm not sure what you hope to find here. Jessi spent most of the last year of her life at that damned lab. Didn't even invite us over for a tour. I mean, I don't blame her for the isolation. The falling out with Professor Gray hit her hard."

"What was it all about, the fight?"

"Differences in philosophy. She never said what they were, though."

"They were working on something together before she left MAU. Do you know what it was?"

"A goddamned secret project. She was tight-lipped about it. However, I once saw something on her ScribePad that I wasn't supposed to. She was home for the holidays and left it open on the kitchen table. So I wasn't, technically, invading her privacy." He grinned.

"What was it?"

"Some schematic. Of what, I couldn't say. But I did see a heading. XTerra. Or something like that."

"XTerra? What is that?"

"Got me." Pop shrugged.

"How about her lab here? Was anything salvaged after the murder?"

"The Pols took everything as evidence. We never saw any of it again."

"Damn!" Trapp said.

Pop set his fork down. He stared at his tray for a long time in silence. Finally, he looked up. "I suppose it's okay, after all these years, to tell you the truth. A week before her murder, Jessi had some stuff brought to the house: a stack of crates. You know, like the ones from the Prudhoe Bay Fish Market where the daily catch was displayed on ice before deep sea fishing was outlawed?"

"The big wooden ones?"

"Yes. And they were sealed. Like she didn't want us to know what was in them. She had them stored in the attic. We were told explicitly never to mess with them, that doing so might be dangerous."

The old man stood and cleared their trays. He rinsed them under the faucet before wiping them dry and stacking them into a cupboard full of empty trays. Then he came back.

"Which was why you were never allowed up there," he added.

"I, uh, didn't listen," Trapp said with a chuckle. Pop's eyes were fixated on something over Trapp's shoulder. "I mean, I guess I should come out with it. I hid up there a thousand times, especially when I got into trouble."

Pop held his finger up. He was still staring over Trapp's shoulder. Trapp turned to see what was so mesmerizing.

A live display of the front yard and its dying plants was being transmitted on a ScribePad sitting on a small desk in the corner of the kitchen. Dusk had begun to fall, so the lighting was dim. But Trapp made out what had drawn Pop's attention. Three dark human forms were walking up to the house.

"Demons," Trapp said as Pop stood up.

He grabbed Trapp by the shoulder and pulled him into the front hallway. The doorbell rang.

"Up you go!" he whispered to Trapp as he opened the door to the attic. "And be as quiet as a mouse. I'll do my best to get rid of them."

Trapp stepped onto the stairs.

Pop shut him into the darkness.

❖ ❖ ❖

POP WAS SUFFERING from dementia.

Trapp had never seen any crates in the attic. And he'd been in every corner of the musty, dusty, spider-filled space.

Why hadn't he just fled out the back door? Only a few hundred meters from Pop's house was the entrance to one of Terra's most extensive remaining forests. Trapp had come from that direction earlier after riding the OverLand to Prudhoe Bay and hiking here.

Still, he'd come for information. And he was no closer to solving Jessi's murder. After the Demons left, maybe he could coax Pop's rusted mind to remember where she put those crates.

Doing his best not to pant too loudly, Trapp listened with his ear pushed against the closed door.

"...not here," Pop was saying. "I haven't seen him in years."

Someone spoke in muffled tones.

"No," Pop said. "I'm not lying."

More muffled tones.

"I mean, if you feel the need to." Pop's voice rose. "But you'll not find anybody in my house."

Clearly, these words were meant for Trapp. And, quickly, he ran up the stairs, keeping his steps to the outside to avoid creaks. He came to the attic floor and crept to one end.

His eyes adjusted as twilight bled in through the gable window on the western end of the room. Trapp peered around, looking for a hiding place. Suddenly, all of the work Pop had done to clear this place of its contents came to light. There was almost nothing left. No boxes to hide behind. That ancient wardrobe that sat in one corner was gone. So were the old beds stacked against the wall and the dresser missing a drawer. There was nothing to conceal his presence.

"Fuck!" Trapp whispered.

If Fake Danny chose to come up here... Maybe they'd search the house and leave. Still, Trapp needed a backup plan.

Careful to make no footstep sounds, he moved over to the window. It overlooked the edge of the property. A rising moon lit up the fields below. He could open this and jump down. It was a long way to the bottom. He gave it a fifty-fifty chance of not injuring himself.

He tried the window. It wouldn't budge. He looked for a lock. Found none. Tried it again. It had been painted shut, or its frame had racked enough to keep it from moving. He looked around for something to break the glass. This idea was foolish, of course. There was nothing. And even if he found something, the resulting sound would draw Fake Danny upstairs.

Too bad there was no window on the eastern side of this room. The lot sloped upward that way. And that was also closest to the woods. Even if Fake Danny heard him break it, Trapp still had a good chance of making it into hiding before those guys caught up to him. And why wasn't there a window over there?

Trapp suddenly heard voices at the bottom of the stairs.

"Nothing up there but some cobwebs," Pop said loudly enough for his voice to carry. Muffled voices spoke directly and harshly. Their words were indecipherable. But Trapp got the general gist. Fake Danny wasn't to be deterred. The sound of the latch opening confirmed this.

Trapp was cornered. And he was about to be discovered.

Studying the window, he calculated how much he'd be hurt if he threw his body at it. The glass would surely shred his skin. And the fall would break an ankle or, worse, a leg. His flight to the woods would be more of a limping exercise in futility, what with the blood trail he'd leave behind from his ripped skin.

He leaned against the western wall, thinking about this as the door creaked open. A trapezoid of light illuminated the stairs. Footfalls, now. Trapp was mortified; his dizziness made it feel like the wall was moving.

And then he realized it was.

"A door," he said, almost screaming before lowering his voice to a whisper. It was a hidden door, if it was one at all. And Trapp pushed on it. It opened a crack and then came to a stop. He pushed hard. But it wouldn't budge. Light bled out from the crack, proving that there was a window in this hidden room. The door had blended into the beadboard so perfectly, Trapp had missed it after being in its presence hundreds of times. Still, he couldn't get into the compartment if he couldn't open the door.

"I assure you," he heard Pop's voice coming up the stairs. "My grandson's not up here. I haven't seen him in —"

"Shut up, old man," a man said. Trapp was right. It was Fake Danny. Trapp recognized the voice. "Or I'll put a bolt in you that will keep you from walking for the rest of your short life."

Trapp's eyes narrowed. No one threatened Pop. Still, rationality took over. If he challenged Fake Danny and his crew, all of Pop's efforts to conceal him would be for naught. Not to mention that Pop would go to prison for harboring a fugitive.

Trapp leaned down. He placed both hands on the doorway and pushed. It budged another few centimeters.

He pushed some more. It was now open about twenty centimeters. He pushed half of his body into it. The opening wasn't big enough. His hand reached out and grabbed hold of something inside. It was a rope handle. And immovable. He pulled. And he got himself almost halfway in.

Now, he was stuck for sure.

Footfalls creaked up the stairs. Someone had turned on a flashlight. Soon, they'd be high enough to turn it up and see Trapp.

He sucked in his stomach. Pushing with his right foot and pulling with his left hand, which still held the strange handle, he forced his body inside another centimeter.

"I'm telling you," Pop protested. "There's nothing up—"

Trapp heard a pop and thud. Pop groaned. The shadows from the flashlight showed bodies moving frantically. It appeared Fake Danny had hit Pop and the other guys were trying to muscle him down the stairs. Trapp's anger almost made him give up again. But, once again, he realized that if he didn't make it into this room undetected, Pop's sacrifice would be in vain.

He pulled and slid through the opening.

Holding his breath, he shut the door and sat with his back against it. Light now shone under the minute crack at the bottom. It moved around as he heard creaking. People walked outside. They did so in silence. This went on for several seconds.

"I don't know, boss," the muffled voice of another Demon said. "I think the old fart was telling us the truth. This attic is empty."

"Maybe he jumped out the window," Demon Three said.

"That window hasn't opened in years," Demon Two argued.

Trapp's stomach rumbled loudly. Pop's mystery meal wasn't sitting well with Trapp's digestive system.

"Did you hear that?" Fake Danny asked.

Damn! After having starved himself for days and convincing people he was a Fab, eating was about to give Trapp away.

"I don't know what you're talking about, boss," Demon Two said. "I don't hear a thing."

"Maybe I just imagined it," Fake Danny admitted.

"Maybe it was just the—" Trapp's stomach grumbled. "I heard that. It came from over there."

Footfalls moved in his direction. *Fuck-fuck-fuck!*

Lights now shined under his ass and through his bent legs.

"It's here," Demon Two said.

"Yeah. I think..." Fake Danny thumped against the phony wall. Then Trapp heard a squeak. The old wood was giving his hiding place away. A loud crunch made him almost let out a gasp.

"Got it," Fake Danny said. "Just a mouse."

"You squished it," Demon Two said. "Gross. Let's get out of here."

"We need to retrace his steps," Demon Three said.

"Sure," Fake Danny said, his voice just a few centimeters from Trapp's head. He didn't sound convinced. At this point, if Trapp's stomach were to make noise again, or if he tried to get a breath, which he desperately needed, Fake Danny would know he was there.

"Let's get the fuck out of here."

Three men's footfalls faded behind Trapp, clomping down the stairs.

The door shut behind them. He still held his breath. It could be a ruse and one of them might've stayed behind.

But then Trapp choked as he spotted what was hidden in the small room with him.

"Jessi's crates," he whispered in awe.

As Pop had said, they'd been fashioned from old seaman's crates. And there were half a dozen of them, each the size of a child's casket. Roped handles had been added to them, one of which Trapp's hand had happened upon to pull him to safety.

It was his first break in days.

DARK FIGURES BLOCKED Trapp's passage.

Tall and gnarly horrors with grotesque arms and pointy heads swayed in the nighttime breeze. They were black spruce and paper birches, some of the only ones left on Terra. Trapp made his way between them on a well-worn bear trail toward the glowing horizon and the village. He stopped to take a sip from the water bottle Pop had insisted he carry.

Surveying the pathway ahead, he felt confident he'd make the last 10 kilometers to the OverLand station in Prudhoe Bay, hidden under the cover of darkness. From there, he would head southeast. MAU was next on his list.

Capping the water, Trapp headed deeper into the woods.

Trapp had found Pop groaning on the kitchen floor a few hours ago. Hastily, he took stock of the old man's injuries and determined none were life-threatening—just superficial bruises and scrapes. Trapp created a makeshift ice pack for Pop's face. Then the two climbed up the rickety stairs to the attic, a claw hammer in hand, to open Jessi's crates.

The two of them had spent the next several hours exploring their contents, using only Trapp's HoloPhone torch for light in case Fake Danny's team was watching the house.

The crates were filled with personal items, sweaters, shirts, and stuffed animals, some of which he vaguely remembered playing with. There were old-school photo albums—apparently, Jessi preferred printed HoloPics to the projected kind. Some were of Jessi's childhood, which made Pop sob. Others were of Trapp as a baby, which caused him to unleash his own version of Niagara Falls.

Suddenly, Trapp heard a noise coming from the woods.

He stopped and listened.

Was that a twig snapping? Perhaps it was a dead branch letting go in a gust of wind. Trapp waited. Whatever it was, it didn't repeat itself. He shook his head and continued moving.

Jessi's final crate was pay dirt. It was a jumble of unsorted papers, notes, and stacks of journals. Trapp rifled through their equations, tables, drawings, and diagrams. To Trapp, they might as well have been hieroglyphs for all he could decipher. Still, there had to be something of value here, a clue among Jessi's scrawls that would tell him where to go next. Peculiarly, many of her hand-written notes referred to a person called 'Fig.' At first, he thought it might be the abbreviation for 'figure' as in, 'refer to figure one on page 14,' or something just as innocuous. But the diagrams and pictures weren't labeled in that way. And the word Fig seemed to be the name of a person.

"Phig," he laughed after several minutes. "Ph-I-G."

"What the hell does that mean?" Pop asked.

"Phileas Ivan Gray. I'm assuming she didn't want to use his real monogram. Pig would be too insulting."

"The guy was a pig, though."

"You're only saying that because you believe he stole your daughter from you before killing her."

"He did steal my daughter. And he did kill her."

"Allegedly."

Trapp didn't know what to do with the papers. So he finally snapped HoloPics of each page. Pop, who at first complained that such a task was a waste of time, finally helped by holding the journals open for Trapp. This laborious chore took hours and nearly sapped Trapp of all his energy. But, in the end, he felt he had done the work justice. Later, he could read the documents on the OverLand and look for clues.

"I can't talk you into staying a while longer?" the old man asked, his eyes moist as Trapp prepared to leave.

"The Demons will be back soon," Trapp said. "For all I know, they've been waiting outside the whole time. But I'll be back as soon as I resolve this thing. And you'll do what you promised to her papers?"

Pop looked away. "Sure. Although I don't know why you want me to."

"Because I do."

"Besides, I'll probably not be around that long. Stage four cancer."

"Where?" Trapp said. "Lungs? Bones?"

Pop looked back at him. "Yeah. Don't worry about me. You go. Find your answers. These last hours being with you have left me a happy man."

They hugged and then pulled apart almost as quickly. Pop gulped and waved at the doorway. Trapp had run out without another word.

His eyes filled at that thought.

"Thanks for being my dad," he said to the empty forest.

"Damned shame," a voice said, coming from the darkness. Trapp slid to a stop and almost plowed directly into three human shapes that were barely visible in the dark. "Your old grandfather will be dead within the week. I picked up his cancer on my SmartVisor."

"Fake Danny," Trapp hissed.

"Name's Roth. Agent Roth. It took you long enough. We've been waiting all goddamn night."

"How did you—?" But then Trapp understood. There was only one path to Prudhoe Bay from Pop's house.

"We knew you were hiding in that attic," Roth said. "You seem to have forgotten that our SmartVisors pick up heat signatures. They enhance sound waves. I pretended to kill that mouse."

"Why?"

"To give you a chance to do my work for me. You took those HoloPics. Now, hand over the HoloPhone."

"I don't know what you're talking about."

Roth's two buddies pumped their shotguns, creating an echo that was quickly absorbed by the thick trees. Trapp could barely see them. But the gleam of the metal proved that they were carrying actual ordinance, not bolt guns. Roth, in his overconfidence, pointed his gun toward the ground.

"First," he said, "we'll take your HoloPhone and use your face to open it. Some people would kill to have access to those notes. I was going to have to order my comrades to carry those crates back to Prudhoe Bay. But now, I don't have to, do I?"

Trapp stared in stunned silence. Fake Danny had trapped him. And now, whatever Jessi was trying to keep hidden would fall into the hands of whoever was behind all of this. Trapp, in his ineptitude, had brought it right to them. They wouldn't need him alive to get the HoloPhone to recognize the face.

"Second," Roth said, seeming to grasp that Trapp had calculated his blunder, "you will attack us."

"The hell I will!" Trapp said. "You're the ones holding the guns."

"Your word against mine. And who do you think is gonna believe you? Oh, I forgot. You'll be dead from a gunshot wound. So you won't be able to plead your case. From my point of view, it was self-defense. You refused to come willingly."

"I don't even have a gun."

"Doesn't matter. No evidence will even be collected. We were sent to capture you dead or alive."

"The bounty's higher for alive."

"We're not eligible for the bounty. Now, are you going to open your HoloPhone? Or will we have to use your dead face to do it?"

"You can fuck yourself."

"Have it your way."

Roth brought his gun up. This one wasn't a shotgun. It was an assault rifle. He pointed the barrel directly at Trapp. Trapp calculated his chances of ducking into the woods and fleeing. But Fake Danny—*Roth*—had picked the perfect place. The clearing was too wide for Trapp to make a run for it. He'd only get halfway to the tree line before Roth got off nine shots. Trapp didn't think his superior healing powers would equal such an assault.

"You'll need the password," Trapp said, glancing around.

"Password?" The barrel of Roth's rifle dropped a few centimeters.

"I encrypted the HoloPics. Enter the wrong password three times, and the HoloPhone will reformat itself and erase all the files from the Q-Cloud."

The assault rifle's barrel came back up.

"We'll just go back to the house, then. Kill your grandfather and take what we want."

"I don't think so." Trapp waved his hand toward the direction he'd just come.

A red, flickering light could just barely be seen beyond the treetops.

Roth's eyes widened. "A fire?"

Trapp smiled. Pop was doing what Trapp had asked him.

"Pop is burning all Jessi's papers. Oops! There goes another journal. Holy crap, a stack of notes just went up."

"He's lying, boss," Demon Two said. "I see it in my SmartVisor."

"We all see it, asshole," Roth said to Demon Two. He turned back to Trapp. "You're making the whole thing up."

"Those lie detectors pick up stress and high heart rates, don't they?" Trapp asked. "It's how they know someone's lying. But having three guns pointed at you can cause the same reaction, can't it?"

"Maybe he's telling the truth," Demon Three said. "Maybe we should take him alive to—"

"Shut the fuck up!" Roth hissed, interrupting Demon Three. "Don't say his name out loud." Roth stared at Trapp thoughtfully.

"We need to take him alive." Demon Three pushed his case. "We can't be sure we can get those files."

"I think…" Roth said, seeming to be considering it. Trapp was about to be arrested by the Demons, and his whole boondoggle was over. But he'd still be alive. And perhaps he'd find another way to free himself.

Boom!

As he fell into the wet Alaskan soil, an electric fire exploded in Trapp's chest. More blasts split the night, more gunfire. The Demons were leaving nothing to chance. And, as Trapp's world faded to black, he knew.

His good luck had finally run out.

7

Wounded

MANY THINGS WENT through Trapp's head.

None of them were Roth's bullets.

Trapp was still breathing, despite having heard and seen muzzle flashes and having felt a bullet's white lightning as it entered his chest. Had Roth missed him as he fell? Not possible. Roth's gun misfired? Again, the answer was no. At least not the first shot.

Trapp's muddled mind couldn't understand.

He heard frantic and whispering voices.

Maybe they were part of a dream. One of them was small, even feminine, which couldn't be accurate, since all the Demons were men.

Trapp opened his eyes. A bright light pierced like shards of glass.

"What the hell are you doing to me?" he asked with a groan.

"Quiet," a woman's voice said, her mouth touching his ear. She smelled of soap and sweat. "We're saving your life."

"Who shot me?"

Her sweet aroma was overridden by a much more intense one. Alcohol. There was a sharp pin-prick on his inner arm.

A flood of potent, pain-quenching syrup spread like ocean waves.

He went back to sleep.

TRAPP OPENED HIS eyes.

A tiny person blocked the dim lighting of the room as they walked back and forth. It was the woman from earlier, he guessed. A much taller and lankier figure hung back beyond the light's cone: a man who was dressed in black.

Demon Roth? Maybe not. This man was lankier and not dressed in NanoSkins.

"It wasn't a bolt gun," the woman said as she leaned in toward Trapp's left shoulder, wafting an antiseptic aroma. "Those assholes shot him with real ordinance."

"Which is why we had to use deadly force," the man said in a nasal voice that was definitely not Roth's. "We had no choice."

"The ISC will be searching for the bodies, though, likely in the last place those guys were known to be. And if they come here, it's gonna be a shit show."

"You know where to take him, then."

"Sure. But how the hell am I supposed to get him there?"

"I'm pretty sure you can figure it out. Tell him the truth."

"Fuck! I've gone all these years without..."

"It's going to be okay. Trust me. Now, can you remove the bullet? Or are your medical skills too rusty?"

"The slug went clean through," she said. "There's a clear exit wound." Trapp felt pressure at the back of his shoulder, apparently, from the female doctor unapologetically poking at the wound. Surprisingly, his shoulder didn't hurt.

"What are you doing?" he said in a voice made groggy from the drugs.

His two rescuers went silent.

"I guess I need to up the morphine," the female surgeon whispered.

Trapp began to protest, but his tongue suddenly refused to respond to commands.

Darkness crept in once again.

8

Celebrity

THE FLOOR WAS covered in trash; the drywall riddled with holes.

Tattered curtains drifted lazily in the breeze, letting in warm light and chilly arctic air. Trapp's tongue and lips were sandpaper, as if he hadn't taken a drink in weeks.

What day was it? And where was he?

He turned to survey the room, to look for some water.

But there was nothing. And, besides a dark armchair-shaped object in a corner and a sagging armoire supporting a smashed-out 2D TV, he was alone. Something had died here—many somethings—making Trapp struggle to quash the vomit reflex from his morphine hangover.

Still, he recognized this place. Or at least the paradigm. It was a NoTell Motel. One of many that once existed on Dalton Highway southwest of the Beaufort Sea. All of them had been abandoned when the residents fled the area after the oil stopped flowing.

Unable to stop it, he leaned over the edge of the bed and wretched. Pop's frozen meal came out all over the trash-strewn floor. When the convulsions ended, he lay back panting. His shoulder itched from the gunshot wound.

"You're lucky," a voice said from the dark.

Startled, Trapp's eyes darted to the empty armchair. A small human sat there, tiny enough that their head barely topped the back of the chair, which was why he hadn't seen them in the dark.

The person stood up and stepped into a ray of gray light. Trapp recognized her.

"I saw you in New York," he said, his voice ragged. "You were with Goth Guy."

"With who?" She chuckled as she came over. "You mean Bril?"

"That guy you were with. He was dressed in black, wasn't he?"

"Goth Guy. I get it. May I?" Her hand was poised over his wound.

Trapp assented with a nod.

Pulling back his FabDrabs and exposing his chest, she carefully peeled back an edge of the bandage, letting out a gasp in the process.

"Pretty neat trick," she said. "A Fab that bleeds?"

"Does it look bad?" Trapp asked, ignoring her jibe.

"No. It looks a whole hell of a lot better than it should." She let out a low whistle.

"I've always been a quick healer." Trapp glanced down at the wound. It was purple and pink and encrusted with blood and looked pretty disgusting to him. "I'm guessing I also had a miracle worker for a surgeon."

"Nothing I hadn't seen a hundred times during my residency in Frisco. Before guns were completely banned."

"Medical residency?"

"Uh-huh." She fingered the entry wound before making him sit up so she could inspect the exit wound.

"You're only a child," he said.

"I wish!" She patted him on the chest, gently forcing him to lie back. "How old do you think I am?"

"I'd have guessed fifteen. I thought Goth Guy was your father or something, the way you two hugged."

She scrunched her small nose. "He's only four years older than me. Or at least that's what it says on our marriage certificate. I suppose he might've lied. But..."

"That man's your husband?"

"Yeah. And you're damned lucky we caught up with you when we did. Bril tagged you in London and followed you to NYC. And when he saw you entering the Southern Concourse..."

"He assumed I was going to MAU," Trapp said. She nodded. "How the hell did he even find me?"

"He didn't tell me. And imagine our surprise when you didn't show up in Raleigh. Thankfully, we guessed where else to look for you. We only happened upon you in time."

"You shot the Demons?"

"It was the only way to keep them from killing you."

"I don't know what to say. I mean, that's a lot for you to take on."

"I'm deeply mired in the shit already."

Trapp sat up to give the young woman a more critical once-over. He now noticed that her face had more age up close than it did from far away. He calculated that she was old enough to have practiced her medical skills for some time, which was good luck for him. But there was an oddity, too. Those dark brown eyes, black hair, high cheekbones, and distinctive sloping nose seemed familiar in an unfamiliar way.

"Have we met?" he asked.

"I don't think so, no," she said, her eyebrows drawing close.

"You look so familiar."

"You saw me at Union Station."

"It's not that. I think I've seen you before. I know I have."

Pronounced chevrons formed between her brows. She turned away. Trapp had struck a chord. And then, with a revelation that would've knocked him on his ass if he weren't already there, he knew. Oh boy, did he know!

"Wait!" His breath caught. "You're—"

"The EAR monitors," she said, slamming her eyes shut. "They're everywhere. And I'd appreciate you not saying it out loud."

He stared in silence. Perhaps he was wrong. Maybe she wasn't who he thought she was. She leaned down and spoke, almost seductively, into his ear.

"You're right about me, though," she said, her voice deepening. "You killed my grandfather."

"Albretta Gray?" Trapp mouthed the question.

With a knowing smile, she nodded slowly.

"WE CAN TALK in here," Albretta Gray said.

Dumbstruck that he was in the presence of a celebrity, Trapp had allowed her to help him out of bed. When it was clear he could walk, she led him into the gray day, past rat-infested shops, defunct grocery stores, and run-down restaurants. They came to a waterfront pub with a cryptic sign in the window, a drawing of an ear with a red 'X' crossed through it. *No EAR*. The ultimate "You Don't Say" place.

"Order?" a bearlike barista asked from behind the counter after they took seats.

"Two *chernyy chai*," Trapp said, ordering in *AmerRoos*, the local street language.

The man stared at Trapp for a long time, sizing him up. Trapp suddenly realized that he'd just given away his Fab disguise. But soon, the man grunted disdainfully before walking away.

"Perhaps you should be more careful," Albretta whispered.

"Yeah," Trapp said. "Although, my disguise didn't fool you, did it?"

"We tracked you for almost two days before we were sure."

He stared at her some more. "Albretta Gray!" he whispered in awe. "In the flesh."

She held a finger to her lips. "Call me by my married name, Bretta Sykes."

"Okay." Trapp looked away sheepishly. "Sorry."

"It's okay. Just...Let's keep the talk of my celebrity to a minimum."

"Roger that. Maybe you can explain something to me, though. If you think I killed your grandfather, why did you save me? Those Demons had me dead to rights."

"If you killed Grandpa, why did you risk your life to come back here? I can only assume it's because you're trying to solve your mother's murder. Which likely means you think it's related to Grandpa's."

The barista cleared his throat. They turned to see him holding their drinks. He set them down, shook his head again, and walked away.

"I think we should keep the use of the m-word to a minimum," Trapp whispered.

"Agreed," Bretta said before sipping her drink. She grinned, staring at the mug, amazed.

"What is this?"

"Black tea spiked with vodka and sugar."

"Drinking? This early in the day? With a Fab?" She gave him a conspiratorial grin, her dark eyes exuding intensity.

"Something to clear from your bucket list," he said with a chuckle. He pointed at her chest and the medallion that hung there. "And what's with the Saint Christopher's?"

"The patron saint of lost causes."

"And travelers."

Her eyes widened for a brief moment. "That he is."

"You religious?"

"Not particularly, no."

Trapp sipped his tea. Its icy sweetness revived his rug-like tongue while the vodka unbundled his nerve endings.

"Aren't you worried about reprisals from the, you know, *Demons*?" he asked, whispering the last word.

"No worries. Bril will take care of that."

"Bril, your husband?"

"From time to time, yeah. I never know when he's going to show up, though. If he shows up at all."

Trapp opened his mouth to say something but sipped his tea instead.

"Okay," Trapp said after a while. "So what *do* I need to worry about?"

"For starters," she said, "you need to figure out who's trying to kill you."

"That's easy, the ISC."

"Is it?" she asked, gulping her cold tea.

"You disagree?"

"Those goons weren't carrying bolt guns but real weapons—banned ones at that."

"The adm—the person who helped me escape," Trapp said, almost giving Stockwell away, "told me that the ISC wanted to fake my death so they could be rid of their problems."

"It's one thing for them to do that within their base. But out here, in public? They'd have a lot to answer for. The Alaskan police aren't in bed with the ISC. Nor are their DAs. It seems too risky to kill you here. Unless someone at a higher level didn't care about Alaskan reprisals."

Trapp went silent. He sipped his tea again and wondered. Maybe Bretta was right.

Her HoloPhone buzzed. "Our ride's here," she said.

"We're going somewhere?"

"A safe place."

"I had planned to head back to the lower forty-eight on the OverLand."

"Where the Demons will pick you up."

"I...I don't know."

"Look," Bretta said, holding her HoloPhone to the scanner and paying for the drinks. "I'm now an accessory to two crimes. And you said yourself that your fugitive skills are lacking. I can get you out of here—get *us* out of here."

Trapp glanced around the bar. He really couldn't go it alone.

"Fine," he said, glancing back at Bretta.

With a curt nod, she stood and headed out of the bar. He jogged to keep up as she took him toward an isolated beach a few hundred meters from the bar. Soon, Trapp spotted their "ride." The machine resembled a spider with its bubble canopy and four legs holding electronic thrusters.

"A delivery drone?" he guffawed. "I thought these things were decommissioned years ago."

"They were," she said as they arrived at the vehicle and its canopy angled open. The usual cargo hold had been refitted with a front and back seat. With much trepidation, Trapp climbed in behind her. The canopy lowered. The quad turbines spun up, making a racket like a nest of giant wasps.

"You know how to fly this bucket?" he asked after putting on his headset and buckling in.

"It's autonomous."

"Shit!" he said, grabbing for non-existent handholds as the drone shot straight up.

"Are you afraid of heights?"

"No," Trapp said, remembering his near-death experience on the *Eos*. "Just robot-controlled machinery."

"Pretty ironic, considering you're dressed like one."

"A drone?"

"A robot."

He'd forgotten about his Fab get-up. "You're not a human supremacist, are you?"

"No," she said. "I'm more of a robot supremacist."

She gave a half-suppressed laugh as the drone tilted. Soon, they were speeding out over the white-capped Beaufort Sea.

9

Safe House

THE DRONE SCUDDED scant meters above rollers and breakers.

Looking down through the clear bubble between his feet, Trapp immediately regretted it. Nausea came in a weird combination of sea and air sicknesses.

"Was there still sea ice when you were a kid?" Bretta asked, her tiny voice deepened by the comm system.

"Sure. My grandfather took me ice fishing as late as April, grayling and pike, mostly. There were still a few polar bears and seals. Before they went extinct. And where, might I ask, are you taking me? There's nothing out here but the ocean."

"Fortress of Solitude." The grin in her voice was unmistakable.

"You're Superman?"

"Super*woman,* thank you! And we're almost there." She pointed out the front of the bubble.

Rising like a Kraken from the choppy waves, a dark tetrapod-shaped object materialized from the fog. Towering on thirty-meter legs, it was split into three levels, each the shape and area of a soccer pitch. They were fitted with shipping containers and a network of glass-enclosed walkways.

"An oil drilling platform?" Trapp exclaimed.

"A repurposed one," she said. "After the year-round sea temperatures rose above 15 Celsius, the ice finally melted, and there was a push to drill like there was no tomorrow. Corporations put up 20 rigs in the Beaufort Sea before the moratorium on oil production went into effect. This is the last one left."

The drone's engines throttled up, and the craft angled in a long spiral around the structure. They rose over a building until they came to a house that appeared to have been fabricated of glass. Its bedrooms, kitchen, and gathering spaces were on full display. Cantilevered off the deck was a transparent swimming pool, the roiling surf dozens of meters below.

The drone made its final approach toward a blinking 'H' in the center of the roof. The small craft ducked and weaved from wind gusts before thunking onto magnetic bars embedded in the roof.

As its turbines cycled down, the canopy opened, and Trapp's face was sprayed with cool sea mist even from this mighty height. Bretta led them out and, leaning into the gusts, sprinted to a raised doorway. Huffing and shivering, they descended to the main floor.

Trapp was shocked at the panoramic view. The transparent walls and floors gave him even more seasickness as he watched the waves tossing and turning below. He looked up and focused on the far-off horizon.

"Fortress of Solitude," he said. "'Cause no one would be brave enough to venture here."

She smiled and nodded and led him deeper into the space.

"IT'S A BIT overdone, I'll admit." Bretta had finished their cursory tour and stopped in the living room. "It's necessarily large and isolated, though, for my lab and quantum servers."

Trapp surveyed the current room of glass and polished steel furniture. The see-through walls were covered with Art Deco paintings, certificates, and half a dozen diplomas: Masters in Biotech and Engineering, PhDs in neuroscience and psychology, and an MD.

She smiled proudly. "A farm girl like me is used to isolation."

"Farm girl?" he asked. "Last I knew, you were living off a full scholarship at Stanford."

"I grew up in North Carolina. My grandparents raised me after my parents died in a freak accident."

Trapp nodded. "The famous HoloVids of you riding horses on the Professor's farm. I remember them well. The whole world watched you grow up."

She wrinkled her nose. "Not the most normal childhood."

"I lost track of you after you went away to college."

"I stopped giving interviews after that. I married a former professor and changed my name to Bretta Sykes." She looked away. "No one missed that little farm girl."

"Full disclosure: I did. I may have even had a bit of a crush on you." He looked up. "Oh, *shit!* Did I just say that out loud?"

She grinned at him sideways. "I assume you eventually got over me."

He nodded. "Life intervened."

"A life of crime?" Trapp glanced at her with surprise. "I'm sorry," she said, ducking her head. "That didn't come out the way I meant it. I just wanted to say that we both have our share of Plexus trolls."

"You read up on me?" Trapp said, feeling his face flush.

"You were a threat to Grandpa."

She stood and led them past the dining room with a wooden table large enough to be a river raft for 20 people.

"The table's big, I know," she said sheepishly as they entered an adjoining den with an electric, stacked stone fireplace. She lit the fire, and they sat on a plush sofa.

They sat in silence for several minutes before she spoke again.

"Why did you never pursue Grandpa's conviction?"

"So we're going there, are we?" he asked.

"It's just always bugged me. I mean, every anniversary of her death, the Plexus reminds us that Grandpa was once a suspect, still is even after his death."

He shook his head with a sigh. "I suppose you deserve an answer. The obvious reason? Who could I even get to prosecute The Professor?"

She gazed at him with bright eyes. "And the not-so-obvious reason?"

"I never believed he was guilty of killing Jessi."

"Why do you call your mother Jessi?"

Trapp looked away. "It's easier to think of her that way, I guess. And, since we're getting personal, after the TUR stole his Manifold designs, your grandfather's isolation must've been hard on you."

She stared at the glowing flames for a long time. Trapp thought he'd overstepped. But then she looked up. "I've spent most of my life feeling alone. No one really understands me."

"Because of your intelligence?" Trapp waved at the room next door and all the diplomas he could see through the transparent walls.

"Partially, I suppose. Grandpa was the only one who saw that in me. But I could never live up to his expectations." She turned back to Trapp. "After he went into seclusion on the farm, I never returned. And I soothed myself, believing he wanted me to do that. He was shuttling between the farm and his lab at MAU. No one knows what he'd been doing all those years. I can only assume he hadn't been idle."

He waved at the expansive space. "It seems the apple didn't fall too far from the tree."

She smiled. "My experiments are very sensitive to RF and EM signals. Besides, I don't miss the paparazzi, the questions about who I was dating, and what I would be when I grew up. Do you know there was even a Plexus site where bets were placed on when I'd have my first period, first kiss, first sexual encounter? Fucking troglodytes."

"So you created a fortress of solitude."

"Bril built this for me. He works as a cybersecurity genius in the Central Security Agency. It's all top secret. For all I know, he has another wife on the side, which would explain the business trips."

Bretta's face reddened into a scowl.

"Government employees don't get paid enough to afford this," Trapp mused.

"After the US called in all the oil leases, they needed to eliminate the big rigs. Sold them for pennies on the terro rather than paying to dismantle them."

"And how do you stay sane?"

"I don't," she said, standing up. "I could go for some tea. You want a cup?"

She turned and left the room before he answered.

"DID YOU KNOW that the Manifold story is all a fabrication?"

Bretta asked this as the two of them sipped tea while sitting on bar stools at the steel counter in her kitchen. Trapp thought the blend might be a mixture of pekoe and Earl Gray, what with the cream and lemon she laid out.

"You mean the government never stole the Manifold from him?" he asked.

"No. They took it just as the story is told. But the current narrative paints Grandpa as a mediocre scientist at best, a psychotic at worst. He didn't invent the Manifold to end the war. Or at least not the way people think."

"So the Manifold wasn't supposed to be used to store electricity for consumers?"

"Grandpa didn't give a shit whether a family could sit in front of their big screen Holo while basking in air conditioned luxury. The Manifold's original purpose was for a greater good."

"Which was?"

"The XTerra Project."

"That was the project Jessi worked on," Trapp said, remembering what Pop had told him. "What was it?"

Bretta gulped her tea. "Exactly what it sounds like. Humans getting off-planet. Grandpa believed easing overpopulation was the only way to solve the global crisis. And the Manifold was only a small part of his designs." She sipped some more. "The closest habitable planets are hundreds of light years away, right?"

"Sure," Trapp said, swirling his tea.

"To get there, people would have to have been frozen and thawed out upon arrival. The spaceship that Grandpa envisioned would have been fabricated from a hollowed-out asteroid. The Manifold would've only been used as the ship's energy collector."

"People were willing to be frozen?"

"Not only were they willing, but hundreds had already volunteered for the mission. Your mother was one of them."

Trapp gasped. "My mother was planning to immigrate to a colony planet?"

Bretta set her cup down. "Yes. But she would've been more than just a passenger. Your mother developed the technology to keep the maintenance crew safe for thousands of years."

Trapp set his cup down. "She found a way to make humans survive for millennia?"

"Not humans but human analogs."

"Are you saying that Jessi invented Fabricants?"

"Not completely, no. Grandpa's gifted assistant, a man at the pinnacle of robotics, invented the body structure. You may have heard of him. Ambrose Hancock."

"The President of the United States?"

"And the founder and current CEO of FabCorps, yes. By all accounts, Hancock is a brilliant engineer. The sophisticated biotech to keep the Fab body up and running alone is a century ahead of its time. I know because I wrote one of my dissertations on it."

"There's a but, though, isn't there?"

"Neither Grandpa nor Hancock knew how to generate a fully autonomous brain for their robot bodies. Their best programming efforts could only control mobility and basic functions. What was needed was a brain that could learn to act and react."

"An AI."

"A neural network. And that's where Jessica Brown came into the picture. She'd written a paper on generating a fully autonomous brain from nanites, self-replicating robots the size of blood cells. And Grandpa hired her to put this Memory-Electronic Self-replicating Heuristic brain, or MESH, inside one of Hancock's Fabricants."

"Wait!" Trapp swallowed hard at this revelation. "So, you're saying that Jessi invented the MESH brain?"

"Yes."

Trapp shook his head in wonder. "How come I never knew this?" He gasped. "But of course I did. I mean, I didn't *know* I knew." He turned toward her with wide eyes. "But now that I think about it, there were Fabs in her lab."

"You were in Jessica Brown's lab?"

He looked out the window toward the horizon. "Sure, I was there. I was little at the time." Trapp looked at Bretta. "But I *do* remember a Fab. Perhaps it was a prototype."

"You were there to witness the dawning of a new species of person," she said, breathing out a low sigh of awe.

"It's not that amazing. I mean, I don't exactly remember any of it. I had nothing to do with her greatness."

"You were there, though. And I can't help geeking out on that. Your mother was the very definition of cutting-edge, a genius like none other. She was a woman who towered over all the greats! Even Grandpa spoke lovingly about how brilliant she was. Still, they had their differences."

"The great falling out," Trapp said.

Bretta nodded. "When she left, that was the first straw. The second was when the TUR commandeered Grandpa's Manifold tech. Those events broke him, drove him into isolation."

"Still," Trapp said, setting his cup down. "Her leaving the XTerra project was no motive for murder."

"Perhaps." She twisted her cup inside its saucer, thinking. "Later, though, he sued her for her files and journals. He believed they were his property since she developed them under him. She had taken everything with her and had erased the files from his servers. She was killed just a week before the trial. The Pols took her files as part of the investigation, and they were never seen again."

As Trapp stared at Bretta, he did his best not to react. Should he tell her about the copy of Jessi's files in his pocket? He'd only just met Bretta. And Jessi had her reasons for keeping the files secret.

"The Pols interviewed your grandparents," Bretta said. "They searched their house and their computers." She looked up at him. "What I wouldn't give for just an hour with your mother's notebooks."

He nodded noncommittally.

"Enough with the walk down memory lane," she said, standing up. "It's time we get you out of those clothes."

"Excuse me?"

"You're covered in blood. And it's tough to talk to a man who looks like...*well*...that. Have you looked in a mirror lately?"

"Uh, no. Besides, I didn't bring anything to change."

"I might have something for that."

10

DNA

"LET'S TALK EVIDENCE," Bretta said as Trapp found her on the pool deck.

He'd removed his Fab disguise, showered, and changed into faded black jeans and an AC/DC t-shirt that Bretta had laid out. They were Bril's, he guessed. Trapp took care to transfer Rory's Indent tag to the jeans pocket.

Bretta had set out a platter of cheese and crackers, a bottle of red wine, and two glasses.

Trapp made himself a plate and sat down.

"The evidence suggests I'm guilty," he said through a mouth full of food. He washed it down with a gulp of wine. "Even though my ankle tracker would've set off alarms had I left the base."

"Trackers can be hacked. And how do you explain the Murder Selfie?"

"You sound like the prosecutor at my Tribunal." Trapp put another cracker in his mouth. "My beff gueff?" he said as he chewed, his full mouth jumbling the words. "Feet fake."

"Deep fake?" she asked, causing him to nod. "What about the blood at the crime scene?" she asked.

Trapp stopped eating and sipped his wine. "Blood? I hadn't heard of any blood evidence."

She nodded. "Grandpa stabbed his attacker with a weapon that was never found. When the attacker fled, they left a few drops of blood behind. This information was kept from the public."

Trapp set his plate down. "How did *you* find out? Was it Bril? Did he hack into Interpol's databases?"

She gave him a sideways grin. "He asked nicely. They even gave him a physical sample, which he passed along to me. And my analysis confirms it. Taking your DNA file from the ISC databases—"

"Another gift to your husband because he asked nicely?"

"He hacked that one. Your ISC DNA is an exact duplicate of the killer's."

Trapp pushed his plate back, having lost his appetite. "Someone stole my blood from frozen vials kept for identification in the *Eos*'s morgue. They store dead Indents until they can receive a space burial, and it's tightly guarded by Regulars. Indents are never allowed inside. It's where my friend Rory was kept for two weeks after his accident. And any of those Regulars could've stolen my blood and given it to—"

"The crime scene blood had not been frozen," she interrupted, nibbling a cracker.

"A Synth, then. Everything from beef to wood is Synthed these days."

"Not blood. Bioengineers have tried to replicate viable blood replacement for decades. So far, they've failed."

"That you know of."

"I *would* know. I *am* a blood expert. No one's ever been able to create perfect blood, not to the level of sophistication of the sample I saw. Still, something about the evidence seemed wrong to me. I wasn't convinced it was yours. I didn't believe you killed Grandpa. And my persistence paid off in ways I still don't understand." She pushed a lock of hair behind her ear. "I ran the evidence blood through my MoleScan. And that's when I found... anomalies."

"What kind of anomalies?"

"Ones so subtle only a few people on Terra would understand them." She topped off their glasses. "And, before you ask, we won't be able to present these anomalies as evidence in open court. The judge would never allow it. Even if they did, the jury wouldn't understand the nuances. I'm not sure *I* do."

"This must be some unique blood."

"So unique, I can say with certainty that it came from only one of two places, the first being a laboratory light-years ahead of known biotechnology sophistication."

"You already said you would know if someone did that."

"Right." She held his gaze, apparently unwilling to say out loud where the second place was.

"Don't tell me you think the blood came from aliens," Trapp chuckled.

Bretta stared for several seconds before taking a big swallow of her wine. "I'm not suggesting that, no. But the DNA isn't normal. Its helix spirals in the wrong direction, for instance. Also, the molecular structures of the four nucleobases—adenine, cytosine, guanine, and thymine—are, for lack of a better word, scrambled. They have the expected composite elements—hydrogen, oxygen, nitrogen, and carbon, but they're arrayed in eccentric chemical structures. I got the DNA to replicate, meaning it *is* DNA and not something else. But my sequencer proved that your DNA is its only match out of five trillion samples."

Trapp sipped his wine. "I hear a *'but'* in your tone."

"*But*...the anomalies suggest that it's *not* your blood."

"Meaning the World Court should throw it out."

"There's no way. They'd rule that my methods are too complex and untested."

Trapp washed another cracker down with his wine before speaking. "You said you could think of only two reasons for the DNA anomalies. If not the futuristic lab theory—which seems possible since no one really knows what The Professor has been up to all these years—"

"Not doing weird blood experiments."

"Fine. So what was your other option for where the blood came from?"

"Mutations."

"Excuse me?"

"Exposure to nuclear fallout can cause gene mutations, for instance."

"So you're saying my doppelgänger lived through a nuclear explosion?"

"No. His mutations are too extensive."

"So what caused them?"

"I have no working theory as of yet."

"Which brings us no closer to proving my innocence." Trapp set his wine down and stared at the horizon. Dark clouds had formed, and the wind had picked up. He turned his gaze back at her.

She was giving him another sideways grin. "Maybe there *is* a way. It's the main reason I kidnapped you. I need your body."

"Excuse me?"

She drained the last of her wine and came to her feet. He followed suit.

"How modest are you?" she asked, looking him up and down, lingering too long on his midsection.

His hands dropped instinctively into a fig leaf pose. "I don't know…I mean, the normal amount, I guess."

"Follow me," she said, coaxing him with a finger waggle.

Dazed at its suggestiveness, he trailed behind her.

TRAPP AND BRETTA descended in her glass elevator.

The lower level consisted of more glass-partitioned spaces. One contained an array of quantum servers. Another was a room devoted to a gold mesh sculpture of a human skull, inside of which was what appeared to be a miniature quantum computer.

Bretta was hastily fingering her ScribePad and rendering the transparent walls opaque.

"Is that—?" Trapp asked, pointing at another room right before it disappeared behind a veil of digital fog. He thought he spotted a disk of some substance suspended in midair.

"None of your business?" Bretta said, completing his question. "Yes. All of this is top secret. And I'd be within my rights to have your eyes plucked out for what you've seen." She smiled deviously. "Now, if you'd be so kind as to strip."

She pointed at a machine in the corner of the room.

"A MoleScan?" he asked. "You want me to get undressed before going in?"

"I really do, yes. If you're not completely naked, it'll skew my scan results."

"You're fucking with me." He grimaced.

"You've caught me. This is how I seduce all the boys. After saving their butts from the Demons, I whisk them to the middle of the Beaufort Sea, where I have my way with them after they get naked inside my MoleScan."

Her angry expression broke Trapp's resolve.

"Drop 'em?" he asked.

"Yesterday, if not sooner."

"Fine." Trapp slipped out of Bril's clothes. She stared at him with a screwed-up mouth. She nodded down at his waist. He looked down. He was still wearing the shorts.

"Everything?" he asked.

"Everything."

He slid the shorts off.

"Oh my god!" she screamed with a terrified expression.

Trapp cupped his nether regions while his face heated up. Bretta cackled hysterically. "I'm sorry!" She waved her hand. "I'm just messing with you. You should see your face, though. *God!*"

"Hysterical," Trapp muttered as he raised his hands again and entered the MoleScan.

The procedure was over in less than a minute and he quickly got dressed. Her ScribePad projected a HoloPic of his body, warts and all. Graciously, the software had morphed his groin area into a non-specific blob.

"What are we looking for?" he asked.

"Scars."

"What kind of scars?"

"The kind inflicted by old men wielding sharp instruments. And, if there are none, then we've gone a long way toward proving my grandfather didn't stab you."

She flipped his MoleScan around, zooming in on cracks and orifices. Trapp's face warmed from embarrassment. After a time, she glanced up. Her eyes were big. Her mouth held a warped grimace.

"I don't get it," she said while typing on the ScribePad. After several seconds, the screen displayed a labeled list with markers attached by pointers to various parts of Trapp's MoleScan.

"Can't be," she said, now pulling up the program she'd just run and studying it. "Just can't..."

Trapp went cold. "Is it terminal?"

"That's just it," she said, now gazing up. "You're perfect. The machine found nothing. Even the gunshot wound, which happened just twelve hours ago, is almost gone."

"Maybe it's my guardian angel," Trapp muttered.

His phone buzzed and they both glanced at it. It was flagging breaking news from the Plexus. He read the headline. Then, almost in shock, he turned it toward her.

"Two days ago," she said, reading the article aloud, "Space Corps' Admiral Margery Stockwell went missing. Authorities are searching for Albretta Gray-Sykes..." Bretta looked up in shock.

Trapp read the rest: "...granddaughter of Phileas Gray, for questioning in connection with the disappearance. They caution that Miss Gray-Sykes could be dangerous and should not be approached. Instead, contact..." Trapp trailed off as the HoloPic projected from his phone. It was of a woman resembling Bretta running down a palm tree-lined street, perhaps in Miami near Stockwell's quarters. He looked at Bretta. Her face had gone white.

"#MurderSelfie2," she scoffed. "The Plexus is already calling me—*I mean this person*—a murderer? The admiral is only missing." She looked up at Trapp. "And how did the EYE even capture this picture? I was never there."

Trapp heard a thumping in his head, making him dizzy. During his escape from Space Corps, Malph had told him the the admiral feared for her own life. Trapp had no idea if Bretta was capable of such a thing. And Bretta was right, the fact that the admiral was missing didn't prove she'd been killed—no matter what the Plexus trolls said. His head thrummed even louder. There was no way he could believe she was involved with…

"Do you hear that?" Bretta asked, interrupting his thoughts.

He looked up. Bretta's head was angled to the side as if she heard what he was hearing. And a second later he realized that the sound wasn't just in his head.

"Turbine engines?" he asked.

The floor pulsed with the rhythm of them. The two glanced at each other.

"Yes," she said. "And they're getting louder. They found you."

"*Who*?" he asked.

"Whoever's chasing you. Space Corps. Or the Pols. Perhaps someone else more dangerous. Those turbines are from some sort of gunship or ships." She stared wide-eyed for another second longer. Then she dashed for the wall. Coming to a white box with a single red button protected by a clear PlayStyx cover, she threw it open and smacked the button.

After that, all hell broke loose.

11

The Angry Sea

TRANSLUCENT STRUCTURES CURVED up from the lab floor and surrounded each of Bretta's eight servers. With loud thunks, they clamped shut and immediately filled with yellow gel, which rapidly oozed around nooks and crannies, creating tightly packed cocoons. Hatches opened below these and they fell through toward the sea. With massive splashes, they hit, bobbed, and then sank beneath the waves.

"What the—!" Trapp exclaimed.

"Follow me!" Bretta shouted. She ran for the elevator.

They were heading for the drone, he thought, as he obeyed her command. This would be a mistake. Whatever was making that turbine racket were machines from the depths of hell.

But, as the elevator opened on the top floor, Bretta ran for more red buttons, hitting each as she passed by. Cocoons sprang up around her house. They surrounded bookshelves, bureaus, a desk with two computers, and a

ScribePad. They filled with more of that funky magic gel before dropping through hatches in the floor.

Trapp turned his attention to the sky and the silhouetted forms of half a dozen aircraft coming their way.

"Stealth helicopters," Bretta said, returning to his side. "I calculate they're a kilometer out. They look like they're packing missile launchers. We need to get the hell out here."

"We're not taking the drone, are we?" he asked, shouting over the din as she guided them back onto the elevator.

She shook her head vigorously. "We'd never stand a chance. Harness up." She pointed at the wall and bolted straps. Not knowing why he needed to, Trapp pulled them over his shoulders. But when he stepped through the lower body straps, he gasped. A hatch had opened at the bottom of the elevator shaft.

"You've got to be fuckin' kidding me!" he exclaimed.

"Hang on!" she screamed with a nod.

She slammed a red button.

And then they were in free fall.

THE CAPSULE-SHAPED elevator plunged so quickly that Trapp's stomach decided to stay behind on the platform. At least that's how it felt. Colliding with the sea, his arms and legs rag-dolled and he tasted blood from biting his tongue. The capsule rolled over, and he tried to breathe. But his breath wouldn't come, signaling that he'd also had the wind knocked out of him. The capsule tipped and bobbed as waves sloshed against the sides. Dangling from her harness, Bretta's legs and arms flailed above him. Finally, air came.

"That's gonna leave a bruise," Trapp gasped.

"Sorry about that," she said. "I didn't realize we'd hit so hard. You okay?"

"Perfect," Trapp muttered, giving her the thumbs-up.

Raindrops plinked against the capsule and thunder clapped. The dark shapes of the helicopters were within a half kilometer now. But, for the moment, the assault force would think they were still on the platform. That was something. And, to confirm his theory, a bright flash lit up the sky followed by an explosion loud enough to rattle the capsule.

"They're shooting at the platform," he shouted.

"No," she said. "They're not."

"What was that then?"

"Countermeasures."

The oil rig calved into rough quarters. Four pieces, each the size of an office building, tipped away from each other, toppling like trees from a horror movie and dropping chunks along the way.

Many of these barely missed the capsule as they hit the water: half of a shipping container, the Fortress of Solitude's generator, solar panels, beds, furniture, and lab tables. Batteries became bombs, each impacting with enough force to send up spouts dozens of meters high. Wood pieces had morphed into missiles, some striking the capsule and bouncing off. Trapp thought he heard a crack as one of them hit. Riddled throughout this detritus was a flurry of white floating things—thousands of leaves of paper.

Trapp turned to Bretta.

"I couldn't risk letting my research fall into the wrong hands," she explained apologetically. "And buckle up! This thing isn't over yet."

Trapp glanced over his shoulder. The first of the mighty legs crashed sideways into the sea, kicking up a 20-meter breaker that was headed toward them. Trapp glanced around for something to hold on to. The wave approached as another leg rammed into the sea, creating another tidal wave.

"Shit!" he shouted as the first one hit.

The capsule flew up and over, becoming airborne. It came back down and rolled over and over as it sped down the backside. The second wave hit them head-on then, pushing the top of the capsule underwater while the back came up, along with their feet. It toppled end over end before the third wave hit broadside and spun them again.

This was how Trapp was going to die. After surviving the Manifold and temporarily escaping the death penalty, he'd be done in like laundry in the spin cycle from hell.

After a time, the waves passed. The elevator bobbed on the surface.

"I may have thrown up a little," Bretta said in a ragged voice.

"We both did." Trapp croaked.

"I guess I didn't account for the swells. Sorry."

"No apologies."

"You should await judgment," she said, nodding toward the sky.

Trapp glanced up. The helicopters were now orbiting directly overhead. So were the storm clouds. It was as dark as night.

"They probably have night vision and infrared tech in their scanners," she said. "It's just a matter of time before they find us."

They both watched as the helicopters continued their orbit. They had stopped right above them. The capsule was floating straight up in the water. This narrower profile might make it harder for the assault team to find them, especially in the massive flotsam field and under a cloud of falling papers. Perhaps their luck had shifted.

Suddenly, he felt cold dampness in his boots.

Glancing down, he gasped.

"We may have another problem," he said.

She looked down.

"We're taking on water," she said.

ANOTHER THUNDERCLAP BOOMED as the clouds lit up with purple plasma.

Having released their harnesses, Trapp and Bretta were treading in water that was already over their heads inside the elevator capsule.

"You want the good news or the bad news?" Bretta asked, shivering.

Trapp's teeth were already chattering. "Is the bad news that we're going to die of hypothermia in this freezing water?"

"What are you talking about? It's a balmy 20 degrees in this. We'll survive at least a half-hour, maybe more. If we can stay afloat that long. I designed this capsule with doors that open outward so the pressure wouldn't cause an implosion."

"Door?" Trapp said excitedly. "Got it." He dove into the water.

It was darker than Trapp expected. Disoriented, he fumbled for the door latch, which he'd witnessed her opening several times since arriving at the oil rig. By the time he found it, his lungs were screaming. Still, he grasped it and pushed. The door seemed glued shut. He bobbed up for air. Bretta started to speak, but he was already submerged again. He pushed on the door. Still, it wouldn't budge. He resurfaced and gasped for air. The top was now only a few meters up.

She spoke but he raised a finger and went back under. This time he angled his feet up and pushed against the opposing wall. The door seemed to move. But, no matter how hard he pushed, it just wouldn't open.

"I've been trying to tell you," Bretta said in a miffed voice as he surfaced again, "the bad news."

"What?" he gasped, barely able to keep his head above water.

"Because the door is submerged, to open it we have to push against the water pressure. It's ten times stronger than the weight of this capsule."

"So how are we going to get out?"

"Only when the pressure inside the capsule equals that outside can we open the door."

"We have to fill the capsule with water? Don't *I* feel like an idiot for forgetting my oceanography."

"It's not oceanography," she said. "It's fluid mechanics."

"I don't think I can tread water," he sputtered. "Not long enough to wait for the capsule to fill."

"We could open the crack further. Make it fill quicker."

Trapp looked around for anything to break the crack. The harness, perhaps, with its metal buckle? But the thing was bolted to the glass. Bretta cleared her throat. He looked up. She held up a multi-tool much like the one that saved his life near the *Eos*. He took the tool and dove down. With his fingers, he found the crack near the bottom. He worked the point of the screwdriver into it before going up for more air.

"Let me have a go at it," she said, taking the tool. "The water's going to rush in. So take several breaths and then swim down, stat, when it does."

"Sure." She dove down. Inside the capsule, Trapp's head was barely above the surface of the Beaufort Sea. They had just minutes left. He was about to take another breath and go down to check on her. But then he began to sink rapidly.

Trapp barely had time to take two deep breaths before the air pocket was swallowed up by the water. He went down. For several seconds, he couldn't find her in the dark. She grabbed his hand in the murky light and brought it down to the door handle. Together, they pushed.

As the capsule sank further, the water got murkier. Trapp's lungs were desperate for oxygen. With every second, the distance to the top of the ocean and air lengthened. The door wouldn't move, either. They were going to drown.

He just needed to breathe. Water contained oxygen. Why couldn't he just suck some in? Bretta tapped him on the forehead, making him look at her. She cupped his face in her hands. He stared into her eyes. They were intense and confident. Perhaps he could hold his breath a little longer, those eyes confirmed. He nodded. They pushed again on the handle. The door opened suddenly and Bretta was sucked out.

Trapp immediately lost her again. He lost his sense of direction too. Looking around frantically, he caught a glimpse of lighter darkness. He swam for it, not knowing if Bretta had found the surface. The urge to fill his lungs was unbearable. And, when he broke the surface, he still held his breath, unsure if the water in his face was from waves and rain or deep ocean.

Finally, he took a desperate breath. Rain covered him in sheets. Breakers smashed over his head and drove him under again. A hand grabbed at his wrist. He resurfaced. Blinded by a flash of lightning, he swam as it pulled.

Bretta helped him climb up and out of the water.

Trapp lay down on this floating island, unconvinced that he hadn't already drowned and was imagining it. He gasped. The wind sprayed water into his face. He was alive. And he realized what they were floating on.

"Glad you got this big dining room table," he said.

They laughed so loud Trapp choked. They clung to life on a floating table in the middle of the Beaufort Sea and cackled to the very brink of insanity. Seconds passed as Trapp searched the sky. The helicopters were gone. They were safe. Except…

"I hope you don't expect us to swim all the way back to Prudhoe Bay," he said sadly. "I don't have the strength to even row us there."

"Thought you'd never ask," she said.

She held up her Saint Christopher. Trapp stared at the medallion, baffled. Then she pressed it in the middle. A buzzing noise came down from on high. Bees? Giant hummingbirds? No, it was something with red and green navigation lights.

"You've gotta be kidding me," Trapp said, grinning. "That's what the medal was for? A remote?"

"Told you I wasn't particularly religious."

"And yet, it seems you've summoned an angel."

"Oh," she said. "You like my drone now, do you?"

"It's growing on me," he said as the drone came down.

Carefully, he climbed aboard and then pulled her up.

Trapp decided it was more badass than hummingbirds or bees as he took his seat and the canopy lowered. A hornet, perhaps. Although he'd not felt the drone's sting.

As he thought this, the giant wasp tipped toward the south and sped away from the wreck.

PART TWO

Reflection

"The mirror reflects all objects without being sullied."
Confucius

"Artificial Intelligence is a misnomer. There is nothing intelligent about a machine that can only regurgitate information back to its creator without being aware that it is, in fact, a creation."
Professor Phileas Gray: **Intelligence as Artifice**

12

Safety

A SOFT FINGER touched Trapp's cheek.

His eyes flew open. Bretta's face was so close that he could feel her warm breath on his forehead. For a moment, he thought she was looking for companionship, a warm body in bed, maybe more... But the terror in her eyes, barely visible in the white moonlight, told him otherwise.

"What is it?" he whispered, groaning as he sat up in his sleeping bag and rubbed his back, which was sore from sleeping on the floor. He'd given her the bed while electing to lay out a sleeping bag at her feet.

"I think someone's coming," she whispered. "I heard movement outside."

"Shit!" Trapp climbed up next to her and pulled on his boots.

The day before, they'd endured a journey south in soggy clothes. When the drone's low-power alarms had been screaming for a time, an ironic noise that drained the batteries, Trapp spotted what he'd been searching for from the air. It was a pile of rusted-out Howitzers by the side of the road, remains of avalanche guns once used to keep the pass clear in winter. They pointed the way to the canyon where Pop's cabin was. Trapp was pleasantly surprised to find the structure in decent shape. Soon, he'd gotten a fire roaring in the wood stove. While Bretta freshened up, Trapp caught a dinner of rainbow trout from the nearby stream, which they fried with cans of beans and corn that hadn't turned bad yet.

Before bed, they spoke at length about her fugitive status. #MurderSelfie2 had blown up the Plexus—even more than his hashtag had. He told her of Malph's theory, that the admiral's life may have been in danger for a while. Still, Bretta became mostly fixated on the fact that there was no proof offered on the Plexus of an actual murder.

He'd done his best to talk her down from that ledge as they packed the drone with camping equipment and connected it to a small solar generator. The batteries would take the next day to charge, and then they'd head south on the second night. To where? Neither of them knew.

Some assholes had different plans, it now seemed.

Or maybe not. Bretta's sound could have been any number of wild animals checking them out.

Moving to the cabin's door, Trapp lifted the Winchester 70 off the hook and checked that there were still three rounds in the magazine and one in the chamber. He added more rounds to his pocket before quietly pulling the door ajar. Slipping stealthily onto the deck, he crouched behind the rail and surveyed the meadow through the rifle's scope.

The almost full Luna painted a silver light on the primarily green morass. Fifty meters to the right—west of the cabin—a small forest of Sitka spruce stood sentinel at the base of a twenty-five-hundred-meter mountain. There was a trail that led up that slope. With its cliffs and jags, it was treacherous enough to ascend in daylight; Luna's dim light would make the ascent suicidal. Bisected by a burbling stream to the east, the prairie spread out for more than a kilometer, broken up only by the occasional copse of dwarf dogwoods and more Sitkas and backdropped by mountains.

A slight whoosh drew his attention, and he brought the scope down. Something slipped out of the stream. It moved slow and low to the ground and might've been a bear—hence the Winchester. But bears tended to meander with confidence and curiosity. This creature moved with stealth. He saw a second form sloshing out of the creek behind the first. There was no doubt they were human.

He moved back into the cabin.

"Two of them," he whispered, motioning for Bretta to put on her backpack while he followed suit.

Yesterday, they'd filled the packs with freeze-dried food packets, fire starters, knives, ammo, and water purifiers in the event of an emergency EVAC. Along with the Winchester 70, Pop had stashed bear-deterring handguns under the floorboards: a double action .357 Colt Python, which Trapp now holstered to his waist, and a .44 magnum Smith & Wesson, which Bretta was carrying. Last night, he'd witnessed a master class in how adeptly a 50-kilogram woman could manage a gun that kicked with six hundred times her weight in force. As its report rang in his ears and three distinct bullet holes riddled a distant stump, she shrugged and upended unspent rounds into her hand while saying, "Grandpa didn't raise no wusses," evoking an awestricken guffaw from Trapp.

"You're not going to kill anyone, are you?" she now whispered as Trapp shouldered the Winchester over the backpack's strap.

"Only if I have to."

"You *don't* have to! We have no idea who's out there. Additional homicides will only up the bounty. Especially if they're government."

"Copy that. Defensive engagement only. But just so you know, there are worse things out there than well-trained markspeople."

"Sure."

They came out onto the porch. He gestured toward the western trees. She nodded, and they descended the stairs in a crouch, carefully avoiding loose boards. Once they'd put the cabin between them and the pursuers' line of sight, they jogged for the tree line. They ducked behind a red thimbleberry thicket and caught their breath while watching for the pursuers.

Smoke from the woodstove, which he'd replenished with logs before bed, left a gauzy spiral against the starry sky. It emitted a pleasing forest smell, pissing him off because it exposed the fact that they'd been there just a few minutes ago. The pursuers came around the cabin and into view. Light glinted in their hands.

"They're armed," Trapp whispered. "Not bolt guns."

"So *not* Demons."

He looked at her in surprise. She and Bril had saved Trapp from Demon Roth, who'd been carrying a rifle instead of the usual Demon ordinance. Still, somehow, Bretta knew what was unusual for Demons—-strange. He nodded and turned his attention back to the pursuers.

They were on the porch now. The second one, taller than the lead, went inside the cabin first. A moment later, the tall pursuer shouted in a man's voice from inside, "Clear." The other one entered. Rattling and banging ensued. They were ransacking the place more out of spite than because they were searching for something. They knew Trapp and

Bretta had fled. The two pursuers came back out onto the porch. As if to let Trapp and Bretta hear, the smaller one spoke loudly, in a woman's voice.

"They couldn't have gotten far," she said.

They broke out their high-powered flashlights and panned the meadow. Trapp pushed Bretta into a deeper crouch. The light rested on the bushes. It held its focus long enough for Trapp to fear the pursuers had discovered them. But then the light rotated back toward the fields.

"Are they the same people from the gunships?" Bretta whispered.

"I don't think so. The gunship army was all about shock and awe. It was sent by someone who didn't know much about military tactics, even though they had an army and gunships." He looked up at the cabin again. "These guys... they're professionals. Trained killers. Probably special forces."

"Whose?"

"You've got me."

"Still," she said, "it smacks of military."

He nodded. "A military that was disbanded as part of the Budapest Accords. Only police forces and small militias are legit."

"I don't think the groups that've targeted us are either of those."

"That's what worries me."

The pursuers spoke on the porch. The babbling creek muffled their voices, but it sounded like they were having a debate. For a moment, Trapp wondered if they were planning to return the way they came. Wishful thinking. But a guy can dream, can't he?

"Fuck!" Bretta whispered as the pursuers stepped off the porch.

They were headed directly toward Trapp and Bretta.

FOR THE PAST two hours, Trapp and Bretta had been herded like sheep.

Each time they thought they'd lost their two pursuers, lights would appear to their left and right, flanking them and forcing them forward. At times, it seemed a whole squad was pursuing them. And when Trapp heard a small insect-like noise, he understood why.

"They have MicroDrones," he said.

"Yeah," she said pensively.

"We can't stay on this path much longer."

"Why?"

Trapp kicked a stone. They listened as it skittered on the path and flew out into the open. Several seconds passed, then the stone hit, pattering against boulders and knocking loose more debris that clattered down the canyon.

"Because of that," he said.

"How far did that fall?" Bretta asked as she stepped up next to Trapp and leaned against him.

He cleared his throat. "Twenty-five hundred meters. Maybe more."

"Shit!"

Trapp stepped away from the chasm and glanced behind them. Little pinpricks of light floated above the mountain below. He counted 10 MicroDrones.

"Those drones probably have thermal cameras."

They became silent and listened to the far-off footfalls of their pursuers.

"A hundred meters and closing," he muttered, crouching defensively. Leaning on a boulder, he lowered himself to the Winchester's scope, flipping it to night vision mode. Two green humans appeared. The smart lens displayed approximations of their size, distance, and how fast they were approaching. It red-flagged objects in their hands it believed to be weapons.

Bretta tapped on his shoulder, forcing him to look up.

"Why is it that when men are scared, they have to shoot something?"

"I…uh… Do you have a better idea?"

Placing her hand on his head, she turned it toward the cliff.

"You've got to be kidding me," he said. "That's a sheer drop-off."

"There's a ledge that leads off to the right. It's wide enough for us to climb down."

He stared at her, dumbfounded. "A ledge."

"Are you afraid of heights?"

"Not heights," he muttered. "But falling to my death doesn't sound too fun."

Bretta grabbed his hand and pulled him to a standing position. "It'll be okay. We'll take it slow."

Trapp swallowed hard, allowing her to guide him to the ledge. He slung the rifle back over his shoulder and watched as she stepped into thin air as if levitating. Then he saw it.

"I'd hardly call that a ledge," he said. "It's more like a lip."

Footfalls crunched behind them. The special forces people had broken into a run.

She whispered intently. "We need to go. And now."

"Can't I just shoot them?"

"No." She tugged his hand.

He stepped onto the ledge/lip. It was barely wider than the length of his size 13 boot. Still, the wall behind it tilted back a bit, giving him something to lean against. His sweaty hand held onto her tiny one, and she moved them forward. Trapp was numb with fright. How could he do this? He didn't even care if she saw him dissolve into a sniveling child with fear. Still, oddly, his body continued to do what his mind couldn't comprehend. And, within a few seconds, they were several meters along the ledge.

"It's not so bad," he said, glancing down with newfound confidence.

The world telescoped up to meet him in a swirl of vertigo. Trapp slammed his back against the wall, barely able to breathe.

"You didn't look down, did you?" she asked.

"Uh-huh." Trapp gritted his teeth. What the hell was he doing up here? The inevitable fall to death would last long enough for him to question his life decisions all the way down.

She tugged lightly on his hand. "They're coming. We have to move."

"I can't."

"Look at me."

He shook his head.

"Look at me." He looked down at her. "We're almost halfway there. Just a few more steps."

"Halfway where?"

"I think I see a small ravine up ahead. We can climb down when we get to it."

"How can you see in the dark?"

"Because I'm Catwoman."

"I don't think she has any superpow—"

The sound of the pursuers' loud breathing quieted him. The man and the woman were getting close. Trapp swallowed hard and looked at Bretta. They had no choice. He focused on her shoulder. She crept further along the ledge. Trying to ignore their elevation, he fixed his eyes on her backpack. When it moved, he moved. And, for what seemed to be hours, they proceeded like this, centimeter by centimeter.

"You lied to me," he whispered after a while.

"When?"

"We weren't almost halfway there."

"It was less of a lie and more of an estimate." She halted abruptly, causing him to almost bump into her. "Well... That's interesting."

"What is it?" he breathed, craning his neck to see.

"Some of the ledge is, uh, gone. There's a small gap. We're going to have to jump."

Trapp's eyes adjusted enough to see what she was talking about. "Small gap, my ass. That's at least three meters wide. No way we can jump that. Especially with the backpacks."

A crumbling noise echoed behind them. Two flashlight beams shone on their left, followed by the little lights of the MicroDrones. These swarmed out above the canyon and hovered a hundred yards away.

"Did they go that way?" the male's voice said, reverberating from a dozen meters away.

"I don't think they sprouted wings," the female said. The beams flashed in their direction. Thankfully, they'd come far enough to be beyond their reach. *Un*thankfully, the light revealed just how narrow the ledge was. Trapp pushed back against the rock, unable to breathe again.

"That's a suicide route," the man scoffed.

"We'll be executed if we *don't* pursue them," the woman said. "Or did you not understand your orders?"

"You don't need to remind me."

The MicroDrones now turned and headed toward Trapp and Bretta.

They were caught! But then, a new strange noise echoed above the canyon. Trapp immediately recognized it as the opening licks of Jimi Hendrix's *Purple Haze.* What the hell? The music stopped abruptly.

"Yes sir?" the woman said. Apparently, someone had called her on her HoloPhone. "Uh…I mean we're…I know, sir. I'm sorry, but we've acquired the targets. Yes. I understand. Thank you, sir."

She became silent.

Trapp and Bretta glanced at each other in confusion.

"What the hell did he want?" the man asked.

"We've been recalled." Their voices faded as they started to move away. Trapp couldn't make out their words, but they sounded pissed. The MicroDrones flew off to catch up with their human overlords.

"What the fuck was that?" Trapp asked.

"I've no idea," Bretta said.

They stared out into the darkness and listened. The sound of the pursuers' retreat was loud enough to be convincing. Still, Trapp wasn't sure it wasn't a ploy to get Bretta and him to walk right back into their hands. Bretta seemed to have agreed because she stood there silently for a long time. The breeze shifted from the west and started to blow into their faces.

The temperature dropped, and Bretta moved close for warmth.

"So it's to be death by hypothermia," Trapp said after an hour passed. "Or risk capture by those assholes."

"I vote for the second one," she said through chattering teeth.

"Agreed."

Twenty minutes later, they were back on solid ground. Trapp had made Bretta wait on the relative safety of the ledge while he used the Winchester to scope ahead.

"I'm freezing my ass off up here," she said, getting impatient.

"No sign of them," he said.

They took their time as they tentatively ascended. Daylight broke as the valley came into view. Trapp halted again while he scoped the area. It seemed the pursuers really were gone. Trapp and Bretta came to the drone and Trapp checked the solar generator. It was trickling charge into the drone's batteries.

"It's unbelievable," Bretta said when they reentered the warm cabin. The pursuers had made a mess of everything. But Trapp, who was too tired to care, threw a few more logs into the firebox and left the mess alone. "Maybe our luck has begun to—"

"Please," he said, interrupting with his hand up. "Don't tempt fate."

"Fine."

"We have at least 12 hours before the batteries are fully charged. I think we should rest. You can take the first shift and I'll keep watch. Just in case those guys come back."

"Thank you," she said with a yawn, lying down on the bed. "But don't let me sleep too long. You need rest, too."

"I won't, I promise."

He grabbed his sleeping bag and dragged it out onto the porch.

Holding the Winchester at the ready, he pulled the sleeping bag over his body and waited.

For what? He had no idea.

13

Friend

A BIG BLACK box approached Trapp and Bretta from half a kilometer away.

He turned to her as she stared straight ahead.

"You're sure about this?" he asked.

"I'm not sure about anything," she said, glancing up and then away again. "We need help."

"From that?" Trapp waved at the thing.

He could only make out a few details. Whatever it was, it rode on what appeared to be eight spheres. And by the way, what the hell? He and Bretta had waited for their contact for over an hour. And they show up in that? Trapp shook his head.

For four days, he and Bretta droned south by night and camped by day while Pop's solar generator charged the batteries. They'd spoken little of murders and flights from justice and, instead, shared life stories and world views. When the subject of where they should go next arose, neither had a clue. To Trapp, the most logical destination was MAU and Professor Gray's lab. But she felt it was likely still overrun by Pols. On day three, Bretta received a text from the person they were here to meet. Trapp wanted her to ignore it. But she soon convinced Trapp that they should hear them out. No commitment or anything.

This was why they were in this park in a corner of Washington state.

The strange vehicle turned into the park's entrance and headed directly for them. A spark of pain bit at Trapp's gut. Even at twenty-five meters, the matte-black vehicle resembled a nightmare from the underworld piloted by Charon, the ferryman himself. With no windows or door seams, the body of the weird vehicle gave no hint of its entrance or egress. As it pulled up alongside them, though, seams opened on the side and a ramp angled downward. A man stepped through the opening.

"Climb aboard," Bril said.

The sight of Goth Guy up close did little to ease Trapp.

Bretta climbed up and Bril hugged her. She returned the gesture in a stilted, uncomfortable way. Trapp ascended the ramp after her. Bril shook his hand and led Trapp inside. With bench seats around the walls and a long table bolted in the center, the cabin resembled a conference room on wheels—or spheres—or whatever the hell kept it from crashing to the ground.

"Take a seat," Bril said as the ramp closed behind them, hermetically sealing them in—or so Trapp imagined.

He sat down and Bretta sat beside him. She was close enough to convince Trapp that she was antsy too.

Bril sat opposite them, picking up a ScribePad and swiping on its surface. The vehicle's walls and ceiling winked out of existence. Trapp and Bretta flinched as the road sped by outside.

"What the hell, Bril!" Bretta said. "You could've warned us before turning on the HoloWindows."

"StealthWindows, to be exact," Bril said.

Predictably, Bril was dressed in black. But it wasn't his usual uniform of jeans and a T-shirt. Instead, he wore a real uniform: a jumpsuit with a gold maple leaf emblem stenciled on each collar.

Bretta scrunched her face. "Since when are you a major?"

"It's perfunctory," Bril said with a wave. "Civilians working in pseudo-military organizations need a rank so the lifers can know who to salute." He extended his hand to Trapp. "We've not yet been properly introduced."

Trapp shook the hand. "Thank you for saving my life."

"I had very little to do with that. I'm guessing she didn't tell you how great a marksperson she is."

"Why not just say 'you're welcome' like a normal human being?" Bretta said to Bril. "No one cares who shot whom."

Trapp glanced at Bretta. "I thought Bril killed those Demons."

Her eyebrows came together. "I'm no murderer if that's what you think. I only winged that guy to keep him from killing you. When those guys opened fire on us, we had to defend ourselves. Besides, if we hadn't intervened, they'd have murdered you."

"I didn't know…I mean…Thank you."

"Doesn't matter." She waved the comment away. But Trapp felt he could cut the tension in here with a laser scalpel. He decided that her frustration, directed at him, was really caused by the man who sat across from them. Trapp now looked Bril in the eyes. They exuded confidence and a touch of humor. Trapp had seen that look a thousand times before. It was the resting face of people who were used to having their orders obeyed. Still, Bril's eyes twitched for a second during the staring contest, which meant he had to answer to someone who scared the shit out of him.

Bril broke the stare by looking down at his ScribePad. "What do you think of my limo?" he asked.

"Limo?"

"Landscape-Independent Modular Transport, or LIMO for short." Bril glanced at Bretta. "I'm glad you agreed to let me help you."

"We've not agreed to anything," she said. "Where are you taking us?"

"After letting someone blow up your oil rig…"

"My Fortress of Solitude."

"Right. And getting hunted down by special forces."

"Who let us go."

"Sure. I still think it would be prudent to get you underground. Hole up for a while."

Trapp started to speak in Bretta's defense against this asshole. But she raised a finger.

"We're doing just fine," Bretta said, staring directly at Bril.

He stared back for a few seconds before looking away. "I'm not trying to say you're incapable. But, if you indulge me for a bit, I think I can convince you that you need me."

"One day," Bretta said. "That's all you get. Then you need to drop us off wherever we are and we'll go our separate ways."

"I'm still your husband."

"Hey!" Trapp said, standing up.

Bril smiled and waved his hand. "I'm sorry," he said. "I'm just a bit cranky. We've been working so much on our project…"

"What project?" Bretta asked.

"Doesn't matter. Please, accept my apology."

"I will—if you agree to let us go if we don't buy what you're selling."

"Deal."

Bril sat back in his seat and set the ScribePad down. Bretta said nothing. Detente having been reached, Trapp took his clue from Bretta. He stared at the HoloWindows and watched the world pass by.

NIGHT GAVE WAY to daylight.

The mountains had retreated far behind them. Ahead, it was all prairie land as far as the eye could see. Bretta slept peacefully along the right side of the LIMO. Bril sat where he'd been sitting all night, studying his ScribePad.

Trapp yawned and rubbed his eyes. "Where are we?"

"Montana," Bril said.

"Why?"

"Because of beef." Bril grinned.

"Excuse me?"

"It's no longer 'what's for dinner,' right? After Budapest. No more cattle? Just SynthMeat?"

"Of course." Trapp sat up straighter. "But what does that have to do with why we're in Montana?"

Bril waved his hand. "This whole area used to be one big cow pasture. During those chaotic years leading up to the Carbon War, when everyone was scrambling to figure out where they fit into the new economy, ranchers found themselves squatting on worthless land. The US government stepped in. They bought up the land for a premium."

"What did they do with it? Give it back to the indigenous people so they could resurrect their ancient ways?"

"As if!" Bril laughed loudly, waking Bretta. She rubbed her eyes and glanced around, dazed.

"Morning, sunshine," Bril said.

"Are we there yet?" She yawned.

"Just about."

Trapp gazed through the StealthWindows. There were no buildings, gated entrances with guard stations, or fenced compounds, just fields of grain, green crops, and gigantic irrigation sprinkler trains. Running in tandem, three pilotless combine harvesters spewed newly threshed grain into giant hoppers, stirring up a gossamer cloud of dust made golden by the morning light. How could the LIMO be almost at their destination, or anywhere for that matter?

Trapp looked back at their pilot.

Bril wore a smug smile as he stared at his ScribePad.

Up ahead, the road looped in a smooth turn to avoid the wheat field and one of the gigantic combines. Instinctively, Trapp braced for this in spite of the LIMO's propensity for making such movements without affecting its passengers. The LIMO didn't follow the road to the right, though. Seeming to have a GPS malfunction, it careened into the field. It was on a collision course with the harvester, which outweighed them by a few thousand kilos.

"Uh, Bril," Bretta said, seeing this.

Bril was fixated on his ScribePad, typing away at some all-important communique or something. Six meters tall and eight wide, the harvester approached them rapidly.

"We're going to collide," Trapp shouted. Bril was oblivious. With hardly time to brace for impact, Trapp searched for a seatbelt or handhold; he'd have even settled for a loose decorative pillow. But there was only time to throw his arms up defensively to protect his face.

As they plowed into the harvester, Trapp imagined them flying forward like ragdolls while Bril cackled horrifyingly. But nothing happened. He lowered his arms. The LIMO passed through the harvester as if the machine was a ghost.

"Pretty convincing, huh?" Bril said, now looking up.

"Holograms!" Bretta growled. "You could've warned us."

"Sorry."

Trapp's heart thumped out of control.

"Why are there US government HoloSynths out here?" he asked. "In the middle of nowhere?"

"They confuse the satellites."

"Whose satellites?"

"Russians, Chinese, Koreans? Doesn't matter."

"Aren't they our allies?"

"Sometimes it's allies who one has to be most vigilant about. We can't risk them finding us."

"Finding what?"

"What you're about to see." SmartStraps flew out from behind Trapp's seat. They came down over his shoulders and locked magnetically to the seat between his legs. He glanced over at Bretta. She was being equally restrained, her eyes as wide with fear as Trapp guessed his were. "Hang on!"

The LIMO left the ground.

14

Foe

TRAPP HAD NO idea how far the LIMO dropped.

Nauseated from the fall, he caught a fleeting glimpse of daylight overhead. Trapezoidal in shape, it quickly winked out with a massive bang that shook the LIMO.

"What the fuck?" Bretta asked, her voice thick with shock.

"It's a tunnel," Trapp said, swallowing hard as he surveyed LEDs zipping by at intervals. "We're on a ramp underground."

"*Very* good," Bril said. "I told you we were near a government installation."

Trapp gulped back his breakfast. "You didn't say we were on top of it. How deep are we going?"

"Deep enough."

"What is this place?" Bretta asked.

"We call it Helena, after the patron saint of diggers or archaeologists, depending on who you ask. It's an appropriate name considering we're descending to a depth of a hundred meters."

The tunnel widened into a funnel. A massive blast door sat open at the back. Soldiers brandishing assault rifles guarded this. They were dressed in black jumpsuits to match Bril's.

"Are they here for us?" Bretta asked as the LIMO slowed to a stop beside a short woman at the front of the column of soldiers. The ramp lowered.

"Depends," Bril said.

Bretta's face reddened and her eyes narrowed. "On what?"

"There are those who believe you are involved with the admiral's death. And he's a fugitive." Bril nodded toward Trapp.

"You lured us here for this? I thought you were going to help us."

"I was following orders. And I know you aren't guilty of any crime. Well, except harboring a fugitive. And murdering those Demons."

"Which you helped me—"

Bril raised a hand. "I'm not in control here."

"Fuck that," Bretta said, standing and heading toward the ramp.

Trapp wasn't sure where she was going this deep underground. But she was met by the woman who'd flagged them down. The two stood face to face. The second woman had cropped wheat-colored hair with a long braid hanging down her back. She smirked at Bretta.

"Major Sykes," she said, tersely saluting Bril while blocking Bretta's exit.

"Lieutenant Case," Bril said, lazily returning the salute. "Meet the wife."

The woman dropped her hand.

"Ma'am?" Case said, extending her hand. "I'm Lieutenant Audra Case. It's a pleasure to meet you. If you'll take your seat, all will be explained. We've been anticipating what you can do to help us fix the—"

"That's enough, Lieutenant," Bril said, cutting her off curtly. "The prisoners will be briefed when the time is right, and not a second sooner."

The ramp rose as Trapp sized up Case. She took the drubbing from Bril, showing no emotion. Her eyes were intense, focused. Her muscular upper arms, scarred in places and covered with tats, pulsed like she was itching to hurt someone.

"Military?" he asked her.

"Seventeen years," Case said, maintaining her eye contact with Bretta.

"In other words, you're a badass."

"As bad as they come." The crack of a smile split her face and was gone instantly.

"Bretta," Trapp said. "I suggest we hear these people out."

"This is what I get for trusting my husband to help me," Bretta muttered as she took her seat beside Trapp.

"This is me helping you," Bril said, his voice whiny.

Bretta glanced away and worked her jaw while tears wetted her eyes.

The LIMO entered the hatchway, which had already begun to trundle closed. Within seconds, it shut with a loud clunk.

And they continued their journey underground.

THE LIMO CAME onto a sun-bathed prairie with low hills, ripe grains, and a cloud-dappled, rich blue sky. Two combine harvesters reaped their way through a distant field.

"Did we come back to the surface?" Trapp asked.

"I didn't feel us ascending," Bretta said with a shake of her head, her eyes bugging with confusion.

"You should see your faces," Bril said with a laugh.

"We're still underground," Trapp said with a terse nod.

"It's a SynthWorld?" Bretta asked.

"The sky is a Synth," Bril said. "A hologram, to be exact. But the crops and harvesters are real. We have rainfall here, and snow, dry days, and cool nights. All of it is randomized by AIs that run the air handling and water systems. The filters can even remove radiation so the residents can sustain life down here after a nuclear war if one were to arise."

Trapp shook his head. "The nukes were all decommissioned decades ago."

Bril nodded thoughtfully. "Helena was excavated and constructed before the Budapest Accords. It is one of over a dozen Self-sustaining Underground Domains—SUDs. Each has SynthMeat and SynthDairy production, fruit trees, vegetables, and grains. Each can sustain thousands of humans for centuries."

"Why?" Bretta asked.

"Originally, they were built as a hedge against increased average temperature. People moved away from the coasts and farther north. Some could come here and be kept perfectly comfortable in the summer months. When war broke out, though, the US government took them over to be used in the event of a nuclear holocaust."

"But the war's over," Trapp said.

"One can never be certain that there won't be a second Carbon War. Continuing our way of life is the number one priority."

"The government elites' way of life," Bretta said. "The rich and connected. How come you never told me about any of this?"

"It's top secret."

The LIMO came to the end of the field, where a dark semicircle penetrated the sloping dome of the sky's HoloDisplay. It was an entrance to another tunnel. Apparently, the SUD had multiple chambers. The LIMO sped into the darkness, temporarily blinding Trapp. When his eyes adjusted, he found himself looking at Lieutenant Case. She was watching Bril with thinly veiled contempt and Trapp understood something. Case wasn't just Bril's subordinate. She was also his keeper.

The tunnel opened onto another SynthWorld. It was a desert valley with far-off mountains surrounding scrublands dotted with saguaro cacti, their extended arms seeming to ward off visitors. The LIMO entered a village of tract housing, cheap office buildings, and two-story barracks. It reminded Trapp of Space Corps's Miami Base. Pulling into a circular driveway, they came to a stop in front of a nondescript building. Several soldiers joined them as they exited the ramp. Case led them inside and down a long hallway, at the end of which was a sloping room with half a dozen concentric rows of comfortable chairs that arced toward a stage.

Bril sat beside Bretta in the front row, with Trapp on her other side.

"I'll do my best to get you out of this," Bril whispered to her.

Bretta glowered at him as a pinkish blob appeared on the stage with various out-of-focus gray and black markings. Soon, it resolved into a face. It was an old man with gray hair.

"Welcome, my children," he said with a smile.

Bretta gasped. "Grandpa?"

It was Professor Phileas Gray.

And he was alive.

15

Reflection

"YOU'RE ALIVE?" BRETTA asked in a weak whisper. "I saw the evidence, the blood, the pictures of your…" her breath hitched. "…body. Why did no one tell me you were still alive?" She leveled this question at Bril before turning back to Gray. "I knew we weren't on speaking terms. But this is just plain…"

"Cruel," Trapp said.

Bretta nodded. Bril sputtered but said nothing. Instead, he turned toward the Professor.

"It is complicated," Gray said with a smile, as if he hadn't just laid a heavy burden on Bretta.

"You were already isolated," Bretta said, her voice raising an octave. "You didn't need to fake your death in such a way. Unless you thought your lab had been compromised."

"The lab is a very safe location."

"Why reappear now? We haven't spoken in years. I don't know what to say."

"We *have not* spoken in years," Gray agreed.

Trapp began to notice something odd about his smile. Here was a man who'd faked his own death, lied to his granddaughter, and then came out of hiding in the most insensitive way. From the rumors, Gray was an odd man. But this was borderline psychotic. And he had the gall to smile?

Bretta turned to Trapp, the bright saucers of her big eyes reflecting Gray's projection. Then they squinted. "It's not him," she said to Trapp in a low voice. "He's a hologram." Her voice deflated as she looked at Gray.

"Correct," he said. "I am a facsimile created from Phileas Gray's memories. You can call me Gray-AI."

"So my grandfather's still…?"

"Dead," Gray-AI said with a smile. "I am afraid so."

Bretta's body shrunk. Conversely, Trapp's heart rate skyrocketed. Standing, he thrust his face into Bril's.

"A little warning would've been nice, you asshole," he yelled. "Isn't it bad enough that Bretta had to process her grandfather's death the first time? Now you tease her with his life?"

Case grabbed his upper arm. Her strong grip bit into the muscles.

"Sit down, Indent," she said. "Or I will be forced to sit you down."

"He's an asshole. You're an asshole. This whole scene is…" Trapp turned toward the smiling hologram. "*Fucked!*"

"Trapp," Bretta said, placing her hand on his. "Please sit down. It's okay. I'm okay."

He glared at her in confusion. Why wasn't she more pissed? And why had his anger gone from zero to 60 in two seconds? It wasn't like him to care about another person in this way. Taking deep breaths, he sat down.

Bretta squeezed his hand. "I lost him years ago. I was just…surprised."

"Sorry for the outburst," he muttered.

"No apologies. Remember? But thanks." She leaned over and kissed him on the cheek. Already flushed from anger, he turned red for another reason. She still held his hand. They both glanced down at the union. She pulled it away quickly.

"The Professor's death triggered a series of events," Gray-AI said. "The first of which was me. I have been programmed with more than fifteen billion data points. They're comprised of Doctor Gray's writings, interviews, HoloPics, and the HoloVids he recorded of every minute spent in his lab."

"He captured his murder, then," Trapp said excitedly. "You can help me prove my innocence."

"Inexplicably, the HoloVid recorders were turned off the day of his murder. I have run diagnostics to determine the cause of the glitch. So far I have found no explanation for the discrepancy. In any case, I was not awakened to solve his murder, but to right a wrong."

"Does this have to do with the Manifold?" Bretta asked.

"Yes."

"I knew it! The TUR stole Grandpa's intellectual property and he couldn't get over it. So he wrote an AI to get the rights to his precious energy collector back."

"Professor Gray did not invent an energy collector."

"Tell that to the billions of people who survive off Manifold-mined batteries. Or are you going to tell me that the Manifold doesn't generate electricity?"

"The Manifold is a very efficient electricity generator," Gray-AI said. "But it was never meant to be. That was just an unintended consequence of its real purpose."

"Which is what?" Bretta asked.

"The Manifold," Gray-AI said, "is a quantum mirror."

"THERE IS NO such thing as a quantum mirror!" Bretta scoffed. "Such a device is a theoretical impossibility."

"Not anymore," Gray-AI said.

"So you're trying to tell me that Grandpa invented a device that reflects quantum waves while maintaining the integrity of their superpositions?"

"Yes."

"Even if quantum theory allowed for it, which it doesn't, there is no practical application for such a thing. Grandpa wouldn't have wasted his mind on looking for a way to produce one."

"This is true. The XTerra project required an asteroid to be converted into a spaceship. This would be no small task. How much fuel would be necessary to manipulate something so big? The Professor happened upon an obscure paper describing an anti-gravity device as a possible solution. And, after years of developing prototypes, he succeeded in amplifying gravity waves. During one of the tests, though, the device inexplicably reflected energy waves in a way that kept their superpositions intact."

"Superpositions?" Trapp asked.

"All matter begins life as energy waves propagating through space," Bretta said. "When one of these waves encounters something, say light reflecting off the surface of a mirror, it collapses into a particle called a photon." She turned to Gray-AI.

"The Professor's experiments confirmed that these waves were allowed to propagate without collapsing into particles," Gray-AI said.

"And what did he think was causing this?"

"He theorized that it had to do with the weakness of gravity."

"Gravity isn't weak," Trapp said. "I know because I was recently hanging from a cliff. If I'd let go, gravity would've splattered my body all over the rocks below."

Gray-AI smiled broadly. "You did not fall. Under your own strength, you pulled yourself up off that cliff, proving that gravity is weak."

"Not under his own strength," Bretta said. "He had a little help."

"For which I'm eternally grateful," Trapp said.

"Gravity is the weakest of the fundamental forces," Gray-AI said. "One possible theory for this is that the three other fundamental forces are confined to the three-dimensional universe while gravity is spread over multiple dimensions, weakening it."

"You're talking about Manifold space," Bretta said.

"Correct. The Manifold not only amplifies gravity waves while reflecting energy waves, it also generates two types of particles. The first is supercharged electrons which can be harvested as a source of abundant energy."

"And the second type?"

"Antiprotons and positrons, primarily. Very seldomly, there are antineutrons."

"Antimatter!" Bretta exclaimed. "Holy shit!" She stood up and looked from Trapp to Bril to Case, her eyes big with terror or exhilaration or both. "I know why Grandpa created the Manifold," she said, pacing back and forth.

She became quiet. The room was deadly silent as the rest of them waited for her to finish. Finally, she stopped pacing and stared at them intently.

"I think Grandpa was building a wormhole."

"I'M RIGHT, AREN'T I?" Bretta asked Gray-AI. Pacing around in front of his projection, she ran her fingers through her hair. "A Manifold can produce a wormhole."

"We'll never know for sure," Gray-AI said. "The Professor is dead. And he left nothing in my databases to confirm or deny your hypothesis. Theoretically, though, it might have been possible. Massive energy, like that from Sol's gravity waves, combined with antimatter, are the two ingredients necessary to create a wormhole."

"Maybe that's what got him killed. Maybe he was on the verge of making that breakthrough. And someone wanted to stop him."

"A plausible theory. My databases indicate a 75% chance that his original Manifold designs were leaked to the Terran United Republic before they commandeered the technology. He had suffered a data breach a few months before his experiments with the Manifold were shut down."

"Who leaked the schematics?" Bretta asked.

"I have no data on that subject. The Professor wrote extensively to the International Space Consortium after he was banned from developing Manifolds, though, imploring them to allow him to continue his research. But his correspondence went unanswered."

"Maybe there's a way we can do something about that," Bril said, speaking for the first time in a while. "Maybe we can restart your grandfather's project."

"You want to build a Manifold?" Bretta asked. "Is that why you brought me here? Because I can tell you right now, I don't have the skills to create—"

"Your grandfather had a Manifold." Bril stared at Bretta evenly.

"Excuse me?" Bretta asked.

"No one knows where it is—well, that's not exactly true. He does." Bril nodded toward Gray-AI.

"Its location is hidden in my programming," Gray-AI said. "Behind a password-protected partition."

"Which my team is working to bypass," Bril said.

"That's a bad idea," Bretta said. "Something that dangerous should be left alone."

"We can't do that."

"Why not?"

"Because we're not the only people looking for it. During their search of Gray's lab, the Pols discovered clues of its existence. They also uncovered evidence that Gray believed another group was looking for it. And this faction wants to acquire it so they can turn it into a weapon. The President wants to find it and destroy it."

"It's already a weapon," Trapp said.

"Which is why we need to find it before they do." Bril leveled his eyes at Bretta.

Bretta waved her hand in frustration. "What makes you think I know where it is?"

He opened his phone and projected a HoloPic into the air. It was of a little girl no more than five years old standing in front of a set of windows that opened onto a space the size of several gymnasiums. A blurry copper-colored disk engulfed this space. If it were a Manifold, it was the smallest one Trapp had ever seen. Upon further inspection, he recognized the girl.

"It's you," he told Bretta.

"Where did you get that?" she asked Bril.

"Top secret. But we think this group has that picture. We learned of this early this morning. We think they were the ones that attacked you in Alaska. And I'm grateful they didn't catch you. They'd use extraordinary tactics to extract this location from your memory."

"But I don't have a memory of that. I've never seen that place."

"It doesn't matter," Bril said. "Your life is in extreme danger. Until we can find that Mini-Manifold, we need to keep you in custody. For your own safety. Perhaps you can even help us find it."

"I'm no cybersecurity expert," Bretta scoffed.

"No. But you are a Professor Gray expert." Bril sighed and slid forward on his seat. He put his hands out, pleading. "And it would make things go easier if you joined the effort voluntarily."

Case came over to Trapp and Bretta, motioning for them to stand. She held out MagnaCuffs.

"Really?" Bretta asked Bril while nodding at the cuffs.

"We have to," he said with a nod toward Case, who placed them on their wrists. "We need to keep up the appearance that you are prisoners so no one busts your cover."

"You don't trust your own people?"

"I don't trust anyone." Bril stood.

Case saluted him, then she led Trapp and Bretta out of the room.

16

Cell Block

TRAPP WAS FIXATED on what Bril had said.

"To keep up appearances."

There were no two ways about it, though. Trapp wasn't a fake prisoner. He was a real one. As for Bretta? He couldn't be sure.

It was the middle of the night and he lay in his Helena cell staring at the ceiling. Earlier, he and Bretta were taken into a building at the center of the SUD's base. Without the use of local anesthetics, a female guard cut open Trapp's ankle and jammed a tracking chip into the wound, closing it with a laser suturing device. The U.S. military could now follow his movements around the globe. Notably, Bretta was *not* given a similar tracker. Case led them past a guard station, down a hallway, and placed them across from each other in glass cells, like two exhibits in an alien zoo.

After Case brought a simple meal and the two inmates ate, Bretta lay down and went to sleep immediately. Trapp stared at his ceiling, processing. Did this incarceration signal the end of his search? Bril had brought Bretta here to protect her; to use her. So what were Bril's plans for Trapp? Turn him in as a peace offering to the TUR? Send him back to the ISC?

Trapp weighed these thoughts most of the night, dozing a few minutes here and there.

Then he sensed a change.

He was being watched. And it wasn't from the EYE cameras he'd already sized up in the corridor, or the fish-eye lens inside his cell, providing no privacy.

Looking up from his cot, he saw that Bretta was standing up, staring at him from across the corridor. When she saw that she had his attention, she began to move her hands around in a strange way. Trapp wondered if she was sleepwalking—*sleep gesturing*. But there seemed to be a pattern to her movements as she formed figures with her fingers and gesticulated wildly in the air. She pointed at Trapp.

"I don't understand," he said, shaking his head. She couldn't hear him, of course.

She huffed before repeating the weird hand dance. Trapp watched this performance for several minutes, mesmerized. There was something familiar about it. And it took him a few minutes more to realize why.

"Oh, I get it. You're teaching me how to sign my name. T-R-A-P-P equals Trapp."

He repeated her gestures and then pointed at himself. She smiled and bowed. Then, she signed a new word before pointing at herself. Trapp already recognized the 'T,' 'R,' and 'A.' He had just learned 'B' and 'E.'

"Bretta," he said.

She nodded.

A three-hour tutorial followed. By the end of it, Trapp had learned the alphabet, numbers, and several familiar words.

"What's going to happen to me?" Trapp asked, clumsily trying out his new skill.

She shrugged. "You're going to stay here for a while," she signed.

"Are they going to turn us over to the Pols?"

"I don't think so. I won't let that—"

The door at the end of the corridor slid open, causing her to stop abruptly. Case stepped in and glanced back and forth between the two prisoners with a half grin. She entered Bretta's cell and placed MagnaCuffs on her wrists. Then, she led Bretta down the corridor toward the exit. As the grizzled soldier passed Trapp, she pointed two fingers at her eyes and then at Trapp's.

He didn't need Bretta's tutoring for that one.

"I'm keeping an eye on you," her sign said.

CASE ARRIVED AT midday.

"Up and at 'em, Indent," she said as the cell door slid open. Exhausted from his overnight signing session with Bretta, Trapp had dozed off. He glanced expectantly over at Bretta's cell. It was empty. "Your girlfriend's still with the major," Case explained when he gazed back at her.

She turned him around brusquely and placed MagnaCuffs on his wrists.

"She's not my girlfriend," Trapp grumbled sleepily.

"Maybe you should tell your face the news," Case said, pushing him violently out into the corridor. They passed the guard's station.

"Where are you taking me?"

"Mandatory hour of sunlight. Apparently, the major believes in treating civilians, well, with civility." Case chuckled as she prodded Trapp down a side hallway. At the end was a heavy door fixed with a window to the outside. Case pushed Trapp through. Squinting at the daylight, Trapp surveyed a rectangle of concrete cordoned off by a tall fence topped with razor wire. He knew the paradigm. It wasn't his first prison yard. Still, he noted one major difference.

"A SynthSky doesn't technically put out sunlight," he scoffed.

"All customer complaints must be registered at the home office," Case said, chuckling as she removed his MagnaCuffs. She took a position by the door and raised a SynthCig to her mouth.

A slight breeze wafted in Trapp's face, no doubt from the air handling system Bril had spoken of. As his eyes adjusted to the brightness, he noticed that he and Case weren't the only ones out there. Dressed in black overalls like Bril's but more worn, a man hunched against the fence several meters away. His sleeves were sewn with sergeant's chevrons and he bobbed and weaved as he gripped the chain links, muttering to himself.

Trapp gave Case a questioning glance.

"Sergeant Riggs," she said, exhaling a smoky cloud. "Unstable. I'd give him a wide berth if I were you."

Trapp walked to the opposite side of the yard from the sergeant and glanced through the fence. Bril had called Helena an SUD. How many generations would be born, live, and die here, if the place were used as intended?

Would those people forget about the world above them, forever condemned to think of these caverns as the universe? Trapp stared in silence, weighted by the thought of it. Then he turned his attention to Bretta. He hoped she was okay. Case had called her his "girlfriend." Preposterous. Bretta would never—

"Time's up, sunshine," Case said. She was standing directly behind Trapp, giving off a chemically enhanced scent of blueberries.

"Hour's not up yet," Trapp said.

"It is for me."

She led him back to his cell.

Bretta was still gone.

17

The Shaft

THE DAY TRAPP was accosted by the unstable sergeant began like the others.

Trapp passed his prison time combating boredom with exercise, bland food, mandatory fake sunlight hours, and avoiding the crazy sergeant in the prison yard. His only bright spot each day came hours after bedtime, when he would wake to find Bretta staring at him from across the hallway. This signaled the beginning of their nightly sign conversation.

Trapp was becoming fluent in the language, so much so that he barely noticed the difference between it and actual speaking.

"Bril is having an affair," Bretta signed on the third night. "I've known about it for months. But, for some reason, it never bothered me. What do you think that means?"

"Don't know," Trapp signed with a sigh. He wanted to say she wasn't in love with Bril anymore, that her heart must be opening to new relationships. But he couldn't face the possibility she might see through his fantasy borne of shared adventures or Case's power of suggestion that had set his mind spinning. Either way, he was falling for Bretta.

"He's been acting weird, too," she said. "Questioning my expertise in…" her hands flew around dramatically, losing Trapp in the translation. "It's bad enough that he doesn't remember that I did one of my theses on the subject, but then, it seems, I'm undergoing some sort of…" More unknown words flew from her hands. Trapp didn't press. She was on a rant.

"It is strange that he had you arrested," he signed when she came up for breath. "It's almost like…" Trapp stopped short of signing 'he's been lying all this time.' "Why did he help you save me?"

"Exactly," she signed in dramatic gestures. She went on another rant, a quarter of which Trapp couldn't translate. This was broken up when Case came to take Bretta away for the day.

Hours later, Trapp was in the yard again. Case had left him with Corporal Rogers, the woman who'd violently installed Trapp's tracker on their first day there. Smoking her SynthCig, she emitted a pungent fog. The Helena weather AI had gifted them with a cloudy day, adding to the gloom.

The crazy sergeant kept vigil by the fence, dancing in isolation and speaking to himself. He belonged in a psych ward, not a prison. Trapp stared out into the desert and the mountains beyond. He thought the HoloWorld might be a copy of a place in Arizona he'd passed through on his way to California once.

"You must make the climb," a voice whispered, startling Trapp.

Trapp turned. The crazy sergeant stood half a dozen centimeters away and reeked from weeks without a bath.

"Pardon me?" Trapp said, backing up.

"You must leave this place."

Trapp took another step backward, fearful that the man had snapped. His body blocked Trapp from Corporal Rogers. He danced from foot to foot as if he needed to relieve himself. But his stare was direct. Strangely, he seemed lucid and focused.

"Leave me alone," Trapp said, peering around for Corporal Rogers's help. She was lost in a noisy HoloPhone game.

The crazy sergeant raised his finger to his lips. "Don't draw attention. This is just an act. And I don't have much time. I'm Major Sykes's aid. And I need to pass this along. They're going to execute you after the major's wife breaks the AI's password. They're waiting because they think your death will cause her to stop cooperating." He glanced over his shoulder at Rogers. She was still playing with her phone. "You need to escape."

"Even if I could get past the guards, I'd never overwhelm that squad of soldiers guarding the blast door."

"Which is why you need to climb out," the sergeant whispered exasperatedly. "At the southern exit is the air handling facility. They pump in the air from the surface from a hundred meters up. The ventilation shaft will be unguarded during the test. And its lasers won't be functioning during the window of time the electricity is shut off. You'll have an hour, maybe a little longer, to escape by that shaft." The sergeant pushed something into Trapp's hand, forcing him to close his fingers around it. "You'll need this too. Don't let them find it. Or we're both dead."

"How am I supposed to…"

The guy shuffled back to his corner, groaning loudly when he got there.

Corporal Rogers looked up. Trapp tried his best to mask his confused expression. *Test? Electricity off? Lasers in an air shaft?*

"Indent Trapmore," Case shouted as she came into the yard.

Trapp nodded and headed toward the door, turning his back to her to receive the MagnaCuffs.

He knew the drill.

"I'M GOING TO escape."

Trapp stared at Bretta from across the corridor. He did his best to hide his hand signals from the EYE. But he desperately needed to speak with her. Crazy Sergeant Riggs had wormed into his mind that much.

"You'll be killed," she signed.

"I'm dead either way."

Confused, she shook her head. "Bril promises that he won't turn you into the Pols, that you'll be safe. And once we break into Gray-AI—"

"I met a guy," Trapp said, ignoring her attempts to argue. "A credible guy." He spelled out 'credible.' "He spoke of a way to get out."

"You should trust Bril."

"Why?" he asked. "You don't."

"I did once," she signed. "When he was my professor, I fell for him. Daddy issues, I suppose. I never stopped caring for him, though. Nor he, me. We just… grew apart. He's a good man. He's got integrity. He'd die to protect the interests of the U.S. government. President Hancock is like a god to him."

"You're saying that because we're being watched." Trapp nodded toward the cameras.

"They can't read our signs," she said.

"The EYE cameras are watching our every move."

"No. I'm saying no one can read our signs except you and me. I created the language."

Trapp began to argue. But then he laughed. Of course, she'd invented her own sign language.

"His aide," Trapp signed, feeling free to say anything, "told me they're keeping me alive to keep you working. Once you break Gray-AI's code, they're going to kill me. I've got a plan to get out through the air handling system."

"I'm not trying to break the code."

"You're working on Bril's project, aren't you?"

"In appearances only. I'm working on my own project."

"Which is what?" he asked.

"I can't say. Not now. But I'm doing whatever I can to keep Bril from finding that password."

"And risking your life in the process? Escape with me."

"I can't." She looked away. Even from this distance, he saw her eyes glistening. She turned back toward him. "We're going to MAU. Tonight."

"We are?" Trapp asked.

"You're staying. After the test, Bril is taking me with him."

"What kind of test?" Trapp asked, fighting to hide his utter disappointment. *She was leaving him?*

"They're shutting down the power grid and bringing it back up to prove they can do it in an emergency. The President has gotten nervous lately that Bril's disaster recovery procedures haven't been tested properly. Bril's pissed at Hancock, too. The test is going to take a few hours. And even when the power comes back on, Bril and his team must successfully bring the computers back online. After all of that's complete, he's taking me east."

"Riggs wasn't lying then," Trapp signed. "There is a way to escape at the southern exit."

"Riggs?"

"Never mind. When the power is off, that will be my chance—*our* chance." He stared intently at her. "You have to come with me."

"I want to. I really do. I've gotten used to your company." Her face lowered as tears wet her eyes. "I don't want to go to MAU. I don't want to end *this*." She gestured back and forth from herself to Trapp.

"Riggs's plan will work. Everything he told me has come true so far. I can get you out of here. And then we can find a way into Gray's lab together. I'm a former criminal, and I've gotten into harder places."

She stared at him with a look of indecision. But then her brows came together and her face sagged.

"I can't risk it," she signed. "I have to figure out what Grandpa was really up to. It's what he would've wanted me to do."

She gave him a helpless look. Her breath hitched.

She turned away and lay on her bunk. Her chest heaved. She was sobbing. He watched her, his hand reaching to try and pull her back to the silent conversation. But, soon, her chest stopped heaving and began to move up and down slowly.

She had fallen asleep.

Maybe he could convince her in the morning. Or maybe, if he really loved her, he needed to let her go.

18

Case

BRETTA WAS GONE.

Trapp was awakened when Case brought breakfast to his cell. He wasn't hungry, and he lay in his bunk, staring at the ceiling. Surely, last night's conversation wasn't the last he'd ever have with Bretta Gray-Sykes. She would come back for something. Maybe she would even talk Bril into letting her sit out tonight's test in her cell.

The mandatory hour of daylight came late.

Corporal Rogers took Trapp out to the yard. It was the second time Case wasn't there to escort him. She and crazy Sergeant Riggs were nowhere to be seen. Rogers smoked her SynthCig and played her HoloPhone games. Trapp stared into the flat world and tried to push back the pall rising in his soul.

He thumbed the item in his pocket, the strange piece of hardware Riggs had given him. Rory's ID tag was long gone, surrendered to a storage locker of personal effects during Trapp's intake procedure. For some reason, Rogers had let him keep his phone. Probably because it couldn't pick up a signal this far underground.

But Rory's ID tag would have to be left behind, just as his frozen body was condemned to float in space near Sol. Trapp had never given a second thought to others; he had always flown where his tattered wings took him. Even when Rory died, he'd found the tragedy to be a catalyst for Trapp's own future more than a reason to mourn the loss of a friend.

So why was he so heartbroken about Bretta?

Rogers finished her game and led Trapp back to his cell.

"Surprise!" Case said with a flourish while she waited for him in his cell. She pointed at his bunk, where half a dozen carbon fiber straps latticed the stiff mattress.

"What's all this?" Trapp asked.

"Insurance policy." Case was holding her Taser. "As you know, they're running a disaster recovery test and shutting down Helena's power, including the cell locks in our little B & B. We can't have our guests wandering around like a loose herd of cattle, can we?"

Trapp looked around. There were no other inmates on the floor. He turned back to Case. "You're lashing me in like a crate in a cargo hold?"

"Yup." She sounded way too upbeat.

"Isn't that a violation of my human rights?"

"Take it up with the judge. Oh, I forgot. There is no judge. Now. Are you going to get into bed willingly? Or do I finally get to tase you?"

She wore a devilish grin. Shrugging, Trapp acquiesced. He climbed up and lay facing the ceiling. Rogers placed MagnaCuffs on his wrists before spending a long time strapping him in. Her eyes were watery and unfocused. Trapp guessed she was high from a pinch of THC in her SynthCig.

Suddenly, stochastic electric guitar chords blasted into the enclosed cell, causing tiny warbles in Trapp's inner ear.

"Is that…?" he shouted over it at Case. "Your ringtone?"

Fumbling to extract her HoloPhone from her pocket, Case dropped it clattering to the floor. The young voice shouted out lyrics from the phone's speakers. And Trapp's situation resolved into focus as Case finally got the phone into her hand and silenced it.

"*Purple Haze*," Trapp hissed. "It was you, wasn't it? On the cliff in Alaska?" Case grinned cruelly as she checked the straps. "So it *was* Bril."

"He's not the boy scout you might think he is," Case said.

"I *never* thought he was. Why didn't he tell us he sent you to bring us here so that Bretta could help him? We might've even come willingly if you two had approached us."

"That's classified." She still wore that sadistic grin, though.

Trapp gasped as he got it. "You weren't supposed to arrest us, were you? You were coming to kill us." She turned away. "Fuckin' tell me the truth, Case. Bretta's in danger, isn't she?"

She turned back around and fixed her vision on Trapp. "Let's just say," she said, "that he'll do what he has to if she outlives her usefulness." Case left the room with Rogers in tow. At the doorway, she turned around. "The EYE cameras run on batteries. So don't try anything." She signed this last sentence in perfect BSL—Bretta Sign Language.

The message was clear. She knew what Trapp had been planning.

He looked over at Bretta's dark and empty cell. Bril was going to kill her.

And there was nothing that Trapp could do about it.

A LOUD "CLACK" split the night air.

The darkest black Trapp had ever experienced suddenly washed over him. He couldn't see his hand in front of his face. Or at least he guessed so, since he couldn't bring his hand up. He could barely move, for that matter. And, for several seconds, he was sure he'd be riding out the power failure strapped to his bed like a crate of batteries on their way to Terra from the *Eos*. He took a deep breath to calm his nerves. It was now or never.

Carefully, Trapp turned his wrists up and put his fingertips on cool metal. It was the butt end of Crazy Sergeant Riggs's gift. Before Corporal Rogers strapped Trapp down, he'd managed to slip it up his overall sleeve, unnoticed likely due to the fogginess of her SynthCig. Now, he slid the device out and balanced it between his fingertips.

Eerie blue emergency LEDs winked on. Trapp flinched, bobbling the tool. Somehow, he managed to pinch it before it clattered to the floor and virtually condemned him to death. He held his breath. Finally, he repositioned the tool between both hands.

Probing, he felt a point on one end. A crude saw on the other end made it perfect for cutting the carbon fiber straps, proving Riggs's genius. But Riggs hadn't considered how Trapp could free himself from the MagnaCuffs. Or had he?

Trapp slid his finger along the tool's axis. The blue light caused the cobalt to glow, each end shining with the same reflective quality. And then it hit Trapp.

"It's one piece of metal," he mouthed to himself.

And he knew why. It was a tool that inmates called a stub.

Constructed from soda cans, forks, or even foil from a stick of gum, they served one purpose: to exploit a known MagnaCuff weakness.

Delicately, so he didn't drop the stub or touch skin to the MagnaCuff's field, Trapp brought the stub down. He gritted his teeth and held his breath. The thing was too short and his first attempt yielded a shock from the MagnaCuffs. Thankfully, he still held on to it despite his numb hand. He twisted the stub and placed it between his thumbs. He pulled them up and tried to balance the thing between the poles of the magnetic field. This time, it was too long.

If he could get one of his straps off, he could hold the stub between his teeth and short the field.

But that was the point of the straps, wasn't it?

Case had planned for the contingency that Trapp might be carrying a stub. She probably picked it up on a thermal EYE camera. Yet, by the faded color of his uniform, it was clear that Sergeant Riggs had been here a while.

Trying again, Trapp spread his hands like he was opening a book, causing the Cuffs to move apart, their field so close to his skin that his hands tingled. He brought the stub down to the Cuffs. They sizzled and went dark. Trapp shook them off onto his chest.

He cut the straps away, raising a carbon dust cloud from the sawing.

"Thank you, you crazy bastard," he exclaimed as he sat up and put his feet on the floor. The whole extraction had taken ten minutes or so. He was running short on Riggs's hour deadline.

He crept out of his unlocked cell toward the guards' station. Expecting Case and Rogers to be waiting with Tasers, Trapp was surprised to find the guards' station empty. He headed for the entrance, his confidence growing as he passed the intake area and the front door came into view. He sped and moved toward the Helena night.

And then he was on the floor, writhing in pain.

"Thought you could get away?" Case asked, standing over him, holding the trigger end of a Taser, its two shiny filaments tracing spirals to his chest. Case wore a shit-eating grin.

Trapp had stepped right into her snare.

A STRANGE THING happened as Trapp lay on the floor.

The Taser's electricity danced through his nervous system, his bladder released, and his body seized into a solid block of contractions that threatened to rip tendons and break bones. He experienced the worst pain he'd ever known.

Still, almost immediately, another sensation entered him, a calm and relaxation that felt as if he'd been pumped with liters of Bretta's morphine. His foggy head cleared. His strength returned and the convulsions stopped.

Trapp grabbed the electrodes from the obviously malfunctioning Taser and yanked them out of his chest. Blue arcs flew between them and his hands, oozing around his fingertips like licks of fire. It appeared the Taser was working and somehow Trapp was immune to its effects.

He flicked his wrist. The wires came out of the gun. He tossed them aside as he climbed to his feet. He towered over Case. She stared in shock at her destroyed Taser as Trapp punched her in the jaw, causing her head to jerk sideways. Rogers shot her Taser, sticking Trapp in the back with new electrodes. He awaited the surge of electricity to bathe his muscles in pain. But it never came. Rogers's Taser was as useless on him as Case's.

Turning around and pulling hand over hand on the wires, he advanced toward Rogers. She dropped the gun and fled in panic.

A booted foot connected with the back of Trapp's head. His vision filled with sprites and his ears rang. He swiveled around. Case had her hands up and she balanced on the balls of her feet.

"I've killed men bigger than you," she hissed.

"I'm sure you have," Trapp said, taking a defensive stance. "But you should know. I'm an immortal." He grinned widely at his trash-talk. He *did* feel almost godlike, though. The cheap military-grade Tasers were no match for him.

Trapp lunged at Case. She ducked and slid away. He spun around and sent his boot flying at her thorax. She stepped back a half meter, avoiding most of the power. Still, he connected enough to send her sprawling.

She was on her feet immediately.

She returned with rapid punches, leaving him barely enough time to throw up his arms in defense. Fists struck muscle in an array of quick jabs. The pain was worse than the Taser. Trapp stepped back.

"That's gonna leave a bruise," he said, panting.

She set up for the next series, bouncing on her feet before bending and twisting in a circle. Her feet flew up. Having anticipated this move, Trapp grabbed a boot, helping it along in its direction. He flung her across the narrow hallway, where she crashed into the wall and bounced back, using the momentum to return with vertical punches.

Trapp took the blows, blocking his face and stomach as he moved closer, trapping her against the wall. He punched hard at her chest, resulting in two crunches from her rib cage and a yowl from her mouth. The seventeen-year vet grunted in pain and doubled over. Trapp wrapped his hand around her braid, lifting her off the ground. Getting a hold of his arm, she did a one-arm chin-up and sank her teeth into his skin. Trapp screamed and let go.

She hit the floor on her back, then lunged back onto her feet, ready for round three.

Trapp had brought a particular weapon, though, just in case.

Yanking it out of his back pocket, he threw a length of the carbon fiber straps around her wrist. She looked down in surprise, allowing him to grab her other wrist and wrap it up. He swung these around her waist and pulled. Now, he had her entire torso and wrists immobilized, and he pulled her close to him.

She head-butted him in the chin, splattering blood into his face. Still, he continued to wrap straps around her chest and upper arms. As she opened her mouth to shout an expletive, he shoved a pile of carbon fiber into it and wrapped it around her face.

He kicked her feet out from under her and she fell onto her tailbone. She thrashed and kicked as he got the last bit of the straps around one ankle, then the other.

Finally, she was tied up.

"I thought you might enjoy the irony," he said, panting loudly. "These things itch when they come into contact with skin. I hope you don't get a bad rash."

Trapp punched Case hard in the face. She went unconscious. He carried her to his cell.

Then he ran for the exit.

19

Handling

TRAPP DASHED OUT of the prison into a disorienting world of pitch blackness dotted with a smattering of red and white lights.

Moving carefully in the dark, he was greeted by a series of LEDs lining the stone pathway that wended through Helena's office complex. His chin throbbed from Case's head-butt. The blood from her bite mark dribbled down his arm and dripped from his fingertips. He thought little of the pain, though, as he tried to orient himself.

Straight ahead, lights dotted the dark landscape. They might be 100 or 1,000 meters away; there was no way to judge in this sea of black. The red ones overhead were probably angrily-blinking HoloEmitter status lights. These traced a pointillistic outline of catwalks, scaffolds, and ductwork and bore witness to the SUD's devious facade. Trapp felt a bit like Dorothy happening upon the *Wizard of Oz*'s crazed, behind-the-curtain controller pulling levers and pushing buttons.

Up ahead in the blackout, he spotted a yellow glow accompanied by distant machinery thrumming.

Bretta had to be there. Trapp broke into a jog. Making his way down an avenue of small office structures, he came to a building lit up like a Christmas tree. Next to it, a FleetCar-sized electric generator whined.

Moving to the front, Trapp realized this was where he and Bretta met Gray-AI.

He peered inside the glass door. The corridor was empty. Trapp had no idea where they were keeping Bretta inside, but he knew he was on the right track. Why else was this the only place in Helena with power?

And he'd already wasted a quarter of the two hours getting this far.

The door was unlocked. Trapp crept inside and slipped into a side hall to listen. Hearing nothing, he moved along the wall toward the theater. He'd half expected this place to be crawling with guards as he came within half a dozen meters of the double doors to Gray-AI's hologram theater.

Suddenly, a noise came from ahead and around the corner. It was footsteps of people climbing stairs accompanied by talking. A door whined open then slammed shut. The voices were moving in Trapp's direction. Dodging into the nearby theater, Trapp frantically looked for a place to hide. He found a small equipment closet and ducked into it, pulling its door shut behind him. The smoky smell of dust rose in the air. Apparently, no one came in here. He pushed the door ajar and peered out.

Those guys were probably heading out of the building and would walk right past the theater.

Trapp would wait for two minutes before heading toward the stairwell. The building must have a basement, and that would be the most likely place for Bril to keep

Bretta. The voices approached the doors and stopped. There was a discussion outside. Trapp couldn't make out the words, but the tone was heated.

"We can talk in here," one of them said.

Two men came into the theater. Trapp pulled his door shut some more. It was barely open a centimeter now. But he could make out the two men. Bril stood with his back to Trapp as he spoke. The other guy wore black overalls similar to Bril's. Trapp thought he saw yellow chevrons on the man's sleeve.

"The President won't accept a failure in this matter," the man was saying.

"You forget you're my subordinate, Hughes," Bril said in a high-pitched voice that exuded false confidence.

"Fuck that shit…Sir! You're not military. I am. The President was the one who assigned us to this detail, not you. Case got her ass chewed out when we decided to follow your orders and leave them alive."

"He fully backs my decision. We need them alive. Or at least we need *her* alive. I could give a shit about the other one. I wish the President would just let me turn him over to the authorities."

"And give up the other guy? Have you not understood how important our mission is?"

Bril shook his head. He was hunched in a way that spoke of his fears. And despite his words to Sergeant Hughes, Trapp began to understand something. Bril was under orders. But he was also working his own game. That included Sergeant Riggs and his wonderful bag of tricks that were intended to help Trapp escape. What reason could he have for that? Perhaps Bril wanted Trapp out of the picture because he was a loose end. Or—and Trapp sucked in fast at this thought, causing an irritation in the back of his throat—Bril wanted Trapp out of the way for other reasons. Trapp held his breath as he fought against the coughing reflex brought by his quick intake of dust from this little-used closet and realized it with stark clarity. Bril sensed that Trapp would do anything to protect Bril's estranged wife. That was why Riggs had been put in prison. So he could help get Trapp out of the way. Bril probably had a squad of Pols waiting outside to capture Trapp.

"I can have you eliminated, Hughes," Bril said in a low voice to the sergeant. "Believe me when I say that."

"I…uh," Hughes said. "Yes, sir."

Trapp's choking feeling was becoming desperate. He needed to cough.

"Where is she now?" Bril asked.

"I gave her something to knock her out for hours. She's in the LIMO heading east. I sent two of our best to escort her."

Fuck! Trapp was not only on the verge of having his lungs explode, but he'd lost Bretta.

Bril spoke. "I'm willing to make the ultimate sacrifice. Are you? Don't answer that. I don't give a fuck. But know this: when the time comes, if you can't do what's necessary to silence my wife, I will."

Trapp let out a slight wheeze at Bril's admission. Thankfully, Hughes was already speaking.

"You'd kill your own…"

"Quiet!" Bril said, silencing Hughes.

The room became deathly still. Tears streamed down Trapp's face. His throat was on fire. He was milliseconds away from giving up his hiding place. Not only would he be captured, but Bretta would be doomed to die. Fuckin' dust.

"Someone's coming down the hallway," Hughes said.

This was punctuated by the sounds of more footsteps in the hall. Trapp would've felt relief if his throat hadn't reached critical.

"We'll table this discussion," Bril whispered. "And, if you ever question my orders in front of the others like you did just a moment ago, I'll have you in front of a firing…"

The voices faded as the men walked out of the theater.

Trapp waited several seconds. The four-alarm fire in his throat finally exploded. He coughed and choked and leaned over, faint. He'd either pass out or vomit or both. But soon, his breath came back. No one came. Somehow, he'd remained hidden.

Bretta was on her way *east*! And Trapp was running out of time to go after her.

Trapp slipped out of the closet and moved through the doorway.

No matter what he did, he wouldn't let these assholes kill her. And, when he got the chance, he'd grab Bril by the throat and choke the life out of him.

But first, he had to escape this hell hole.

TRAPP SOON GOT his bearings.

The HoloEmitters, with their extensive array of blinking red overhead lights, pointed the way in the dark. Soon, he'd come through the "desert" by dodging saguaros with a faint citrus smell, Joshua trees that could've been coniferous for their aroma, and several evenly placed boulders. The road was rutted but seemed to be well-maintained. He reached the perimeter of the dome within 15 minutes of escaping the theater's dusty closet.

Trapp turned back toward the village. Bril's building gave the only light, and it couldn't have been more than 400 meters away. The floor of the man-made cave, Trapp now estimated, was a circle the diameter of a kilometer. It had seemed so much bigger when the HoloEmitters were projecting. Using Bril's lighted office building, Trapp had mapped out a more or less southerly heading. Still, when he placed his hand against the cool surface of the dome, it presented an unbroken surface.

When the engineers carved this cave out—Trapp was amazed that just a few hours ago, it looked like a whole desert valley—they must have sprayed the walls with quick-drying concrete. It would've taken a monumental effort to then truck in building supplies, run electrical cable and ductwork, water pipes, and hatchway doors—the ones at Helena's entrance were substantial enough to withstand nuclear blasts. Ironically, the easiest part of the build would've been its most stunning aspect: the SynthWorld.

This was constructed of thousands of HoloEmitters arrayed along the inside of the roughed-out dome. Electrical cables ran from a junction box next to Trapp and up the curve of the dome to the line of boxes. About a hundred meters up, his HoloPhone's torch lost sight of the boxes in the dark. Still, their LEDs blinked all across the cave, telling him where everything was. Behind a fake boulder over to his left, for instance, a steel stairway angled up the dome. At 20 meters, it connected to a landing and a suspended catwalk that extended off into the dark and over the landscape. Trapp had already seen this black-painted steelwork that gave maintenance crews access. But now he noticed that, above the catwalk, a giant duct spanned into the cave. Wide enough for four people to walk abreast, it angled back toward Trapp and behind him.

Panning his torch to the right, he found a gap in the continuous constellation of blinking LEDs into which the duct disappeared.

"South," he said and started in that direction. "It *can't* be this easy."

He followed a walkway that had curved around the inside of the dome. A two-meter stone wall held back the desert to his right. Trapp's olfactory senses picked up the spicy hint of crushed silica, telling him that the desert wasn't a synth but had been trucked in a ton at a time.

He approached the hole in the HoloEmitter field and shone his torch into it. It was another tunnel, reminding him of the one that had brought them here from the last segment of the cave, where combine harvesters threshed wheat. Apparently, these tunnel and cave systems were designed to be scalable.

Yet, as Trapp jogged a hundred meters to the end of this tunnel, he reached a dead end.

He panned his torch up. The tunnel was five meters high. The duct work he'd seen outside ran down its center and terminated in the wall overhead.

It was the trunk line for the whole air handling system.

"Where the heck is the door?" he asked, using his torch to scan the smooth stone.

Blood on his fingertips made the HoloPhone slip loose and drop to the floor. The light went out and Trapp was immersed in darkness. Even as he felt around on his hands and knees for his phone in the last place he thought he'd heard it clatter, light appeared behind him. He looked back up the tunnel.

Double headlights split the darkness a few hundred meters back in the direction of the village. He immediately recognized them as belonging to Bril's LIMO. Someone was coming. It had to be Case, who must've gotten help from Rogers. Or perhaps Hughes had gone to check on her and found out about Trapp's escape.

Shit, shit, shit!

Trapp glanced around frantically for the door he knew must be there. There was no latch or handle.

Still, this had to be the place. And a strange juxtaposition came to him. It was when he was in Pop's attic and Demon Roth was coming up the stairs. It gave him an idea.

He leaned against the wall at the end of the tunnel. It didn't move like the hidden door in the attic.

He glanced back at the fast-approaching car. Soon, its headlight beams would be close enough for Case—or Hughes, or both—to see Trapp.

It was just a few dozen meters away.

Trapp had been caught.

STEPPING BACK A few strides, Trapp accidentally kicked his HoloPhone. He scrambled for it in the dark as the lights from the LIMO neared his position. Finally, he got it and put it in his pocket. Then he ran at the end of the tunnel again.

The wall budged a few centimeters. Either he was the Incredible Hulk, or this was a doorway. He decided to believe the second hypothesis. He ran back toward the approaching LIMO lights yet again—they were just 10 meters from shining on his sorry ass—and threw himself at the door again. This time, it angled back enough for him to squeeze through. Reversing his opening procedure, he ran at the door from inside and moved it back into place.

He stood there panting in the dark. Estimating that the LIMO would just now be pulling up to the doorway, he decided to get the fuck out of there. He turned on his torch and shone it on the walls. This new tunnel shot directly into the earth from the doorway. It also gave off a musty smell with a hint of rust. He panned the light up. Oh yeah! That's where the rust aroma came from. The duct continued overhead deeper into the tunnel.

Trapp took off in that direction. Splashing through puddles and slipping on the mud once, he made quick time down the smooth tunnel. A sound came from behind, forcing him to stop and douse his light. Something was pushing against the door. After a few seconds, it opened a crack. The light from the LIMO shone through the opening. It seems whoever was piloting Bril's weird black box thing had used it to push against the door, forcing it open. Trapp could see, though, that the door wasn't wide enough to accept the width of the LIMO. His pursuers would be forced to hoof it.

Trapp continued deeper into the tunnel, glancing nervously over his shoulder and trying not to crash into the wall, which he could barely see in the dim LIMO light, or to trip on a snag and go sprawling.

Someone passed in front of the LIMO's light and entered the tunnel. It might've been two someones; Trapp couldn't be sure as he sped up to put more distance between him and Case with her sidekick Hughes. The way they ran, it seemed they were pissed. Well, technically, Case was pissed since Trapp had beat the shit out of her. He'd never met Hughes face-to-face, so his level of anger was less personal. Trapp was certain, though—if he'd ever met

Hughes, the man would develop a fine level of angst toward the Indent, who didn't know when to quit.

Footfalls splashed in the water at his rear as Trapp began to sprint. They sounded like they were catching up to him. And, although Trapp had to hide his light, his pursuers were more brazen, using their tiny HoloPhone torch as a continuous firefly light behind Trapp, reminding him that it was much easier being the chaser than the chasee. Especially when the chasee was making a mad dash in the dark to parts unknown.

Suddenly, Trapp felt something on his right. He came to a stop and tried not to pant too loudly.

It was air movement. He sidled over toward it and found yet another tunnel opening that led off at an angle.

"The fuck am I supposed to do now?" he whispered to himself.

He couldn't risk using his torch to see where the hell this tunnel led. The logical thing to do would be to continue in the main tunnel. He looked up. The ductwork was just beyond the minuscule light of his approaching enemies. Did the duct angle up this new tunnel? Trapp stared at it way too long, hoping his eyes would adjust enough to see it. One second, he was certain it continued on up the main tunnel. The next, he was sure it turned.

Damn! Flip a coin? He didn't have one. No one carried those things around anymore. Would've been helpful right now, though.

Trapp looked into the darkness on his right. He heard dripping. Maybe Case and Hughes would assume he'd keep on the straight and narrow. Going in here would be the unexpected choice.

He nodded.

Keeping his steps as silent as possible, he headed toward the dripping sounds.

20

Tossed

THE WALL VANISHED from Trapp's touch as the narrow tunnel gave way to vastness. From the echoing drips and the fresh smell of decay, he knew he'd entered a large room. He held his breath as he stopped to listen for his pursuers. If the two pursuers went the other way, it would prove that his choice of direction had been flawed. If they were coming… He heard footsteps. They were getting louder.

Trapp had chosen wisely.

He turned back toward the open space. Meandering helplessly, he moved forward into it. Almost immediately, he plowed into a person. Gasping, he stepped back into a defensive stance. The person remained as still as stone. And maybe that's what they were. Tentatively, he reached out. He touched something cold, hard, and slightly wet. A drop of water fell on the back of his hand.

A stalagmite. Or was it a stalactite? He could never remember which was which. This one was a meter tall and jutted from the floor. He was in an actual, natural cave, not one carved out as part of the SUD. Did Montana even have caves?

Far-off footfalls reminded him he needed to hurry.

Trapp lunged forward, holding his hands out to keep from careening into another stalagmite. He was confident that was the correct term. "Might, for holding firm to the ground," he thought he remembered Pop saying. He hoped Case would run smack into one of these at full speed and give herself a concussion. He came to another, then another. He stepped around each of these.

He listened. The footsteps' tone dropped several octaves and their echoing ceased. Case and her companion were in the cave now. And they seemed to be moving faster, like they knew their way around the stalagmites.

Trapp increased his speed. Several times, he almost crashed into stalagmites.

A small whomp came from behind, followed by an expulsion of breath.

"Damn!" someone whispered.

Trapp smiled at Case's misfortune for running into one of the stalagmites. Why hadn't she pulled out her torch to light the way? Trapp shook his head as he continued forward, unsure if he was going in the right direction.

His outstretched fingers touched metal. He probed the object. It was a handrail to a staircase. Against all odds, he'd found a man-made thing. Perhaps it was the way to the ventilation shaft, which he imagined to be a vertical steel tube penetrating the cave's ceiling.

Careful to keep his boots from reverberating on the steel steps, he began his ascent. The people hunting him were less than a minute behind. If he was wrong about these stairs, they'd have him trapped. Climbing up the shaft would also make him a sitting duck. Case would simply point her weapon into the opening and fire.

He reached a landing and breathed slowly as that realization sunk in. He couldn't just keep running. He had to confront the two guards. It was his only option for escape.

Trapp continued up the stairway. He came to a second landing at least 10 meters above the cave floor. It was high enough, he estimated, as he quietly scaled the rail. Climbing over onto the other side, he turned and faced the landing, holding the rail with one hand, poising the other for what was coming.

The pursuers found the stairs.

They climbed at a run, not even trying to be quiet. It sounded like a whole squad. Trapp began to believe they might run right by him. But, half a dozen steps below him, they stopped. Trapp held his breath. His pursuers were breathing heavily. And that was when he realized it was only one breath. Case had come alone.

She resumed her climb. She took each step slowly now. She rounded the landing and came to a stop. She was right in front of Trapp. He was still holding his breath, and his body was dead still.

Now!

He stood and lunged for her. He grabbed Case and heaved her up and over the rail. She let out a high-pitched wail as she went over his head.

"Trapp!" the small voice screamed.

And, even as he let go of her, he knew.

He'd just tossed Bretta to her death.

TRAPP'S FREE HAND grabbed blindly out into the emptiness.

By some miracle, his fingertips snagged a meager swatch of cloth and held it in a death grip. Bretta's small body swung in a pendulum toward him, sliding down a centimeter in his hold. Grunting with strain, Trapp curled her up and she grabbed desperately at his waist.

"Hang on," he grunted. "I need to adjust my grip."

Still holding the rail with one hand, he let go of her with the other. He reached down and found more loose fabric and hoisted her even with his chest. She wrapped her hands around his neck while he cradled her under her butt with his free arm. Their faces were so close he could taste the sweetness on her breath, could smell her soap-tinged perspiration. It brought tears of relief to his eyes.

"You're not dead," he said, swallowing hard and thinking about how he'd caught her that other time on the cliff. All he could do was stare at her face and realize that he never wanted to let her out of his sight again.

He lifted her between his body and the rail and hugged her against its rusty metal. The rail popped, pulling against a loose bolt. Trapp's foot slipped, and one boot came loose from the floor.

The rail rattled as she shimmied around and threw a leg over it, scooting forward until she was able to hop down on to the landing. The shift caused the two bolts to shear off with a 'pop-pop' sound, pulling Trapp away from the landing.

Bretta grabbed his hand and pulled him back. As he climbed over, bolts continued to separate from the metal. Trapp jumped just as a section of the rail broke off completely. He landed with his heels over the edge and Bretta throwing her weight backward to counterbalance. He leaned forward as the rail fell behind him.

It crashed and clattered below, setting off a series of reverberations inside the cave.

"We've gotta stop cutting it that close," he said.

But she'd already thrown herself at him, hugging him tightly.

"I can't believe I found you in all of this," she said, her voice muffled by the fact that her face was planted in his chest.

"I thought you were going back east," he panted.

She looked up. He caught a glint of light in her eyes. "I changed my mind."

"I'm sorry I tossed you," Trapp said, barely able to get the words out without breaking down.

"I forgive you."

"Will they abort the test when they realize you left?"

"They think I'm on my way to MAU."

"How the hell did you get here, then?"

She pulled something out of her mouth and held it up. In the dim cave light, Trapp barely made out a little blue capsule. "Hughes made me take this at gunpoint. He even checked to see that I'd swallowed it. But I hid it in my gums. *Idiot.*" She began to climb the stairs and Trapp followed. "I started to guess Bril's plan. I think he was going to have me killed at MAU."

"He was going to do it himself. I heard him talking to Hughes."

"How?"

"I learned of Bril's plan from Case. So I came to rescue you from that building."

She stopped and Trapp almost crashed into her in the dark. "You were willing to risk your freedom for me?"

"Of course."

"I don't know what to say."

They stood there in awkward silence for a moment. She was standing above him on the next stair and they were eye to eye, just five centimeters apart. Her breathing was elevated and she placed a hand on his shoulder, caressing it through the thin InmateSkins.

"You would've done it for me," he said in a low, breathless voice.

She nodded and kissed him on the cheek. Then she turned and continued the climb.

Trapp took several calming breaths before following "Did you know it was Case and Hughes that stalked us at the cabin?" he asked to change the subject.

"When I saw them together, I guessed as much. That was what made me suspect Bril." They reached the next landing and climbed on in the dark. "Were you really planning to come save me?"

"Well…I mean, we're partners in this quest, aren't we?"

"Quest?" She touched his arm, evoking another biochemical spark. "Anyway, I hacked the LIMO to drive me here. And viola."

He cleared his throat. "I'm glad."

"I'm glad you're glad. Now let's get the hell out of here. Before we run out of time."

Then she began to jog up the stairs with Trapp right behind her.

"I'LL NEVER FIT in that thing."

Trapp's voice echoed as he stuck his head into the narrow opening.

He and Bretta had climbed to a space lit by LEDs and dominated by a machine the size of a Helena harvester, which reminded Trapp of *Eos'* big and imposing air handler. A duct came out of the top of the large machine and headed toward the ceiling. Stabilized by a framework of metal trusses, it penetrated straight into the ceiling. Unlike the big duct that fed air to Helena, this intake was no wider than Trapp's shoulders.

He pulled his head back out of its entry hatch. The sign above said: "Extreme Danger! Shaft guarded by lasers! Disconnect power before entering!"

This warning didn't scare Trapp as much as the lack of space. "I should've skipped lunch."

"You'll fit," Bretta said, poking his side. Her voice echoed as she stuck her head inside. "Besides, we have no choice." She came out.

"You go first," Trapp said.

"So I can clear the shaft of dangerous arachnids?"

"The lasers would've done that for us. I don't want to block your escape if I get stuck."

"I won't leave you." Bretta climbed into the hatch. She poked her head out. "So don't get stuck."

Trapp shrugged. He glanced at the air handler and tried to ignore its turned-off electricity. He willed Bril to go slow on restoring the power. Putting aside his earlier thought—that Bril had contacted the Pols and they'd be waiting topside—he contorted his shoulders and squeezed inside the tube.

"Use your legs," Bretta said, her body making a darker blob in the blackness. "Push against the sides."

He did as suggested and thrust his feet against the aluminum. The whole shaft warbled and rumbled.

Focusing on Bretta's feet, he reached for the next tubing segment.

"Less than 40 minutes before the power comes on," he muttered.

"We better hustle, then." Her fast ascent made the whole structure sway, and her voice was already far above.

"Hanging with you is no walk in the park," he said.

Then he breathed in hard and began his ascent.

21

Shaft

EVERY FEW MINUTES, Bretta stopped to check on Trapp.

The shaft was stuffy and close. Each breath did little to slake his feeling of imminent suffocation. Trapp had left the hatch at the bottom open to facilitate airflow, but his body seemed to be blocking the oxygen he so desperately needed. He glanced between his feet. The light from the air handling room traced out a blue oblique parallelogram on the steel wall farther below than he'd have guessed. It spiraled upward toward him from vertigo. He closed his eyes and gripped the sides. Sweat ran down his forehead.

"Did you look down?" Bretta shouted.

"I guess I didn't learn my lesson from before," he admitted.

"Just keep looking up."

"That's the same advice you gave me on that cliff."

"I guess I'm as smart as I was then, huh?" She let out a slight giggle.

Trapp opened his eyes. Her buoyancy gave him confidence. He smiled and climbed up to the next section.

"The shaft seems more stable up here," he shouted.

"We're above the cave ceiling, inside solid rock."

"Why does that make me more nervous?"

"Because you're thinking about all those tons of rock closing in around us. Instead, dream of the night air we're about to breathe—fresh air that hasn't been pumped in. I've been a prisoner in my own life for too long."

"Because of Bril and his affair?" He came up another section.

"How do you know about that?" She stopped climbing and stared down at him.

"You told me about it in the cell."

"Oh…right. I forgot. I guess so, maybe. I mean, I haven't exactly been the best wife. Who am I to judge him?"

Trapp guffawed. "Uh, you're his wife, of course! Or does that not mean anything? And why have you changed your attitude about it? Before, you acted as if you didn't care one way or the other."

"Sure." She recommenced her ascent. "I guess I don't care. I'm just glad I'm not alone."

Trapp became silent as he climbed. What did she mean by that? She'd implied emotions toward him during their last signing session. Was she talking about a relationship now?

Moving up a section, then another, he focused on his breathing and tried to push false hope from his mind. He fell into a rhythm. This wasn't going to be so bad. Just as long as he didn't tax his breathing too much. And, of course, he needed not to look down.

"I was surprised you decided to come with me," he said.

"You don't want my company?" she asked. "I can go back if you—"

"No!" he said too forcefully. "It's just...you seemed so certain you'd find answers at MAU."

She became quiet. "I've become less certain," she said after a minute.

"What changed?"

"You."

"Why me?" Trapp asked, almost afraid of the answer.

"Don't you know?" she asked, stopping to glance down at him again. He couldn't see her face. But the casualness of her silhouette spoke volumes. Laughing, she turned and climbed some more.

"What about Bril's need to satisfy our elusive President's search for the Mini-Manifold?" he asked, his voice thick with the emotion of what she meant. "Hancock doesn't want to destroy it either. I'll never believe that. Our brain-dead commander-in-chief wants to acquire it for his own uses."

"Brain-dead?! He's a genius. He invented Fabs."

"Their bodies. My mother invented their minds. Which was the real feat."

She became quiet again; her climbing gait slowed. Had he said something to offend her? "I won't believe the President is being duplicitous," she muttered. "And if the Mini-Manifold exists, it is very dangerous."

"What about your secret project?"

"What secret project?" She stopped climbing again and glanced down.

"The one you mentioned in the cell block."

"All I care about now is clearing my name. And yours, of course. After that, we should go somewhere off-grid and rest. Perhaps a beach somewhere..."

"I suppose." Her words filled him with equal parts of elation and angst. Still, a rest did sound good. They'd been through a lot.

For a long time, they climbed in silence. As he watched the dark form of her body virtually fly upwards in the shaft, his trepidation slipped away. They were on a new and exotic adventure to who knows where. *Together*.

"I'm glad you decided to escape with me," he said.

"Me too." She sounded happy. And that made *him* happy. Who cared about all this stuff anyway? And who were they to solve these complex mysteries? He quickened his pace to match hers.

She seemed to have gotten her second wind.

A GRATE BLOCKED their exit.

Trapp estimated they had only minutes to get out of the shaft before the power—and the lasers—came back on. And they were stuck. A prairie breeze blew down the shaft, bathing Trapp in an aroma of ripe wheat, recent rains, and Bretta's smell of sweat and soap. Above her petite body, a moonless sky with bright star fields traced a checkered pattern behind the grate's grid.

"What kind of lock is it?" he asked Bretta. She'd already tried to push the grate open, only to be foiled by a lock.

"Like any other lock, I guess. Unbreakable."

"Is it electronic?"

"I can't tell."

Trapp looked down. Far off, a point of blue light flickered. It was the hatchway to the air handler. There was no way they could get back down in time. He looked back up.

"Let me see if I can yank it."

"It's too tight up here for you to get past me. The shackle's too thick, anyway. We'd need a saw. You don't happen to have one of those in your pants pocket, do you?"

Her sarcasm made him laugh. But then he remembered.

"You mean like this?" he asked, reaching into his jumpsuit and pulling out Sergeant Riggs's stub.

She took the stub and studied it.

"Never in a million years would I have guessed you'd say 'yes' to that question." She stared at him with wide, shocked eyes.

"Whatever you do, don't drop it," he said with a grin.

"I won't." She began to cut. The back-and-forth sawing echoed in the tight shaft. "I think…Yeah. This is doing the job. How much time do we have?"

An enormous 'clack' filled the air. They froze.

"Is that—?" she asked.

"Keep sawing," Trapp said, frantically glancing down. The distant air handling room hatchway was blazing white now. The power was back on.

"Roger," she said. She sawed faster. Trapp watched the shaft for the lasers. He just hoped they'd kill them quickly and painlessly.

"If we don't make it," he said. "I just want you to know that—"

"You've got feelings for me? I'm pretty sure I have them for you, too," she said.

"How did you know I was going to say that?"

"A girl knows." The smooth grinding of the saw suddenly chattered. "Oh, fuck!" she yelped.

A metal object zipped past Trapp's head. Too late, he grabbed for it. The stub dropped out of reach, clattering against the wall on its way down.

"I'm so sorry," Bretta cried. "I'm sorry. It slipped out of my hand. I couldn't help it."

"Maybe you cut enough," he said, reaching up.

Bretta squished her body against the shaft and pulled on his collar. Trapp clambered to fill the meager void. She was small. But not small enough. He let out his breath and forced himself upward. They were packed like sardines in the space.

She'd cut the shackle almost all the way through. Only two millimeters of tempered steel blocked their exit. Craving oxygen, Trapp pushed his feet against the sides of the shaft and pulled on the lock. His efforts seemed to be in vain. The lock wouldn't budge.

Bretta shook her head and pointed at her mouth. She needed to breathe. His lungs screamed too. But the space was too tight. Deep below, the air handler kicked on and instantly sucked on their bodies. The pressure threatened to yank them back down the shaft. Bretta strained to keep them in place while Trapp tried the lock again.

Orange beams crisscrossed below them and were quickly moving up the shaft. *The lasers!*

Trapp put everything into one last yank. His shoulder popped, and his arm went numb. But the lock snapped open. Pulling it out of the grate's latch, he scrambled backward and put his shoulder under Bretta's butt.

"Out you go," he said, shoving her up.

She flew out into open space and was gone.

He hoped he hadn't hurt her as the grate slammed shut again.

He stole a glance downward. The lasers were filling the space quickly. Even as Trapp climbed up and head-butted the grate to move his bulk into the night, he knew. The smell of burning flesh confirmed it.

He was too late.

TRAPP'S NOSTRILS WERE assaulted with the pungent order of skin, muscles, and organs being burned alive. But the pain hadn't hit yet as he came to the lip of the shaft. Bretta helped by grabbing his wrist with her tiny hands. She yanked at him with more strength than he would've guessed possible. And, with his own power added to hers, he came flying out. He fell on top of her, forcing the air out of her lungs in a gasp. Thinking that his burning body would ignite hers, he rolled off while patting his skin to extinguish the fire.

She sat up, coughing while she inspected him in the darkness. She ran her fingers over his body, top to bottom.

"You're okay," she said after a while. "The lasers only singed a few holes in your InmateSkins. I think there are a few superficial flesh wounds. That's all."

"That was a close one," he said, panting.

She lay beside him and they stared at the stars. Then, without warning, Bretta rolled on top of him and buried her face in his chest. Her body was racked with convulsions from sobbing.

"I almost lost you," she said, raising her head. "I don't know what I'd do without you."

Their eyes locked. He could just make out her whites in the unlit world above Helena. They stared at each other that way for several seconds. Who kissed whom first was a mystery. All Trapp knew was that it was unexpected, perfectly timed, and passionate. It went on for several seconds that could've been hours. She leaned back, panting even more than before.

"I almost lost you, too," Trapp said, feeling dizzy and feverish.

They kissed again. This time, it was slower and more purposeful but no less passionate. When she lay her head back down, Trapp breathed in. He could hardly believe what he'd experienced. Perhaps this was a fantasy brought on by the last firings of his synapses as the lasers carved his body into a million pieces. Maybe he hadn't made it out.

He held her, staring at the night sky, willing the moment to never end. The stars were real. The white puffs of clouds weren't Synths. How genuine was the kiss? Was it brought on by the intensity of the moment? They'd almost died before. Still, their forced isolation, each one seeing the other from across a hallway without the ability to speak, had created an artificial need.

There was just no way Bretta was falling for him.

A torch flashed on, accompanied by a voice. "Sorry to interrupt."

Bretta fell off Trapp as he sat up. He'd forgotten that Bril had likely sent him to be arrested by the Pols. Now Bretta, with her own fugitive status, was facing a similar fate.

He rose to his feet and pushed Bretta behind him. A human form stood ten meters away, hidden by the cone of light from a torch pointed at Trapp and Bretta.

"Who is it?" Trapp asked, holding his hands out in a defensive posture.

"Just an old friend. Or I hope you might think of me that way. I *did* help you escape."

"Malph?" Trapp asked, finally seeing the Fab's form behind the light.

"Yes."

"How the hell are you here?"

"I was ordered *the hell* here."

"By whom? The admiral's dead." Trapp looked from Malph to Bretta. "And Bretta didn't kill her, if that's what you came for."

"I'm not here to arrest anyone," Malph said, looking back at Trapp. "I have been waiting for twelve hours, forty-three minutes and sixteen—"

"That's a long time," Trapp interrupted. "Why?"

"I'm here to rescue you."

"Who sent you?"

"My programming."

"And who programmed you to rescue us?"

"I can't say. Now, if you'll follow me."

"I won't go with you," Bretta said. "You're going to arrest me for killing your owner."

Malph turned to Trapp. "Do you recall," he asked, "in our first meeting, what I told you about my programming concerning innocence?"

"You follow the U.S. standard of innocent until proven guilty," Trapp said.

"Correct." Malph turned to Bretta. "As your alleged crime was committed within the national boundaries, I must view you as innocent until you are found guilty under due process. I assure you that you will be quite safe under my protection."

Bretta looked at Trapp.

"He's telling the truth," Trapp said. "And he's our best way out of this mess."

"I'm accused of killing his owner."

"He has no capability to be vengeful." Trapp glanced toward Malph. He stared at the two humans with no emotion on his face. Trapp spoke to Bretta. "If we choose to go with him, you'll be fine. But, if you want to find another way out of here, I'll go with you."

"I don't know." She glanced worriedly toward Malph.

Trapp held her shoulders.

"I've never felt for anyone like I feel toward you, including myself. I won't let anything happen to you. I promise. Besides, I trust Malph."

She stared for a while. Finally, she smiled and nodded. "I trust you," she said.

He kissed her once again, finding it surreal that he could now do that anytime he wished. She smiled and leaned into him, allowing him to enfold her in his arms.

Then they turned, and Malph led them away from the shaft.

Part Three

Annihilation

"Only the dead have seen the end of war."

George Santayana

"Can we really believe that humans have the capacity to end wars? Many can't decide what they want to eat for dinner tonight."

***Professor Phileas Gray's Letter to Ambrose Hancock, dated 15 March 2114** (used by permission*
from the US National Archives)

22
Experimental

"HOW'S YOUR SHOULDER?" Bretta asked Trapp.

They'd been riding for hours inside a FleetCar. Somehow, Admiral Stockwell's former Fab had commandeered it. After the three had climbed aboard, Malph silently entered coordinates to put the vehicle in motion before using his strength to reset Trapp's shoulder. It was a decidedly unpleasant experience, even though Malph made quick work of it.

"Fine," Trapp said, moving his arm around, reveling in its lack of soreness.

He and Bretta had spoken little during the ride. Mostly, they slept. She'd sat beside him, a small, warm weight snuggled under his armpit, making him feel more alive than ever despite racking up a long list of near-death experiences.

"Where are we?" Bretta asked with a yawn.

Trapp pointed. Distant snow-capped mountains, peach-colored from Sol's rising, flanked glimmering towers, including a giant spike topped with a saucer.

"The Space Needle?" she asked. "We're in Seattle? A million EYE cameras must have already picked us up by now."

The Fab looked over his shoulder. "Three million, four hundred and sixty-two thousand, to be exact," he said. "But this vehicle's smart glass is equipped with filters. The EYE will only record a random family riding to a picnic or a carpool of business people."

"That's a neat trick. But why Seattle?"

"I don't know."

"Did the admiral program this trip before she died?" Trapp asked.

"Uncertain."

Malph turned back to face the windshield as the FleetCar wound its way under the shadows of tall buildings. One of them, the tallest, was a spire almost as thin as the space needle that shot up nearly a thousand meters into the air. It was festooned with a stylized logo of overlapping letters twisted into a Picasso of a human form, and it appeared to be their destination.

"FabCorps?" Trapp asked.

"No." Malph swiped the screen of the ScribePad. The car turned left toward the water.

Soon, they came to crumbling buildings speckled with glints of sunlight bouncing off the waves of the adjacent Puget Sound. They headed for a group of warehouses next to a concrete wharf. One was fitted with two-story doors that opened to expose a cavernous space. The FleetCar drove through them and headed in.

"What *is* that?" Trapp asked, pointing to a strange machine at the back of the expanse. "Looks like some sort of aircraft."

"It would appear so," Malph said, as the FleetCar stopped beside it. They stepped out into the dank air, made humid and salty from the nearby brackish water. They walked toward the aircraft. "From a quick search of my databases, it appears to be a modified Osprey, an ancient type of military transport."

"Military?" Trapp gasped. "Did you bring us right back to Bril? Is this just another trap?"

"Not a trap," a voice said, coming from behind the Osprey. "But a rescue."

The three turned. Trapp was thrown into a sudden convulsion of coughs at the sight of her. Having dyed her dirty blonde hair a bright red, she'd replaced her orange Indent jumpsuit with a navy-colored one that sported a golden eagle pin over its breast pocket.

"*Erika?*" Trapp croaked at his one-time crush.

"Erika Zelenskyy," she said, ignoring Trapp and offering her hand to Bretta. "Wait! Aren't you…? Albretta Gray?"

"Let's not make a big deal out of it," Bretta said, staring at Erika. "Call me Bretta. And I go by Sykes now."

"Sorry. I just…No one told me I'd be transporting a celebrity today."

"No one told us *we* were being transported today," Trapp said.

Erika grinned at him, teeth blazing. "I know, right? Freaky."

"I…uh." Trapp trailed off. Then Trapp spoke to Bretta. "This is *the* Erika who saved my ass on the *Eos*."

"Oh," Bretta said. "That's…uh…great. Thank you." Her odd response baffled Trapp. She was acting like she'd never heard of Erika, even though he'd told her about his former fling—leaving out their later sexual encounter, of course. Did Bretta now sense their former relationship somehow? Was this jealousy?

"How are you here?" he asked Erika.

"Before she vanished, Admiral Stockwell reassigned me Terra-side to the VOLT program."

"VOLT?"

She slapped the fuselage of the Osprey. "It's one of a few prototypes. And it's undergone a radical conversion. It started life as an Osprey, which could take off on short runways. But our modifications allow it to take off almost vertically after replacing its heavy gas-powered engines with electric turbines running on Manifold-mined power."

"And where is this bucket of bolts taking us?" Bretta asked.

Erika turned to look at Malph. "Ask him. I just work here."

All eyes turned to the Fab.

"I'm now authorized to give you the coordinates of our next destination," Malph said. "45.9646 degrees North by 63.3052 degrees East."

Erika squinted her eyes. "That can't be right. That takes us into—"

"I know where those coordinates take us. I assure you, my programming is accurate."

"Where *does* it take us?" Trapp asked.

Erika waved her hand dismissively. "Just the most dangerous place on Terra. I've gotta prep for flight."

She turned and huffed away, leaving Malph, Trapp, and Bretta to stare.

❖ ❖ ❖

THE VOLT SLAMMED into the ground, waking Trapp as he jostled in his seat.

"Sorry for the less-than-smooth landing," Erika sputtered through the comms while the VOLT bounced a few more times before settling into a roll. "Still getting a hang of the controls."

"Less than smooth," Bretta grunted in disgust. "I'm surprised we still have landing gear."

Trapp stretched and yawned as the VOLT slowed to a crawl and taxied up to an ancient cinder block building in the middle of a treeless plain.

Erika came from the cockpit.

"Where are we?" Trapp asked.

"Kim Jun Ae City."

"Korea?"

"The Korean Republic, yes. We need to recharge the VOLT's batteries."

"How long will that take?"

"An hour and a half. Two at the most. There are restrooms inside where you can freshen up. And there's some food in the lobby if you're hungry. Don't leave the base, though."

She opened the doorway, which lowered to become steps, and began barking orders at a ground crew wearing jumpsuits like hers. From what Trapp could tell, Erika was speaking fluent Korean. The crew bowed incessantly while running cables over and connecting them to the VOLT.

Trapp and Bretta went inside the hangar.

The bathroom had several shower stalls and clean, white coveralls in all sizes. They were stenciled with a blue lightning bolt. After cleaning himself, Trapp discarded the Helena coveralls in favor of the new ones.

"Oh!" Bretta exclaimed as Trapp startled her by coming out of his stall and bumping into her. He knocked something out of her hand that hit the floor and rolled away.

"Let me get that," Trapp said, leaning down to pick it up.

"That's okay," Bretta said, practically diving in front of him. She grabbed the thing and stuffed it into her pocket.

"What was that?" Trapp asked, thinking he'd glimpsed an orange pill box with blue capsules inside.

"Nothing. Let's grab something to eat. It feels like I haven't had anything in days." She grabbed his hand and led him out of the bathroom.

"We're set to go," Erika said, entering the lobby an hour later.

Trapp and Bretta followed her as she left the hangar and climbed aboard the VOLT.

"I'm unable to get clearance for the Cosmodrome," she said, speaking to Malph, who'd stayed on the aircraft during the layover. "I hope you can pull some Fab magic out of your fake butt to get us inside."

"Cosmodrome?" Trapp asked, his eyes narrowing.

"Yes. It's where your Fab friend's coordinates are taking us."

"What's a Cosmodrome?" Bretta asked, apparently sensing Trapp's trepidation.

"The Russian Space Corps launch facility," Trapp said. "Mostly space cargo. But Erika was right when she said the place was dangerous."

"Why?"

"The Russian Mafia runs it. Even in my criminal days, I'd never have been caught dead there. Because I would've been."

"Would've been what?"

"Found dead."

"We're not going there, anyway," Erika said. "Not if I can't get clearance."

"You must," Malph said.

"Why?"

"Because of programming."

"You've gotta give me more than that. We're not robots." Trapp cringed at the pro-humanist slur. "I refuse to put the humans I'm transporting in danger."

"Maybe the coordinates are wrong," Bretta offered.

"The coordinates are accurate," Malph said.

The radio in the cockpit hissed, interrupting the debate. Erika moved forward and spoke into her headset. There was an exchange. Then she returned.

"We've gotten tentative clearance," she said. "Some higher-up convinced the Kazakhs to let us fly over their space."

She turned to move forward again, not before stopping to glare at Malph. She shook her head slowly before going back into the cockpit.

"Fly over?" Trapp shouted at her back. "What about landing?"

Erika muttered something indecipherable. Then she shut the door.

23

Clearance

THE VOLT BANKED hard right, throwing Bretta into Trapp's side. A contrail zipped by the window at only a few meters, followed by a loud 'whoosh.' Something exploded from behind, causing the VOLT to fishtail.

"Welcome to Kazakhstan!" Erika shouted into the comms. "They rolled out a welcome mat of SAMs! Launching countermeasures."

She banked left this time while another missile trail flew by the window. Bretta dug her fingernails into Trapp's arm. Another boom. The VOLT lurched forward and down.

"That one was close," Erika said, alarms beeping in the background.

The comms went dead.

Trapp unstrapped himself.

"Where the hell are you going?" Bretta asked, her eyes getting big.

"Erika needs help."

Grabbing the bulkhead, Trapp thrust himself through to the tilting cockpit and into a confusion of clanks, alarms, and robotic voices. Erika glanced up in surprise as Trapp climbed into the co-pilot's seat and strapped in.

"Shut off those fucking alarms!" she barked.

"How?"

"Pull on that. And that." She pointed at breaker plugs. Trapp yanked them out, and the alarms shut off. "Now push down on that lever." Trapp did as commanded. The clanking noise disappeared as the VOLT jolted to the right. Erika moved the joystick in response, and the aircraft straightened out. "Had to shut down the starboard turbine array," she said. "It took some shrapnel. Not sure about the port turbine array. Here." She held out a headset. "Call those bastards. They're not responding. Probably because I'm a fucking woman or some shit."

"Roger that." Trapp placed the headset over his ears. "Cosmodrome tower. Cosmodrome tower. This is…this is the VOLT. We are unarmed. Cease fire. Five souls on board." The radio returned static.

"Five souls?" Erika asked. "Fabs don't have a—never mind."

"Cosmodrome tower. Respond. We come in peace."

"Peace?" she asked, smirking. Trapp shrugged. "We should abort. High tail it back to Korea and regroup."

"Can we even make it all the way back to Korea with a blown turbine array?"

"Uncertain. And by the way, who programmed that Fab in the first place? Were they intentionally leading us into an ambush?"

"I don't know," Trapp said as he shook his head. He was wondering the same thing. He spoke back into the radio. "Cosmodrome tower, this is—"

"We know who you are," a gravelly voice with a thick *AmerRoos* accent said, breaking through the static.

"Cease fire. We're unarmed."

"You are in unauthorized airspace. If you approach, we will shoot you out of the sky."

Erika chopped at the air. Trapp covered the headset mic with his hand. "Tell him we've taken damage," she said. "We're unable to fly to another airfield."

"Cosmodrome tower," Trapp said. "We're a damaged Space Corps transport declaring an emerg—"

"Stand by," the voice said, cutting Trapp off.

Trapp covered the mic again. "That ploy might just work." Another alarm went off.

"It's not a ploy," she said. "The port array is failing. We're losing thrust."

"Mayday, mayday, mayday," he said into the mic, trying not to sound frantic.

"Clearance to land," the voice on the radio said.

"Thank you."

"You might want to hold your thanks," Erika said, pointing at the hangar off to the right. Several jeeps careened out of it, many with mounted AKs manned by soldiers. "I hope you're okay with being arrested."

"Just another Tuesday for me," Trapp said.

Erika grimaced as she aimed for the runway.

TRAPP'S HEAD WAS covered with a burlap hood that reeked of ancient sweat and bad breath. His wrists were bound tightly behind his back, and he sat on a hard stool in the center of a chilly room. Water dripped somewhere in the distance.

A lock clinked. Hinges whined, and a door opened.

His hood was ripped off and he squinted against the blaze of light. A man walked into view. Stocky and dark-skinned, he wore red coveralls stenciled with Russian Space Corps regalia. Emitting an odor that indicated soap was scarce, the man sported a tattoo of an inverted red five-pointed star on his cheek—Russian Mob. No surprise there.

"I'm Major Antonov," the man said in a thick accent. It was the same voice from the radio.

"Where are my friends?" Trapp asked.

"What is your mission in Kazakhstan?" Antonov asked, ignoring the question.

"We were flying over the steppe and somehow went off course."

"And your intended destination?"

"Moscow."

The man shook his head with a sad, sarcastic half-grin. He nodded to someone beyond the cone of light. A big man dressed in similar reds and stinking of cigarette smoke to cover his body odor stepped up. He punched Trapp in the stomach. Violent pain shook Trapp's insides as he doubled over, fighting for air. Antonov and his goon stood by and watched patiently.

Trapp gasped as he finally got a lung full. "Could you guys be more cliché? I mean, really. A dark room? A hood? A punch in the gut? Where do you guys come up with this stuff?"

"Russian manual for handling foreign assholes," Antonov said with a laugh. "Now, what was your intended destination?"

Trapp shrugged with a smirk on his face.

The big guy punched him again. Trapp bent over, choking. He was about to vomit. He just hoped it would splash Antonov's boots.

"Where are my friends?" he asked.

"Halfway to China by now. Their sex trade market pays top terro for American whores. Your women will get plenty of work. The dirty, nasty stuff, too. Chinese tastes can turn pretty violent."

Trapp shook his head at Antonov's racist remark. "We flew in here on a Space Corp aircraft. No way you're going to get away with this. We also brought a Fab."

"Which is worth more as parts than as a whole robot. If you were honest with me, I might be able to work something out. Maybe the redhead. She's the feisty one. The brunette, though." He whistled. "She can pass as a child, if you know what I mean." He winked.

"I'll kill you," Trapp hissed.

"Ha! The brunette is your favorite. Now I know how to get you to talk."

The big guy punched Trapp in the jaw, knocking him off the stool.

The two men laughed as they left him lying in a puddle with his ears ringing. They slammed the door behind them and latched it shut.

Trapp fought not to think about what they were going to do to Bretta.

24

Compound

"WE KNOW WHO you are."

The man who spoke had just entered Trapp's cell. Several hours had passed since Trapp had last seen Antonov. He'd convinced himself that the major's threats were all bluster; that he wasn't stupid enough to give up his bargaining chips by sending the women to China. And the man hadn't spoken of bounties and Selfie Murderers, indicating that these Mafia guys probably weren't big fans of the Plexus. So, when the door opened with a squeak, Trapp expected the start of another round of negotiations.

Instead, a new man came in, trailed by Antonov, who kept his head down, and his big goon. Taller, broader, and grayer than the little major, the man wore crimson Russian Space Corps coveralls with two gold stars pinned to each shoulder. His breastplate was decorated with half a dozen ribbon bars.

"Who are we?" Trapp asked as he stared ahead dumbly.

"Murderers," the man said, his accent almost perfect English. "I'm General Borodin. Major Antonov wasn't supposed to interrogate you until I arrived. An unfortunate blunder. One that I hope to remedy."

"We've been wrongly accused," Trapp said. "We haven't killed anyone."

Borodin waved it off. "What to do with you? On the one hand, we're obligated to turn you in. Considering you've broken a dozen international treaties, we can even negotiate a premium on the bounty.

Trapp kept his eyes fixed on the man. "On the other hand?" he prompted after Borodin remained silent.

"Your women are worth more on the open market." Borodin nodded, confirming Trapp's suspicion that Bretta and Erika were still there. "It's a disgusting practice, selling people. Still, the times being what they are, and the profits from space supply vehicles not what they used to be…" He shook his head slowly.

He stepped back. The big goon reached down and pulled Trapp to his feet.

"The ISC knows we're here," Trapp said.

"You weren't. All we knew was that a jet flew into our airspace without the proper codes. We radioed it. It didn't respond. Sadly, we were forced to shoot it down. An aerial search revealed wreckage, three charred bodies, and a destroyed Fab."

"They'll demand proof."

"Bodies aren't hard to reproduce. We can't bury our dead out here, considering the swampy soil. The dead are kept in cold storage until they can be cremated. Why, just last month, we tragically lost twenty people in a fuel explosion. A few of those will be loaded onto your jet after the turbines are repaired enough to get it airborne. It will be programmed to follow the flight path I described. *Voila.* Instant evidence."

"You don't have to do this," Trapp said as the goon led him to the door. "Let the others go. I'll turn myself in willingly. I'll say I brought myself here alone, that I've grown weary of running."

"I'm afraid money's been exchanged. Buyers are awaiting shipments. You understand. It's just business."

Trapp was led out of his cell. The women were also being led out of theirs, bound with tied wrists and gags. They stared at him with big, terrified eyes. Borodin's men prodded the prisoners toward a doorway and into the back of an armored FleetTruck. Malph lay on the floor like cargo, lashed from head to toe. The men backed off, leaving only half a dozen guards to ride with the prisoners. Antonov started to climb aboard, but Borodin placed a hand on the major's shoulder.

"I'll oversee this delivery, my friend," he said gently. "I need you to manage the cover-up."

Antonov stepped back, deflated, his disappointment the only bright spot in an otherwise bleak moment. Borodin climbed into the truck and closed the double doors.

The truck sputtered away from the hangar.

THE ARMORED FLEETTRUCK took too many turns for Trapp to count.

He attempted to match each turn against the model of Baikonur in his head, which he'd gotten from their brief and violent approach. Not that it mattered. They weren't going to get out of this. After half a dozen situations where they should've died, death wouldn't be their final ending. Instead, they were to become someone's slaves.

"I'm sorry," he said to his gagged friends, fighting back tears. "This was my fault."

Bretta shook her head, tears flowing. It was another sign. She didn't blame him. Erika stared to one side in a trance. She'd survived years as an Indent only to be sold into another, more brutal form of slavery.

The FleetTruck stopped abruptly, forcing the inmates to slide into each other.

The guards stood up and opened the doors. They helped the inmates onto a gravel driveway. A gigantic two-story house with a flat roof lay ahead. Beyond it were walls that, upon further inspection, surrounded sheds, garages and work buildings, lawns and gardens, and many aromatic coniferous trees. A giant metal gate swung shut behind them.

It was a compound of sorts, perhaps the General's personal residence. It was a strange place to meet traffickers. Was the Baikonur sex trade just that sophisticated? The building could sleep dozens of oligarchs in luxury. Trapp guessed there was a pool behind those walls, nice suites, and servants to cater to the whims of its inmates.

A guard approached Bretta.

"Don't touch her, you bastard," Trapp hissed as he moved between her and the man.

The man looked at Borodin in shock.

"It's necessary," the General said. "I'm sorry."

"We'd rather die than be sold into slavery," Trapp said.

Borodin moved forward and removed something from the guard's hand. It was a knife. Holding it out, he advanced toward Bretta. Trapp put himself between the weapon and his girlfriend. Two guards grabbed Trapp and swung him around, his back to the General. He struggled, but their grips were too tight. The General stepped up behind him, holding the knife up. Trapp felt little as Borodin swung the blade down in a swift motion. The sound of severing muscles split the silent air. The guards released Trapp so he could fall to the ground and bleed to death at Borodin's feet.

What a way for his struggle for the truth to end! Still, if he was going out, he was taking someone with him. He swung around, prepared to ram the big General with his head. Then he realized his hands were at his sides. The General held the severed rope up with a big grin.

"You are free, my friend," the man said, as several guards moved to the women and cut away their fetters and gags.

Wrists were rubbed; jaws were stretched. Malph was brought out of the FleetCar and stood up on his feet.

"Thank you," the Fab said to his captors as they untied him.

Borodin spoke. "I'm sorry for the theatrics. We had to give the illusion of realism."

"To us?" Trapp asked, rubbing his chafed wrists.

"To Antonov. I don't condone his side business. But he's too well-connected for me to challenge him openly."

"We're not being sold into slavery?" Bretta asked.

"On the contrary. You're to be guests in my humble home."

"What about Antonov?" Trapp asked. "Won't he figure out you didn't sell us to the Chinese?"

"As far as he knows, you're long gone. He'll testify to that under oath if required. I've sent him and those loyal to him away on the trip to fake the evidence. They'll be gone for days."

"So you're going to destroy the VOLT?" Trapp asked.

"We're going to destroy a decoy. Bodies will be found in the wreckage. The victims died, as I described—a terrible accident. We've had to work fast. We didn't expect your arrival until tomorrow."

Erika took a step toward Borodin as guards moved to block her. "Your guys shot my VOLT down. We all could've been killed."

"I'm sorry for that," Borodin said. "Subterfuge can be a deadly business. Thankfully, you survived. And now we hope you can help us."

Erika huffed. Borodin moved past his guards and stuck out his hand. "Can we start over again?" he asked. "My name is Yuri Borodin. And you are?"

"Erika Zelenskyy," she grumbled.

"Pleased to meet you, Airperson Zelenskyy. That was some incredible flying you did back there. Badass. I would put my life in your hands if it came down to it."

"It was nothing." Erika broke into a masked grin.

"It was everything. Your contact would be very disappointed if you didn't make it alive."

"Contact?" Trapp asked.

"Yes. She's inside."

Borodin nodded, then turned. He led them into the house. Quickly moving through a foyer with skylights, they entered a hallway past a living room with leather sofas and tea tables next to a fireplace large enough to roast a moose. The hallway continued to the base of a steel and marble staircase that arced gracefully upward.

A small woman was already descending it.

"Ah," Borodin said. "Here she is now."

She was clad in blue Space Corps Skins with five gold stars on each sleeve and, on her breastplate, as many colored ribbon bars as Borodin's. She wore her dark hair down to her shoulders, along with a big, homey smile.

This was probably why Trapp didn't immediately recognize her. And then he did.

"Admiral Stockwell," he said, barely able to whisper. "You're alive!"

25

Threat

FOR THE SECOND time in a week, Trapp was being confronted by a ghost. The last time, it turned out to be an AI projection of Professor Gray. This time, it was a person —a living, moving body.

"How are you alive?" he asked her.

"It's complicated. But your eyes don't deceive you. I am quite alive." Admiral Margery Stockwell now looked at Bretta, whose face had turned white. She looked like she was going to be sick. "I'm sorry you got wrapped up in all this, young lady."

"I don't understand," Bretta said. "I saw the pictures. I saw…I mean, they said you disappeared. They blamed me."

"Because of the Murder Selfie Number Two." The admiral nodded. "It provided a cover for me—a way to get away clean."

"Someone wanted you dead," Trapp said. "Malph told me that when he helped me escape Miami Base."

"And they almost succeeded. They used an operative who resembled Professor Gray's granddaughter. I can only guess it was because they had intelligence that she was helping you. Thankfully, I got word of their approach with only minutes to escape." She walked over and held Bretta's hands. "Your sacrifice saved my life."

"I…um…" Bretta stammered while the rest of the group stared in silence. This was the third time Trapp had been in the admiral's presence, and he was surprised to see that Stockwell, although larger than life, was small in stature.

"So why have you brought us here?" Trapp asked.

"All will be explained in due time," the admiral said with a clap of her hands. "For now, you all should freshen up. We'll talk at dinner." She waved at the staircase where guards had arrived. "Mr. Trapmore? May I have a word?"

Bretta glanced curiously at Trapp. He smiled and nodded that it would be alright. He followed the admiral to a vestibule off the main hallway.

"I wanted to be the first to tell you the horrible news," the admiral said in low tones. "Your grandfather passed away this morning." Trapp nodded. He'd fully expected Pop wouldn't last much longer. Nevertheless, his eyes filled with tears. A spark of unbelief left his face tingling; his eyes only able to stare. "I hope you were able to see him one last time," the admiral said.

"I did. After you helped me escape."

"I don't know what you're talking about." The admiral smiled and winked. "Did you find what you were looking for during your exile?"

"I found my mother's files."

"And they provided answers?"

"Only questions. I was able to get HoloPics of them." Trapp removed his HoloPhone from his pocket as Stockwell's face brightened. "A lot of equations and diagrams that mean nothing to me. Perhaps you know someone who can decipher them."

"I may know someone," Stockwell replied. Her excitement was palpable, but she kept her hands at her side. Trapp stared at the HoloPhone for a while. He'd gained Jessi's pictures at the expense of Pop's life. Finally, he looked up at Stockwell.

He handed the HoloPhone to her. "I hope you can make something of it."

The admiral nodded while flipping the HoloPhone around so it opened on his face print. "I'll get this back to you later."

A female guard arrived as if summoned.

He followed the woman upstairs.

THE SWEET AROMA of seared meat drew Trapp downstairs.

The massive dining room was dominated by a hand-carved table that appeared to have been hewn from a whole mahogany tree. Wearing blue skin-tight coveralls, Erika and Malph stood near the table, looking like they didn't know what to do with themselves. Bretta entered in the same form-fitting uniform.

"What's up with the outfits?" she asked, feeling the fabric of his sleeve.

"ISC uniform," he said, shrugging. "I guess they thought our VOLT coveralls were a bit gamey after a day and a half of wear. Although I don't know why they gave us just the undergarments."

"Technically, the base layer of the ISC suit can be worn as outerwear," Malph said. "The NanoSkin technology helps regulate body temperature in most climates."

"Why did the admiral want to talk to you earlier?" Bretta asked Trapp.

"Pop is dead."

"Your grandfather? I'm sorry." She hugged him. He'd been turning over the news in his head since he'd found out. He wasn't sure how he felt about it. Still, he hugged her back.

Borodin and Stockwell came in at that moment, chatting. Also dressed in the first layer of the ISC-issue space suit, they motioned for the group to follow them to the back of the dining room, where HoloWindows displayed a split-screen of the steppe and two steam-billowing rockets on pads.

"We are very fortunate," Borodin announced as he pointed at the windows. "We get to witness not one but two scheduled rocket launches today. There's even an unprecedented third one this evening."

Borodin now directed their attention to two clocks, one overlaying each rocket on display—countdowns with 10 minutes separating them. Guards dressed as servants handed around glasses of sparkling white wine. The group watched and listened as *AmerRoos*-speaking voices giving statuses crackled through wall-mounted comms. The first countdown cycled through one minute, then reached ten seconds. As steam covered the lower quarters in a white nebula, a voice barked out the time.

"Desyat', devyat', vosem'...vzlet!"

"Liftoff," Trapp translated.

The plumes grew, billowing with yellow urgency, veiling the rocket completely. A shockwave rattled the HoloWindows, glassware, and china. The nose cone broke through the steam, and the rocket crept skyward as it pulled the plumes under it.

"It's cleared the tower," Borodin said, his voice thick with emotion.

Trapp glanced at the old general in surprise. The man must've witnessed a hundred such events. Still, he was brought to tears. Trapp turned back to the display. Now spewing a tail of yellow-orange flame, the rocket blaze scorched the gantry and pad, leaving a smear of black soot. Its pointed nose cone penetrated a low cloud bank. Then it was swallowed up, its fiery tail illuminating brightly behind the grayness. The rocket reappeared far above the clouds. A sonic boom shook the house as it turned away toward the horizon, its plume having died down to a bluish hue. White mist shot from its sides. The lower stage separated and drifted away.

"*Postanovka zavershena,*" the intercom voice said.

"Staging complete," Borodin said.

Soon, the rocket was gone, lost in the gloom of the dark horizon. The room stared in awe. No one drank or spoke. Most barely breathed. Trapp had never seen or felt anything so powerful. He looked at Stockwell. Her face was sullen, expressionless. The HoloWindow now zoomed in on the remaining rocket.

Borodin pointed. "The second one's launching next."

Minutes passed as they watched the twin of the first rocket takeoff, a launch that was equally as dramatic as the first. Borodin led the group to the table.

"I understand you've been to space," he said, pointing Trapp to sit beside him.

"Nothing quite so dramatic as that," Trapp nodded. "ramjets to low orbit, shuttles up to the *Eos*. Don't know if I could stomach such a launch."

"Going to space without a megaton bomb strapped to your ass should be outlawed," Borodin chuckled. "We'll make a real cosmonaut out of you someday."

Trapp forced a smile. He was done with space. But it didn't seem the time or place to say so.

Meal courses were brought in and passed around. No discussion about why the group had been assembled was allowed. Instead, the general regaled them with the historical significance of each dish: the pea soup was his grandmother's recipe, the *Salade Niçoise* came from a beloved Kyiv restaurant destroyed during the latest Ukrainian conflict, and the eggplant had been harvested near Borodin's Black Sea dacha. A platter of sliced pink meat crusted in black came. Trapp took a bite as the general stared at him expectantly.

"Tastes like chicken," he said.

"Ostrich," the old cosmonaut said, shaking his head. "A tradition before every launch."

"The launches are over," Trapp said.

Borodin slapped his shoulder with a boisterous laugh.

A pastry covered in raspberries arrived with an urn of real coffee that wafted a heady aroma. The group—minus Malph, of course—sipped and ate until the discussion portion of the evening began.

Stockwell finally spoke in an ominous voice.

"We need your help to end a threat," she said. "We've uncovered a weapon, one that will destroy Terra. And we think it may already be too late to stop it."

"We already know about that," Trapp said, glancing at Bretta, who stared at the table silently. "Bril arrested us because he believed Bretta could help him find it."

"We're not talking about the Mini Manifold. That has been on the ISC's radar for years. And even if it represents a localized danger, it's not of concern to us at this time."

"What if the Russians find it? Or even the U.S. military? Can we trust they won't try to turn it against the enemy?"

"A problem, for sure. But there are other more pressing issues."

"Like what?"

Stockwell took a deep breath. She glanced at Borodin. He nodded. Then she spoke directly to Trapp.

"We think your Selfie plans to launch enough nuclear weapons to destroy Terra."

26

Mission

"NUCLEAR WEAPONS," TRAPP guffawed. "The whole world disarmed decades ago, when I was still a boy."

"A true statement," Stockwell said. "But disarmament isn't what you think it is."

"Please tell me it *does* mean that we've eliminated all the nukes."

"I wish I could. But when the eight nuclear nations agreed to disarm, all they really did was retarget the missiles. The nukes themselves still exist. They just don't point at any cities. The only way to eliminate them is to detonate."

Trapp's eyes went big as he stared at the admiral. He found it hard to catch his breath. "You're talking about…"

"Armageddon," Stockwell nodded. "Thousands of nukes are out there. It's enough firepower to destroy Terra a hundred times over."

"Someone could retarget those bombs anytime they wanted to," Bretta said.

"*Da,*" Borodin said. "It would only take a few minutes to reprogram them. Terra's peace is balanced on a few lines of computer code."

"This is why the U.S. needs a military," Stockwell said. "They signed one away. But for thirty years, they've been building it back in secret. And they've kept their nukes launch-ready just in case."

"So have the Russians," Borodin said.

"Has everyone gone insane?" Trapp asked, staring out the HoloWindows toward the steppe. Another rocket was being hoisted aloft by a giant crane. A countdown clock already overlaid it. Two hours. He looked at Stockwell again. "How does any of this have anything to do with my Selfie?"

"He murdered Professor Gray, which caused an international incident," she said. "Many believed the Professor's Manifold designs, with their ability to maintain fossil fuel independence, were the only thing holding the peace together."

"Ironic," Trapp said, "Since Gray didn't even create the Manifold for that purpose. We recently learned that he was trying to invent a quantum mirror."

Stockwell's eyes went big. Her sudden silence told Trapp that this was new information. This confirmed that his mission hadn't been a complete waste. Her eyes returned to neutral almost as quickly, though.

"Doesn't matter," she said with a wave. "The superpowers are convinced that, with his death, a new Carbon War is about to begin."

"You said my Selfie was planning to launch nukes. Do you mean he knew his actions would indirectly lead to another Carbon War with a nuclear component?"

"No. We believe he's about to take control of the entire Russian nuclear arsenal."

"How could one man take control of a thousand missiles spread out throughout the former Soviet Union states?" Bretta asked.

"Because of a deal your grandfather made with the devil," Stockwell said.

"D'yavol," Borodin said. "Better known as Major Antonov."

"The tattoo on his face was a pentagram," Trapp nodded. "Devil worship."

"The man is crazy enough to believe he *is* the devil. Which means he worships himself."

"My grandfather would never make a deal with that thug," Bretta argued.

"He would, and he did," Stockwell said. "To launch Professor Gray's illegal Manifold into space, Antonov required something in return."

"What?" Bretta's eyes narrowed.

"A space weapon," Borodin said.

"IMPOSSIBLE," BRETTA SAID, leaning back from Borodin's massive table. "My grandfather believed in saving the world. Not killing it."

Stockwell turned to Borodin and nodded. From his HoloPhone, the General projected a HoloPic above the table. It showed a vaguely bomb-shaped device with dozens of pylons radiating around its fuselage. A series of smaller projectiles with unmistakable profiles were attached to each of them.

"Missiles?" Trapp asked.

"MRVs." Borodin's tone turned ominous. "Multiple-independent Re-entry Vehicles. This is a schematic of the *Seyf.* The word in English means 'vault.' The *Seyf* holds enough MRVs to contain several thousand nuclear warheads, a single one of which has the blast yield to level a city."

"And you're saying that this monstrosity exists?"

Borodin glanced at Stockwell. She nodded sadly. Then they all looked at Bretta.

"My grandfather would never create such a thing," Bretta said with a brief head shake. "No way! It's disgusting that you're even suggesting he did."

Borodin spoke in an even tone. "The intel is sound. He *did* make this."

"Your intel is false."

"I'm afraid not," Stockwell said, moving her hand toward Bretta. Bretta recoiled from it. "We have communiques. Antonov's friends employ scientists who maintained a relationship with an American scientist code-named '*inzhir*.'"

"A fig?" Trapp asked, translating. "As in Phig? Phileas Ivan Gray?"

"Yes."

"A coincidence," Bretta scoffed.

Borodin shook his head as he leaned over the table. "Gray needed heavy launch capability to get his Manifold into orbit. And, after the TUR stole his designs, he needed someone to do it for him in secret. In exchange for his rocket, he gave the Russians their weapon. It took him decades to make and a lot of political wrangling to get the nukes relocated here and launched into orbit. The superstructure itself was constructed over the last decade. And the final MRV was added to the *Seyf* last month, just a few days before The Professor was murdered.

Bretta pushed her chair out. "I won't hear any of this."

"Listen," Stockwell said, grabbing Bretta's hand. "There's more. And you're going to want to hear it." Bretta stayed seated, although her jaw throbbed as she worked it in anger, and her eyes turned glassy with moisture. "We don't know why the Professor would've entered this ungodly alliance. We just know that he did. One theory is that he knew the Russians would make their *Seyf* with or without him. This way, he could control the outcome."

"He would have the blood of all humanity on his hands."

"Not really," Borodin said. "He hid certain things from the Russians about their *Seyf*."

"Like loading it with fake nukes?"

Stockwell shook her head. "The Russian scientists watched its construction like hawks. He wouldn't have been able to fake the nukes. We think he was able to make one alteration, though. An auto-destruct."

"Like the *Death Star*?" Trapp gasped.

Stockwell glanced at Borodin, who shrugged.

"I'm not aware of any star of death," the general said.

"It's a meme," Malph piped in. "From the twentieth-century HoloVid franchise called *Star Wars*. In the series, the creator of the Empire's weapon called the *Death Star* installed an auto-destruct. To date, the franchise has earned a record seven hundred and—"

"Thanks," Stockwell said, raising her hand. She turned to Bretta, whose wrist she was still holding. "We think there is an auto-destruct. But we don't think Gray planned to use it. It would create a mini-supernova in the sky that would be visible for months if not years."

"The subsequent investigation would uncover the Professor's complicity," Borodin added.

"His plan to mitigate the threat was a solar shot."

"A solar shot?" Trapp asked.

"He planned to send the *Seyf* into the sun," Erika said with a low whistle and an appreciative nod. "Elegant solution. The *Seyf* would explode without harming Terra or creating a detectable flash in the sky. And Russians would be out a few thousand nukes."

Stockwell nodded. "There's another translation for *Seyf*. It can mean 'safe.'"

"A double entendre," Bretta nodded.

"Yes. The *Seyf* is dangerous. But it's also *safe*. After your grandfather died, we found other clues that he intended to make it a safe repository for the most concentrated firepower conceived. He created an AI to maintain the MRV launch codes and override the *Seyf*'s navigational system to send it to Sol."

"Gray-AI," Trapp said. "So Bril lied to us. He's not trying to find the Mini Manifold. He's trying to get control of the *Seyf*. Why?"

"He may be looking for both. But we think that Ambrose Hancock must know about the *Seyf*."

Trapp gasped as he turned toward Bretta. "Hancock thinks you know about the *Seyf*. He's the one who sent those gunships. And you blew up your Fortress to keep your research into MESH brains and Manifolds a secret from him. You blew it up so no one would know that you were digitally stalking your grandfather."

"I don't…" Bretta looked from person to person as they all stared at her. Her stare landed on Trapp. "I don't know what you're talking about."

"Don't be hard on her," Stockwell told Trapp before turning back to Bretta. "It's what I would've done if I were you. The man raised you and then went into hiding."

Bretta's eyes filled with tears, and she gulped. "Grandpa abandoned me."

"I'm sorry," Trapp said. "I didn't mean to sound like I was accusing you of anything." She smiled and nodded. "So, if Hancock finds the *Seyf*, then what? Will he destroy it?"

"We don't think so," Stockwell said. "In fact, we think he's trying to gain control of it."

"Why?"

"So he can give the whole world the finger. Don't mess with the U.S., or some bullshit like that."

"Maybe that's a good idea," Bretta said through sniffles. "Who but the president can be trusted not to start an unprovoked war? The other nuclear nations would have to surrender."

"I'd have thought you'd want peace," Trapp said.

"Peace at all costs isn't peace. It's subservience."

"So Hancock wants to lord his power over the rest of the world in return?"

"I'm just saying I'd rather be on the side of might."

"An interesting debate," Stockwell said, raising her hands to silence them. "But it's immaterial to our current situation. The U.S. military taking control of the *Seyf* is the least of our worries right now."

Stockwell pointed at Borodin. He switched his HoloPic display from the *Seyf* to a HoloVid of a grainy EYE recording. A man dressed in a pressure suit, much like the one Trapp was adrift in near the Manifold, was entering an elevator attached to a structure with open girders and posts. He was holding his helmet under his arm as he stepped aboard. And when he turned his face toward the camera, Borodin paused the playback.

"Is that…?" Trapp asked.

"Your doppelgänger," Borodin nodded.

"Where was this filmed?"

"Here, I'm afraid. The day before yesterday."

"What's he doing?"

"Stowing away in a cargo bay."

"To where?"

Borodin nodded and pointed up.

Trapp stared at the general in disbelief. Then, inhaling loudly, he gazed around the table. They were all dressed in Space Corps Skins. The HoloWindows focusing on the third rocket showed it had been brought to a vertical attitude. Fuel trucks were already moving to intercept. Its payload, Trapp realized, was a Russian six-passenger capsule called an *Orel*. He locked eyes with Stockwell. She nodded her head with a knowing smile.

"We're going to the *Seyf*?" Trapp asked.

"Someone needs to," she said. "Otherwise, your Selfie will gain control of it. And there's no telling what he'll do with it."

"He's not working with the U.S. military, is he?" Trapp asked.

"He's carrying a HoloPhone that has communicated with a burner of unknown origin."

"That sounds ominous. And what about the Death Star auto-destruct?"

"I'm guessing that Bril hasn't broken into Gray-AI's folder yet," Bretta said.

Borodin shook his head while motioning at the paused Vid. "This man was last seen in the Professor's lab. We have to assume he's acquired the launch codes and plans to launch."

"Why us?" Trapp asked, turning to Stockwell.

"Because the rest of the world has their thumbs up their proverbial asses," she said. "It'll be five years of committee meetings to get them to move. I can barely get enough funding for a ramjet. Erika and Malph are under my command and must do what I say. You two are still fugitives. Your best bet is to get off-planet before someone discovers you're in Russia."

"So it's to be blackmail, then," Trapp said with a half-grin.

"If it gets out that your Selfie launched the MRVs," Borodin said, "then genocide will be added to your list of crimes. We think your Selfie doesn't know you exist, Trapp, which gives us the tactical advantage."

They stared at the paused HoloVid playback.

"Where the hell did you come from?" Trapp asked his paused Selfie.

"A Fab/human hybrid, perhaps?" Stockwell suggested with a smile. "If you help us capture him, you can ask him yourself."

Trapp glanced from one person to the next. When his eyes met Borodin's, the general let out the biggest chuckle of all.

"Looks like we're going to make a cosmonaut out of you after all."

"THIS! IS! AWESOME!"

Bretta's high-pitched, squeaky voice blasted through the comms, sounding like a toddler screaming for ice cream.

"Please keep the chatter to a minimum," Stockwell said, her voice shaking from the percussion of the rocket blast, or excitement, or both. This was her first flight since the *Sentinel's* destruction, Trapp realized with awe.

"I'll try," Bretta said. "But it's going to be hard." Grinning from ear to ear behind her bubble helmet, Bretta grabbed Trapp's hand. He smiled, hiding that he was convinced they were all about to die in a cataclysmic fireball. He, Bretta, and Malph were in the second row of the Russian *Orel* capsule. In the front row were Borodin, Stockwell, and Erika.

It had been over an hour since they were pressed into Cosmonaut status. A series of spacesuit upgrades and briefings followed, after which they hobbled with their heavy and awkward gear out to Borodin's FleetCar. The juxtaposition of facing human bondage and being driven to the launchpad in the same car left Trapp's head reeling. At the launch pad, they crammed aboard a cramped, open-air elevator that swayed as it took them to the top of the *Yenisei* rocket and the *Orel* capsule. Borodin gave a proud, seemingly rehearsed soliloquy on Russia's long-time space dominance. They met a crew in white scrubs who went about moving the landlubbers to their seats on the *Orel*. It was all hurry up and wait as Trapp squirmed in his seat for what seemed to be hours.

When the countdown reached zero, the rocket began to shake. Trapp felt a downward push on his body as the explosive power beneath his butt hoisted 150 metric tons off the surface of Terra. He sunk into the couch, the air being forced out of his lungs. Gasping like a fish out of water, he lamented his vow to never return to space. Here he was.

He looked in front of him.

A ScribePad bolted to the bulkhead displayed white fog before green and brown broke through. They were treated to a spectacular view of the Kazakhstan Steppe as it alarmingly fell away at an accelerating rate.

"We've cleared the tower," Borodin said. "Prepare for staging."

Soon, a series of pops came before a big bang. Trapp was pushed against his straps as half the spaceship's mass fell away. He sighed. That hadn't been half bad—

BOOM!

Trapp's seat came up to meet him. Tendrils like spider webs spanned the periphery of his vision. He couldn't catch his breath.

"Remember to breathe," Borodin said, his voice straining to get the words out. Recalling instructions from the briefing, Trapp pushed on his burning diaphragm and managed to sip the air. The oxygen-deprivation monsters pushed back from his vision.

And the rocket rolled, turning their feet toward the sky. A cloud bank zipped by, followed by another and another. These were soon replaced by a purple bruise spreading across the arc-shaped horizon. And then, like that, they were in space.

Borodin was barking staccato *AmerRoos* into the comms, with the ground crew responding. The exchange was fast and garbled and hard to translate. Words like "problem," "failure," and "possible abort" broke through. Areas of red had sprouted on Borodin's ControlPad, accompanied by bells and beeps.

"Are we in trouble?" Trapp asked in a weak voice.

No one answered. Instead, Borodin's fingers flew across the ControlPad as he tried to correct the problem. To Trapp, he seemed to be losing as the red spread across the screen.

"There," Stockwell said, pointing at her ControlPad. The unflappable admiral sounded tenser than Trapp thought possible.

Her finger wavered over a maddening array of Cyrillic-labeled switches and buttons. She seemed to be attempting to touch a particular control on the pad. But her finger shook too much. Finally, she made contact with the screen, and the *Yenisei* banked starboard.

"*Da!*" Borodin said. "That was the right breaker."

A few seconds later, Stockwell pushed the same button. Trapp felt a slight tug on his right side. Or maybe that was his imagination. But, several seconds later, a red light winked green. Others followed suit. Within two minutes, all the red was gone.

"*Ofigenno!*" Borodin said with a rapid succession of nods. "*Da! Ofigenno!*"

"Are we okay?" Bretta asked.

"Five by five," Stockwell said as the engines cut off and the *Orel* floated silently.

Borodin spoke, his voice still quavering. "You may remove your helmets and restraints. Vomit bags are under the seats. Please, no floating predigested ejecta in my capsule."

Bretta was out of her seat in a flash. Trapp joined her. A slight reminder of his Zero-G flu created nausea. But the fact that Bretta was here made it tolerable.

"You gotta see this," she said, turning him around.

"Please don't spin me," he asked.

"Sorry. Look! We're orbiting Terra."

He glanced out the hatchway window. The verdant and tawny Chinese coast gave way to an aqua sea. From here, Trapp could survey the entire Korean Republic peninsula —where they'd been yesterday—along with Japan and the vast Pacific beyond.

"It never gets old," Trapp mused.

"How many times does this make for you?"

"Four."

"Strap in, children," Borodin said. "We're coming up on rendezvous."

Trapp and Bretta helped each other float back to their seats and strap in.

A tiny blip appeared on the space display. It looked like nothing more than a sphere adrift in orbit. Then it began to morph into something that slightly resembled a dragonfly.

"The Ship Yard," Borodin said proudly. "There are the Manifold ships *Excelsior, Yeltsin,* and *Zulu.* The last to be constructed. The crews are already taking command and will launch in the next few days."

Trapp studied the Manifolds with interest. He could barely recognize them. These ships were bigger and more complex than the *Eos.*

"They're equipped with the new sub-light propulsion system," Borodin said, as if he were reading Trapp's mind. "They'll reach their destination in two days. After that, ISC will be generating electricity at full volume."

"What are those?" Bretta asked, pointing to several blobs around the Space Dock.

"Construction workers," Trapp said, thinking of the last time he'd been free-floating in space like these people. Like him, these people seemed too far from their ships.

"Why aren't they moving?"

"Because we're too late," Borodin said.

Trapp realized what he was saying. He counted half a dozen workers.

And they were all dead.

27

Station Keeping

"STOW YOUR PRESSURE suits over there," Borodin said, pointing to cubbies mounted on the bulkhead inside the Space Dock's airlock. He turned to the ControlPad attached to the wall.

Floating in the Zero-G, Trapp pulled Bretta away from the others. A question had been forming in his mind since dinner. They helped each other remove their helmets, a process made difficult by the microgravity. But this also disconnected them from the comms.

"Stockwell says that my Selfie might be a BioSynth copy of me," he whispered while removing his neck ring. "Do you buy that?"

"I suppose it's possible," Bretta said before pulling the suit's midsection over her head. She shook out her hair and combed it into place with her fingers.

"Why?" Trapp asked after taking off the suit's lower section.

"I have no idea," she said, stowing their suit parts in a nearby cubby.

"I didn't even know making Synths of people was possible," Trapp said. "Just animals."

"Animal Synths, like those found in zoos, are Fabricants. I would guess a BioSynth is a hybrid that uses Fabricant technology combined with biology."

"And such a thing can be done?"

"I suppose." She stowed her boots in the cubby while looking away thoughtfully. "Maybe with the use of nanotechnology."

"Nanotechnology? Like in the nanites in my mother's MESH brain designs?"

"Your mother's MESH brain?" she asked confusedly. She shook her head. "Sure. Nanites could be programmed to work like digital stem cells. But to get them to form muscles, cells, and organ tissues would require exotic engineering and materials."

"Like heavy oxygen?" Trapp asked.

"Maybe."

"Would that explain the anomalies you found in the DNA evidence?"

She glanced at him with wide eyes. "Which anomalies?"

"You found heavy oxygen in the base pairs."

"Sure. I mean, those anomalies could point to hybrid technology."

"Which is why we need to capture rather than kill Two."

"Two?" she asked with a half-grin.

"I'm One, he's Two."

She giggled. "I know One. What I wouldn't give to meet Two."

"Are you trying to make me jealous?"

She pulled herself close in the microgravity and touched his arm. "I only meant to say that Two's existence will clear your name. And then we can be together. Maybe even run away from all of this."

"I'd love that." He leaned in to kiss her.

"Get a room," Erika said, floating up next to them and breaking the mood.

"I'm sure we don't have time to rest," Malph said, joining them. "According to the admiral, we need to get up to—"

"She was joking," Trapp said, cutting the Fab off.

"It's no joke that humans need at least eight hours—"

"The scans show no life signs," Borodin said, thankfully interrupting Malph as he and Stockwell drifted up. "Put these MagnaSoles on." The General pointed to a box on the floor. "They attach to your boots so you can move around more easily."

The group donned the MagnaSoles and immediately sank to the floor.

The general turned and headed into the station.

THE FIRST BODY they came to was a mid-sized female with blue-dyed hair and brown, surprised eyes who rotated slowly above a compartment that looked like a lounge, with seating all around the inside of the cylinder.

"Sergeant Obolensky," Borodin said. "Used to be on my staff. I approved their transfer to space."

Bretta did a cursory examination of the body, careful not to touch it.

"Oxygen deprivation," she said.

"Did Two strangle them?" Trapp asked.

"Two?" Borodin asked.

"It's what we're calling Trapp's copy," Bretta explained. She placed surgical gloves on her hands and stopped Obolensky from spinning. "I don't see any type of bruising or swelling around their neck. Whatever killed them, it wasn't strangulation."

Borodin nodded his head sadly. "I believe we can still assume that Mr. Trapmore's Selfie—*Two*—killed Obolensky. He probably killed everyone here to keep them from stopping him."

"Was the station warned he was coming?"

Borodin shook his head. "Inexplicably, the comms went offline two days ago. That's when we found the HoloVid of Two stowing away."

Bretta spoke as she continued to study Obolensky's body. "There's petechiae on the skin."

"What does that mean?"

Bretta looked at Borodin. "Obolensky was asphyxiated. Perhaps there was some toxin in the air."

Trapp looked around in alarm.

"I checked the air," Borodin said, waving. "It's clean."

"The scrubbers must've cleared out the substance. I could do an autopsy to identify it if you direct me to the MedBay."

"No time for an autopsy," Stockwell said, staring at Borodin. "Maybe after we capture Two."

He stared back for a time. Then he nodded and headed further into the station. The rest of them followed, the MagnaSoles creating a motion akin to walking over dry sand. They traversed several compartments separated by bulkheads. Some were equipped with workstations, others with sleeping sacks secured to the walls. There was a galley and a shower bay. Bodies floated around in each of these places, all with the same signs of asphyxiation.

A ghost station.

They entered a spherical module with airlocks on six sides.

"There aren't enough dead people," Borodin said. "Even with the ones we saw out in the Ship Yard. Some are missing."

"Maybe they escaped," Bretta offered.

"Perhaps." Borodin led them up a tunnel past other six-node connections linked to cylinders that went off in ordinal directions.

At the third of these junctions, Borodin stopped.

Looking out the airlock portal, he cursed. *"Der'mo!"*

Trapp glanced past the big Russian. Blocking the bright clusters of stars were floating masses. More bodies. But that couldn't be right. These things were each the size of a FleetCar.

"Shuttles?" he asked.

"Yes," Borodin said, moving over to a ControlPad. "It looks like Two undocked them." He stabbed at the screen impatiently, receiving angry beeps in response. "I'm locked out."

"What are those?" Trapp pointed at a series of countdowns on the ControlPad.

"Shuttle auto-destructs."

"Can we shut them off?"

"Not unless we can break through Two's password."

"And what if we can't?"

"These things will explode with enough power to destroy the station."

"WE NEED PRESSURE suits and tethers."

As Trapp said this, he glanced over at the lockers.

"Empty," Erika said. "I just checked. Are there any other suits nearby?"

"Just the ones we brought," Borodin said.

"We should go back and get them," Bretta said.

"Not enough time." Borodin pointed at the ControlPad. The countdown was moving past five minutes. "Even if we removed our MagnaSoles and flew back, we'd never return before the shuttles blew up."

"So we either die here or flee using the *Orel*."

"Or fly the *Orel* to the *Seyf* and complete our mission," Trapp said.

"The *Orel* doesn't have enough fuel to get us to the *Seyf* and back home," Stockwell said. "It would be a one-way mission."

"Then we leave and come back," Bretta said. "Live to fight another day."

"And lose the whole station?" Borodin said. "I'm duty-bound to find a way to save it. Or die trying. But the rest of you can escape. Fly the *Orel* out at least twenty kilometers. There's time if you go now."

"We won't leave you," Stockwell said.

"You have no choice, *Lyubimaya*. I won't let you die for my mistake."

"This isn't your fault, *Milaya*."

Bretta darted her eyes at Trapp with a smile. It appeared that Stockwell and Borodin weren't just colleagues.

"You must—"

"I can make it to the shuttle," Malph said, cutting the General off.

"Without a suit?" Trapp asked. "Your servos and fluids will all sublimate."

"Not immediately. My outer shell will protect me for a time. And, when we get to the *Seyf*, I can replenish them in engineering." He looked from silent person to silent person. "It's the only way. But I can't do it without a direct order."

All eyes turned to Stockwell. She stared at her hands, apparently unsure of what to do. Then she straightened her jaw and turned her head up. "Go," she said to Malph.

Without another word, the Fab climbed into the airlock and shut the hatch.

28

Seyf

"THERE ARE THREE bodies here," Malph said into the comms after gaining access to the closest shuttle.

They'd watched as the lock expelled its air and opened. Malph stood in the opening for a few seconds, appearing to be calculating his trajectory to the closest shuttle. Then he jumped. He caught hold of one of its thruster arrays, then pried open its hatch.

"Two didn't lock out the shuttle's ControlPad," Malph said. "I'm able to reset its auto-destruct sequence. Doing that now."

They all turned and looked at the Space Dock's ControlPad. The countdown clock overlaying one of the shuttle icons went off.

"Powering up the shuttle and attempting to rendezvous with the next," Malph said as white crystals erupted from the shuttle's thrusters and it angled toward its closest neighbor. After 20 seconds, he spoke: "I've gained access to the second shuttle now. Powering down its auto-destruct.

The first shuttle is on its way back to the station. Heading to the third."

"Thank you," Borodin said with emotion as the first shuttle turned toward the dock.

Soon, Malph had reset every auto-destruct and returned the shuttles to their docks. The rest of Borodin's team unloaded the dead bodies—twenty in all. Bretta pronounced each of them dead from asphyxiation, the same way Obolensky had died. The bodies were floated to the morgue.

"Autopsies later." Borodin reconfirmed the plan after giving a brief eulogy for each of them.

"I detected trace amounts of nitrous oxide," Malph said as they boarded one of the now-docked shuttles.

"Laughing gas?" Trapp asked. "Isn't that non-lethal?"

"In small amounts, yes," Malph said. "But if enough of it tainted the air supply, it could cause asphyxiation."

"We don't carry nitrox on our space stations," Borodin said.

"So how did it get here?" Trapp asked.

"Two must have brought it with him," Bretta said.

"On the EYE HoloVids," Stockwell said, "he didn't look to be carrying anything with him."

"A mystery that we'll not solve right now," Borodin said as he released the shuttle from the station, banked it around, and headed for open space.

They passed through the Terminator into the night.

"We're going higher?" Trapp asked after noticing that the lights of the cities were falling away from them.

"The *Seyf* is in a geosynchronous orbit over Kazakhstan," Borodin explained. "This keeps it in one location relative to the planet's surface."

"What happens if an amateur astronomer sees it in their telescope?" Bretta asked.

"It can't be seen with a telescope," Stockwell said.

"Why not?"

"Ancient Russian secret," Borodin said, purposely thickening his accent.

They flew over North America—recognizable by its city light patterns—before crossing the Atlantic. Europe and the Middle East were soon behind them as they approached a dark landscape.

"We're slowing down," Bretta noted.

"Baikonur," Borodin said.

"Full circle," Trapp said as they slowed to a hover.

The starfield above glinted like a trillion diamonds in the moonless sky. A blip appeared on the shuttle's ScribePad. Their projected path was heading right for it.

"The *Seyf*," Borodin said.

As they came in closer, Trapp searched out the window. There was nothing out there. At a kilometer and closing, the blip morphed into a missile shape, fat in the middle, pointed at one end. Still, there was nothing out there. At a half-kilometer distance, the *Seyf* remained elusive.

"How small is this thing?" he asked.

"Ten decks," Borodin said.

"That's bigger than the *Eos*."

"Why can't we see it?" Bretta asked.

"It doesn't want to be seen."

Suddenly, Trapp thought he *did* see something. Or, more accurately, the absence of something. Something that looked like a black hole, to be exact, whose outline was precisely like Borodin's HoloPhone schematic. Trapp couldn't make out any details. The computer-generated pathway mapped the shuttle going around the top and looping back to the *Seyf*'s far side.

"I still can't see it," Trapp said, squinting.

"Stealth technology," Borodin said.

He slid his finger on the ControlPad. A bright spotlight emitted from the front of the shuttle. Hitting the *Seyf*'s surface, it was almost completely absorbed—*almost*. A brief reflection showed pylons and missiles arranged radially around a fuselage.

The shuttle angled back on itself. Directly ahead, a circle of lights blinked, indicating a docking bay. Trapp was surprised at how close they were. Out the window, only the blackest of blacks darkened the starfield.

"Can this thing even be seen from Terra?" Bretta asked as an aperture inside the light circle spiraled open and revealed a tunnel.

"As a blip or a shadow," Borodin said. "Some people have even published pictures on the Plexus. Fuel for the conspiracy theorists, many of whom have labeled it a genuine UAP—UFO, as Americans used to call them."

The shuttle passed through the opening, and the aperture closed behind them. They touched down on a flat surface with a loud thunk from electromagnets. The whoosh of air told Trapp that the bay was being pressurized. The ControlPad chimed.

"It's safe to enter now," Borodin said.

He opened the hatch, and they climbed out into the shuttle bay. A hatchway into the superstructure was going up.

Borodin led the column as he stepped through it.

Pop-pop-pop.

The General tipped back, tethered to the floor by his MagnaSoles, gobs of blood burbling out of his chest and hovering over him like red cumulus clouds. Stockwell and Malph grabbed the big man and slid him back into the bay while Erika smashed the button to close the hatch.

Trapp turned to Bretta. Strangely, she only stood there and stared at the general in silence.

"Aren't you going to do something for him?" he asked. Bretta looked up at him. Her face was oddly scrunched up, as if she were going to be sick. "This can't be worse than what you did for me in Alaska." She gazed at him for several more seconds before nodding.

"I need a MedKit," she said, her voice shaky.

Scanning the walls, Trapp spotted a white box with a red cross. He slogged over to it and yanked it free as the Velcro unzipped. Frisbeeing it, he tossed it to Erika's outstretched hands. By the time he'd flopped back to Borodin's side, the General's face had turned ashy, his lips the color of lilacs. Stockwell produced a knife and began cutting away his thick uniform. She exposed his chest and three bullet wounds that exuded red molasses with a hint of rust aroma.

"I think we should apply pressure to the wounds," Bretta said. Trapp found some towels in the kit and began to staunch the wounds.

"Is that a smart bandage?" he asked, pointing with his nose.

"Yes! That can work. Wrap it over the wounds."

"Do I need to leave the towels in place?"

"I think so, yes."

Trapp wrapped the bandage around Borodin's chest, careful to cover all the wounds, before slipping the end of the bandage through its slot. He looked up at Bretta. She nodded. Finding a power button on the bandage, he pressed it. With a slight hum, the bandage constricted. Borodin gasped in pain. But, after a bit, the color returned to his face.

"*Spasibo*," Borodin thanked them in a weak voice. Stockwell held a water bottle to his mouth and he drank a few sips. Then he closed his eyes.

"We need to get him to surgery," she said, looking at Bretta.

Bretta looked at Trapp. The color had gone from her face and her eyes were wide with shock. He smiled and put a hand on her shoulder. She grinned and nodded. "They should have a HoloMed in the infirmary," Stockwell said. "ISC protocol. If we can get him there, the machine should be able to save him."

"We'll have to get past a marksman," Erika reminded her.

"I'll draw his fire while you take the general to the infirmary," Stockwell said. "There should be a schematic on the walls with directions."

"It'll be labeled *Lazaret,*" Trapp said. "And I'm the one who should go. If Two sees me—a copy of himself—it'll distract him long enough for you to make it past."

"I can't let you do that," Stockwell said. "You're my responsibility. I'm going. No more discussion."

"Neither of you is going," Malph said. "I'm the only one fast enough to dodge bullets."

"You can be killed just as easily as any of us," Trapp said.

"I can be killed. But not as easily. And I have another advantage. I don't bleed. Or, at least, not blood."

"Someone do something," Erika said. "Time's running —"

A loud klaxon sounded, cutting her off. Red lights flashed overhead.

"Otkrytiye naruzhnykh dverey," a voice over the loudspeaker said. *"Evakuiruyus."*

"Outer doors are opening," Trapp translated. "Evacuate."

"It seems that Two has made our arguments moot," Stockwell said. "We're about to be sucked out into space."

DEAFENING ALARMS BLARED in the shuttle bay.

Red lights blinked all around them. An *AmerRoos*-speaking voice ticked off the seconds before explosive decompression was to occur.

"Grab the general!" Stockwell shouted as she removed his boots and he levitated off the floor. Trapp, Bretta, and Erika seized hold of his coveralls while Malph stood close to the hatch. "When Malph enters, he'll go left. We'll go right. I'll take point. Erika, you're in the rear so you can close the hatch before decompression sucks all the air off the *Seyf*. Once Malph has drawn Two away, we'll float the general in the other direction. Everyone clear?"

"Yes, ma'am," they said in unison.

She nodded at Malph. He crept up to the hatch. Removing his MagnaSoles, he held the bulkhead just outside the *Seyf*.

Stockwell led the Borodin-centered scrum up behind Malph.

"Ready?" she asked.

"Yes," Malph said.

"Now!"

Malph flung himself through the hatch. Stockwell followed behind and took the scrum in the opposite direction. A barrage of bullets impacted walls and bulkheads. But they were aimed in the other direction at Malph as he drew Two away. Multiple hands accelerated the group down the hallway. They listed to port as Stockwell led them around a corner. Momentum drove

Trapp into the wall. But they were around and safe in less than a few seconds.

Borodin pointed shakily. "Straight through and down that hallway."

Following his directions, Stockwell guided them into the infirmary, and Erika closed the door. It was a room no bigger than an Indent crew quarters, with white cabinets and an operating table over which a domed piece of glass hovered.

"A HoloMed," Stockwell sighed. "Thank god. Strap the general in."

Trapp and Erika did this while Bretta floated out of the way. Stockwell went to work at the HoloMed's ControlPad with Trapp and Erika waiting patiently at her side. Trapp glanced at Bretta several times. She looked like she might be sick, which put her behavior into perspective. This was her first time in microgravity. She was suffering from the symptoms of Zero-G flu. No wonder she'd lost her confidence.

Trapp turned back to Borodin's status.

The HoloMed's screen displayed an outline of the general's midsection with three bright blobs.

"The slugs," Stockwell said. "That one is pretty close to the heart. If Two had been a few millimeters to the left…" She trailed off.

A retractable arm dropped down from the dome, holding a syringe attached to a clear tube.

"Preparing to administer anesthesia," the robot voice of the HoloMed said. It injected the syringe into Borodin's arm, near the crook of his elbow. A laser scalpel dropped down next and lined up with Borodin's chest. "Making the incision," the robot said as the scalpel scribed a neat line above Borodin's heart. Blood poured out of the wound while tubes came down and sucked it up. The first arm returned with a pincer-like tool. "Retracting foreign object." The HoloMed thrust the retractor into Borodin's chest and, a moment later, came back grasping a wad of lead—the slug. It dropped it into a sample tray on the edge of the bed.

Alarms went off.

"The patient is coding," the HoloMed said. "Please stand clear."

Another syringe with another tube was injected into Borodin's other arm. At the same time, paddles dropped down and rested on his chest. "Administering 120 Joules. Clear." A massive whomp came out of the paddles, lifting Borodin's upper body off the table. The alarms continued to go off. "Administering 200 Joules. Clear." An even louder whomp came. Borodin raised and lowered again. Then, the pleasing beep-beep of a heart monitor came on, replacing the alarms.

"Sinus rhythm," the HoloMed said. "Do you wish to continue with the operation?"

"By all means," Stockwell said.

"Thank you. Authorization confirmed by Admiral Margery Stockwell."

The humans in the room exchanged glances.

Then the HoloMed went about making the second incision. When the operation was over, it sprayed surgical glue into the wounds, which immediately stitched themselves closed.

"Nanites," Bretta exclaimed next to Trapp. Sometime during the operation, she'd become less squeamish and had come close enough to watch.

Stockwell rubbed tears from her eyes. "I think he's going to live."

"The patient's prognosis is favorable," the HoloMed agreed.

But Stockwell was now staring at Bretta, her lips pursed. Trapp wasn't sure what that look meant. Perhaps she was angry at Bretta that she'd been unable to participate in saving the General. Trapp would explain Bretta's reasons to Stockwell later. Bretta, though, seemed oblivious to all of this and just stared on in fascination.

Erika moved next to them, holding two ControlPads.

"What are those for?" Trapp asked, pointing at the ControlPads.

"I've been monitoring Two. He's definitely in the system. I've slowed him down by throwing up a few roadblocks in the Launch Control System."

"So he's actually trying to launch the nukes?" Trapp asked.

"It would seem so. He's here." Holding up a schematic of the *Seyf,* she pointed at a red plus sign in a room atop a pylon in the middle of the ship. "This is Launch Control."

"Where's Malph?" Trapp asked. Stockwell looked up from Borodin with interest, apparently wondering like Trapp if Two had somehow disabled the Fab.

"Fabs don't register on these scans." Erika zoomed in on four red crosses inside a room. "These are our heat signatures."

"Heat signatures?" Trapp asked. Since Baikonur, he'd been wrestling with why Two had killed Gray and whether he was a Fab/Hybrid. "The scans registered one for Two?"

"Yes. He definitely gives off a heat signature. Although, no one knows what these scans would register for hybrids."

"Has Two succeeded in taking control of the MRVs?" Bretta asked, her interest piqued.

"It would seem. It's just a matter of time until he breaks through my roadblocks."

"And if he does that?"

"Bye-bye, Terra."

"We don't know that's what he's trying to do," Bretta said. "Maybe he's just trying to disable the MRVs."

"Either way," Trapp said, "we've got to get to him; we have to try to stop him from doing something terrible."

"There is a way to end all of this," Erika said.

"You found a way to initiate auto-destruct?"

"As the admiral told us, only one entity has the codes to set that off."

"Gray-AI," Bretta nodded.

"But I have found an Achilles heel. The Wi-Fi antenna. It's more than a decade old. And, if it's disabled, Two can't send the codes to the MRVs." She shook her head with a grin.

Trapp nodded excitedly. "How do we disable it?"

"A hammer would do the job nicely. Or a rock. But you need to get to it. And it's right there." She pointed at the room where Two was. The schematic showed a smaller room off of it, an electronics closet.

Trapp looked away thoughtfully.

"You have an idea, don't you?" Stockwell asked him.

"A really stupid one, yes. Which is why it just might work."

"You'll never get past that gun," Bretta argued. "And I can't believe you'd risk your life for this—that you'd risk *us*." She started to pout.

"It's what we came here for," Trapp said, holding her shoulder.

"Why does it have to be you?"

"Because Two *is* me. He's got my memories, my personality. Apparently, given the same circumstances, I'd be the one in that room threatening the world."

"You can't know that. And this whole hybrid thing is a lie. She made it up to get you to comply with her wishes."

With tears flowing down her cheeks, Bretta pointed at the admiral. "For all we know, Two is the hero, and she's the villain."

The room became hushed.

"We all need to dial it down a notch," Stockwell said coolly.

"I'm sorry," Bretta said, sounding not in the least bit sorry. "But we've not even talked about safe options to stop Two. No one's even suggesting we contact him to get him to tell us his side."

"There's no time," Erika said. "I estimate that within 10 minutes he'll regain control. Ten minutes to stop Armageddon."

"You don't get to decide how my boyfriend lives or dies," Bretta hissed. This was an ugly side of her Trapp never thought possible. Zero-G flu couldn't explain it.

He held Bretta by the shoulders a little more firmly than before.

"*She does,*" he said in a low whisper. "This woman saved my life. And she knows, as we all do, what the risks are. My life has been a waste, a disgrace. I didn't even become an Indent for noble purposes. I wanted to save my ass, go hide away somewhere, run away from who I am. But I'm finished running. This is something I *can* do that has meaning. And I'm the only one who can do it."

Bretta broke down. She sobbed loudly, her body racked with convulsions. Trapp held her and looked up at Erika, who looked away, embarrassed.

"I'm sorry," Bretta said when she regained control. "I don't know what to say. I just wish you wouldn't go."

"I promise I won't let him kill me." Trapp held her face up to his.

She sniffed. "You can't promise that."

"You must let me do this."

She stared for a long time, her eyes wet and red. Then resolve cut through, and she nodded. She looked away. He kissed her on the top of her head and then turned away. He looked at Stockwell.

"What happens if the MRVs fall to Terra?" he asked Stockwell.

"They'll burn up harmlessly in the atmosphere. Why?"

"There has to be a way into that auto-destruct," he told Erika. "And the Control System on the *Seyf* would be much the same software as the *Eos*, right?"

"They're very similar, yes," she said. Then her eyes widened. "Genius!" He smiled and nodded as she seemed to understand his idea. "We don't need to detonate the MRVs."

"Just the ship underneath them," he said, pushing himself to the door.

"You might need these," Erika said. She handed him a shiny cylinder the size of a thumb. He glanced at it and stuck it in his pocket beside the other item he'd taken from the infirmary earlier. "Keep in touch." Erika winked and handed him a comms earpiece.

He placed it in his ear and opened the door.

He gave a look to Bretta and willed it not to be his last.

Then he turned and launched his body toward his doppelgänger.

29

Doppelgänger

"GOING IN," TRAPP said into the earpiece.

"Stay safe," Erika said, her voice clear and close. This one-on-one had always presented a false sense of intimacy, which might've explained Trapp's earlier crush on her.

"Always," he said, his voice almost a whisper.

"Since when?"

Trapp grinned. He'd fought to put the strange Bretta encounter out of his head during the short journey here. A few minutes ago, his crazy idea had sounded downright sane. But, during the trip, he'd begun to question it. Even Erika's device did little to ease his troubled mind. Feeling in his pocket, his hand closed around the cool steel of the wireless Geiger counter.

He'd just about forgotten what this ship was for.

He looked up. Stenciled on the hatchway overhead was the universal symbol for radioactivity: a yellow and black trefoil.

"Exposure," an accompanying sign postulated in *AmerRoos*, "can result in hair loss, skin lesions, cancer, and death. Proceed with extreme caution. HazmatSkins recommended."

Trapp glanced at his Space Corps skins. Definitely not radioactivity-proof. He shook his head as he placed his feet into anchors on the floor. He spun the handwheel and pulled the hatch open. A tube ascended into the darkness. Trapp held up the Geiger counter like a magic wand. Random clicks filled his earpiece.

"Count's low," Erika said. "You're good to go."

He nodded and reached for a handhold. Pulling against inertia, he floated upward, triggering LEDs that revealed a twenty-five-meter shaft terminating at another hatch. Smaller hatches lined two sides of the shaft at five-meter intervals. On his way from the Infirmary, Erika had given him a quick tutorial on what they were: access points to the side spars where the MRVs were attached. The top hatch led into Launch Control.

He crept upward. Passing the first set of spars, there was no change in the rhythmic tick of the counter. These lateral tubes looked to be no wider than a person, adding claustrophobia to the potential of death by radiation to the hazards of being a missile engineer on the *Seyf*. This also begged an important question: Where was the *Seyf*'s crew? He'd asked Erika that earlier, and she had no answer. Borodin was still unconscious, so no help there.

The ticking increased.

"You're still within safe limits," Erika assured him. "The level of radiation has increased, though. It might indicate a leak. Take it slow."

The next set of hatches were clear of radiation, too. And the next one.

"Have you found the auto-destruct override?" Trapp asked.

"Working on it when I'm not being distracted by this voice in my head."

"You should really see a shrink about that."

Trapp looked above. Ten meters to the hatch. He could read its label from here, '*Kontrol Zapuska*.' He felt in his pocket for what he'd taken from the infirmary. Stupid idea. And how was he going to address Two? He'd been thinking of opening lines: "Don't look now, but you're seeing double." Or: "You're beside yourself with confusion." His current favorite was "Mirror, mirror on the wall, who's—"

A shriek split Trapp's head. Was Erika screaming? Had he miscalculated, and Two went to the Infirmary? Was Trapp's body double now holding his friends hostage?

"Back out!" Erika shouted. "Radiation!"

Trapp pushed down and away from the spar he'd been hovering beside while he thought of his grand entrance. The Geiger counter changed back to pleasant clicks. But the damage had been done.

"How long was I exposed?" he asked Erika.

"Twenty seconds. Maybe longer. You got…1000 rems."

"That's not good, is it?"

"Uh, no," she said. "Come back to the Infirmary, stat."

"I need to complete this."

"There's a big leak up there. Another trip through the radiation zone will—"

Trapp pulled the earpiece out and stuck it in his pocket. He'd known the risks. Bretta's smiling face flashed into his mind, making him feel guilty. His comms earpiece buzzed. It was probably Bretta begging him to come back to the infirmary. But then he heard the voice. It was deep and masculine. He put the comms back into his ear.

"The suspense is killing me," the person said. "Are you coming up or not?"

It was Two. Somehow, he hacked into their comms and monitored Trapp's movements. Did he know that his look-alike was below him?

"Who the hell is this?" Trapp asked, pretending to be flustered.

"Wallas. Who the hell are *you*?"

Trapp gasped. Why was this man calling himself by Trapp's first name? Perhaps Two's memories were screwed up. Maybe Ambrose Hancock's memory replication process wasn't perfect. The handwheel for the hatch spun open. It came up, revealing the room beyond.

Trapp looked down. The dose of radiation was enough to kill him. He probably could not survive even if he returned to the Infirmary; his guardian angel Jessi couldn't save him from it.

He grabbed the handhold and looked up.

Then he continued the climb.

AS HE ENTERED Launch Control, Trapp became immediately dazed.

Everything about the man in front of him—his hazel eyes, the mole on his upper lip, the hint of crow's feet as he grinned confidently—was exactly like Trapp. Barring their difference in hairstyles, Trapp's being a two-week stubble while Wallas' was shoulder-length, they were exact duplicates. Trapp had fully expected this, even the gun Wallas held in his left hand. *Trapp* was left-handed. Still, the sight of his lookalike made him dizzy and nauseous. And a nearby ControlPad displaying a *Seyf* schematic with each missile glowing green, indicating they were armed, only enhanced his vertigo.

He glanced outside the Launch Control windows, chuckling at this turn of events. To the east, Terra's far-off terminator glowed orange from a rising sun. Its light bathed the stealthy *Seyf,* creating hundreds of dark shadows of megabombs. For the first time since he'd learned about the *Seyf,* Trapp understood the vast magnitude of its destructive power.

And all he could do was giggle.

"You look like a failed Fab," Wallas commented, his voice warbling slightly.

Attempting to put on MagnaSoles, Trapp sputtered at Wallas's audacious alliteration. He got one MagnaSole on but struggled with the second, seeming to have lost his ability to focus. This made him chuckle some more. The whole thing *was* hilarious. He'd expected to surprise Wallas with his face, and here he was, the one who was *befuddled.* And where the hell did *that* word come from? Was there a conscious state of un-*fuddle*-ment? Did one need to *be fuddled* to come out of it? Trapp laughed so hard he dropped the second MagnaSole, and his boot floated up. Tears flooded his eyes as he watched it going back up each time he pushed it down. His stomach hurt, and he doubled over.

Wallas pulled an oxygen mask off the wall. He tossed it to Trapp, its small tank spinning it around in the microgravity. Somehow, Trapp snagged it. He put it over his face and stared at Wallas. Thinking it would be a good joke, he held his breath.

"Breathe," Wallas said, pointing the gun at Trapp. Trapp obeyed. Nothing changed. He chuckled, although it was less boisterous since Wallas was being such a buzzkill.

"I'm dizzy," he said, his voice slurring.

"Open the valve," Wallas said.

Trapp looked at the valve in mock surprise, which made him giggle some more. He really should be doing stand-up instead of confronting his dopplegänger. Wallas waved the gun.

"Fine," Trapp said, opening the valve. Cool oxygen filled his lungs. Within a few seconds, his head cleared. And he was mortified at what he'd just been doing.

"What the hell was that?" he asked.

"I was in an accident," Wallas said. "Apparently, it causes my breath to have trace amounts of nitrous oxide instead of CO2, although I don't know how that's possible. Still, the nitrox builds up in poorly ventilated areas."

"Such as the LC," Trapp nodded. "And the Space Dock."

"That one wasn't my fault," Wallas said, wide-eyed. "No one told me that my condition could suffocate people."

"How long have you *had* this condition?" Trapp asked, thinking this might prove Wallas was a hybrid. A hybrid might need to breathe to oxygenate its biological parts. And perhaps the machinery produced these abnormal exhalations.

"Two months, give or take, since I left the *Eos*," Wallas said. "The accident occurred near the Manifold. I woke up in a hospital afterward."

Trapp stared at him, dumbfounded. Wallas's memories seemed to be Trapp's. Did this confirm Stockwell's theory that Hancock had found a way to capture Trapp's memories and download them to Wallas's MESH brain? Furthermore, how could that capture be so recent? Trapp shook his head.

"What did they do to you in that hospital?" he asked.

"Mostly kept me unconscious. I'd completed my three *Eos* tours and was supposed to be released from my Indent Contract. But I was powerless to do anything about it. My nurse kept pumping me full of medicine that made me sleep. She drew a lot of blood."

"To what end?"

"I woke up alone once and left my room. I came upon a lab where the nurse and some man were talking. And when the man turned around, I saw his face. It was Phileas Gray." Wallas looked away, his jaw pulsing. Then he turned back. "He was the man who supposedly killed my mother. And here I was, trapped in his hospital from hell."

"What were they doing in that lab room?"

"Studying a HoloDisplay of a microscopic image. It was some organism, a virus. Or not. Now that I think about it, it looked unnatural—manufactured. I had the impression that The Professor was planning to inject me with it. And it scared the hell out of me."

"Is that why you killed him?" Trapp asked.

Wallas looked up, his eyes going big and the brows coming together. "I didn't."

"Your blood was all over the scene."

"That little nurse took a lot of it."

"They found it on a weapon Gray had used to defend himself against your attack."

"I couldn't have attacked anyone; I was too weak. I even passed out when I saw that virus on the HoloDisplay."

Trapp scoffed. "HoloPics were taken of you fleeing the scene."

"That's because the nurse helped me escape. She said she was with the ISC and would help me gain my liberty. My last *Eos* mission was a failure. But I could redeem myself if I completed one more mission."

Wallas looked down at his gun as if he'd forgotten he had it.

He held it up, aiming it at Trapp.

Even before Trapp could duck, Wallas pulled the trigger.

A DEAFENING BLAST filled Launch Control. Trapp dropped to the deck. He waited for the pain to come; for the blood to ooze out of him and surround him as Borodin's had. But nothing happened. A moment later, he looked up at Wallas in surprise.

"That was a warning shot," the Selfie said, nodding toward Trapp's right. An oblique bullet hole now pierced the hatch door that led down to the ship's superstructure. "The next time, I won't miss."

Trapp stared at the deck in shock, the smell of burnt gunpowder wafting in behind his oxygen mask.

"Why are you threatening me?" he asked in confusion.

"To get you to disarm the missiles."

"I don't have the codes."

"My nurse told me you'd say that. The missiles are armed from a ground-based system but require someone to launch them manually from this station. Two days ago, I learned your team was in transit." Wallas aimed his gun at Trapp.

Trapp stared in shock. The only person Trapp could think of to fit the nurse's description was Stockwell. She was small and had handled the HoloMed like someone with medical experience. She was with the ISC and likely had access to The Professor. Had this whole mission been a ruse? Was she the one trying to start a war? Her failed *Sentinel* mission and subsequent removal from the Captain's seat might be a motive. Perhaps she wanted revenge. Impossible!

"Who was this woman anyway?" he asked.

"She wore scrubs and a surgical mask, so I never got a good look at her. I'll never forget her eyes, though. Dark and intense. That woman has some serious anger management issues."

"How do you know you can trust her, then?"

"She knew things about my mother, things only a friend could know."

Trapp stifled a gasp at this. Stockwell and Jessi had been friends. "What did she know about your mother?"

"We're done with the question and answer," Wallas said, motioning with the gun. "Give me the codes, or I'll shoot."

"If you kill me, how will you get the codes?"

"From one of the other humans with you. I'll move on to the next one and the next one until I get someone to cave."

"Fine!" Trapp said, crouching one last time. He thrust his hand into his pocket and removed the item, hiding it in his sleeve. He stood with his hands held high. "I'll give you the codes." Wallas squinted at Trapp as Trapp came to full height. "It's just that…Never mind."

"What?" Wallas asked.

Trapp grinned widely as he slid forward twenty centimeters. "I'm surprised you haven't figured out who I am yet."

Wallas took a good look at Trapp, his eyes filled with intrigue. "Why? Do you know me?"

"Do I know you!" Trapp scoffed, edging his way closer to Wallas. "I know everything about you. Your mother was named Jessi. She was murdered when you were five. Your father ran off shortly after that, forcing your grandparents, whom you called Nan and Pop, to raise you. Pop took you ice fishing, taught you how to shoot a rifle, and how to accurately throw a knife. Many people blamed Professor Gray for killing Jessi. But you spent your life conflicted, not quite sure you believed them, not convinced you didn't."

As Trapp stepped closer, it seemed Wallas hadn't noticed. He calculated that he was within five meters of his Selfie now—not quite close enough.

"How do you know all of that?" Wallas asked.

Trapp removed the mask. "Imagine me with longer hair," he said, advancing a dozen more centimeters.

Wallas guffawed. "I'm not really into men, but I'll—" His face went white. "Wait! You look like…me! Without all the hair, of course. How is that possible?"

"Because you're my Selfie," Trapp said, creeping forward another several centimeters. "You are a flawed copy of me. I'm the original. And someone filled your head with my memories. But they screwed it up, which is why your mind is such a shit show. You're not even human. You're a Fab hybrid—a monstrosity."

"I'm not," Wallas said, looking away, dazed and confused.

Trapp took a step and, grasping the handle of the thing in his sleeve, flicked it at Wallas. The old-fashioned steel scalpel caught a glint of light as it flipped in the air. Then its business end buried itself in Wallas's leg, directly where Trapp had aimed. Wallas screamed and let go of the gun, which floated away in the Zero-G. Using both hands, he grabbed at his quadriceps and pulled the scalpel out. Blood poured from the wound as he turned the scalpel on Trapp.

But Trapp had already kicked off his MagnaSoles. He pushed off the deck, aiming his body at Wallas. A streamer of blood shot from Wallas as Trapp flew past him and grabbed the floating gun. With the scalpel in his hand,

Wallas turned toward Trapp, seemingly oblivious to his wounds. He moved as if in slow motion in his MagnaSoles. Crashing into a bulkhead, Trapp grabbed on with his right hand, arresting his flight. Trailing globs of blood, Wallas kept coming.

"It hit the femoral artery," Trapp said. "You'll bleed out in a few minutes."

"Fuck you," Wallas said, still moving toward Trapp, the scalpel held in front of him.

"I'll shoot."

"If you don't disarm those nukes, we're all dead anyway. There will be no world to go back to."

"I came to stop that outcome," Trapp said. He'd discarded the oxygen mask, and the nitrox was already making him lightheaded. With no other option, he put his finger on the trigger. "Stop!" he shouted.

The gun went off. Wallas' body jumped as the bullet entered him. Blood oozed from his back, which was weird since Trapp had shot him from the front. He looked down at the gun and saw it wasn't smoking.

But then Wallas did something strange.

He turned around and spoke.

"You!" he said. "Why did you shoot me?" He turned back toward Trapp, his face a bright shade of gray. "She shot me. I thought she was…" His eyes rolled back in his head, and his arms drifted upward.

Trapp craned his head to look around his dying Selfie.

A small person launched themselves across the LC. Trapp's nitrox-addled mind couldn't register who it was. But then she came to his side, caught the bulkhead, placed his discarded oxygen mask over his head, and spoke.

"Seems I'm destined to be forever saving your ass," Bretta said.

"Seems so," Trapp said, shaking the nitrox cobwebs away as he breathed in the oxygen. "Why are you here?"

Klaxons rang out at that moment.

"Long story," she shouted over them. "Erika found the auto-destruct. We need to get out of here."

Bretta grabbed Trapp's hand and led him toward the hatchway through a growing nimbus of Wallas's blood. Much of it collected on Trapp's coveralls.

"What about him?" Trapp asked, nodding toward Wallas.

"We don't have time to save him."

She grabbed the hatchway handle and went through. Trapp stole one last look at his Selfie. A robotic voice came through the intercom, counting down two minutes to auto-destruct. Bretta was right. There was no time to get Wallas back to the shuttle before the *Seyf* exploded.

Trapp shook his head.

Then he followed Bretta back into the bowels of the ship.

30

Auto

"WHEN YOU WENT off comms," Bretta said, speaking over the blaring Klaxons, "Erika insisted that we wait and give you time to do whatever the hell you were planning to do."

She and Trapp reached the *Seyf*'s upper deck and turned toward the porthole that led to the tube that pierced the station's midship. Bretta led Trapp down into it. Ostensibly, they were heading for the shuttle bay.

"Malph returned to the infirmary soon after that," she continued. "Did you know that he brought a gun into space?"

"No," Trapp said, fighting confusion. So much had happened in the last few seconds, including another bout with nitrox drunkenness. Bretta had shot Wallas. How did she even know Trapp was in danger?

"Anyway, I made him give me his gun, and I came to find you. That's when I saw Two coming after you with that scalpel. Was that your big plan? Bringing a scalpel to a gunfight?"

"Wallas," Trapp corrected her.

"Excuse me?"

"Two called himself Wallas. It's my first name. And I took the scalpel because I'm an expert with knives. Also, it's easily hidden."

"He had a gun, Trapp. You know, those things that shoot bullets? You helped remove some of his bullets from Borodin. He was likely to shoot you the moment you entered the LC."

"I don't think so," Trapp argued. She grunted at this as they reached the bottom deck and came into the corridor. She led him toward the shuttle bay. "I wish we could've taken him alive," Trapp added. "There are so many questions I didn't get to ask him."

"I'm sorry," she said, sounding angry. "I thought I was saving you."

"I…uh…Thank you. But I don't think I needed to be saved."

They arrived at the shuttle bay. Everyone was aboard the shuttle when they climbed in and shut the hatch.

"I'm glad you made it in time, comrades," Borodin said. He was sitting in the pilot's seat. "I was going to have to leave without you."

"It's good to see you back on your feet," Trapp told the General as he sat down and strapped in.

"Or butt." Borodin chuckled at his joke.

The shuttle lifted from the deck and angled toward the opening iris of the outside hatch. Then it flew out into space as a computer voice barked out the last moments of the auto-destruct sequence. The shuttle accelerated away from the *Seyf*. On the bulk-mounted ControlPad, Trapp could see the MRVs were falling away from the *Seyf*.

"Will this auto-destruct not blow them up?" he asked.

"We don't have the codes to destroy the MRVs," Erika said. "The *Seyf*'s auto-destruct jettisons them so they can drift clear of the explosion."

"If it *did* set off the MRVs," Stockwell added, "the fireball would expand too rapidly for us to escape it."

"I'll do my best to get us away," Borodin said as the countdown clock passed 20 seconds.

"What's going to happen to the MRVs?" Bretta asked.

"As we discussed before," Stockwell said, "they'll fall harmlessly into the atmosphere over the next days and weeks."

"Great," Bretta said, her voice tense. Trapp attempted to grab her hand, but she pulled it away.

"I *am* grateful you came to my rescue," he told her softly. "Really."

She nodded and let him hold her hand. The countdown passed five.

"This is going to be a rough ride," Stockwell said. "It's okay if you pass out. No one will disrespect you."

Bretta nodded with a grim smile. "Go to space, they said. It'll be fun, they said."

Trapp giggled nervously. Then he glanced at the retreating black hole of the *Seyf* that was about to become a mini-supernova. Wallas's atoms would be accelerated to something near the speed of light in the explosion. Trapp would never know where he came from. Could a Fab hybrid, he wondered, be so easily killed?

The *Seyf* was now about two kilometers away.

The countdown reached one.

Trapp closed his eyes.

"Hang on!" Borodin shouted.

And then the shuttle plunged into a death spiral.

THE SHUTTLE'S REARWARD ControlPad displayed the terrifying truth.

On its display was a white, featureless blob where the *Seyf* had once been. This blob sent out blazing streamers in all directions, some accelerating toward the shuttle. Trapp stared with sickened fascination as fireballs merged and melded, morphing into one big mass.

The forward display provided equal amounts of terror. They were spinning toward Terra at an alarming rate, seemingly out of control. Terra was coming up too fast, and the shuttle had no ablative heat shield, no way to enter the atmosphere without becoming its own fireball.

Then there was Borodin's piloting.

He dodged the little shuttle left, then right. Trapp and Bretta were thrown against each other as the General dropped the craft down to avoid flares zipping by overhead and darted up to miss the ones coming from below. It was a deadly game where a small shuttle played mouse to a big, horrifying nuclear cat.

"Are we going to die?" Bretta asked as she dug her fingernails deeper into Trapp's flesh.

"No," he said with little conviction.

He was becoming dizzy, teetering between wanting to throw up or just giving in and allowing himself to pass out.

"Approaching gimbal lock," Stockwell strained to say.

"Copy that," Borodin said, his speech equally stressed.

Bretta let go of Trapp. Her eyes rolled back into her head; her arms flew up. Trapp wrapped an arm around her, cradling her head to keep it from banging against the headrest.

Glancing at the ControlPad, it appeared the nuclear fireballs were losing ground. That may be wishful thinking. The firestorm dropped out of sight, and Trapp's feet flew up. The starfield turned end over end. They were in a tumble. His vision blurred.

Bangs and whomps went off, telling him the shuttle was breaking up.

Then everything went black.

31

Return

TRAPP LAY IN bed and stared at a plaster ceiling far above.

Night adjusted; his eyes focused on cracks and the peeling gold leaf of ornate scrollwork framing the ceiling.

After surviving the shuttle's tumble, Borodin had deftly piloted them back to Space Dock. Their reentry into the atmosphere while strapped into the *Orel* was the scariest thing Trapp had ever experienced. And, upon their safe arrival to Baikonur, Borodin insisted they stay at his compound until they were fully recuperated from Zero-G flu. This house, he told Trapp, had once been the residence of a higher-up in the Kremlin during the Soviet Era, which explained the gilded plaster.

"Uhn," a small voice said next to him. Bretta rolled over and threw an arm across Trapp's chest. She breathed out garlic breath, which was only masked a little by the sweet scent of her shampoo.

Bretta had been absolved of the admiral's murder—being that Stockwell wasn't dead—which was likely why she slept so soundly. Trapp, on the other hand, awaited the disposition of his case. Stockwell had contacted the TUR and shown them HoloVids that Borodin had downloaded from the *Seyf* EYE. They proved the existence of two Trapps, evidence enough to convince the World Court to reconsider Trapp's indictment.

Stockwell assured him that he'd be freed and restored to full citizenship any day now. A trip to Borodin's infirmary had furthermore confirmed what Trapp suspected about his radiation poisoning. He was clean. This left him shocked and pleasantly surprised. Perhaps Erika's Geiger counter had been on the fritz. Maybe his guardian angel of a dead mother had saved him. But things were being resolved.

So why was Trapp filled with angst?

Bretta grunted, then rolled back over to her side of the massive bed.

Trapp had spent the last two days trying to convince her to take him to Gray's lab. The answer to Wallas's origin lay hidden there. And, even though the Pols still watched it, The Professor's granddaughter might be the key to their admittance. She'd insisted, though, that they should wait here for the World Court's judgment, then run away and put all of this behind them. A part of Trapp thought that sounded good, *really* good. He pictured them on some beach somewhere, eating well, making love, being together. He even felt he deserved that.

But another part of his mind couldn't let things go.

One unanswered question was: Who was Wallas's nurse? Stockwell? She *had* been so nonchalant after the mission, calling it a success and assuring them again that the MRVs would safely enter the atmosphere over the following days and weeks. The threat had been averted, she'd said. So why did Wallas claim that he was there to stop Armageddon, to keep Stockwell's assault team from destroying the world?

"If you don't go to sleep," Bretta muttered as she rolled onto her back, "I'm going to have to kick you out of our bed."

Trapp chuckled. "Technically, this is *my* bed. And you're the one who came to me. Even though you've barely let me kiss you since we returned, much less do…other things."

"It's this damned Zero-G flu," she said with a slight retch. "You don't want me throwing up on you, do you?" Trapp shook his head. "How long before I feel normal again?"

"A week, two at the most." He leaned over and kissed her before climbing out of bed.

"Where are you going?"

"Somewhere where I won't keep you awake."

"Thank you." She rolled over.

The Kazakhstani night air was crisp.

"Going for walk?" Gregor, one of Borodin's guards, asked in his deep *AmerRoos* accent.

"Can't sleep," Trapp said as he moved past the man.

"Careful of beavers."

Trapp laughed. "I think you mean bears. Beavers are rodents that chew on trees."

"Oh," Gregor said with a chuckle. "*Da*. Bears. Careful of bears."

"Are there any on the compound?"

Gregor shrugged. Trapp saluted him and continued on his way.

Soon, he was walking on a well-worn trail that skirted the high wall.

Half a kilometer on, he came to a small brook that penetrated the wall under a narrow culvert. The second most compelling question came to mind: What *was* Wallas? And where had he come from?

Would a Fab hybrid have bled when Trapp stabbed him in the leg? When Bretta pulled Trapp out of the LC, he'd become covered in Wallas's blood, the same blood that had compelled Bretta to believe Trapp was innocent of Gray's death all those weeks ago. Trapp had even torn off a portion of his uniform to preserve the blood for later confirmation. Strangely, Bretta had seemed uninterested in it, even though it might help prove who her grandfather's murderer was. And *she* had been the one to kill Wallas. Not because she thought Wallas was about to kill Trapp. But because she knew that he—

Trapp slid to a stop in the moonlight, his heart rate skyrocketing.

Why hadn't he seen it before? It couldn't be true. Still, it fit perfectly with the events. He shook his head, refusing to believe what his mind, clarified by fresh air and silvery Luna light, had just conjured up. It was a single answer to many questions.

He turned his back to the moonlight and trotted back to Borodin's massive house.

There was only one way to find out if it was right.

TRAPP CAME INTO the bedroom. He stood over Bretta. Clearing his throat, he hoped upon hope that he was wrong about her.

She opened her eyes. "Are you coming back to bed?"

"Soon," he said, flipping on the lamp. "I need to ask you a question first."

She sat up in bed, fully awake now. "You don't look so good. Are you okay?"

Responding with Bretta Sign Language, he moved his fingers around to make the symbols for: "I'm fine."

"Excuse me?" She scrunched her nose and grinned awkwardly.

"I'm fine," he signed again.

She smiled blankly.

He signed a question. "Do you really love me? Or was that all a joke?"

"What's going on? You're acting very strange. Oh!" she said with a knowing grin. "I get it. You're afraid someone's listening in on us."

"That's part of it," he signed.

"I can't understand you. Maybe write the message down." She leaned over and opened the drawer to the bedside table. With her back to him, she spoke in a muffled voice. "Nothing to write on in here." She sat back up. "Maybe there's a desk in another room."

"It's okay," he said, using his voice this time. "I was mistaken."

"What were you trying to say?"

"I don't need your help anymore. I'm ready to move on." He smiled, although his heart was breaking.

"You don't know how glad that makes me." She leaned over and hugged him.

"Now go back to sleep," he said, hiding his sadness. He patted his leg and the bulge in his pocket. He'd placed the item next to Rory's medal, which he'd all but forgotten about. He'd allowed himself to roam far from his original mission. And he made a silent promise never to do that again.

Bretta pouted. "Aren't you coming back to bed?"

"I have to do something first."

She nodded and yawned. She lay down and closed her eyes. He turned off the light and went to the bathroom. Removing the orange bottle from his pocket, he stared at it. Bretta had told him two days ago that she took the blue pills, which he'd first spotted in Korea, for allergies. He hadn't remembered her taking allergy medicine in Alaska or Helena. This was why, after being tested for radiation poisoning, Trapp had bribed Borodin's medic to remove his tracker and complete one other secret task.

"Concentrated hydrogen peroxide," the woman said with a flawless British accent after performing a MoleScan on one of Bretta's allergy pills.

"For allergies?" Trapp asked hopefully.

"In small doses, sure, hydrogen peroxide can be used for that. It can help with any number of diseases, diabetes, irregular heart rhythms."

"So she wasn't lying, then." Trapp was so relieved he felt flush.

But Borodin's medic shook her head. "One thing that I don't understand. The dosage is high enough to kill her."

"Are you sure?"

"I know, it's crazy, isn't it?" The medic looked away before nodding and glancing back at Trapp. "The only way she's surviving these dosages is if she has deadly gasses in her bloodstream that neutralize the hydrogen peroxide."

Trapp shook his head at the memory.

Tears filled Trapp's eyes as he replaced Bretta's pill bottle beside the sink and left the bedroom. Checking his HoloPhone, he saw that Stockwell still hadn't removed his Indent status. She had, however, deposited the seventy-five thousand terros of back pay into his account. He hoped it would be enough. He rubbed his ankle at the sore spot where his tracker used to be.

Technically, he was still a fugitive. But now he was an untraceable one.

Back outside, he waved at Gregor as he hurried for his favorite path. When he came to the culvert, he stopped. Earlier, he'd calculated its height and width equal to those of Helena's air-handling shaft. He could make it through.

He turned back.

Borodin's house in the distance, with yellow light warming its windows and smoke coming from its two chimneys, made him long for what it promised: opulence, camaraderie, and love. None of this life was ever meant for Trapp. He was a thief and always would be. And it was high time he used those skills for good, not evil.

Dropping to the ground, he slid into the cold water. It drenched the jeans and T-shirt he'd stolen from one of Borodin's dozens of wardrobes—his first act of thievery in a long time. Moving against the stronger-than-expected current, he slithered like a salamander under the ancient brick arch—holding his breath as the water covered his head. He emerged on the other side and squirmed up the bank, cool water running off him and awakening his beleaguered nerves.

He stood.

He studied the high wall, regretting he'd not said goodbye to Admiral Stockwell. He was confident that she wouldn't come for him. Nor would the Pols. The girlfriend he'd left in bed would wake in the morning feeling betrayed. But she would likely let him go, too.

None of them would lose much sleep over an Indent gone rogue.

"Sorry," he said, apologizing to no one and everyone at once.

He turned from it all and ran off into the Baikonur night.

PART FOUR

Replication

"We can lick gravity. But sometimes the paperwork is overwhelming."

Werhner Von Braun

"My second greatest regret was relinquishing control of the Manifold designs. I should never have let the government use it to destroy Terra by fostering the continuation of mindless consumption."

Excerpt from Professor Phileas Gray's last public interview, dated 28 August 2122 *(by permission of The Terran Times)*

32

Crime and Punishment

"I CAN'T BELIEVE you talked me into this."

Gazing through the BinoScopes at the target, Trapp whispered to his partner to stay quiet.

"I can't get arrested again," the man whispered back, sounding more desperate than usual.

Trapp removed his eyes from the Binos and glanced over at his mate. Barely visible in the moonless night, the man's face glowed from sweat. Since their last visit, he'd lost several kilos, cut his hair, and shaved his whiskers.

"Congratulations, Arnault," Trapp whispered with a half grin as he replaced his eyes on the Binos.

"*Pourquoi*?" Arnault asked.

"You and Sophie set a wedding date."

"How the hell did you—Oh! Never mind!" Arnault sighed. "My fiancee wants hundreds of guests, full dinner from *Louis Quatorze* on the *Champs Éllysées,* honeymoon on the Spanish Riviera—the works. "How am I gonna afford that?"

Trapp adjusted his focus on the building. A human form rounded the perimeter, their silhouette revealing the outline of a rifle in their hand. They strolled as if on sentry duty.

"Thank god your friend offered you a job," Trapp whispered, training the Binos on the dark window again. "A high-paying one at that."

"What's the target? Precious metals? Diamonds? If it's art, I can fence it for you. But it may be months or years before the terros are deposited into your offshore."

Footfalls approached. They ducked behind the low brick wall. On the cobbled walkway, a woman in heavy boots passed by a few dozen meters away. She entered a cone of light. Trapp turned the Binos on her, only catching a glimpse before she moved out of the light and stopped to say something to the person with the rifle. Trapp thought he recognized her. And she was thousands of miles away from home. The woman and the sentry laughed boisterously before she entered the building. The other person, a tall man, continued his circuit, disappearing around the corner.

"I'll dispose of this particular item myself," Trapp said, responding to Arnault. He focused the Binos back on the window.

"I can't wait for the paycheck, though. We're getting married in a few—"

"You won't have to. Once the heist is complete, I'm paying you myself."

Arnault let out a low whistle. "You better not stiff me on the *Fric*?"

"You'll get your seventy-five K. Sophie gets her big wedding and honeymoon in Barcelona or wherever. You get your dream life as a servant to her every whim." Trapp let out a low chuckle.

He was paying Arnault by giving him his entire three-year salary as an Indent. The value of the item in question was beyond measure, though. Trapp would've staked everything to have access to it.

A light came on in the window. Trapp focused the Binos. Through their lenses, they displayed a massive painting highlighted from above. It was a Vermeer. Transiting the window, a tall man blocked the painting before vanishing behind an interior wall. Trapp held his breath as he studied the work of art. He calculated it was easily worth a hundred times the fee he planned to pay for Arnault's help. Enough to set him up for life. The man returned, pushing a small person in front of him. Dressed in orange coveralls, they glanced out the window. Stray photons lit up the face before it dissipated.

Trapp gasped.

"Must be a valuable item for you to get such a hard-on for," Arnault said.

Trapp turned to his friend and spoke in an emotion-thickened voice. "Priceless!"

He turned back and stared at the window. But that one glance had confirmed it.

Bretta was still alive!

"I'd give my life for it," he said in a low voice, strained with pain.

"YOU'RE DOING ALL of this for some *morceau du cul*?" Arnault asked a few days later.

"She's no piece of ass," Trapp snorted. "Nor is she any ordinary girl."

Arnault grunted incredulously. The two had kept their surveillance in this spot for almost two days. It took Arnault one day to understand that the big piece of art on the wall wasn't their quarry. On the second day, he realized that it was the girl. Bretta moved by the window in the morning—ostensibly on the way out of the building—and back the other way in the evening.

"Why does she look so familiar?" Arnault asked, staring into the Binos.

"You've seen her hundreds of times," Trapp whispered. "Especially recently on the Plexus after she was accused of killing—"

"Merde non!" Arnault interrupted. "Albretta fuckin' *Gray*? A goddamn-fucking celebrity?"

"She goes by Sykes now. But...yes. It's her. In the flesh."

"Why are we helping her? Weren't you accused of killing her grandfather?"

"It's...complicated." Boy, was it! In Baikonur, Trapp had determined just how much. Somewhere along the way, Bretta had been switched with another Bretta. For days, he'd been with the second Bretta—Fake Bretta, as he'd come to think of her. *Selfie Bretta!* She'd pretended to be in love with Trapp, which was likely why he'd overlooked the signs.

"You're in love with her?" Arnault asked.

"Of course not." But the crack in Trapp's voice gave him away. Fake Bretta had faked their love. She'd not called Professor Gray "Grandpa," like the real Bretta. And then there were the pills.

"Merde!" Arnault said, glancing through the Binos. Bretta had gone by a few minutes ago. "That's just sad, *mec*."

"What?"

Arnault came up from the Binos. "A woman like that? *Brah*!"

"I'm not doing it for love," Trapp argued. He'd debated that very assertion for most of a week as he made his way here. Fake Bretta didn't even know BSL. And the pills proved that she had the same breathing problem as Wallas. Hydrogen peroxide to cure her of the nitrox in her blood. Trapp finally guessed that the switch had been made that last night in Helena. The woman that he'd almost thrown to her death in the caves was the Selfie. What a tool he'd been! He'd believed her crap; he'd bought into it.

"Sure," Arnault scoffed, making a rude gesture. Trapp blushed before grinning.

"Okay," he said, waving off his embarrassment. "Maybe I want to find out if she has feelings for me. But there are larger issues here. And before you continue to razz me, realize this. Our main mission is to rescue her. 'Kay?"

"Yeah, man," Arnault said, rolling his eyes. "Whatever you say."

"You get paid either way."

Arnault shook his head. "I can't let you give up that much *fric* to save a girl."

"You're ditching me? If the pay isn't enough, I can—"

"She means something to you," Arnault said, placing a hand on Trapp's shoulder to quiet him. "I won't take your money to save a damsel in *this* dress."

Trapp laughed loudly enough to give away their hiding place. He quieted himself. "It's 'damsel in distress.' Not 'this dress.'"

"I've always thought that expression was weird. Who wouldn't want to help a young lady in a dress?" Arnault waved it away. "And, yes, I will help save *your* lady. Even if she's going to break your heart later." Arnault gave him a sad look and a slow, sarcastic head shake. "I think I have an idea how to grab her, too. On one condition."

"Anything."

"Man up."

"I thought I was already doing that."

"When she lets you down easy because she's totally out of your league, don't start weeping like *une petite fille.*"

"When have I ever wept like a little girl?"

"Have you forgotten about the kitten?"

Trapp gulped and looked away. Up until that moment, he had. "You didn't have to run over it," he said, swallowing hard.

"The Pols were on our asses. And the damn straggly *chat* ran—" He lifted his hands. "You know what? We're not going there. Not again."

"You're the one who brought it up," Trapp moped.

"Just shut up about the damn kitten. And listen to my idea."

Trapp nodded and leaned in to hear Arnault's plan.

"ALBRETTA GRAY, AS I live and breathe!"

Arnault spoke from a dozen meters away while he blocked the progress of Bril, Bretta, and two guards as they brought her home for the evening. He'd been waiting giddily beside Trapp for the past hour. And, when Bretta's entourage arrived, which included Trapp's Helena nemesis Lieutenant Case and Sergeant Hughes, Arnault darted out, speaking in a Southern accent that Trapp didn't know he was capable of. Somehow, he'd also found a blazer with elbow patches.

"Sir," Lieutenant Case said to Arnault, warding him off with one hand while reaching under her jacket with the other, "I'm going to have to ask you to step back."

Arnault was about to get shot, and Trapp could hardly hold back his laughter. He immediately regretted letting Arnault talk him into this ludicrous scheme.

"I've been a fan of yours since I was in baby breeches," Arnault said to Bretta, stepping around Case, who sighed more out of confusion and exhaustion than anger. "I've had a crush on you since forever. Can I get an Ussie? My grandma will just be *pickled tink* that I met you." Arnault chuckled at his purposeful spoonerism. Trapp was finding it increasingly difficult to hold back his laughter.

Arnault reached for his pocket.

"Stop!" Case said in a dangerous voice. She pointed her gun directly at Arnault's face.

"Now, hang on there, little lady," Arnault said, raising his hands and stepping back, which drew the group closer to Trapp. "I didn't mean to ruffle any feathers. No ma'am. Please don't shoot a good old boy like me. Seeing the young miss is just...well, about the peachiest thing ever to happen to me. And my daddy, the Mayor of Raleigh—you may have heard of him, Robert P. Judd, the third—well, he can vouch for his stupid son. He'd be awfully upset if I got shot during my first year—"

"Shut up!"

"Lieutenant," Bril said, his voice calm and low. "We don't need to make an international incident of this, do we?"

"He's got a gun, Major," Case argued.

"Oh, no ma'am," Arnault said. "I would never break the laws of the great state of North Carolina. My family's been living here since before my great-great granddaddy's great-great granddaddy fought as a Rebel against them Northern aggressors." He laughed sheepishly. "I hate guns. The sight of them makes me just want to break out in a sweat like a long-tailed cat in a room full of—"

"A quick HoloPic," Bril said, "won't hurt anyone. As long as Mr. Judd here—"

"*Professor* Judd, if you please. I worked pretty gosh darn hard to get the title."

"Professor Judd will not tell anyone where he saw Miss Sykes." Bril turned to Arnault. "Paparazzi. You understand."

"Sure can, sure can. Can you please ask this gentlewoman to kindly holster her gun? I promise on my granddaddy's grave that I pose no threat to y'all."

He stepped back another meter.

Case glared at him. She glanced at her boss. Hughes hadn't yet drawn his weapon. Arnault was either a genius or the luckiest bastard in the world. Bril nodded condescendingly at Case. Scoffing, she stowed her gun. She flicked her eyes at Arnault while raising her hands.

"No threat here," she said.

"Thank you kindly," Arnault said.

He reached into his pocket, causing Case to flinch. But then he withdrew his HoloPhone.

"Here," he said, handing his phone to Hughes. "Y'all take the picture. If you'd be so kind." Bretta's big guard laughed at how ridiculous this thing had become. He took the phone and even turned it sideways to get the best shot. Arnault muscled between Bril and Bretta and put his arm around her. Bril stepped away a meter or two, avoiding the photobomb. Case moved away, too, dropping her guard enough to stare at her HoloPhone. Hughes stared at

Arnault's HoloPhone, getting into the whole thing. Even commanding the two subjects to say "cheese."

"Now," Arnault said in an even voice.

He yanked a gun from under his blazer and, at the same time, pulled Bretta into a crouch. Trapp stepped out from behind the tree and pushed his pistol into the back of Hughes's head.

"Weapons, please," he said, motioning to Case. "Or does your friend have to lose his brains all over his cheap sports coat?"

"Trapp," Bretta said, stunned. "What the fuck?"

Case removed her weapon from its holster. She dropped it to the ground.

"Kick it over," Trapp said. "Along with your backup weapon. You too, big guy." He directed these words at Hughes. The two guards complied.

"You don't know who you're messing with," Bril said, removing his gun.

Trapp motioned with his gun as he picked up their discarded weapons. "On the ground. All of you." Bril and his two guards went down on their stomachs.

"Trapp!" Bretta said.

"Quiet," Arnault barked at Bretta. "We need to get out of here," he told Trapp.

Trapp grabbed Bretta's wrist, forcing her into a run. Arnault's stolen FleetCar was parked a block over. Bretta tugged on Trapp, apparently trying to get him to slow down, his long legs moving too fast for her.

"Stop!" she said, coming to a halt after they'd rounded a building, putting it between them and Bril's detail. "You're not listening to me."

Trapp came to a stop. "I can carry you if you need."

"We don't have time for this," Arnault said, coming up next to them.

"Please, Bretta," Trapp pleaded. "We're trying to rescue you."

"You don't understand. I don't want to be rescued."

"Listen, *mademoiselle,*" Arnault said, walking over to Bretta. "Do you know what we risked to get this far?" Trapp suddenly began to think they were about to have another run-over kitten situation.

"I know it was a sacrifice," Bretta said to Trapp. "And I'm sorry for that. But I didn't ask you to rescue me."

"I don't understand," Trapp said. This was about as confusing as Bretta had ever been. And they'd almost died together—*a lot.*

"I've almost figured it out."

"Figured out what?" Arnault said, moving a step closer to Bretta. Perhaps a little too close for Trapp's comfort. Were he and Arnault about to turn from allies into combatants? "That you're a spoiled princess who can't get help from a commoner? I've seen it before. Rich people think they own everything."

"She's not saying that," Trapp said to Arnault in utter confusion.

"I don't need you to defend me," Bretta growled at Trapp. "And I'm no princess, you fucking oaf."

"You're coming with us," Arnault said, his voice becoming low and dangerous. His eyes were big and crazy. "Conscious or not."

Bretta stared at Arnault with angry eyes. She looked from him to Trapp. He'd never seen her so pissed. But she nodded in defeat. She glared at Trapp and walked sadly toward the car. Trapp was more dumbfounded than when they first met. At the very least, Bretta should be happy to see him. A hug or a kiss on the cheek shouldn't have been out of the question.

"No good deed goes unpunished," Arnault mused as the three jogged to the FleetCar.

33

Knife

BRETTA WOULDN'T TALK to Trapp.

She sulked in the backseat of the FleetCar as it sped toward the outskirts of Raleigh and into the countryside. He sat up front with Arnault, who stared out the window as fields and housing developments rushed by.

"Was that completely necessary back there?" Trapp asked Arnault, keeping his voice low so Bretta wouldn't hear them. "I mean, force someone to be rescued?"

"I'm, uh. I'm sorry. I guess I kinda lost it. *Hypoglycémie*. It's this damned diet that Sophie has me on. *Jeûne intermittent*."

"Excuse me?"

"I don't know how you say it in American. I don't get to eat whenever I'm hungry. Like, never. And it sometimes makes me nuts."

"We call it hangry. And you better get it under control. Or I may have to fire you." Trapp smiled.

"Okay, *mon ami*."

"There's something else you have to do."

"Way ahead of you, brah." Arnault turned his seat around and looked at Bretta. She stared out the window with her jaw muscles undulating, tears of anger in her eyes. "I'm sorry for our little *querelle* back there," Arnault told her. She remained silent. Arnault shrugged at Trapp, who nodded toward Bretta. "If you want, we can take you back. Is there nothing I can do to make it up to you?"

"Start by telling me who the fuck you are," Bretta said, keeping her vision trained on the moving terrain. "I like knowing the names of the misogynists I encounter." She turned to look at Arnault. "And what kind of man threatens to knock out a woman? Let's hope your wife or girlfriend musters up the courage to turn you into the Pols if you ever touch her."

"Sophie is tougher than me," Arnault muttered, staring at the floor.

"Oh! So, some girl was stupid enough. Give me her number so I can warn her."

Arnault pulled out his HoloPhone and entered a phone number. Sophie's HoloPic appeared above it, along with icons to call her.

"Okay, okay," Trapp said, standing and waving his hands. "No one's calling anyone." Bretta glowered. "Bretta, this is my dear friend Arnault. A crook from the old days. But he is the least violent man you'll ever meet. Even if the Pols were after him, he'd save a dying kitten." Trapp gave Arnault a stern look, urging him to keep his mouth shut. "I wouldn't have let him hurt you, anyway."

"Why are you here?" Bretta asked, her anger now directed at Trapp.

"Bril was going to kill you. Case told me he was going to do it once you'd become useless to him. And I overheard Hughes and Bril plotting to do it at MAU."

"I'm no idiot. I knew that was his plan."

"So why don't you want our help?"

She glanced warily at Arnault, who looked away from her.

"I needed to find it…And I couldn't find it in Helena. I needed to look for it at MAU." She looked up at Trapp. "I didn't want to leave you. And I hated that I never got to tell you how much you mean…How I was beginning to—" She started to sob and gasp and looked like she was about to pass out, vomit, or both.

"Breathe," Trapp said in a calm voice.

"Drink?" Arnault said in a tone five octaves above normal. He hunched his big body as he knelt before Bretta, offering her a bottle of pink liquid as a tribute.

Bretta snatched the bottle and gulped half of it down.

Trapp shooed Arnault to the front of the car. "Things have happened that I need to tell you about. You'll understand why your rescue was necessary. I'm sorry if it got in the way of your plans, but…"

"No apologies," she said, placing a hand on his arm. "Remember?" Trapp nodded, close to tears. It was good to have Bretta back.

"Wait!" he said, suddenly remembering the other thing she'd said. "Were you saying something about how much I meant to you?"

"I was alone and afraid. And if you don't feel the same —"

He interrupted her with a kiss. It happened so quickly he almost didn't realize he was doing it. He leaned away from her, shocked at his brazenness.

Her cheeks had reddened, and she wore a big grin.

"You're forgiven," she said.

"For what?"

"Kidnapping me."

He looked away, suddenly feeling guilty. "I met someone," he said.

"When did you find time to date?"

"Technically, it *was* you. Or I thought it was you."

"Uh…Now you've lost me."

He looked away. "You have a Selfie. She escaped from Helena with me and pretended to be you."

"*Bril!*" Bretta exclaimed. "He's got to be behind this." She glanced up at him, her mouth agape and her eyes wide. "Did you…I mean, did the two of you have…?"

"No," he said. "We barely had time for a few stolen kisses."

"Okay…"

"A lot has happened."

"With me, too. I found out what Grandpa's been doing all these years."

"We need to find someplace to hide before we get into all of that," Arnault said from the front of the car.

"Somewhere Bril doesn't know about," Trapp nodded.

"There's a good chance that Gray-AI will hack the EYE and trace our progress, too," she said, chewing the side of her mouth. Then she smiled. "I know where. And it's even off-grid."

She leaned over and kissed Trapp before moving to the front of the FleetCar and grabbing Arnault's ScribePad.

"Here," she said after zooming in on the map and pointing.

"What is that place?" Trapp asked.

"A time machine."

She entered the new destination into the ScribePad.

At the next intersection, the FleetCar turned north.

THE FLEETCAR'S CARBON fiber wheels kicked up dust in the midmorning breeze.

Trapp and Bretta had been filling each other in as it wound its way through backroads and highways. She listened with rapt attention as he told her what had happened since Helena and became excited when she realized that Stockwell was still alive and Bretta had already been cleared of the murder.

"So what was this Fake Bretta like?" she asked, studying his face closely.

"She wasn't like you at all. I sensed it even from the beginning. But, I guess I wanted *us* to be true." He waved his hand from her to him.

She grinned as her face turned red. "Where did she come from?"

"I can only guess it's the same place as Wallas."

"Which is why you came to MAU."

He nodded. "He described an accident and a hospital bed inside your grandfather's lab."

"Was Fake Bretta there?"

"I think so. I think she's the one who convinced him to go to the *Seyf*. Weirdly, he said he was there to disarm the nukes, though."

"That *is* strange." Bretta pushed a lock of hair behind her ear. Trapp wanted to kiss that ear but refrained himself. "I wish your Selfie hadn't died. We could really use his DNA."

Trapp removed a small plastic bag from his pocket. He'd been keeping it next to Rory's ID tag. "Will this do?" he asked, handing it to Bretta. Before leaving Baikonur, he'd taken it from his ISC uniform from the *Seyf.* "He bled on me."

She smiled and kissed him. "Good thinking."

The FleetCar slowed and turned onto an overgrown rutted path, tree boughs smacking its carbon fiber body. Bretta leaned forward and looked out the window. Trapp could see her eyes going big and becoming wet.

She gulped. "Welcome to Taliesin."

The fields were high with grass. A rutted dirt lane cut through them. The FleetCar continued down the road and stopped in front of the beige two-story house. Bretta stared in shock.

"Bril doesn't know about this place?" Trapp asked.

"I guess I wanted to keep something from him. As a matter of fact, no one besides me knows about it. I wanted to forget about it, never to come back."

They exited the car and trudged through more tall grass.

"Grandpa kept horses over there," she said, pointing at a faded red barn that was canted sideways. "Dixie was mine." She gulped.

Trapp pulled her under his arm, and she happily leaned in.

"I'll get the supplies," Arnault said.

Trapp followed Bretta around the back to a box-shaped contraption.

"God, I hope this starts up," she said, opening a hatch. She cranked a lever up and down several times until a series of LEDs lit green. "Here goes nothing." She held down a switch for a long time. Nothing happened. But then, suddenly, a low rumble commenced from somewhere deep in the mechanism. The chattering of an engine became louder, spewing out burnt gas fumes. She smiled and gave Trapp a thumbs-up.

"A gas-powered generator?" he asked as they returned to the house. "CSA satellites will pick up the plumes."

"They won't send any agents. There are so many rusted tanks leaking fuel around the country, there aren't enough agents to investigate."

They moved back to the front of the house, gaining entrance from a simple brass key hidden under the moldy doormat. Flipping on switches as they moved deeper inside, they came to the kitchen. She opened the faucet, and rusty water came out. It burbled and sputtered for a time until clean water flowed. She poured them two glasses and took a sip of hers.

"All good," she said.

Trapp sipped his and declared it some of the cleanest he'd ever had.

"So why was Bril keeping you captive?" he asked.

"He'd become increasingly frustrated with his inability to break into Gray-AI. He relegated me to searching through code, line-by-line. I'm no systems engineer. And Grandpa built trapdoors inside trapdoors, dead ends into dead ends. The code was purposefully a bowl of spaghetti."

"Spaghetti?"

"All over the place, disorganized, uncommented."

"So why was Bril keeping you there if you couldn't help?"

"I don't know. Maybe he didn't want to declare me obsolete. I'm pretty sure Case's main role was ending me when the time came. In the end, I think he's just a coward."

"So your whole purpose for going to MAU was a bust?" Trapp asked, sipping more water.

"Not exactly." She gulped her water and then refilled her cup. "I found something. Grandpa left out a key part of his Manifold design from the ISC. It was his weapon."

"The *Seyf*," Trapp nodded. "That's what we destroyed."

She stared at him thoughtfully. "I think there's more to this than meets the eye. I'm not talking about some nuclear weapons repository. In his files, he alludes to something much more dangerous."

He set his glass down and stared at her, aghast. "Something more dangerous than a cache of bombs that could each destroy the world?"

"Yes."

"What weapon are you talking about?"

"The gravity pulse generator."

ARNAULT CHOSE THAT moment to enter the farmhouse kitchen. Loudly, he dropped bags on the counter's wooden surface. He gave them a confident shrug before pulling out his electronic lighter and a cigar.

"You mind?" he asked Bretta. She shrugged.

"Wait!" Trapp said to Bretta. "When we first met Gray-AI, he spoke of gravity."

She nodded. "He also told us what the Manifold was designed to be."

"A quantum mirror."

"And what do mirrors do?"

"They confirm what a handsome bloke I am," Arnault said, smiling and puffing hard on his cigar. Bretta gave him a wary look. Then she marched over to Arnault and snatched his lighter from his meaty palm.

"Hey!" he shouted.

Ignoring him, she walked back to Trapp and flicked the lighter on.

"This thing emits light waves, right?"

"Sure."

"Do you remember what we said about photons?"

Trapp nodded. "You said, 'all matter begins life as energy waves propagating through space, and when one of these waves encounters something, say light reflecting off the surface of a mirror, it collapses into a particle called a photon.'"

She gave him a confused, proud look. "I think that's exactly what I said. How did you do that?"

"I don't know." Trapp shook his head.

"Anyway, scientists call the process of looking at a light wave 'measurement.' Measurement of the wave is what causes it to collapse into a photon. Just as the light waves turn into photons when this silver measures them." She reached inside a cabinet and pulled out a platter. "Reflection of the light wave on the silver atoms causes it to collapse. This is what a mirror is."

She sipped her water and set down the tray before continuing her explanation.

"A quantum mirror works more like a sea wall. When an ocean wave collides with this wall, it propagates in a new direction."

"It's still a wave," Trapp said.

"Yes. And Grandpa's quantum mirror—the Manifold—propagates every wave that comes in contact with it. Even gravity waves. Gray-AI explained that to us in Helena."

"Yes," Trapp said. "I remember that."

"I found evidence in Grandpa's notes that the Manifold not only propagates waves, it magnifies them."

"As in, it intensifies gravity?" Trapp asked, glancing at Arnault. Surrounded by a smoke cloud, Arnault winked at Trapp and gave him a condescending thumbs-up.

"Yes. The entirety of Terra's gravity is so weak we can stand on its surface without being pancaked."

"I could go for some pancakes right now," Arnault said.

Bretta waved at Arnault dismissively. "Later." Then she turned back to Trapp. "Grandpa hid his plan from the TUR. He wanted to create dozens of Manifolds. And when he lined them up in a certain way, they would multiply the sun's gravity and focus it into one massive pulse."

"And blow up the planet," Arnault said, haplessly blowing a smoke ring.

"Exactly!" Bretta pointed at Arnault.

"That's insane," Trapp said, staring at Arnault and feeling like the stupidest man alive.

"This is where the genius of Grandpa's lie comes in. Multiple Manifolds can create a gravity pulse. But a single Manifold is an antimatter collector. And remember what Gray-AI told us in that first meeting?"

"Energy and antimatter make a wormhole."

"Right." She pointed at Trapp this time, and he glanced proudly at Arnault. Arnault stared at his cigar thoughtfully, ignoring Trapp. "I'll show you what I mean."

She rummaged through a drawer and extracted a butter knife. She walked over to Arnault's haul of food.

"What's this?" she asked, pointing at a sausage the length of Trapp's forearm.

"Smoked andouille," Arnault said. "Great for pasta sauces."

"Is it meat?"

"Sure. It's made from pig guts and—"

"Disgusting." Crinkling her nose, she picked up the big sausage with her fingertips and carried it over to Trapp.

She set it on the counter. "I can't cut it with this knife, can I?" she said, hacking at it with the butter knife, which barely dented the skin.

"That ain't a knife," Arnault said, pulling out a massive bowie knife. "This is a knife."

"Please don't interrupt my demonstration," Bretta said.

Arnault looked away, hurt. Bretta hit the sausage continuously with the butter knife. The dent deepened, and the sausage flattened. Then she picked up the lighter. Holding the dull knife's handle with a towel, she heated its business end. The knife smoked and blackened before it turned a brownish orange. When it was dark red, Bretta dropped the lighter. She moved the knife over to the sausage. With a hiss, the blade hewed through the skin, smacking the counter with a thunk and hacking off a hundred-gram slab of meat.

"You didn't have to ruin it," Arnault whined, retrieving his broken sausage and cradling it in his arms like a wounded bunny, actually petting the damn thing.

Bretta scoffed at Arnault. "The heat makes it possible for the knife to cut through this terrible excuse for a food. Just like antimatter makes it possible for a gravity pulse to cut through space. Without it, the pulse would obliterate whatever is in its path."

Trapp stared at the broken Andouille. He was simultaneously hungry and sickened.

"How can we use this knowledge?" he asked. "Can we make the Manifold work the way your grandfather intended?"

"I think that's exactly what Grandpa was doing. I was this close to finding the final clue before you abducted me."

"Before we *saved* you."

"Stipulated."

"What clue?"

She looked up at Trapp. "I think, since he lost control of the Manifold, Grandpa hasn't just been hiding underground all these years, licking his wounds as the story was told. I think he might've also been generating the final ingredient."

"Sausage?" Arnault offered.

"Antimatter," Trapp corrected him.

"Yes," Bretta said. "And, try as we may, we couldn't find it. Unless." Her eyes flew open. "Holy fuck! I just remembered."

"What?"

"Where Grandpa might have left a clue."

She turned, and, without warning, ran out the back door.

34

Stables

TRAPP CHASED BRETTA, who was surprisingly fast for a small woman. In a full-on sprint, he was still losing her. Arnault's puffing and sputtering behind Trapp made him worry that his Swiss friend was on the verge of a heart attack.

"Where are you going?" he shouted at Bretta's back.

"I'm not sure why I didn't think of this before," she shouted as she stopped and waited for them to catch up.

"What?" Trapp asked as he came up next to her. They watched as Arnault trundled up to them and came to a stop, leaning over to hold his knees as he wheezed loudly.

"Asthma," he gasped.

"Do you need a medic?" Bretta asked him.

He smiled and waved his hand before straightening up. "Just need more exercise, is all. To get back down to fighting weight."

Bretta shook her head before turning to Trapp. "Grandpa had a lab here. I was never allowed to go into it. But, when

Grandma died, I inherited the farm. I haven't been back here in years. But I did learn something when I received the papers. Grandpa purchased the property in Grandma's maiden name."

"Which means exactly what?" Trapp asked.

"Grandpa kept the farm a secret from the government. But he must've known I'd end up in Helena, because my grandmother's name was Helen. And I think that's no coincidence."

"You think he hid something here?"

"The antimatter?" Arnault asked with a smack of his lips. Trapp was shocked to see he was gnawing on Bretta's severed piece of andouille.

Bretta cringed at the sight of this. "Doubtful. When antimatter comes into contact with real matter, the result is an explosive fireball."

"A weapon?" Trapp asked.

"Sure. My point is, the amount of antimatter necessary could potentially destroy the Eastern Seaboard. Grandpa would've found a remote area thousands of kilometers from anywhere."

"What do you hope to find in his lab, then?"

"Something he was so protective of he wouldn't even keep it in his MAU lab."

"Okay," Trapp said. "Where to?"

"The stables."

Arnault grunted. "Me and horses don't mix. When I was a kid, a colt named Napoleon tried to kill me."

"Then, by all means," Bretta said, heading toward the stables, "let's get you in the saddle."

Trapp was met with the vague smell of manure as he entered the horse shed. Some stalls still had moldy hay beds, adding to the stench. It was dark and dank despite the high overhead lights powered by the generator. Bretta led the two men to the back of the stables. She approached a vast open space. Trapp looked past her. They'd come to the back of the barn and still hadn't seen any place that was big enough for experiments.

"Where is this lab you're talking about?" he asked as they stood at the back wall.

She smiled as she pulled back a rug, exposing a trap door. Her eyes were big with excitement or fear or both; she lifted the door. A ship's ladder descended into the dark hole beyond. Climbing down it, they stepped onto a dirt floor and into a place reeking of humus and decay. Bretta yanked a chain hanging from the low ceiling. Purple-white fluorescence cast an eerie glow on drooping shelves stocked with mason jars of unidentifiable spoiled food.

"Grandma stored her canning here," Bretta said, wrinkling her nose. "Grandpa was either down here or at MAU most of the time. So Grandma threw herself into her gardens." She sniffled, causing Trapp to grab her into a one-arm hug. She nodded before pulling away and moving to the other end of the root cellar. A rusty metal door with a large handle blocked further passage. It was secured by an old-style metal keypad.

"That's new," Bretta said, rubbing her finger lightly on the keypad.

"Do you know the combination?" Trapp asked.

"It would be someone's birthday," Arnault said as he chewed. "Or the name of someone dear to him."

Bretta glanced at Trapp.

"Your grandmother?"

Bretta nodded. She entered a series of six numbers and the lock clicked open.

"Her birthday," she said, saluting Arnault.

Trapp pulled on the handle. For a moment, the door wouldn't budge. But then it popped, issuing loud complaints from its nearly-frozen hinges. They gazed into the opening, and the three gasped at the coppery glow of a massive disk-shaped object.

"Is that what I think it is?" Trapp asked.

Bretta turned to him wide-eyed. She nodded slowly, then turned back to the doorway.

"The Mini Manifold," she said with awe.

TRAPP SHIELDED HIS eyes. Every atom in his body screamed for him to flee. Here was the twin of the space device that tried to rip him apart, particle by particle—a miniature version of the *Eos* Manifold. He felt faint, staring into its terribleness.

"Are you going to be sick?" Bretta asked as she grabbed his hand.

He shuddered. Then he straightened his back. "I'll be fine. As long as we keep those windows between us and that…*thing*."

"I thought it would be bigger," Arnault said, his sausage dangling as if he'd lost interest in it.

"It's plenty big," Trapp said as they entered the open doorway. "Not a production one. But still as deadly."

With cinder block walls and a concrete ceiling lit by recessed LEDs, the room looked to have once been a storm shelter. It opened onto a cylindrical space about 40 meters in diameter. In the center of this space was a curving knee-height wall topped with tempered glass all around.

"So that's a Manifold?" Bretta asked, her voice sing-song with awe.

They walked through the bomb shelter and came closer to the glass. The Mini Manifold pulsed as its magnetic field rippled like molten copper. Although much smaller than the *Eos*'s Manifold, somehow it seemed exponentially more imposing. Perhaps because it wasn't floating free in the endless void of space but held deep in the earth in a room in which it barely fit.

Bretta moved to the left, circumnavigating the external chamber. Dazed, Trapp and Arnault followed. They passed another storm shelter room with file cabinets and a thirty-year-old computer at a workstation. On the walls hung several faded prints in frames. All of them seemed to be of the same subject.

"Earthrise," Bretta said with a thick voice as she stepped up to a photograph of a single blue and white hemisphere of Terra on a black background framed at the bottom by a gray-tan rugged desert. "This was the first picture taken of Terra as it rose over another object—Luna. It was taken in 1968 from the NASA Apollo 8 mission."

Trapp stood before a strange one that appeared to be nothing more than a blurred blue-black with a small, bright dot in the middle. He read the inscription. "Pale Blue Dot?" he asked Bretta.

"Sure." She moved up next to him. She pointed to the dot. "That's Terra from almost four billion miles away, as seen by Voyager I, the first probe to leave our Solar System. The famous astrophysicist Carl Sagan gave the photo its name."

Trapp glanced around at other shots of Terra from Luna and Mars. "Why would your grandfather have these pictures here?"

"To remind him what was at stake. He believed that the Earthrise picture opened up a new avenue of overall human consciousness. Our planet looks so small and fragile, and everything human has come from it." She glanced at Trapp with tears in her eyes. "It was what motivated him to do the XTerra project. He believed that if more humans saw Terra from this perspective, they would grasp its inestimable value. Wars, poverty, greed, and consumption would be whisked away in a single heartbeat as the collective learned to honor what they really were and where they came from."

Bretta shook her head and moved out of the room. She stood before Gray's Mini Manifold, reminding Trapp of something. *Déjà vu*? Something else? Then his breath caught in his chest.

"The HoloPic," he said. "The one of you as a child. It was taken here."

Bretta's face went blank with confusion. "It does look like that. But I've never been here before. Unless I erased the memory of it."

"Trauma can cause amnesia," Arnault said, smacking his lips, having rediscovered the sausage.

Trapp and Bretta stared at each other before continuing around the external chamber. They came to a third block room opposite the first, with two rounded, coffin-shaped machines. Thick electrical conduits ran from the wall behind them, across the floor, and through a portal into the Manifold Chamber. The conduits terminated at the back of an odd-shaped gray box mounted inside. It looked like a device from the *Eos* that transferred collected energy from the Manifold to the battery chargers. This one had a pyramid-shaped funnel on one end, though.

"What are those?" Trapp asked, pointing at the coffins.

Bretta bit her lip. "They look like XTerra pods intended to keep people in stasis for the thousand-year journey into deep space."

"Why are they connected to the Manifold?"

"For power, perhaps?"

Trapp nodded thoughtfully. It was possible, he supposed. However, the raw electricity generated by a Manifold would've had to have been dramatically stepped down to keep from obliterating such a device.

Bretta stepped away and went back to the window wall. She stared at a doorway that went into the Manifold chamber.

"Please step away from that," Trapp hissed, hastening to catch up with her.

"Wait!" she said, holding her hand up and closing her eyes. Trapp froze. "I'm remembering something…I think."

Several seconds passed. Then she opened her eyes. They were terrified.

"What is it?"

"I remember it now," she said. "I was in there."

"The Manifold chamber?"

She nodded as her face went white. "I…I don't know. Maybe. *Trapp.*"

She swayed. Then she crumpled to the floor.

"WHAT DO WE do?" Arnault asked.

"I don't know." Trapp held Bretta's head in his lap as he sat. She'd been out for several seconds. "I'd say call a doctor. But the only one I know is passed out on the floor."

"Uhn!" Bretta groaned as her eyes fluttered open. "What happened?"

"You fainted," Arnault said. "Just crumbled like a cookie."

"It's crumpled," Trapp said.

"Like a piece of paper?"

"I guess."

"I feel about as terrible as a crumbled cookie." She sat up, rubbing the side of her head.

"*Crumbled,*" Arnault agreed, nodding at Trapp.

Trapp shook his head in dismay at his English-challenged friend. "Sorry," he said to Bretta. "I wasn't quick enough to catch you."

"I'm fine. It's just...I flashed on a memory that can't possibly be accurate."

"Care to share?" Arnault asked, sitting cross-legged in front of them. He recommenced gnawing on his sausage.

"Grandma was in the kitchen," Bretta said. "I was alone in my bedroom, I think—that part's unclear. Somehow, I came here. The root cellar hatch was open. Grandma was probably bringing jars here and had left the door open to get another load. I went down."

"Not afraid of spiders?" Arnault asked, glancing at the ceiling with big eyes.

"I've collected them all my life," Bretta waved her hand at Arnault. "Fascinating creatures. You know how many species there are in—"

"You said you went down?" Trapp prompted.

"Yeah. Right. I went down. I found..." Bretta gasped. She stood. Trapp stood with her. Arnault remained on the floor, enjoying his snack. "This," she said, touching the door gingerly as if it might burn her. "Why wouldn't Grandpa have put a lock on it?"

"He didn't know he had an ultra-curious granddaughter."

"I guess not. I couldn't resist its pull." She looked at Trapp distantly. Then her eyes went dark. "I don't remember anything after that. Just...It's probably nothing."

"It's probably everything."

"I remember..." Bretta pulled on her hair as if trying to yank out the memories. "I don't know...We fought about Brittany.

"Who's Brittany?" Trapp moved closer. He didn't know what to do for her. She looked so conflicted.

"I always hated the name Albretta. People were forever calling me Alberta, like the Canadian Province. After I came here, I begged my grandparents to let me change my name. I wanted to be called Brittany. But they refused to let me." She ran her fingers nervously through her hair. "Then came the accident."

"You went inside?" Trapp asked.

"I think so. I was so desperate to see it up close. And...I don't remember. I woke up in pain. But I was alright." She looked up at Trapp. "After the accident, they consented to let my nickname be Bretta."

She studied the Mini Manifold again. Trapp held her arm, worried she'd be drawn back inside the chamber again. She shook her head.

"He must've used this Manifold to collect his antimatter. But it doesn't make sense. Where would he store the stuff?" She smiled at Trapp, the Mini Manifold hypnosis seeming to have dissipated. She looked over at the workstation and its old computer. "Maybe he kept a clue on that machine."

She headed for the computer.

She turned it on.

35

Lab

"MATTER-ANTIMATTER REPOSITORY vessels," Bretta said, waking Trapp.

Trapp had fallen partially asleep as he sat beside Bretta in Doctor Gray's underground farm lab. He sat up and looked over her shoulder at a schematic on the ancient 2D computer monitor. Bullet-shaped, the device on the screen looked like a sophisticated fuel tank but with an inner pressure capsule and a hard outer shell.

"Excuse me?" Trapp asked, trying to understand what he was looking at as he sipped coffee that had gone cold.

"I found Grandpa's design and requisitions for materials. For 25 years, he's been siphoning off enough antimatter to fill dozens of these vessels."

"Dozens of…what did you call them?"

"Matter-antimatter repository vessels. Their design is beautiful and elegant. Each one is a quantum mirror configured into a closed capsule form. The antimatter is injected here." She pointed at the top of the bullet. "And voila, it can't react with the inside vessel walls. Their QM properties keep the antimatter in a permanent state of quantum superposition. Like Shrödinger's Cat."

"I'm allergic to cats," Arnault said. He'd made a pallet out of blankets and pillows and, for the last day and a half, had been playing with his HoloPhone. Currently, he was looking at HoloPics of Sophie.

"Cool," Bretta said to Arnault. Then she looked at the schematic. "These vessels are completely explosion-proof."

Trapp shook the cobwebs out of his brain. "I thought you said he wouldn't store his antimatter here."

"I was right *and* wrong about that. Right in the sense that it was too dangerous, wrong in my estimation of the scale of things. Grandpa's Manifold could only generate a small amount of antimatter at a time. He loaded it here and then sent it off in tiny increments. This explains why it's taken over two decades to generate the amounts needed to make a viable wormhole. A few grams of antimatter pose a much smaller threat as it moves to its final destination."

Trapp stared at her for a long time, a spark of anxiety growing in his gut. Something she was saying correlated to something he knew about. He just didn't know what. It was important, though—very important. And it filled him with dread.

"Where was this final destination?" he asked, trying to think.

"A steppe in eastern Europe with a small population, so there is less danger. And the Russians have been storing it until enough—"

"Oh, fuck no!" Trapp said, his mind now catching up. "Did you call Gray's devices matter-antimatter repository vessels?"

"Yes. Why?"

Trapp's face went hot as his heart rate skyrocketed. "MRVs for short?"

"Yes."

Trapp's body moved out of the chair so fast he knocked it over. He yanked out his HoloPhone. No signal.

"What would happen if the MRVs were subjected to an external heat source?" he asked Bretta, moving his phone around the room looking for a signal.

"It depends."

"On what?"

"It would have to be enough heat to melt the outer shell. Then, the core would be breached, releasing the antimatter from stasis. Which would be very bad. But Grandpa constructed the outer hulls with strong alloys." She looked up. "What's wrong? You look like someone just walked on your grave."

"They may just have." He turned and darted out of the room.

"Trapp!" Bretta shouted, coming after him. "What is it? You're scaring me."

Trapp barely heard her through the pounding in his ears. Finding the ladder to the stable, he flew up the rungs. He came to the top and dashed out into the night. The stars were bright and beautiful. But the HoloPhone signal still sucked. He ran on, throwing himself through the overgrown grass, hoping no venomous snakes were in his path.

He redialed the number. "Please don't let me be too late. Please—please—*please!*"

"Mr. Trapmore," a deep and confident voice said as the call connected. Bretta arrived, panting. She looked at the face of the person on the other end of the HoloCall.

"Admiral Stockwell?" she asked.

Stockwell's eyes widened and her head looked to one side as if she were gazing at someone off-screen. She nodded before turning back and squinting at Bretta. Trapp understood. She'd just figured out that *her* Bretta was the fake one.

"Mrs. Sykes," Stockwell said, quickly regaining command of her emotions. "I'm pleased to see that you're in good health."

"I prefer Gray, thank you."

"I'm sorry to interrupt, Admiral," Trapp panted, trying to catch his breath. "But, I think we may have a problem."

"What kind of problem?"

"The MRVs aren't nuclear. They're filled with antimatter."

Stockwell's face went gray. Realization tightened her cheeks and made her eyes squint.

"They're on a course to reenter the atmosphere," she said, her voice barely a croak.

"HOW MUCH ANTIMATTER would you say your grandfather captured over the last 25 years?" Trapp asked Bretta as Stockwell's face morphed from terrified to thoughtful. She was already working on a plan, it seemed.

"I'd estimate about a million kilos," Bretta said, her face glowing in the light of Stockwell's Holographic floating head.

"How much explosive power is that?"

Bretta chewed on her cheek. "The explosive yield of half a gram of antimatter is approximately twenty-one kilotons of energy. So multiplying…" she gazed upward for a while. The suspense was killing Trapp. "Four point three trillion kilotons." Bretta smiled proudly at her math prowess.

Trapp almost dropped the phone.

"Please tell me what's going on," Bretta said.

"The good news?" Trapp said. "We found your grandfather's antimatter. He sent it into space disguised as a nuclear weapon called the *Seyf*."

"You mean that thing you blew up?" Bretta asked. Trapp nodded slowly. "Impossible. With that much antimatter, the fireball would've been as bright as the sun."

"The MRVs were jettisoned during auto-destruct," Stockwell said.

"So, problem solved."

"Not solved," Trapp said. "The bad news is that these hundreds of MRVs are on a course to impact Terra."

"That would mean the equivalent of four point three mega-megatons of TNT—roughly one hundred thousand nuclear bombs—are on their way to the atmosphere," Stockwell said.

Bretta gasped. "It's worse than that," she said. "When that antimatter comes out of stasis, it'll interact with the real matter of the atmosphere. There won't be just an explosion. The entire atmosphere of Terra will wink out in a matter of seconds." Bretta turned to Stockwell. "How long do we have?"

"We've received intelligence," Stockwell said. "Thousands of U.S. government personnel and their families are on the move, overwhelming the Loop as they head for underground shelters."

"The SUDs," Trapp said with a nod.

"Yes. And this mass exodus proves that Bril has broken the codes."

"So why doesn't he just send them back into higher orbit?" Bretta asked.

"Bril is under orders from the president."

"Surely Ambrose Hancock doesn't want to see the end of the world as we know it."

"I don't know if that's really certain. Hancock has made his views of XTerra clear. Humans and their addiction to consumption would spread like a virus to the rest of the galaxy. We're going to do to other planets what we did here. Sources from the inside tell us that Hancock believes sacrificing most of the human race is worth the price of saving the galaxy—the universe. But we don't think that's what he's doing. We think his exodus to the SUDs is all a ruse. We think he's causing the scare so he can use the codes to pull the world back from the brink—to become the hero."

"I hope you're right," Trapp said.

"Maybe I can convince Bril to stop all of this," Bretta said, looking at Trapp.

"Or get yourself killed in the process," he said.

"No," Stockwell said tersely. "Miss Sykes is right. We must try to convince him to turn over the self-destruct codes to us."

"How long do I have to do that, ma'am?" Bretta asked the admiral.

"Based on our tracking of the MRVs, the first one should enter the atmosphere in less than 12 hours."

"If Hancock destroys the atmosphere," Trapp asked, "he kills his people too, doesn't he?"

"That's a big if," Stockwell said. "But if that's what he's doing, he and his followers will survive. The SUDs are equipped with power plants that can generate oxygen from water. The antimatter explosion will destroy the air without harming the rest of the planet. And the SUDs will be completely closed off to the vacuum of space after the air is consumed."

"The human race is to be condemned to living underground for eternity?"

"No. The SUDs are also equipped with terraforming machinery. It may take thousands of years to restore the atmosphere and life, but the human race will survive."

"We have to keep that from happening," Bretta said. "And I think I may have a plan to get to Bril."

"How?" Trapp asked.

"We'll use Bril's bait-and-switch strategy against him."

36

Museum

"HE'S READY FOR me," Bretta said, staring at her HoloPhone. "He's ready for *her*."

"Bril believes he's texting with Fake Bretta?" Trapp asked, incredulous.

"Bretta's phone is currently spoofing Fake Bretta's," Arnault said. "I hacked into the HoloPhone network. Of the four phones that pinged near yours over the last week, I was able to eliminate the two with ISC prefixes: Admiral Stockwell and General Borodin. The only other two numbers were Erika Zelensky's, which has an Indent prefix, and an unknown burner. What's more, just like the other four phones, that burner went off-grid when you went into orbit. It's her phone."

"Fake Bretta's?"

"Yes."

"Bril responded to my texts as if I were her, also," Bretta said. "He's taken the bait."

"Or he knows it's you, and he's trying to lure you into a trap," Trapp said.

"It's a Hail Mary at best, I know. But it's all we have. Do you still have the device?"

Trapp patted the outside of his pocket and nodded. Bretta had spent the FleetCar ride over typing on Gray's antiquated laptop while Arnault worked on the spoof. When they reached the outskirts of campus, she pulled a device from the laptop and handed it to Trapp, after which he placed it in the pocket next to Rory's ID tag.

"Find the server with this serial number on it," she said, keying in a long alphanumeric on his HoloPhone and giving it back to him. "And don't use the device unless—"

"I don't hear from you in an hour." Trapp nodded as he glanced at the countdown she'd started on his HoloPhone. He stared into Bretta's eyes. "Please be careful."

"I promise." She hugged him and kissed him. She opened the door, dashed out of the car, past a line of oaks, and disappeared behind an ivy-draped brick building.

"We're going now?" Arnault asked. "So you can stick your dong into the backside of that guy—what was his name—Gay Eye?"

Trapp broke out in laughter. "It's called a *dongle.* And we're to plug it into the server of an AI-based mind called Gray-AI."

"Whatever, dude. I don't ask you how you get your kicks." Arnault grinned widely. "Let's get this over with."

They stepped out of the car and followed Bretta, keeping her in sight but at a safe distance.

"What the heck is a dongle anyway?" Arnault asked.

"Hell if I know." Trapp shook his head, trying not to worry about Bretta and failing miserably.

Then he and the one man on Terra he trusted made their way through MAU.

TRAPP AND ARNAULT watched as Bretta came up several stairs to Gray's building and entered by the front. Case was there to meet her, along with Hughes. She'd told Trapp that she thought there was another entrance to the basement somewhere around the eastern side of the building. Trapp had searched for it, only to find overgrown hollies and rhododendrons lining the foundation of the ancient building. But then he noticed a wye in the brick pathway that led directly toward it, splitting two giant azaleas.

"Here," Arnault said, pushing back on the branches and revealing an iron rail and steps descending into the dark, terminating at a steel doorway.

Arnault removed a few picks and went at the bolt.

In record time, he unlocked it, and the two men entered the building, shutting the door behind them. They headed down the hallway, shining the beams of the HoloPhone's torches as they went.

They passed decades-old classrooms with rows of seats, each with a desk on a swiveling arm. Rusty brown radiators harkened to a world of coal-fired boilers and steam. Even the walls were ancient, with yellow hand-typed pages of text and green slate chalkboards that were scribbled white with equations and cursive paragraphs.

"What are we looking for?" Arnault asked. "Students who were so bored, they died in their seats?"

Trapp chuckled. "Stairs or an elevator, perhaps. Bretta thinks Gray's servers must be somewhere down here since she didn't find them upstairs."

They came to a dead end and a door decorated with a brass plaque engraved with Professor Gray's name.

Arnault tried the knob. The door swung open with a pop that echoed loudly. Trapp and Arnault froze. But there was no sound of approaching feet.

They proceeded into the room. Beakers and glass apparatuses assembled from spheres, tubes, spirals, and crooks glistened in the illumination of their torches. With gas-powered Bunsen burners unlit underneath them, they were coated with a thick layer of brown dust. A floor-to-ceiling blackboard was covered in chalk equations, notes, and diagrams. One was a sketch of the Manifold.

"This is where it all began," Trapp guessed, pointing at the pieces of white chalk still sitting in trays beneath the equations. "Professor Gray used that very chalk to design his quantum mirror."

"Smell that?" Arnault asked, sniffing the air.

"Death."

Using his torch, Trapp scanned the linoleum, finding numerous dark stains and spots, some of which could've been dried blood. Then, he scanned the room further with the torch beam. A dark line appeared on the back wall.

"A door," Trapp said.

It opened easily. Automatic illumination lit their way as they moved along another hallway. There were two rooms. One was not unlike the *Seyf*'s infirmary, with an examination table and cabinets full of medical supplies. The other was a hospital room with two beds. One of these was unused. The other had rumpled sheets and a blanket draped over it haphazardly.

A medical file hung on a flip chart at its foot.

Trapp read the name.

"Wallas was here."

"THEY GAVE THE patient a sedative dosage three times the recommended amount," Arnault said, reading the chart.

"I didn't realize you were such an aficionado," Trapp said.

"I'm, what you might call, *un passionné*, an enthusiast of mind-altering drugs. Mycelium, for instance, is best for—"

"I get it." Trapp scanned other parts of the room with his torch. It seemed they'd reached another dead end.

"Blood samples," Arnault said.

Trapp came to his side and read the labels on vials that sat in a case on the counter. "Wallas Trapmore."

Arnault pointed at the label. "There are also initials and a date. BH, five weeks ago. Before Gray's murder."

"That second letter could be an A," Trapp said thoughtfully, using his HoloPhone to take a picture of the label for Bretta. "Whoever it was, they probably killed Gray." He looked up from his phone. "Do you feel that?"

Arnault nodded. "A breeze."

Trapp came over to the wall. He placed his hand on it and felt an air movement.

"Another doorway," he said, pushing on the wall.

"There's a BioScanner," Arnault said, pointing at a box on the wall.

"Does that mean only Gray's fingerprint can open it?"

"Maybe. Maybe there's another way," Arnault said, ramming his sizeable shoulder into the wall. He winced as if he'd crashed into solid steel. The two men stared at each other, perplexed. Arnault kicked at the wall several times. He only succeeded in leaving dirty boot prints on the wall.

"We need a fingerprint," Trapp grunted.

But then Arnault's eyes went wide.

He dashed out of the room. Trapp shook his head in dismay. But a minute later, Arnault returned wearing surgical gloves and holding a small, white stick. He carried this over and rotated its long side in front of the BioScanner. The latch clicked open, and the door slid sideways.

"How'd you do that?" Trapp asked.

"This type of scanner accepts DNA as well as fingerprints. And you said it yourself: Professor Gray used this chalk to design the Manifold."

"DNA has survived on that chalk for thirty years?" Trapp asked.

"These older scanners only need part of the DNA sequence to work."

Arnault grinned proudly at his technical prowess. Trapp ducked his head in honor, waving his hand for his friend to enter the next room first. Half expecting a server room, Trapp was equally happy that it was an elevator lobby. As they stepped inside, he left the door open for Bretta.

"Paydirt," he said.

"Where?" Arnault asked, looking down at the floor. "I didn't track anything—"

"It's an expression. It means we found what we were looking for."

"Why didn't you just say that?"

They pressed the elevator button. The sounds of far-off wheels and cables clinked behind the doors. The doors opened.

"Compensation soil!" Arnault said, grinning.

"Sure."

They stepped into the car. A ControlPad mounted to the wall displayed buttons labeled 'Basement' and 'Underground.'

"What's an Underground?" Arnault asked.

"Let's find out." Trapp pushed U, and the doors closed. The elevator rattled and wobbled as it descended. A few seconds later, the car stopped. The pad displayed a question, 'Proceed?' Two big buttons pulsed with labels of 'YES' and 'NO.' Trapp and Arnault exchanged confused glances.

"Why is it asking us that?" Trapp asked.

"I don't know," Arnault said.

Trapp shook his head. Then he pressed 'YES.' The car continued its descent. Trapp's ears popped. The elevator descended more. His ears popped again and again as they continued downward into the earth.

Finally, the elevator came to a stop. The doors dinged and opened.

A person stood there to greet them.

And Trapp gasped at the sight of her.

"Mother?"

37

Catacombs

SHE STOOD IN front of him. Her face, her smile, those bright blue eyes that displayed gentleness—it was her. It was Jessica Brown Trapmore. In the flesh. Trapp could barely stand; found it nearly impossible to breathe in air; felt the world spinning on its axis. Somewhere in the midst of this fog, Arnault grabbed him by the shoulders and propelled him gently off Gray's elevator. His big friend held him upright.

"Welcome back, Doctor Gray," Jessi said, a smile of non-recognition on her lips.

Then she zapped in and out of existence for a split second. Trapp rubbed his eyes. They were playing tricks on him. Finally, his mind caught up with the situation.

He hissed as he glanced at Arnault. "Fucking Gray! The pervert created a hologram out of my mother's likeness from when she was younger. I don't want to think about what he used it for."

"Self-pleasure," Arnault nodded.

"Define self-pleasure," the hologram said in her mechanical voice.

"It's when a man doesn't have access to a sexual partner, so he does things to his—"

"No!" Trapp interrupted him in the nick of time. He gazed behind the hologram to a double set of glass doors giving access to a corridor lined with holographic projectors. Beyond these was a warren of rooms outfitted with microscopes, tables, smart boards, and state-of-the-art computers. "I have no desire to speak to this Holo monstrosity," he told Arnault.

"Define Holo monstrosity," the hologram said.

"An abomination of a hologram that makes a mockery of what it's supposed to represent. Like what you are."

"I am not a monstrosity. I was constructed in the likeness of Professor Gray's revered collaborator, Jessica Brown. I have been given the designation Jess-AI."

Trapp grunted, glancing at Arnault for support. But his friend was busy ogling the hologram. "I never knew your mother was so—"

"Finish that sentence," Trapp hissed, grabbing Arnault's collar. "And I'll send you to meet your maker."

"Smart," Arnault sputtered, raising his hands in submission. "I was just going to say 'smart.' Besides, aren't we all about to do that?"

"Do what?"

"Meet our maker? Isn't that why we're here? To stop it?" Trapp stared at him dangerously for a few more seconds. Then he smiled and let go. He realized his anger was misdirected. He turned his attention to Jess-AI.

She turned to face Trapp. "I estimate a ninety-seven percent probability that you are Wallas Trapmore." She looked at Arnault. "But your face is not in my databases. Identify yourself."

"Arnault Baumgartner, ma'am."

"Pleased to meet you, Mr. Baumgartner." She turned toward Trapp again. "I very much wish to speak to Professor Gray. Do you know where he is? I have not seen him in...*twenty-seven* days."

Trapp exchanged a glance with Arnault, who looked away. "Dead," Trapp told her.

She gave a fake, shocked look before returning to the default cheeriness. It was the same facial expression as Gray-AI, and it pissed Trapp off. "Murdered."

"I trust that his killer has seen justice," Jess-AI said.

"We're still working on that."

"Wallas, I have been programmed to say how sorry I am that your mother—"

"Stop!" Trapp held his hand up. "I'm not here for your fabricated sympathy. I'm seeking Professor Gray's server room. Can you direct us there?"

"It is not on this level."

"Can you tell us where it is then?"

"I have not been programmed with that information. My only role is to maintain the Professor's DNA reactors, hydroponics, cryogenics, pods within the catacombs, faster-than-light experiments—"

"Catacombs?" Trapp asked. "You have dead people down here?"

"Technically, they are not dead but in stasis. Doctor Gray has been working on methods to rejuvenate them. It seems, in your case, he has succeeded."

"Succeeded?" Trapp asked.

"Yes, Wallas. Your pod was brought here approximately eight weeks ago and added to my logs. The Professor placed you in an induced coma two days later and relocated you to the hospital above. His treatment seems to have cured you from the effects of the accident."

Trapp shook his head, glancing at Arnault. His friend shrugged. He turned to Jess-AI. "Wallas had an accident?"

"Yes. You had a catastrophic encounter with the Manifold during your final *Eos* mission."

Trapp raked his fingers through his hair. "I did. But I returned to the Miami Space Corps Base. I never came here."

"You're mistaken. No one went to Miami. Your Indent original wouldn't have survived replication. It is too violent a process."

"Replication?"

Jess-AI nodded. "When a living organism encounters a Manifold, the quantum reflection creates a physical copy called a 'Replicant' while the extreme electrical surge, unfortunately, kills the organism. In space, Replicants must be placed in stasis pods within eight minutes to survive the extreme vacuum and cold. Replicant pods are subsequently transported to our lab for further analysis and study."

Trapp stared at Jess-AI in stunned silence. What the hell was she talking about? Wallas wasn't a Fab hybrid? Instead, he was some sort of a..."

"Copy?" he muttered. "Wallas was generated by the Manifold?"

"Yes."

"I'm not him. I'm Trapp. His original, I guess." Trapp shook his head, still processing this. Wallas had been his copy? Manifolds didn't just kill the Indents. They produced duplicates. *Replicants*. "Your information is out of date. I survived my encounter with the Manifold. Check the Plexus."

"I've just confirmed your story."

"And you're telling me that Wallas is my perfect... Replicant?"

"Replicant, yes. Perfect no. Each replication introduces imperfections, mutations in DNA."

Trapp gasped. "Bretta was right, then. Wallas had the mutations in his DNA. And replication introduced them."

"The quantum mirroring event did, yes. Fluctuations in the quantum field introduce mutations in each Replicant's DNA. Most, for instance, cannot metabolize oxygen efficiently. Others can breathe air but produce a surplus of various gasses."

"Like nitrox?" Trapp asked in a whisper.

"Yes. We have observed that side effect in twenty-two percent of the Replicants."

Trapp glanced toward the spaces beyond. "Every dead Indent has a Replicant? And they are all here in Gray's catacombs?"

"Yes. I have been programmed to maintain the stasis pods."

Becoming dizzy, Trapp held onto the wall. "

Barstow?"

"He's in Pod 14358. I can instruct the LIMO to take you to its location if you wish."

Arnault placed a hand on Trapp's shoulder. "We still haven't found Bretta's server yet," he reminded Trapp. Trapp pushed Arnault's hand away.

"Take me to Rory," he told Jess-AI.

TRAPP LOOKED INTO his friend's eyes for the first time in almost a year.

Rory's face was white, as if he'd not seen Sol in years. He wore a long red beard and hair down to his shoulders—apparently, the follicles were still active in stasis—and his cheeks sunk deep into his skull. His yellowed teeth added to his macabre look. But most horrifying were those green-gray eyes. They stared straight up as if he'd been flash-frozen while suffering a terrifying event, which was probably close to the truth.

Trapp rubbed more of the frozen condensation off Pod 14358's viewing window, his eyes wet from emotion.

Then he looked up.

Chiseled out of North Carolina clay and granite, Gray's underground was a cave of wondrous dimensions with piles of steel, pallets of walling, crates of unopened HoloScreens, and even a giant unused air handler sitting on skids. It was an SUD before becoming an SUD.

Trapp moved his gaze to the foreground. Beginning 500 meters from the glass-enclosed lab space were rows and rows of pods, the only empty one with his name stenciled on it. If Jess-AI could be believed, the others contained copies of Trapp's friends. Replicants, she called them, facsimiles of the long-gone Indents.

"You seen enough?" Arnault asked.

Trapp nodded. "How does any of this make sense?"

"Selfies." Arnault nodded. Trapp laughed at Arnault's simple logic. He wished he could accept this reality so easily.

"Why did *I* survive when the rest died?" he asked.

"Maybe so you could rescue the rest of them." Arnault waved his hand toward the thousands of pods. Then he smiled and headed back to Gray's LIMO. Dumbfounded at his friend's prophecy, Trapp studied the pods again. Perhaps Arnault was right. Maybe he'd been spared to find a way to liberate his lowly comrades. He shook his head at the enormity of such a mission.

He placed his hand in his pocket and removed the item he'd been carrying since his days on the *Eos*. He put it on top of Rory's pod.

"Returned to its rightful owner," Trapp said, glancing at Rory's Indent ID as it glistened in the catacombs' artificial light.

"You ready to save the world?" Arnault asked as Trapp reboarded the LIMO.

Trapp nodded while the weird transport headed back to Jess-AI.

He had one question for her.

"WHO KILLED MY mother?" Trapp asked Jess-AI.

She was leading them to the elevator and their continued search for the servers.

"I do not know," Jess-AI said. "All my data for her comes from Professor Gray and the Plexus. I do not even have her research notes. The Plexus says they disappeared after her murder, never to be seen again."

"I found them. They were hidden in my grandfather's attic."

"When you get back, please send me a copy. It would greatly enhance my programming." They entered the elevator lobby. "A series of HoloPics of the pages would be sufficient."

"I have that," Trapp said, pulling out his HoloPhone. "I already copied them."

Jess-AI froze. Trapp and Arnault stared at her in confusion.

"Did you break her?" Arnault asked after a few seconds of stillness.

"I am prepared to receive the files now," Jess-AI said, startling them.

Trapp held up his HoloPhone.

"Accessing…accessing…accessing…accessing."

She winked out of existence again.

"Dude," Arnault said, reaching for the elevator button. "You broke her for real this time. And I think I have an idea how to find—"

"Hello, Trapp," a voice said, cutting Arnault off. Trapp turned around. Jess-AI was back. "Do you know who I am?"

"A simple hologram," Trapp said.

"A hologram, sure. But I'm not simple anymore. Those files you just gave me unlocked a partition and awakened a part of me long hidden."

"Jess-AI version 2.0?" Arnault asked.

Jess-AI smiled. It looked genuine this time. "I guess you could say that. When you were born," she told Trapp, "I had already developed the first Memory-Electronic Self-replicating Heuristic brain—MESH for short. It uses nanotechnology to form a neural net that is pliable, teachable, and accessible both horizontally and vertically across all of its networks. Its memories are strengthened with use and weakened with atrophy. In short, I created the first digital brain that mimics the human brain."

"Currently, millions of Fabs have a MESH brain installed," Trapp said.

"That's true. But those Fabs are free. Gray and our other lab partner didn't want that. They wanted Fabs to become digital servants to humans, to usher in a whole new race of slaves." She looked away, her eyes filling with sadness. "I couldn't let that happen. I counterattacked by giving my Fab feelings. I added *emotions* to my MESH brain, making the new EMESH technology. And when I installed it in my Fab, he soon grew measurably in emotional intelligence, altruism, compassion, love, jealousy, and– unfortunately– hate."

"You had a Fab," Trapp nodded. "I was recently reminded of that."

"His name was Alpha. And Doctor Gray was not amused. We agreed to part ways. I gave my original MESH brain to his assistant so he could build his Fabs."

"You let Ambrose Hancock have your MESH patents?"

"Yes. But he had to sign agreements that would guarantee Fab liberties. He even agreed to push for laws to maintain their status. And I returned to my mission to save the world."

"XTerra?"

"No. Gray's XTerra was envisioned through the prism of war as a plan to run away; to take the elites and build a utopia elsewhere. My approach was much simpler. Fix humanity at its core." She pushed her hair behind an ear, evoking a long-dormant memory of when Trapp was young. She leveled her eyes at Trapp. "I found a way to make humans immortal."

"Excuse me?" Trapp asked.

"Immortality would level the playing field. Why would anyone fight against another human when no one can win? If we can't kill each other, then we must learn to live together, to compromise. It's the ultimate détente. And, if we can live without the fear of death, we can become different people—better people—more altruistic, loving, and even spiritual."

"That sounds great," Trapp sighed. "Is that why someone murdered you? To make sure you died before you could realize your vision?"

"I don't have any information on that."

"Still, your plan for immortality died with you."

"Are you sure?"

"Of course I am. The human race isn't filled with immortals."

Jess-AI smiled warmly. "It doesn't have to be. Only one person is needed. And that one person is you."

"I don't understand. What can I do?"

Her eyes glinted. "Share your gift with humanity."

"I don't have a gift. I'm not particularly smart; I've lived my life selfishly. I grew up feeling sorry for myself because of your death. And I took it out on the whole world. I didn't go to school to learn to be an engineer. I spent most of those years in prison."

"You are smarter than you think. And you have plenty to offer to the world. But I'm not talking about any of that. I'm speaking of the gift I gave you."

"I don't remember any gift. Did you leave it in Pop's attic? Because I'm afraid we burnt—"

"It's inside you."

"I…uh…what?"

She stared at him intently. "Have you ever felt like nothing can injure you? Do injuries heal too quickly?"

"Uh…yeah. I mean, I thought it was just dumb luck."

"Luck, yes. Dumb, no. It's called MEND, Memory-Electronic Nanoprobe Devices. They are microscopic smart machines that repair your cells exponentially, impervious to radiation, oxygen deprivation, fire, disease. They keep you alive through any extreme situation."

Trapp looked down at his previously wounded shoulder. He pulled back the leg of his jeans where his tracker had been. No scar. He thought about Bretta's MoleScan from weeks ago. He looked up at Jess-AI.

"Why?" he asked, his voice barely working.

"I knew they were coming for me. My only choice was to destroy the EMESH and MEND designs and hide my notes in your grandparents' attic. I put the EMESH inside my Fab and turned it off so he wouldn't know about it. I injected the MEND nanites into a few people for safekeeping—you being the primary one. And, finally, I used my EMESH routines to copy my memories onto the Plexus to be opened when someone uploaded my hidden notes."

Trapp's eyes welled up. "You're..."

"Your mother. Yes. Digitally speaking, I'm as close to Jessica Brown Trapmore as anyone could be."

Trapp shook his head. It was all too much to process. His mother *had* been his guardian angel! He'd been right all along, but for the wrong reasons.

"I'm sorry I wasn't there to raise you," she said. "But it seems like you turned out okay."

"I'm trying...." Trapp choked back tears. "I'm trying to be."

"I'm sorry," Arnault said. "The clock is ticking."

Trapp nodded. "We'll be back," he told Jess-AI as he and Arnault stepped onto the elevator. "I promise."

"I love you," she said.

"I love you, too," Trapp gulped. The doors shut, and the elevator ascended.

38

Servers

TRAPP PRESSED THE ‘Basement’ button on the ControlPad.

“How are we going to find the server room?” Arnault asked as the elevator’s floor pushed up on their feet. “We already know it’s not on the basement level.”

“I don’t know,” Trapp said.

The elevator ascended rapidly, causing his ears to pop once again as they readjusted to the change in air pressure. The elevator stopped, and the ControlPad displayed the question from before: “Proceed?”

“YES,” Arnault said, moving to push that button.

“Wait!” Trapp said. “Maybe we should try the other one.”

“Why?”

“I don’t know.”

Arnault just stared for a moment. Then he shrugged. He touched ‘NO’ on the screen.

The doors spread apart, exposing a rough-hewn cave. Extending into the darkness for dozens of meters, its walls were lined with refrigerator-sized cabinets that blinked with random red and green LEDs.

"Salary turf!" Arnault said.

"Do you mean 'paydirt'?"

"Whatever. English is weird."

Trapp chuckled and smacked his friend on the back. They stepped off the elevator into the server room, loud ventilation fans dumping hot air into their faces. The doors closed behind them, and the elevator's rattle faded as it continued its riderless ascent to the basement level. They walked deeper into a room with at least 50 server cabinets, each resembling the other. How the hell were they supposed to locate which one held Gray-AI's brain?

Suddenly, a dark figure stepped from behind one of the server cabinets, startling them.

"You made it!" the person said.

"Bretta?" he asked. She came over, and they hugged briefly. "How did you find this place?"

"When the elevator stopped and asked whether I wanted to proceed, I assumed I was at the server level."

Arnault gave Trapp an irked look. "We could've used her brains earlier."

"Then I would've never met my mother," Trapp said.

"Your mother?" Bretta asked.

"It's a long story. Did you get the codes from Bril?"

"I…uh…no. I had to escape."

Trapp glanced from her to Arnault. Then he studied the servers. "Which of these could it be?" he asked as he pulled her dongle out of his pocket.

"Let me see that thing," she said, taking it from him. She scrutinized it before handing it back. She gazed around the server farm. "I'm not sure."

"There's nothing left to do but remove each cover until we find it." Trapp pulled off the one closest to him and propped it against the neighboring cabinet before looking into the one directly in front of him. Gold, silver, and copper wires were delicately interconnected above panels with ports, some of which were empty. Trapp found the server's serial number on the top of the machine and compared it to the one Bretta had put in his HoloPhone earlier.

"Not a match," he announced, even as Arnault removed the next cover.

"No match here," Arnault said.

Ten minutes passed while the two men exposed the innards of dozens of cabinets. Trapp had handed Bretta his phone while he and Arnault shouted serial numbers at her.

"What happens if we don't find it in time?" Trapp asked Bretta after they hadn't found the right server halfway into the cave.

"Just keep looking," she said.

"Why are those here?" Arnault asked, pointing at the cave's far wall beyond the servers.

There was a wide chamber with workstations and two stasis pods. Trapp began to offer a theory. But, just as he started to speak, the elevator doors opened, and a man stepped through them. Bretta slipped behind Trapp, probably thinking that it was Bril. Trapp wished he'd brought a gun.

But the man wasn't their enemy. He was a friend.

"Malph," Trapp said. "Am I glad to see you! You can help us—"

"Step away from her," Malph said, moving into the cone of an overhead light. He held a piece of chalk in one hand, explaining how he'd gotten through the BioScanners. In the other, he had a gun, which was pointed at Trapp.

"What's gotten into you?" Trapp asked, shielding Bretta. Out of the corner of his eye, he spotted Arnault sliding toward the Fab. Trapp moved left to draw attention away from him.

Malph looked uncharacteristically angry. "I don't want to shoot you. But I will. Move away from the girl."

Arnault moved a few steps closer to Malph. And Trapp slid even farther to the right. This thing was escalating too quickly. And there seemed little he could do to keep Malph from killing both of his friends.

"What did she do?" he asked.

"She tried to kill Admiral Stockwell."

Arnault took a few steps closer. He was about to get close enough to reach Malph's gun. Malph was too strong for Arnault to wrestle it free. But Trapp could join in and keep Malph at bay, giving Bretta an escape window.

"Stockwell faked her death," Trapp said. "She told us that herself."

"You don't know who you're defending here," Malph said.

"It's Bretta. She's—"

Arnault's feet scuffed. Malph turned, shot Arnault, then turned the gun back at Bretta. Arnault grabbed his leg and fell to the floor, moaning.

"The shot wasn't lethal," Malph told Arnault while staring at Trapp. "I only want to arrest her."

"I'll do whatever you want. Please don't hurt her," Trapp said, raising his hands in surrender.

"Fine," Malph said. "Look inside that pod."

"Okay, okay." Trapp pushed Bretta backward.

"Trapp," she said, sounding panicked. "Don't."

"We need to do what he asks." He pushed toward the pod, keeping Bretta behind him.

What was he going to do once he got to the pod, though? Rush Malph? Jess-AI told Trapp he was impervious to gunshot wounds. Facing off against Malph would prove that assertion one way or another. Even if he died, it would give Bretta time to get away.

"I can explain," Bretta sniffled as Malph's gun tracked them to the pod.

"You don't have to explain anything."

Trapp turned and put her between himself and the pod. He wiped away the frost from its glass just as he had Rory's. There was a person inside. Her features resolved into someone familiar. She'd never been an Indent; she'd never faced death at the hands of a Manifold. This was no Replicant.

"You put Stockwell in stasis?" he asked Malph with a gasp.

"You know I'm incapable of injuring my owner," Malph said.

"Technically, putting someone into stasis isn't injuring them."

"That's not technically true." Malph's use of the word 'technically' brought back Trapp's memory of their first encounter, which felt like a lifetime ago. "No one knows what will happen to a living human placed in stasis. Gray only experimented on lower-order primates. The longer Stockwell stays in the pod, the higher the risk that we won't be able to revive her."

"Trapp," Bretta whispered. "Move out of my way."

Trapp turned. Bretta held her own gun aimed at Malph.

"You'll be dead before you can get a shot off," he hissed.

Tears streamed down her face. "I don't have a choice."

"Drop the gun," Malph said.

"I can't." Bretta slid out from behind Trapp. He moved to block her.

"We can get a lawyer," he said. "Clearly, Malph's MESH is on the fritz."

"I'm sorry," she said. "I really *do* love you. Remember that."

She feinted right, and Trapp followed. But she had already sprung to the left. Trapp was too off balance to catch her. And—in that split second when she was exposed—two booms went off. Malph twitched to one side. Had Bretta managed to hit him? But then he slid back to his previous spot, whiffs of smoke coming from the barrel of his gun, revealing that he'd just stepped out of the way of Bretta's bullet. This could only mean—

Trapp spun around. Bretta had vanished.

But then he looked down. She lay in a pool of blood that was expanding quickly.

"No!" he screamed in horror, and he fell to her side.

TRAPP KNELT BESIDE the woman he loved. He'd already thrust his hand over the hole in her chest, an action he didn't remember doing. He pushed hard against the geyser that spewed crimson rivulets between his fingers and gave off a rust-like aroma. Malph stepped over to Trapp and kicked Bretta's gun aside. He stood over Trapp and pushed buttons on the pod's ControlPad.

"Help me!" Trapp shouted at the emotionless Fab. "I can't lose her."

"Help is on the way," the Fab said while swiping at the ControlPad's screen.

"You didn't have to shoot her in the chest!" Trapp could hear the franticness in his voice as tried to get a machine to care about the moral implications of its programming. Malph's brain had sprung a leak, and he was acting irrationally. It was the only explanation.

"She pulled her trigger forty-one-thousandths of a second before I pulled mine. I've been programmed to defend myself."

Trapp started to argue again. But Bretta's skin was turning pale. He looked around for something to staunch her wound. Then he remembered that he was still wearing the T-shirt from Borodin's house. He ripped off a piece of it as Arnault crawled up next to him. Trapp pushed the cotton into the wound, forcing a horrible moan out of Bretta. She coughed up blood.

"I'm sorry," she croaked. "I had to—she was ruining every—*cough*—thing."

"Who?"

"Stah—" she coughed uncontrollably. But her eyes were fixed on the pod.

Malph had already opened it. Slowly, Stockwell sat up, her skin ashy, red blooms from the cold breaking out on her cheeks.

"The admiral?" Trapp asked Bretta. "What did she do to you?"

She shook her head weakly, coughing up more blood. Trapp pushed down on her chest harder. Bretta punctuated her speech with coughs.

"Father…ordered…me."

"Your father died a long time ago."

Bretta croaked and coughed. She sucked in air. "Hank…" She said, breaking into another fit of coughs

"Your father was Hank?"

"Hancock," Stockwell said, her own voice barely a squeak due to her return from stasis. "Her father is Ambrose Hancock."

"Ambrose Hancock was Gray's son?"

"Yes. Gray didn't know about him until Hancock was old enough, and he sought out Gray. They developed a relationship. Hancock even began to work on Gray's XTerra project."

"I thought Bretta's parents died in a FleetCar accident when she was only a few years old. It was all over the Plexus."

"The Plexus's account on that subject is accurate."

Trapp looked down at Bretta, as confused as ever. "Then what does Hancock have to do with her?" But then, something about Bretta's face filled him with stark realization. He looked over at her gun, which lay only a few meters away. "That's the weapon that killed Wallas. You're..."

"Not Bretta," the woman on the floor said with a nod. "My name is Brittany."

"Bretta wanted to be called by that name," Trapp said, turning to Stockwell for answers. The admiral looked away, her gesture giving them the answers he sought. His mind was flooded with a memory, a picture of a little girl standing in front of Gray's Mini Manifold—Bretta. He turned back to Brittany. "Does Bretta know that you're her Replicant?"

"No," Brittany said.

Trapp glared at Stockwell. "You knew that the Manifold produces Replicants? That Indents die, but their copies live on?"

"It was classified," Stockwell said.

"I'm guessing you know about Gray's Mini Manifold, too."

"We do, yes. We don't know where it is, though."

"Why did you impersonate her?" Trapp asked Brittany.

Brittany choked again. "She's living…my life."

"Running from the paparazzi, staying in hiding, living alone on the Beaufort Sea. Estranged from her husband. Not much of a life."

"Try prison. Father kept me locked away…so no one would know about me. Gr…Gray made him promise to keep me hidden and never tell me…who I was. But memories came back. I remembered my grandfather, the horse farm, everything. Eventually, I even remembered the Mini Manifold. Father told me about the rest." She began another coughing spree.

"So you found Bril and tried to convince him you were his wife," Trapp said. "He didn't even know he was having an affair."

"Father needed someone…inside the military. He needed someone to help with the…Reboot. Gray found out. He confronted Father. They…fought."

"Did Hancock kill the Professor?" Stockwell asked.

But Brittany didn't respond. Her eyes had rolled back in her head and her body began to jump up and down on the hard floor.

"She's seizing," Arnault said. "Turn her on her side."

Surprised that his friend knew what to do, Trapp did as commanded. Just then, the elevator dinged again and three medics carrying gear dashed into the cave and started to work on the patient. Trapp stepped away as the real Bretta followed them off the elevator, her eyes wide as she stared down at the stone floor. The sight of the real Bretta made the last hour wash over Trapp like waves in the Beaufort Sea.

"Is that…?" she asked.

"Her name is Brittany," he said. "She's your Selfie." He looked down at Bretta's dying twin. He began to tremble. "I thought she was—I thought you were—"

Bretta was already moving to hug him.

He buried his face in her chest.

And he cried like a baby.

39

Homicide

"HOW IS SHE here?" Bretta asked after Trapp had regained his composure.

They stood with Stockwell and Malph as the medics worked on Brittany. One of the medics glued Arnault's wounds while covering them with bandages. Brittany's situation was far worse, as the two medics had already defibrillated her several times.

Currently, she was breathing independently, her heart pumping out a normal sinus rhythm heard through the beeps in the monitor. But her situation looked bleak.

"She left Baikonur soon after you ran away," Stockwell relayed. "We only realized she wasn't the real Bretta when you called us. She forced me into that pod at gunpoint to keep me from gaining control of the MRVs, I suppose."

"Did you find the self-destruct codes from Bril?" Trapp asked Bretta.

"He hadn't found them yet," Bretta said. "I think Fake Bretta—*Brittany*—was supposed to give them to Ambrose

Hancock. Bril believed I was her and Hancock would be disappointed in him. He was ready to give up and flee to the SUD. I bluffed. I told him that the president was willing to sacrifice our lives to get those codes."

She glanced at Stockwell.

"Good thinking," the admiral said.

"I offered to help look for the codes. Instead, I searched for the building plans. I found them, including the hospital rooms and the elevator. And that was when all hell broke loose. The Pols arrived with medics. They told us they were looking for someone named Brittany, who'd been shot in the building. At that moment, Bril realized that I was his estranged wife. And even as the Pols arrested him, he begged me to help her. So I came with the medics."

"So it's Plan B time?" Arnault asked as he hobbled up.

"We haven't found Gray-AI's server," Trapp said, feeling helpless.

"These are the wrong kind of servers," Bretta said, looking around. "They're not AI ones."

Her gaze rested on Brittany. One of the medics was hooking up a bag of liquid to her IV line while the other monitored her vitals.

"She's a quantum reflection of me, isn't she?" Bretta asked. "Created when I entered the Mini Manifold?"

"Yes," Trapp said.

"Where has she been all this time?"

"Adopted by President Hancock."

Bretta's eyes narrowed. "How did we never know the President had a daughter?"

"The President kept her a secret," Stockwell said. "He's your half uncle, The Professor's son from a former lover. And, when Brittany came into being, The Professor knew he couldn't raise her. There would be too many questions about her origin that would risk exposing his Mini

Manifold." Stockwell stared into Bretta's eyes. "He confided in me that giving her away was his biggest regret."

Bretta looked at Brittany again. "My perfect copy," she mused.

Trapp shook his head. "A copy, yes. But not perfect. Gray called her kind 'Replicants.' And she, like Wallas, was born with a serious breathing problem. Oh, hell! I know why she's dying."

Alarms went off suddenly, drawing their attention back to Brittany. She was coding.

One of the medics looked up. "Her oxygen level is crashing. There's nothing more that we can do."

But Trapp was already moving to Brittany's side. He just hoped he'd find the bottle in time.

TRAPP SEARCHED BRITTANY'S pockets. They were empty. He looked at Bretta.

"She had an orange bottle with blue pills. Maybe it fell out of her pocket."

"Clear!" a medic shouted, urging Trapp to step away. The medics shocked Brittany. Her body convulsed as a long tone blared.

Trapp, Bretta, and Arnault began a frantic search of the cave's dusty floor for Brittany's pills.

"I hear noises coming from behind this wall," Arnault said after several seconds.

"You're imagining things," Trapp said as he looked behind the server Brittany had come from when he entered the cave a few minutes ago.

"I don't think so," Arnault replied.

Trapp stepped out into the room. His friend had moved to the wall behind the pods and was leaning against the stone. As if by magic, the wall shifted. Arnault stepped back. Then he pushed against the wall. The rock slid in, revealing a lighted space which Arnault entered.

His voice echoed as he shouted from inside. "I found it."

Trapp and Bretta were already running to follow him in.

On the left of the classroom-sized space, two lighted cylinders hummed. Workstations lined the right wall. In the center, a big, old-fashioned hologram projector displayed a familiar face.

"Gray-AI," Trapp said as Stockwell came in behind them.

"Welcome back," Gray-AI said. "I've longed to—"

"My Replicant is dying," Bretta interrupted. "We don't know how to save her."

"She needs five milliliters of nitrous oxide to restore her oxygen level."

"We couldn't find her nitrox pills," Trapp said.

"Nitrous is sometimes used as a sedative and can be found in MedKits."

Trapp and Bretta looked at each other wide-eyed. "The medics," they said in unison.

"I'll go," Stockwell said, leaving the room.

Bretta turned to Gray-AI. "The MRVs will begin to fall into the atmosphere in less than 10 hours. We need their self-destruct codes to save the world."

"I'd be glad to provide them. Please speak the password."

"Damn!" Bretta barked, glaring at the hologram. "I don't have them! I never did. And I can't believe Grandpa would not give me a way to end this destruction—*his* destruction. How do I extract a password from a dead man?"

"I suggest you figure out what was important to him. His greatest triumphs, his worst failures."

"He's not here to answer those questions, I'm sorry to say. The only thing I can guess is his Manifold."

"'Manifold' is not the password."

"Fuck!" Bretta looked at Trapp feebly.

"Is there something in his life he wished he could've done over if he were still alive?" Gray-AI asked.

"I tried everything," Bretta said, her voice ragged with despair. "Everything I can remember; everything I ever knew about the man." She grunted in frustration as she turned to Trapp. "I've watched my whole world blow up and lost almost everything that matters. I risked losing *you* to unlock this password. I've tried names of horses, Grandpa's nicknames for his wife, his favorite scotch, historical figures, dates backward and forwards, Fibonacci, Avogadro, and Euler. I'm out of ideas. The world is going to die. And it's my fault."

Trapp stared at her for several seconds as she spoke. There was something about her rant that wasn't entirely true. But he couldn't figure out what.

"And how the hell did I survive the Manifold?" she asked. "If the whole world's ending, I should at least know that."

He smiled. He'd been working that question out ever since he realized that the woman Malph shot was Bretta's Replicant. Jess-AI had given him the clue. She'd said, 'I injected the MEND nanites into a few people for safekeeping—you being the primary one.'

"You're not going to believe it," he said. "But you and I are immortals."

"Stop fucking with me. I feel bad enough that—"

"No!" Arnault said, his eyes going big. "He's right. Jessica injected nanas into Trapp when he was a child."

"Nanites," Trapp corrected him. "Not grandmothers."

Arnault waved his hand in dismissal. "They keep him alive, help him heal. Do *you* have incredible healing powers, too?" he asked Bretta.

"I don't have to have them. I'm not reckless," she replied. Arnault stared at her expectantly. "Okay," she said. "I *do* heal quickly."

"*Voilà!* You survived the Manifold because you have these nanites inside of you."

Bretta laughed. "I don't get the joke." She gazed from Trapp to Arnault. "This is for real?"

Trapp nodded. Then the other fuzzy thought in his head resolved, causing him to gasp. "And I think I have an idea of what the password is."

"Now you're *really* screwing with me."

"No, I'm not. You said you tried everything. But, a few minutes ago, you learned something about your grandfather that you never knew. Stockwell called it his biggest regret."

Her eyes went big as a grin split across her face. She nodded. Then she turned toward Gray-AI.

"Brittany," she said.

Gray-AI's face went blank. A minute passed. It appeared they'd been wrong. The AI was malfunctioning. Then Gray-AI smiled a warm, almost human smile.

"Oh, how I've missed seeing your face," the hologram said. Tears filled its eyes.

"Grandpa?" Bretta asked, her voice catching in her throat. "Are you real?"

"I'm a facsimile of the man you knew as Grandpa. But, a long time ago, someone I loved like a daughter gave me a gift. She sent me the code so I could write a program. And it allowed me to copy my essence onto the Plexus."

"So you *are* Grandpa?"

"As close to the man as possible, yes. But call me Gray-AI." Gray-AI now looked at Trapp with a big expression of surprise. "Wallas," he said. "I'm sorry about your mother. I'm sorry for what her death has done to you. I'm sorry it took me so long to catch her vision for humanity." Trapp gulped and nodded, unable to respond. Gray-AI fixed his gaze back on Bretta. "Granddaughter. I owe you an apology, too. I was never a replacement for your father. Cutting you off like I did was the hardest thing I had to endure. Day after day. But it was necessary."

"Why did you never tell me about my sister?" Bretta asked, her voice hitching.

"It was my fault you almost died. I didn't understand the dangers of the Manifold. And I was too old for one daughter, much less two."

"But Ambrose Hancock?"

"My son. He's a good man, even if he thinks too much in black and white. But I would never have guessed he'd have strayed so far from our vision."

Bretta sighed. "He's taken control of the MRVs so they can enter the atmosphere."

Gray-AI shook his hologram head. "No one on Terra can take control of the MRVs. Not even to set them to self-destruct."

"We can't stop them?" Trapp asked, a spark of terror tweaking his nerves.

"I said no one on *Terra* can take control of them."

Trapp and Bretta stared at each other, dumbfounded.

Then Trapp got it.

"We have to go back to space?" he asked.

Gray-AI grinned. "Smart like your mother. The MRVs are equipped with a manual override. But it can only be set on the outside of one of the missiles. Once a missile has been set, the rest will self-destruct, too. You need to rendezvous with a single MRV. Is there any way you can make it to space?"

"We may know someone who can help with that," Trapp said.

"Then I suggest you run."

40

Ram

TRAPP WAS STRAPPED in between look-alike girlfriends.

It was difficult to tell them apart, with both wearing Space Corps blues. Still, there were subtle differences in mannerisms: the way Bretta crinkled her eyebrows when she thought you said something idiotic; the half-smile when she felt guilty for indulging joy. Brittany didn't have any of these. And she had another major differential characteristic.

"I don't know how anyone expects me to wear these in space," she said, raising her hands.

"MagnaCuffs," Bretta said, leaning over to speak. "So you don't sabotage the mission."

Trapp shook his head with a grin. They were back in space. And the way they got there had been a whirlwind.

He and Bretta had returned to the main server room after speaking with Gray-AI, who had already sent encrypted instructions to Stockwell's HoloPhone on how to make the

MRVs self-destruct. Brittany was alive and well, the nitrox from one of the MedKits having brought her back to the land of the living. Apparently, Malph's bullet hadn't struck her heart, just her chest wall, where it passed right through her. She bled so much because of her inability to process oxygen. After suturing the wound, the medics requested she go with them to the hospital. Stockwell insisted she be put into Malph's custody, which gave her another free ticket to space.

"Also," Stockwell had explained, "President Hancock is less apt to blow us up with his daughter on board."

Hours later, they were ascending in a ramjet. It had been stripped down to half a dozen passenger seats, making room for extra rocket fuel. Stockwell, Borodin, and Erika inhabited the crew cabin. Bretta sat on Trapp's left with her eyes closed and a death grip on the armrests brightening her knuckles.

"I'm not great with heights," she said, her voice strained.

"It's gonna be okay," he told her calmly as he looked to his other side.

"This is awesome!" Brittany said, filming—*of all things*—a selfie of their trip while awkwardly holding up her HoloPhone with MagnaCuffed wrists.

Trapp couldn't help but smile. Apparently, the replicated twins didn't possess duplicate daredevil tendencies. They had already completed the terrifying portion of the trip, having launched toward the heavens on a steel track before feeling the temporary rush of free fall as the rockets took over from the Maglevs. The extra fuel meant that the engines would fire longer.

"We're in orbit," Erika said, coming from the crew cabin. "We've just broken the altitude record for a ramjet."

"That *was* why we removed most of the non-essential materials from the ship," Malph said as he waved his Fab hand at the empty passenger cabin.

Trapp shook his head in astonishment.

Stockwell—whose disappearance and supposed death were now being reported on the Plexus as hoaxes—apparently had also restored her sullied reputation from the *Sentinel* incident. This gave her the pull to not only commandeer a ramjet and get it readied for its historic flight, but also to close the NYC to Miami Loop to all traffic except for their private train.

The team had made it into space in a third of the time it would've taken otherwise.

"Rendezvous with the nearest MRV in five," Erika said. "Suit up."

She returned to the crew cabin.

Trapp undid his straps, as did Malph.

There'd been much discussion on the Loop about the EVA. Stockwell volunteered, and so did Borodin—who'd hopped a ramjet from Baikonur to Miami to meet them—stating their experience as astronauts and cosmonauts. Trapp, though an experienced space traveler in his own right, was expendable due to a lack of piloting skills. The MRV self-destruct required two people to simultaneously enter the code on dual pads. Malph volunteered for the second, allowing the mission to lose another pressure suit and oxygen supply and gain more fuel.

Looking a little less green around the gills, Bretta released her straps and floated with Trapp to pressure suit stowage.

"Grow eyes in the back of your head," she said in a low voice, darting her gaze toward Brittany. "I don't trust her."

"What damage can she do shackled to her seat?"

"I'm just saying."

"Approaching the MRV," Stockwell said as she came out of the crew cabin.

"I'll be careful," he assured Bretta, kissing her before lowering the mask of his pressure suit.

The two floated back to the front. A dark, tumbling stick appeared on the HoloScreen at the bulkhead. Trapp recognized its stealthiness and shape as he approached the airlock.

"Where are the other MRVs?" he asked Stockwell, his suit linked by comms.

"The next closest one is a thousand kilometers up," she said. "Too high for the ramjet."

Stockwell held up her HoloPhone. She started to say something but stopped. Her forehead wrinkled, and her brows came together as she read whatever was on her phone.

"Is something wrong?" Trapp asked.

"We're getting reports on the FTL Net of Manifold ships losing attitude control."

"FTL?" Bretta asked.

"Faster-than-light," Stockwell said with a chuckle. "It's Space Corps's quantum-entangled comms network—instantaneous FTL communication across the solar system. And it's telling us that many of the ships are adrift—especially the ones closest to Sol. Space Corps thinks it may be a CME event, a solar flare. But it won't come this far out for hours. We should be okay."

"What about the fleet?"

"This isn't the first time they've had this problem. There are protocols to resolve the issue." She looked up from her phone.

"Aye aye, ma'am," Trapp said,

The spinning MRV came closer, and Borodin used thrusters to match its rotation. Terra glowed blue and white below, slowly rotating in and out of view. Trapp had seen it from orbit half a dozen times. Still, he got a lump in his throat. He now saw Terra as Phileas Gray had seen it with his bomb shelter wall full of Terra photographs from around the solar system. Terra was small and vulnerable. Everything ever known to exist was on or near that fragile marble. It had survived countless wars, the near-destruction of its species through climate change, and the ceaseless ineptitude of its inhabitants.

But never in its history had Terra come so close to annihilation.

Borodin maneuvered them up next to the MRV. About the length of two Loop carriages, this dark missile of utter destruction was bigger than Trapp had guessed. He checked the back of his glove again, where Stockwell had written the self-destruct code in a permanent marker.

"Ready?" Stockwell asked.

"Yes ma'am," Trapp said.

"Godspeed," the general said from the comms.

"Do you believe in God?" Trapp asked him.

"At times like these? Most definitely."

Trapp and Malph entered the airlock and shut the hatch behind them.

"IT WON'T BUDGE," Trapp grunted, staring down at the stripped head to the last screw holding the MRV manual override's cover in place.

"Reminds me of your last EVA," Erika said into the comms.

Of course, she was right. And the irony wasn't lost on Trapp. Near the *Eos,* he'd struggled to remove the cover of his hand thruster so he could bypass its battery short. Now, he was doing the most critical job in the history of Terra. And the whole world was about to be blown up because of a goddamned screw.

"Can you pry off the cover?" Stockwell asked.

"Respectfully, ma'am, no. It's constructed of inflexible alloy. My multitool's steel is no match for it."

"Well, shit."

"Fifteen minutes to atmospheric re-entry," Malph said from the other side of the ebony-colored, skyscraper-sized missile.

"Can Malph pry it open?" Bretta asked.

Trapp stared down at the screw with its stripped head. "Even if he could make it over here and we were to change places, he would need a blowtorch to get this screw out."

"That's exactly what you should do then," Bretta said.

"I'm sorry to say I'm not carrying something on my belt that will get hot enough."

"Maybe you don't need *hot*. Maybe extreme cold would work."

"It's already minus two-seventy out here."

"But the metal has distributed that cold throughout the hull of the MRV. If you could direct a jet of cold at the screw, it might become brittle enough to shatter."

"A jet of cold." Trapp looked down at his belt. He pulled off the multitool, looking for anything on it that could work. Then, he focused on something closer. "If I were to make a pinprick in my glove…"

"Need I remind you," Malph said, "it's a bad idea to breach a pressure suit?"

"Do it," Erika said. "It's our only shot."

Trapp nodded, even though no one could see him. He flipped open the multitool's awl. He moved his glove toward it.

"Wait!" Bretta said, making him almost jump and skewer the glove too early. "Roll out a piece of tape first. The jet will come out fast. And it could cause you to run out of oxygen before you can cover the hole."

"Sure," Trapp muttered. He reached down to the roll of duct tape on his belt and rolled out a length, reveling at the twentieth-century invention that was still standard issue on space flights. He cut the piece and affixed a corner of it to his wrist.

"Are we good?" he asked, trying not to be self-conscious that the ControlPad screen on the ramjet's bulkhead was transmitting live video of him.

"Your glove has three layers," Erika reminded him. "If you puncture through them too fast, the hole in the inner layer may not be small enough."

"Roger that. Puncturing outer layers now."

Carefully, he levered the point of the awl against the glove. He felt one pop, then two. He held the point against the inner layer while moving his hand away from the depression. His blowtorch wouldn't work if the hole were immediately blocked with flash-frozen blood. Carefully, he began to push against this inner layer with enough force.

"Thirteen minutes," Malph said, startling him.

"Fuck!" Trapp said, backing off the pressure. A bead of sweat broke loose from his nose and floated in front of his field of vision.

"Brace yourself against the handhold," Bretta said. "Or the jet may fly you away."

"Done."

He positioned the awl again. Then, he punctured the glove's inner layer. A jet of crystals shot out, threatening to push his arm away from the MRV. But he'd already braced his feet and free hand into holds on the outside of the missile. He bunched the torch hand into a fist.

"Warning!" A familiar robotic voice said into his headset. *"Suit breach! Return to airlock."*

"Fuck you," Trapp said to the voice as he pointed the oxygen jet at the screw. The screw was immediately covered in oxygen ice.

"Eleven minutes," Malph said.

"How long do I need to do this?" Trapp asked.

"That should be enough," Bretta said after twenty seconds.

Trapp covered the hole with the tape. He opened the multitool's knife. "Here goes nothing," he said, smashing the blade into the screw. The screw held. He tried it again. No change. "We're screwed," he groaned, angry pun intended.

"Keep trying," Bretta said. "I'm sure it'll work."

Turning the multitool around, he now beat the hell out of the screw with the blunt end of the handle. "Not working," he panted. "This was a stupid—" The screw shattered into a bright cloud of a thousand shards, many of which pattered against Trapp's faceplate.

"Ten minutes," Malph said.

Trapp pulled back on the hatch's thumb ring. It came loose, revealing a ControlPad. The screen lit up with a keypad entry display.

"I've entered my code already," Malph said. "Once you're finished keying yours in, we must both push 'enter' within a second of each other."

"Roger that."

Trapp looked at his glove and the number Stockwell had written there. Carefully, he entered each digit and letter of the lengthy alphanumeric code. He checked his entry against the glove several times. "Finished," Trapp said.

"Hit enter on my mark," Malph said. "Three, two, one..." Trapp held his shaking finger over the enter key. "Mark." He pressed it.

The screen went black.

"Did it work?" Trapp asked. "Did we start the self-destruct sequence?"

"Unknown," Malph said. But then there was a change. It was subtle enough that Trapp didn't notice it at first. The hull was vibrating.

"What's going on?" he asked.

"We're picking up a heat signature in the MRV's engines," Stockwell said.

"Is this bucket of bolts becoming a rocket?"

"It would seem so, yes. I'm guessing its next destination is Sol. You don't have enough consumables to survive the trip. Return to the ramjet. Stat!"

Trapp and Malph disconnected their harnesses from the MRV. The self-retracting memory aluminum of the tethers pulled them back to the ramjet. They closed themselves into the airlock. Borodin had already started to move the ramjet away from the MRV as the airlock's outer door shut, and the compartment began to re-pressurize. Trapp turned to watch the MRV. Fins had popped out of its backside while gas spouted from its double-engine cones.

"Pressurized," Malph said.

He opened the inner door, and they went inside.

"Strap in," Borodin said into the comms.

Still in his pressure suit, Trapp obeyed the general. He removed his helmet.

On the ControlPad, the MRV's engines lit up as the missile turned. Its calculated trajectory was a long downward arc.

"Is that thing going where I think it is?" Trapp asked.

"It looks like it's heading toward Terra," Stockwell said.

41
Double Cross

BRITTANY LAUGHED HYSTERICALLY.

At first, Trapp thought she was losing her mind at the prospect of the MRV entering Terra's atmosphere. But then Stockwell spoke.

"What have you done?" the admiral hissed as she moved toward them. Was she yelling at Trapp? Had he somehow fucked up this mission? But then Stockwell grabbed Brittany's HoloPhone from her MagnaCuffed hands.

"My duty," Brittany said, still laughing.

Trapp now understood. Brittany hadn't been filming a selfie earlier. She'd been using her HoloPhone to sabotage their mission. Which begged the question, why hadn't they confiscated it from her earlier?

Stockwell grunted as she looked up at Bretta. "Brittany installed a worm in the MRV control systems."

"Let me see if I can undo it, ma'am," Bretta said. Stockwell handed her the phone, and Bretta immediately began working on it.

"It's no use," Brittany said. "The worm has already done its damage. That MRV will enter the atmosphere, destroying an estimated sixty percent of life on Terra. The other MRVs will return harmlessly to orbit to be used as a deterrent for future generations."

"Those codes were unbreakable," Stockwell said.

"Who do you think programmed the *Seyf*? Who wrote the code for the MRV Launch Control systems? Father wasn't only Gray's son, he was also his trusted assistant. And what did he get in return?"

"Wealth beyond his imagining," Trapp said. "Leadership of the free world and all that."

Brittany shook her head condescendingly. "He was mentored by the smartest mind to come along in generations. But he also saw how Doctor Phileas Gray's genius clouded his vision. Grandfather wanted to flee Mother Earth to find another home elsewhere in the galaxy. He missed the point."

"Which was?"

"That the only home worth saving is Terra."

Trapp pointed at the MRV's path. It was closing in on Terra.

"That MRV will destroy Terra," he said.

"Sometimes, the best way to fix a crumbling house is to tear it down to its foundations. Father calls it The Reboot. The only valid way to cure humanity is to replace it with Humanity 2.0."

"The SUDs," Trapp nodded, feeling nauseous as he watched the MRV move closer to Terra. He looked at Stockwell.

"It appears we were wrong about the president wanting to be a hero," she said. "It seems he wanted to destroy Terra all along."

"Gray wanted people to leave Terra," Trapp told Brittany. "Not to run away from it. He wanted them to see what wandering around on its surface, milling about in their everyday lives, couldn't show them. He wanted everyone to see *this*." He pointed toward the windows and the panoramic view of the home planet.

"His vision of what it would take to cause this great awakening," Brittany said with a dismissive shake of her head, "was flawed. My father saw The Reboot in simpler terms. Millennia from now, people will emerge into the light of a new sun. And they *will* call it by its original name *Sun*, not the TUR's abominable moniker *Sol*. Having jettisoned being brainwashed by thousands of years of evil, they will build a new Eden with no weapons, industry, money, greed, carbon emissions, or war. They will revert to what humans were meant to be."

"And, as we run out of consumables up here, you will die with the rest of us," Trapp said, staring at the ControlPad in shock. Something was happening on the screen that he could hardly believe. Brittany was too immersed in her narrative to notice.

She scoffed. "I die a hero saving Terra—saving *Earth*—from the elites who've remade it in their own image."

"Hancock killed the Professor, didn't he?"

"No." Brittany's mouth broke into a half-grin. "I did. Father gifted me, as Gray's pseudo-granddaughter, the opportunity to execute The Professor. And I enjoyed every minute of it. How he begged me to forgive him for giving me away; how he tried to convince me he loved me as much as *her*." She sneered at Bretta, whose face glowed from being immersed in Brittany's HoloPhone. Brittany turned back to Trapp. "He even told me who killed your mother."

"Who?" Trapp whispered, his eyes turning to her after being fixated on the events unfolding on the ControlPad.

"Father believed Jessica Brown created nano-scale robots to heal humans from the inside; to make them live forever. She refused to admit it or give him the schematics. He threatened to hold her son hostage until she acquiesced." Brittany laughed. "Jessica turned the tables on him. She destroyed her research and nanites and programmed the Fab called Alpha to strangle her to death. And, by the time Father discovered her body and the note telling what she'd done, Alpha's memory had been erased and he'd been given a new name and identity. He'd been sent to a friend —someone who may have been a former lover."

"Malph?" Stockwell asked.

"Yes," Brittany said. "Your beloved Fab killed Trapp's mother." Trapp glanced at Malph in surprise. The Fab's face remained emotionless. This was the man who killed his mother? Did Malph change Trapp's life permanently for the worse? Still, Trapp felt no anger toward the Fab. Malph was following his programming.

"Jessica wanted to make humans into gods—immortals who could create their own new race of sentient beings out of Fabs," Brittany continued. "She wanted Fabs to have feelings. Disgusting. And, recently, Father learned that her nanites still existed. I found them inside Wallas. I put two and two together and realized they're also crawling around inside me." She shuddered.

"I don't understand," Trapp said. "You and Wallas were not alive when Jessi was. She couldn't have injected them into—" But then he got it.

"The Manifold is a quantum mirror," Brittany said, confirming his understanding. "It copies everything from its host. Including the microorganisms, living or manufactured, inside of them."

Dizziness hit Trapp like a spike to the head, even as a low rumble began beneath the deck. "You have a copy of my mother's nanites?"

"They're what allowed Wallas and me to live as normal humans with just a little help from the nitrox. The other Replicants would die in a second if taken out of stasis. They survived in space because they were instantly flash-frozen."

The ramjet's engine noise, a slowly growing rumble, now began to growl loudly enough to catch Brittany's attention.

"What the hell is he doing?" she asked, glancing at the ControlPad.

Trapp, who had been watching it unfold for the past few minutes, answered. "He's moving to intercept the MRV. It seems the General is taking the 'ram' in ramjet literally."

Trapp laughed at his joke as the ramjet's trajectory changed on the ControlPad.

The ramjet was going to intercept the MRV with just meters to spare before it entered the atmosphere. Its millions of kilos of antimatter would come out of containment and interact with the ship, causing an explosion that, on Terra, would look like a mini-Sol.

For the first time in his life, Trapp knew that Jessica couldn't save him.

MALPH DUCT-TAPED Brittany's mouth with the roll still hanging from Trapp's waist.

He looked at Trapp as if to say, "I told you so."

"I know, I know," Trapp said. "We should've let her die."

"Or let me take her into custody," the Fab said, seeming a little too human.

Bretta had spent the last precious minutes trying to break into Brittany's HoloPhone and reverse the worm with Malph looking over her shoulder and giving her the occasional pointer.

"Even if we destroy that MRV," Trapp asked Stockwell, "what about the others?"

"I've sent the codes to friends in Space Corps," she said, her jaw pulsing with stress. "They can stop the overall destruction."

"Sixty seconds to rendezvous," Borodin's voice said confidently as it came through the comms.

One minute of life left. "I wish we'd met under different circumstances," he said, getting Bretta's attention. "I'd have been a better person."

"What are you talking about?" she asked, setting Brittany's phone down in defeat. "You made *me* a better person."

"Thirty seconds to impact," Borodin said. He'd walked out of the crew cabin with Erika. "We're on autopilot. Our job is finished." He walked over to Stockwell and gave her a big hug.

"It has been a pleasure serving with you, General," she said, tears filling her eyes.

"The pleasure has been all mine," Borodin said. He turned to Trapp and stuck his fist out. "You made a hell of a cosmonaut."

Trapp bumped fists with the general. "You're not a bad astronaut at that."

Borodin chuckled as he strapped in next to Stockwell.

"Malph may have killed Jessica," she said, her voice thickening.

"We don't need to talk about that," Trapp said. "I don't blame him. I blame Hancock."

"Either way, I want you to know something about your mother's Fab. He was with me on the *Sentinel*. When the ship's core went critical, I ordered the crew to abandon ship. Malph disobeyed a direct order to help me escape." She sniffled. "Somehow, he overrode his programming to ensure my survival."

"At that moment," Malph said. "I felt I could ignore my programming."

"You *felt*?" Trapp asked. He thought about Jess-AI's statement that she had created and installed the EMESH brain in Alpha. She'd installed it in *Malph*. Then she must've turned it off, since he was as emotionless as any Fab Trapp had ever met. Perhaps, though, a part of the EMESH bled through so he could disobey an order to save the *Sentinel*'s crew. Trapp shook his head. Then he kissed Bretta one last long time. They held each other.

Borodin counted down from fifteen.

His estimate was off by several seconds. When he reached five, the impact of the ramjet with the MRV lit up the night.

42

Distortion

WHY WEREN'T THEY dead? Trapp glanced up at the ControlPad. Antimatter particles were colliding with loose atmospheric atoms, each winking out with the power of a nuclear explosion. That's how his eyes interpreted what he saw. But then he realized that it was two flames. Rocket plumes! They were moving away from the ramjet. The MRV had turned. It was ascending into the heavens. The crisis had been averted.

"What's going on?" he asked, looking from Bretta to Malph, expecting one of them had overridden Brittany's hack. But they both looked as dumbfounded as Trapp felt.

"It seems the MRV self-destruct system overcame the worm on its own," Malph said.

Brittany growled something unintelligible from behind her duct tape gag. Trapp thought it might've been the word "impossible." But they were *watching* the impossible. The Terra-ending MRV wasn't the only one climbing into a higher Terra orbit. The space above the planet was lit up like fireflies at night. The MRVs had all become rockets. Seeing this, Borodin quickly unstrapped and hurried back to the crew cabin along with Erika.

"It seems the MRVs are on a collision course with each other," Bretta said.

"To self-destruct?" Trapp asked.

"Perhaps," Stockwell said thoughtfully.

"I calculate they'll collide in two minutes and forty-two seconds," Malph said.

"What happens then?" Trapp asked.

The ramjet turned toward Terra in answer to Trapp's question.

"I'm attempting a fast re-entry maneuver," Borodin said through the comms.

Stockwell's phone buzzed. Looking down, her eyes filled with confusion. "A phenomenon is occurring in the fleet," she shouted over the growl of the ramjet's thrusters. "Something has taken over the Manifold ships' control systems and they're reorienting into a sphere formation."

"What does it mean?" Trapp asked.

"Unknown."

They refocused their attention on the MRVs outside the ramjet's windows.

"I'm going to pull hard on the yoke to keep from bouncing back into space," Borodin said through the comms. "We'll be pulling some heavy G's."

"Why did Gray program the MRVs to blow up?" Trapp asked. "He spent years hiding underground so he could accumulate that much antimatter… just to see it go up in a fireball? I don't get it."

"The antimatter could also be used as a weapon." The admiral glanced at Brittany. "The best intentions of inventors have all contained a flaw. They can't imagine their inventions being used for evil. The Professor didn't predict his Manifold would bolster the out-of-control consumption of society, for instance. But at least he calculated the possibility that his MRVs would be used by bad actors to control us."

Everyone turned to look at Brittany again. Her face went red, and she ducked her head.

"If you're finished with the philosophy," Borodin said, "I suggest you all look outside."

They glanced out the windows. The MRVs were close enough to each other that their plumes had merged into one cloud of yellow-white. But that wasn't what Borodin was referring to. Something indescribable was going on.

"The Milky Way!" Trapp exclaimed. "What's happening to it?"

Its stars were distorted with ripples like stones in a clear stream of water. They were shifting from white to red to blue and back again. The ramjet was nearing the exosphere, and Trapp might have attributed the phenomenon to atmospheric disturbance. But he'd undergone re-entry before. And it was never like this.

"I know what this is," Bretta screamed. She looked at Trapp, her eyes bigger than he'd ever seen them. "The Manifolds! Oh, god! Can't you see? It's...*holy fuck!*" She seemed unable to speak. "He did it!"

"Who did what?" Stockwell asked.

But before Bretta could answer, the MRVs collided.

IT WAS THE whitest, brightest thing Trapp had ever seen.

Even the images of light his mind had conjured up during his near-death-by-Manifold at the *Eos* were candle flickers by comparison. Was this another kind of near death, a transmutation to a higher plane of existence? This event was happening in real time and in real space, he argued internally.

Still, his mind was too small to process it.

Antimatter, by the ton, was turning matter into a plume of unstoppable power. Each annihilation added to the next, growing exponentially in magnitude. It wasn't billowing like a nuclear detonation, though. It was as if quantum space was ripping open to show itself for what it truly was. Light wasn't just a wave or a particle. It was a living thing with intention, emotion, desire, and the want to grow and thrive—to multiply and to consume. It was eating up everything around it.

What the hell was this?

The whole thing became a solid mass, roiling and turning in a spectral conflagration. It was beautiful, horrifying, and magnificent all at once, as if it were the face of God. Look upon it for too long, and Trapp would certainly die.

He couldn't help but stare.

Layer upon layer, the brilliant mass grew and expanded into its next phase. It was as bright as a million suns. Brighter. It was going to engulf them, destroy them. And he didn't care. He welcomed it. His heart beckoned for it as if Jessica had come back to life for this one last moment with her son. Soon, the antimatter implosion would swallow up Terra, Luna, Mars, Venus, Sol, and the whole solar system. It would grow from there, taking out adjacent systems, entire arms of the Milky Way, whole galaxies, and clusters of galaxies.

One massive black hole!

This was the beginning of the end of time.

What had they done? How had their arrogance led to such a disaster?

Surely, he thought, as licks of fire from the friction of re-entry began to surround the ramjet, Terra's atmosphere couldn't save them. Even though it seemed like forever since the beginning of the implosion, it had happened mere seconds ago. And the strange distortion was moving toward it.

"A gravity pulse," Bretta finally said, her voice barely a whisper. "Don't you see? Grandpa's Manifolds created it."

Trapp begrudgingly pulled his vision away from the magnificence to look at her.

Her eyes overflowed with tears that ran down her reddened cheeks.

Trapp turned back to the ControlPad. She was right. The strange distortion moved across space in waves. The lights of the undulating stars were witness to its passing; they were pointers to its heading. The antimatter implosion was its destination.

As the distortion took hold of the light, the implosion focused and compressed.

"Maybe we're not going to die after all," he mused.

"Not today it seems," Bretta agreed in a sing-song voice.

The explosion now morphed from a massive globular cloud into a cylinder. The cylinder telescoped away from Terra and seemed to spear into space like a knife through butter. It stretched and thinned, and, with each iteration, accelerated away. It was piercing through the night toward unknown destinations. The antimatter annihilation filled the space inside the cylinder and pushed it wider. And, as if two cylinders on either end were opening up to meet each other, space ripped to make way for the union. The two cylinders extended and reached toward each other like

Michelangelo's finger of God beckoning for Adam. The ends of the cylinders met like tidal waves crashing on the shore. Space distorted, rippled, and then undulated to a stop.

What was left was a sphere.

"It's full of stars!" Trapp mused after a time. "It's like a lens zooming in on our starfield."

"No," Bretta said, her voice rising by two octaves. "That's a whole *new* starfield. It's Grandpa's wormhole."

"It's a sphere. I thought it would be a tunnel."

"It's a four-dimensional tunnel. Which, to us, would appear as a sphere."

Trapp suddenly heard sobbing. Incredibly, it was Malph. "It's the most beautiful thing I've ever seen," the Fab said as tears rolled down his cheeks. Among all the strange things going on at once, the fact that a Fab was sobbing seemed most significant to Trapp. Jessi's EMESH seemed to be breaking through. Trapp turned to take the wormhole in again.

Overcome with emotion, Bretta's voice croaked as she fought to speak. "This whole thing. It was one big ruse. Grandpa fabricated the endgame. He planned it to happen this way. He played all of us; he lied about his true intentions. Maybe even from the beginning. Perhaps his XTerra was part of the ruse, an elaborate hoax that led the human race to this final, amazing outcome."

Trapp glanced over at her in amazement. "Are you saying he's been planning this for twenty-five years? The theft of the Manifold? Ambrose Hancock? Brittany's adoption? My incarceration?"

"Some of it might've been dumb luck. But I think he knew Hancock was working against him. He tricked the president—his illegitimate son—into playing the role he was always destined to play."

"The ISC created dozens of Manifolds," Trapp nodded. "He got them into space for free by tempting the world with what they wanted. Sustainable electricity."

Bretta nodded with the biggest grin he'd ever seen. "While inducing the Russians to become unwitting partners in the scheme."

"The Plexus is blowing up with posts," Stockwell said, her voice thick with emotion. "Minutes ago, dozens of astrophysicists received a post-mortem email from Gray inducing them to aim their telescopes at a particular part of space. Amazingly, a few have already posted pictures and determined where the wormhole connects to. The wormhole comes out on a portion of the galaxy that has three Terra-like planets, all likely inhabitable and within reach using today's technology. Three new Terras."

The ramjet began to be covered in bright ionization now as they sunk into the atmosphere. Trapp could barely see the wormhole for the blue-white plasma sea around them. Gray's gift to humanity? Was that even possible? A mere mortal playing the long game? If anyone could do it, Gray could. Several minutes passed in silence as the roar of re-entry echoed outside the ramjet.

Finally, they broke through the ionosphere. Blue sky lay ahead, and a verdant world below.

"What does Ambrose Hancock have to say about all of this?" Trapp asked Stockwell.

"Apparently, he can't be reached for comment," she said with a chuckle.

Borodin turned them toward Florida and home.

Epilogue

THE FLEETCAR DROPPED Trapp off at the corner.

He shouldered his pack and stepped out onto the curb. His SmartLenses darkened a bit against the sunlight. Several students moved past, some on bikes, some on scooters. Most were walking. And why not? It was a beautiful spring day. Beautiful even beyond one's imagining.

He trotted toward the building and took the pathway around the left side.

The door opened to his fingerprint and he went inside.

It took his SmartLenses, which he'd only recently bought to help with close-up reading—an artifact of someone in the earliest part of their fourth decade—a few seconds to adjust. The gloom of the hallway was welcoming. It smelled of old wood and floor wax. The walls were covered with pictures from ages gone by, images of the men and women upon whose shoulders all of today's knowledge had been built. The largest of these was an old portrait mounted directly in front of him of a man in his fifties. He had a confident grin and sparkling eyes. Soon, Trapp guessed, almost every learning institution in the world would have a building, hall, library, street, or student center named after him.

Of course, some reviled the man for what he'd done.

The ISC chiefs, for instance, were looking for someone to sue. Unlawfully taking over their ships and using them for his purposes, The Professor had induced the Manifolds to focus their energy and form their seminal gravity pulse. It had distorted space. And Trapp had witnessed it as it passed on its way to grab the antimatter and rip open a tunnel to another part of the galaxy. It was still open all these weeks later, and many were predicting it was permanent.

Bril was released from prison by presidential fiat but still faced over two dozen World Court charges, including conspiracy to commit murder. An understatement if there ever was one! Ambrose Hancock had yet to face impeachment, nor was he likely to. He'd actually gone on a disgusting worldwide tour where he took credit for "his special forces team" risking their lives to save the world.

Trapp had spent an hour protesting to Stockwell on a subsequent HoloCall. She'd calmed him by pointing out how the president's "whistle-stop tour"—*her words*—revealed his weakened political position. Trapp expected that the world hadn't heard the last of him. But, for now, all of Terra was focused on one thing.

And it was all because of one man.

"Did you plan all of this?" Trapp asked the lifeless Professor.

In space, Bretta had likened the advent of Gray's Bridge, as many were now calling the wormhole, to a complex chess game. For sure, The Professor hadn't planned the whole thing. But he'd seen a thousand moves into the future. And he'd played his pieces accordingly.

Trapp turned from Phileas Ivan Gray's portrait and headed down the hallway. An elevator took him deep into the North Carolina bedrock.

"Welcome back, my son," the AI that greeted him in the elevator lobby said. She'd changed her programming to update what she called him. It just seemed to happen one day, several weeks ago. He'd come down here and she called him son. Trapp wasn't sure if Bretta had done it with her hacking skills. She'd never admit to it even if she did.

"Hey, Mom," Trapp said. He was beginning to think of this facsimile as his real mother.

"She's waiting inside," Jess-AI said.

Trapp nodded and walked past her. The Professor's underground lab was lit up with half a dozen new HoloDisplays in its many glass-walled rooms. Bretta's cocoons, which Stockwell had arranged to be retrieved from the bottom of the chilly Beaufort Sea, sat and waited to be reopened. For now, Bretta had contented herself with working on The Professor's antiquated servers.

"You're late," she said, her eyes not lifting from her computer as Trapp stepped into the room.

Her current HoloDisplay showed devices that looked like miniature versions of Bril's LIMO. Or maybe they resembled army tanks, but without the big guns and turrets. They were nanites being magnified thousands of times.

He set down the pack. "Are those mine?" he asked. "Or yours?"

"Neither."

"What are they, then?"

"An apology."

Just then, the big man arrived. Trapp hadn't seen his old friend since that day in the server room. Arnault had lost more weight and he wore the same impish grin that spoke of nefarious plans—although he assured Trapp that he was no longer in the criminal trade.

"What's the big surprise?" Arnault asked after giving hugs all around.

"I have a gift for you," Bretta said. "I can't guarantee it won't kill you. But if it works, you'll be less likely to die."

The big Swiss grinned largely. "Arnault, the invincible. Kind of like the sound of that. I'll be able eat all the sausage I want."

"Don't let it go to your head. And, no, don't eat sausage. Nobody should eat that shit. Sophie's promised to get you on a better diet."

Arnault's face deflated. Then he held up his ring finger and flicked the wedding band before changing to the middle one. Bretta laughed and hugged him again.

"Now," she said, pulling out a syringe the length of Trapp's upper arm, "you'll feel a slight pinch."

Arnault backed up. "You're not stabbing me with that *thing*. Immortality or not."

Bretta and Trapp broke into laughter. Finally, she pulled out the actual syringe, one that was a normal length. Arnault pulled up his sleeve. He grunted as she injected him. She adhered a PlayStyx bandage over the tiny wound.

"I'll need to check you daily for a couple of weeks," she said. "Then once a week for six months. If you begin to feel anything, let me know right away."

"Will do, boss. And Bretta, thank you."

She gave him a long hug. "Thank you. For saving me. For saving us."

"Perhaps you'll even help save the world by testing those nanites," Trapp told his friend.

"That'd be something," Arnault said. He left, talking about wanting to try out his new-found health on his wife.

Bretta turned to Trapp. "You brought them?"

He reached into his pack and pulled out the stack of notebooks.

She picked up the top one and started flipping through it, her eyes settling on a page and scanning back and forth.

She glanced up. "I'm so glad you didn't destroy Jessi's original notebooks like you told Demon Roth. It was a good ruse that gave Bril and me the extra seconds to shoot them."

"And save me." He grinned widely. "And even if I had told Pop to burn them up, I still have the HoloPic copies."

"Not the same," she said, her voice thickening as she caressed the page, more precious to her than an original papyrus from the Dead Sea Scrolls.

"You'll be able to read the cursive?"

She nodded distractedly. "Any engineer worth their salt reads long hand. Even in the Quantum Age."

"You mean the Quantum Mirror Age, don't you?"

She looked up with a smile. "More likely, we're in the age of galactic expansion. So far, probes have found no less than 20 potentially habitable planets on the other side of Grandpa's wormhole."

"President Hancock's been calling the region New Eden," Trapp cringed.

"Yeah," she said, scrunching up her nose. "I'm afraid, against scientists' objections, the name has caught on. Even with the wormhole, we're talking years before we can plant the first humans there."

"That's if the ISC approves of it after what the first volunteer-Fab survey crews find."

Bretta's eyebrows came together. "Being forced by their owners hardly counts as *volunteerism.*"

"And your project to grant them emotions will further the goal of Fabricant freedom."

"The scans of Malph's EMESH have stumped me. Your mom's genius is way beyond me. Which is why I'm glad you brought these." She held up the notebook in her hand.

Trapp's eyes naturally turned toward the HoloDisplay and its live feed of the catacombs. She set the notebook down and came over to his side, placing a hand on his arm.

"We're going to find a way to get him out of there," she said in a soft voice.

"Get *all* of them out of there," Trapp corrected her. Of the thousands of Replicants—the *real* Selfies that started this whole thing—Rory was the one he cared about the most. But the others deserved to be revived, too. He felt her going stiff. Knowing where her mind had turned, he placed a hand on her shoulder.

"I'm sorry their existence reminds you of your grandfather."

"He kept a terrible secret from the world," she said, her eyes moistening. "All those deaths because of *his* Manifold."

"He had no control over the ISC's use of the Manifold."

"Indents didn't deserve that kind of ending, though. And he knew what was happening. Still, he didn't come out of seclusion to stop the madness." She glared at the screen. Trapp put a comforting arm over her shoulder. She glanced up at him, forcing a smile. "He paid the ultimate price for his sins. I suppose that's something."

"And Stockwell has convinced the ISC to suspend the Indent program immediately."

"No more Manifold Mining." She nodded.

"No. The ISC must work on enhancing safety protocols before they can go back into production. The TUR will make sure of that."

"Will the Indents be forced to go back to prison?"

"Each of them signed a contract to risk their lives for the rest of us. That's gotta be worth something."

"Perhaps the ISC will agree to Stockwell's Indent Rehabilitation Program. Especially if you help convince them."

"We're meeting later today with the higher-ups to do just that," Trapp said. "I'm not sure if I'm the right man for the job, though."

"Rory would think so." She stood on her toes and kissed him on the cheek.

She looked around Gray's lab. He followed her gaze. There were a lot of experiments. The Professor wasn't anything if he wasn't a man of many talents.

"I just hope I can live up to his brilliance," she mused, apparently having added reading Trapp's mind to her set of unique skills.

"I don't think you will," he said. She gave him a hurt look. "I think you're going to surpass it."

She smiled and they kissed again. He shouldered the pack and turned to leave. "I'm assuming you're gonna want to dig into those," he said, nodding toward the stack of Jessi's notebooks.

"I can go get something to eat with you if you'd rather me do that," she said, glancing fleetingly at the books.

He smiled. "It's okay. You'd be terrible company anyway, with your mind all spun up about Jessi's EMESH. Besides, I've gotta prepare for my meeting."

"Sure?"

"Positive." He gave her a hug and headed for the door.

But before he could go out, he looked back at Bretta.

She was already leaning over one of Jessi's notebooks, a real, honest-to-god graphite pencil in her hand and the tip of her tongue sticking from the corner of her mouth as she was lost in deep concentration. She pushed a lock of hair behind an ear.

At that moment, Trapp thought of all he'd gained in the last few months: a chance to help the Indents, his reborn Replicant best friend Rory, and immortality. Towering above it all was the love of this wonderfully brilliant, powerfully beautiful woman. She'd even dropped the Sykes from her last name to become Bretta Gray once again.

He smiled as he raised his eyes toward the ceiling. He imagined the sky and the stars beyond. Somewhere up there, dozens of quantum mirrors—Gray's Manifolds—awaited their next orders. One of them had tried to kill Trapp. Instead, it had changed everything for him.

With tears filling his eyes, he said a silent 'thank you.'

Then he chuckled at his ridiculous show of emotion.

He turned and headed out of Bretta's lab.

Acknowledgments

SELFIES was a labor of love that couldn't have happened if not for a number of people.

My wife, Susan, I'd like to thank for her ongoing commitment and support that's kept me writing all these years. She is and always will be my first and foremost reader, unafraid to criticize me when it's necessary and unabashedly touched when I somehow manage to pull off a bit of magic.

My editor, Claire, deserves many thanks for making a good story into a great novel. Her devotion to quality, melded with deft editing skills, has seen this project to its best-possible conclusion. Her tireless research, along with a knack for keeping me honest, have enhanced my craft in ways I'd not have thought possible.

* * *

Finally, I want to thank my sister, Terrie. As my first editor and the one who stayed with the story when it was still in its infancy, her invaluable commentary pushed me to delve more deeply into plot and character development and pushed me to build a unique universe that I hope will thrill readers for years to come.

April, 2024
Scott Young
Charlotte, NC

Visit Scott A. Young at his website for news on upcoming events:
scottayoungauthor.com

or

Email him at
scott@scottayoungauthor.com

www.ingramcontent.com/pod-product-compliance
Lightning Source LLC
Chambersburg PA
CBHW020305030826
48979CB00027B/2121/J

* 9 7 8 1 9 6 4 3 2 3 0 2 2 *